W9-AXC-908

Until We Reach
HOME

**Center Point
Large Print**

**This Large Print Book carries the
Seal of Approval of N.A.V.H.**

Until We Reach
HOME

LYNN AUSTIN

CENTER POINT PUBLISHING
THORNDIKE, MAINE

This Center Point Large Print edition
is published in the year 2008 by arrangement with
Bethany House, a division of Baker Publishing Group.

Cover image courtesy of Bethany House Publishers.
Photography by Steve Gardner, PixelWorks Studios.

Copyright © 2008 by Lynn Austin.

All rights reserved.

Scripture quotations are taken from the HOLY BIBLE,
NEW INTERNATIONAL VERSION ®.
Copyright © 1973, 1978, 1984 by International Bible
Society. Used by permission of Zondervan Publishing
House. All rights reserved.

The text of this Large Print edition is unabridged.
In other aspects, this book may vary
from the original edition.
Printed in the United States of America.
Set in 16-point Times New Roman type.

ISBN: 978-1-60285-346-1

Library of Congress Cataloging-in-Publication Data

Austin, Lynn N.
  Until we reach home / Lynn Austin.
    p. cm.
  ISBN 978-1-60285-346-1 (library binding : alk. paper)
  1. Sisters--Fiction. 2. Swedes--United States--Fiction. 3. Large type books. I. Title.

PS3551.U839U58 2008b
813'.54--dc22

2008038050

To my family:
my husband, Ken;
my children, Joshua, Benjamin,
Maya and Vanessa;
my mom and dad;
and my sisters, Bonnie and Peggy

PART I

Sweden

JANUARY 1897

"It is good to have an end to journey
towards; but it is the journey that
matters in the end."

URSULA K. LE GUIN

Chapter One

ELIN CARLSON WALKED into the barn and everything changed. Her sister Sofia stood illuminated by a shaft of sunlight as she paused from her chores; close beside her, talking softly to her, stood Uncle Sven. His hand rested on Sofia's hair, which dangled down her back in a long, golden braid. Elin remembered the weight of his hand on her own head and for a moment she couldn't breathe.

"Don't tell anyone, Elin."

Her fear erupted in a strangled shout. "Sofia!"

Her sister jumped. Timid Sofia was frightened of the dark and of Aunt Karin's geese and sometimes her own shadow. Sofia pressed her hand to her heart as she turned toward Elin.

"Oh, you scared me!"

"Elin sneaks up as quietly as a mouse, doesn't she?" Uncle Sven said. He chuckled in his good-natured way and settled his cap on his head. He strode past Elin, touching her shoulder briefly as he left the barn, the straw crunching beneath his heavy boots.

"Don't tell anyone. . . ."

Elin's heart pounded. She couldn't seem to move and didn't trust herself to speak. Her breath plumed in the cold winter air. Sofia had returned to her chores, but she stopped and looked up again after a moment.

"What's wrong, Elin?"

"Nothing."

Everything.

Sofia was sixteen, the same age Elin had been three years ago when Uncle Sven and his family had moved in with them. She needed to warn Sofia, to tell her what could happen, what nearly had happened today. But Sofia was so young, so innocent. So happy. Elin had been all of those things, too, three years ago.

"What's the matter?" Sofia asked again.

Elin shook her head and hurried out of the barn, running after her uncle, fear and anger boiling inside. Her boots bit through the snow's crust as she ran. She caught up with him when he halted near the wood-pile. He slowly turned to face her.

"Eh? You want something, Elin?"

How dare he pretend not to know. How dare he smile as if nothing had ever happened. Elin opened her mouth, longing to shout, *"You leave Sofia alone!"* But nothing came out.

Uncle Sven stared at her, his eyes boring into hers, his smile never wavering. Then he bent over, lifting the axe in one hand, a log in the other. He balanced the log on its end on the tree stump, then split it in two with one blow.

"You will be very sorry if you tell."

Elin's anger dissolved, leaving only her fear. She was speechless. Helpless.

She turned away and hurried back to the barn,

aware that everything had changed. She would have to guard her sister night and day from now on. She could never leave Sofia alone with him again. Or Kirsten, either. Kirsten was their middle sister and only eighteen—had their uncle been alone with her, too?

Fear squeezed Elin's chest as she watched Sofia put fresh hay in the cow stalls. The steady *thwack*s of her uncle's axe continued outside the barn. Elin drew a shaky breath, struggling to keep her voice calm. "That's good enough for today, Sofia. Go on up to the house."

"Why? What's wrong with you? Your face is as white as milk."

"Nothing's wrong." She snatched the hay fork from Sofia's hand and leaned it against the wall. "I'll walk with you."

"You act so crazy sometimes," Sofia said with a frown.

No one will believe you, Elin. They will say you are crazy.

Perhaps she was crazy. The pressure in her chest increased as she drew another painful breath and tried to speak casually. "What was Uncle Sven doing in here?"

"You'll never guess!" Sofia's pale blue eyes sparkled with happiness. "He said I could ride to the village with him tomorrow if I wanted to. He said he would buy me a treat at Magnusson's store—anything I wanted."

So that was how it would begin for Sofia. She craved sweets as much as Elin had craved solace after Mama and Papa had died. Uncle Sven had offered Elin soothing words and warm arms and a comforting shoulder. *"You are special, Elin. Do you know that? My special girl."* Now Sofia's trust would be bought with peppermints and licorice sticks.

"You can't go with him, Sofia. I need you to help me with . . . with . . . I need your help tomorrow."

"But Uncle Sven said that I—"

"You and I will go into town another time. Now come up to the house with me." She tried to link arms with her sister, but Sofia pulled away. The happy expression on her sweet round face transformed into anger.

"I don't have to do what you say. You're not my mother!"

"I know, I know. . . . But listen, why are you working out here in the barn, anyway? I thought it was Kirsten's turn to do this. Where is she? And aren't you supposed to be watching the children for Aunt Karin?"

"Kirsten took them for a walk in the woods. She promised to wash the dishes for a week if I switched chores with her."

Knowing Kirsten, she and their three young cousins were chasing after elves or hunting for trolls. Every meandering walk through the woods was an adventure for Kirsten, every boulder a crouching troll, every rustling breeze an elf scurrying away.

12

Elin felt her stomach turn over as she remembered how often Kirsten had worked alone in the barn these past few weeks.

But no, Uncle Sven wouldn't be able to deceive Kirsten, would he? For one thing, she never slowed down or stood still long enough to become ensnared by his lies. And for another thing, she was as sturdy and bold as their Viking ancestors, seldom following anyone's rules, acting more like a boy than a girl much of the time. Kirsten would much rather escape from work altogether and explore the forest than sit by the fire and do needlework. Even her straw-blond hair was unruly, always managing to escape from its hairpins and braids to fly as freely as she did.

No, their uncle would find it easier to entice Sofia. She was gentle and shy, with a quiet, compliant nature. She was built more like Elin, too, with fine, delicate bones. Elin remembered the day her uncle had slipped his thick fingers around her wrist and whispered, *"Look at that, Elin. As slim as a twig. I could snap the bone, just like that."* But those threats had come later, after Elin had grown older and had begun to pull away from him.

She noticed that the sound of the axe had stopped. Her heart sped up. "Come up to the house with me, Sofia. Now!"

"Why are you so angry?"

"I'm not angry. I-I just don't like it when you and Kirsten swap chores. She always takes advantage of you." She steered Sofia out of the barn, quickly glancing at the woodpile. Uncle Sven was gone. Elin scanned the fringes of forestland that bordered their farm in search of Kirsten, certain she would be able to spot her bright red coat and striped blue apron. There was no sign of her, either.

That was another reason why their uncle would choose Sofia. Kirsten could disappear as quickly and completely as a wood sprite, while shy little Sofia never did anything in a hurry. She tiptoed hesitantly through life, as if an unseen harness kept her from galloping down the road into the future along with everyone else. Sofia would be easy prey.

Elin knew it was her fault that Sven had turned to Sofia. Elin had been avoiding her uncle for the past few months, resisting his advances, desperate to break free of him. He knew it, too.

"We must help Elin find a job in town," he'd told Aunt Karin. "She deserves to have a little freedom and some spending money of her own, don't you think?" He made it sound as though he were doing Elin a favor—and before today she had been eager to leave home. Now she didn't dare. Even though she longed to flee as far away from him as possible, she could never leave Kirsten and Sofia behind.

Laughter sounded in the distance as Elin and Sofia neared the cottage. A moment later she saw Kirsten emerge from the woods with her three little cousins. The knot in Elin's stomach loosened as she listened to Kirsten's joyous laughter and watched her and the children throwing snowballs at each other. Kirsten seemed much too happy and carefree to have felt the weight of Uncle Sven's lies.

Sofia broke free from Elin and ran toward Kirsten through the snowdrifts. "How far did you walk? The children look frozen! Aunt Karin is going to be furious when she sees how wet they are."

"We went all the way to the road. And look what we got." Kirsten reached inside her coat and pulled out a small white envelope. She waved it in the air. "We were on our way home," she said breathlessly, "when we met up with Tor Magnusson. He walked all the way out from town to deliver this letter to us. It's from America!"

"Let me see it." Elin reached for the letter but Kirsten snatched it away at the last minute and hid it behind her back.

"How much will you pay me for it?"

"Nothing. Hand it over, Kirsten." Elin's discovery in the barn had made her too upset to cope with Kirsten's games.

"Who is it from?" Sofia asked. She peered behind Kirsten's back, tilting her head as she tried to read it.

"A famous Indian chieftain!" Kirsten said with a laugh.

"It has to be from Uncle Lars," Elin said. "Who else do we know in America?" She turned away and opened the cottage door, stomping the snow off her boots before entering the kitchen.

"You're no fun at all," Kirsten said, handing over the letter. Sofia and their three cousins tumbled through the door behind Elin like puppies, dropping to the floor to remove their wet clothes.

"Hurry up and open the letter," Sofia begged as she pulled off her boots. "Read it out loud to us."

Elin found a filet knife and carefully slit open the envelope, then pulled out the letter. Their uncle in America was upset to learn that their older brother, Nils, had left home. That had been Uncle Sven's fault, too. He and Nils had argued so often that Nils finally had gone to Stockholm to find work, even though the farm rightfully belonged to him. Elin had begged Nils to take her with him but he had refused, unwilling to be "tied down," as he'd put it. He'd never sent them a single letter.

Nils should come to America, Uncle Lars had written. *I could find a job for him here. Or if he wants a farm of his own, there is plenty of land in America, too. It is the very least I could do for my sister's son.*

"What about his sister's daughters?" Elin wondered aloud. She realized then that she would have to take matters into her own hands. Neither her brother nor anyone else was going to rescue them. Kirsten and Sofia were no longer safe in this house. Once Uncle Sven forced Elin to leave home, just as he had gotten rid of Nils, her sisters would become his prey. She had to help them escape. She had to write to Uncle Lars in America.

Elin sank onto a kitchen chair, suddenly feeling tired. This was her beloved home, filled with memories of her parents and of happier times when they all lived here together. But now bad memories had crowded out the good—funerals and fights and unspeakable secrets. Shame engulfed Elin every time she looked at Uncle Sven.

She picked up the knife that she had used to open the envelope and slipped it into her apron pocket. She would carry it with her from now on, until they were all safely away from here. If her uncle came near her again, she would use it to defend herself.

And if he ever laid his filthy hands on Sofia or Kirsten, Elin would kill him.

Chapter Two

KIRSTEN CARLSON KNEW she had done a very poor job of cleaning the cream separator, but she needed to hurry up and finish her chores or she would miss seeing Tor. If another letter came for Elin today, he would be delivering it any time now. A steady stream of letters had been arriving from America for the past few months, and Tor Magnusson always walked out from his father's store in town to deliver them. And to see Kirsten.

One of the machine's parts slipped from Kirsten's fingers as she tried to reattach it, and she huffed in frustration. This was taking too long. She would finish the job later. She left the separator in pieces and sneaked out of the barn into the glorious late March sunshine, taking the shortcut through the woods. She knew the path by heart and probably could have walked it in the dark on a moonless night, especially if Tor were waiting for her.

She raced through the forest, swatting away the branches that caught in her hair and snagged her skirts. When she emerged onto the road she saw Tor in the distance, striding toward her. She paused to wait for him and to catch her breath, savoring the damp, woodsy smell of earth and pine trees. Her hair was in tangles, her coiled braids falling from their pins. She plucked a stray leaf from her sweater and smoothed the loose strands away from her face. She could clean the mud off the hem of her skirt later.

Tor lifted his arm in the air and waved a large envelope as he jogged toward her. "Look, Kirsten! A thick letter this time." She took the envelope from him as he paused to catch his breath. It was much thicker than all of the others had been and weighed considerably more. "What do you suppose is in it?" he asked.

"I don't know. Elin won't read them to us anymore. She says they're private. She's very secretive about it."

"Maybe she has a boyfriend over there in America."

"Ha! Not Elin," Kirsten said with a laugh. "No, according to the return address, it's from our uncle Lars in Chicago. It is a fat one, though, isn't it." She felt the envelope for clues.

"Let's pry it open and take a peek inside." Tor grinned mischievously as he pretended to grab the letter. She slapped at his hand.

"No, we can't. Elin will murder me."

"We'll tell her it got damaged on the voyage." He laughed and the sound of it made Kirsten's heart thump faster than it had when she'd run through the woods. Tor seemed to have this effect on her lately. She'd grown up with him, spending more time with him and her brother, Nils, than with any girl friends. But Tor had become much more than a friend since Nils had gone away. And he seemed to feel the same way about her.

"Come here," he said, grabbing Kirsten's hand and pulling her toward him. "I need a kiss after walking all the way out here."

She glanced up and down the road. "Wait . . . not out in the open. What if someone comes?" She led the way down the path she had taken, then went willingly into his arms once they were hidden in the thick brush. Kirsten knew that nice girls didn't allow boys to take such liberties, but this wasn't just any boy— this was Tor. And she was in love with him.

"I'm tired of keeping a secret about . . . you know . . . about us," Kirsten said when they finally paused for breath. "Let's sit together in church next Sunday."

"We can't." His smile faded into a worried look. "My father says I must sit with our family."

"You're twenty years old, Tor. Can't you sit wherever you want to?"

"Of course I can. But he wants me to sit with our family, so—"

"So I'll sit with you and your family from now

19

on." She lifted Tor's hand, which was entwined with hers, and kissed the back of it. She hoped he would pull her into his arms and kiss her again, but instead he released her hand and took a small step backward.

"You can't sit with us, Kirsten. You don't understand my father."

"I know he's an old grouch who yells at all the kids who come into his store to drool over his candy." She tried to keep her voice light and teasing as she brushed his sandy blond hair off his forehead.

"Don't." He pushed her hand away. Tor's expression had become very serious, for some reason, and his blue eyes had turned dark.

"What's wrong?" she asked. "Are you afraid to tell your father about us?"

"It's too soon. He'll need time to get used to the idea of—of you and me."

"Why doesn't he like me? What did I do, Tor?"

"I didn't say he didn't like you—"

"You may as well have! You won't sit with me and I can't sit with you—what else am I supposed to think?"

"Come on, Kirsten . . ." He tried to embrace her again, but she pushed him away.

"No. No more kisses, Tor. If you really cared about me, it wouldn't matter what your father said." She crossed her arms, waiting for his explanation.

"My father is also my boss, remember? If I make him angry he'll fire me, and I'll never find work in the village. Jobs are scarce all over Sweden, you know. That's why Nils left, isn't it?"

"We could move to Stockholm, too, like Nils did. Then we could be together."

"We could," he said, but his expression told Kirsten that he didn't want to. "Listen, I need to do what my father says for now if I want to inherit the store someday. We can still see each other in secret and . . . and I'll work on my father's attitude in the meantime. All right?"

He opened his arms to her and she went into them, clinging to him. What a wonderful feeling it was to be held this way, to lean against his chest and feel his arms surrounding her. She never wanted him to let go.

"Why doesn't your father like me?" she murmured.

"Let's not talk about my father. Our time together is too short as it is. And I have four more letters to deliver."

Kirsten let him kiss her again until it was finally time for him to leave. "Promise me you won't tell anyone about us," he begged as he said good-bye. "Not yet, anyway?"

"I promise."

She ambled back through the woods, light-headed with love, wishing she could marry Tor Magnusson this instant and run away with him to Stockholm. She was still thinking about Tor's kisses and wondering why Mr. Magnusson didn't like her when she nearly collided with Elin in the kitchen doorway. Elin

21

plucked the thick letter from Kirsten's fingers without a word of thanks and scrambled up the steep stairs to read it in their bedroom in the loft. Kirsten didn't find out what was in the mysterious envelope until later that night, when she and her sisters were getting ready for bed upstairs beneath the eaves.

"I have something to tell both of you," Elin began. She sat hunched on the edge of the bed as if she had a shawl wrapped around her shoulders to protect herself from a biting wind. She always curled up that way, even on the hottest summer night. Elin clutched the envelope in both hands as if it might fly away if she didn't hang on tightly.

"Why are you whispering?" Sofia asked as she crawled into the bed she shared with Kirsten.

"Shh! I don't want anyone else to hear us."

"What's in the package?" Kirsten asked.

"I'll show you in a minute." She paused, and as she inhaled slowly she seemed like an old woman to Kirsten—old before her time—even though she was only eleven months older than Kirsten was.

"Just spit it out," Kirsten said, gesturing impatiently. Elin frowned at her but finally got on with it.

"Now that Uncle Sven has taken over the farm, it's getting too crowded here for all of us. Besides, there's no future for us here in the village. Mama wanted us to have a better life, remember? Before she died she begged us to stay together and to take care of each other. And so . . ."

"We should all go to Stockholm to live with Nils,"

Kirsten said. She slipped into the bed beside Sofia and tried to plump up her pillow.

"How can we do that?" Sofia asked. "We don't even know where he is."

"Don't interrupt," Elin said. "Let me finish."

"And stop squirming, Kirsten," Sofia added. "You're making all the covers come untucked."

Kirsten pinched her arm, making her squeal. "You're such a prissy baby, Sofia. You have to have every hair and pleat and hem perfectly in place."

"Shh! Both of you, be quiet and listen to me. I've been writing to Uncle Lars in America, asking him if we could move there and live with him."

"America?" Sofia's eyes went wide with fear. "Are you crazy, Elin? We can't leave our home."

"Yes, America," Elin said. "And today Uncle Lars sent these." She pulled the contents from the envelope and spread them out on the bed. "Look—boat and train tickets that will take us from the village all the way to Chicago in America. He sent enough for all three of us."

Kirsten snatched up one of the tickets and stared at it, then flung it down again. "I'm not going." She was in love with Tor Magnusson and he loved her. They were going to get married. She would have told Elin the truth then and there if Tor hadn't made her promise to keep it a secret for a while longer.

Elin stared at her. "You're not going? Just like that? Aren't you even going to think about it? I thought you liked adventure."

"I'm not going, either," Sofia said. Her voice trembled with unshed tears. "You can go if you want to, Elin, but I'm staying here."

"Listen, both of you. This is a wonderful opportunity. Everyone who moves to America says it's like a paradise over there. The farms are huge and the crops grow twice as tall as they do in Sweden."

"I don't care what they say," Sofia said. "I'm not leaving home."

"You can stay behind with me and—" Kirsten almost said "Tor" but stopped herself in time.

"No one is staying behind," Elin said firmly. "We're a family. The three of us are all that's left, and we're staying together."

"You're not the boss," Kirsten said.

"How can you even think about leaving?" Sofia asked, her voice rising in pitch. "This is our home. We don't belong in America." She scrunched down beneath the covers as if the matter were settled, then added, "I'm not going!"

"Shh! I don't want anyone to hear us."

Elin's warning came too late. The stair treads creaked as someone ascended, and a moment later Uncle Sven emerged through the loft's opening.

"What's going on up here, eh?"

"Nothing," Kirsten said. She glanced at Elin and saw that she had hidden the tickets beneath a pillow. "Sofia's mad because I kicked all the covers loose, but I'll tuck them back in." She wasn't sure why she had lied, but something about the way their uncle looked at them made Kirsten want to pull the covers up to her chin. She wanted him out of her bedroom.

"You girls are going to wake up the children."

"We're sorry, Uncle Sven. We'll be quieter," Kirsten said.

He lingered several moments longer, as if reluctant to go. "Well, then . . . good night, girls."

Elin stared at the open hatch until Uncle Sven went away. She seemed to have hunched even smaller. When she finally pulled out the tickets again, her hands were trembling.

"What's wrong?" Kirsten asked. "You're shaking."

"We can't let him know we're leaving until the very last minute," Elin whispered, "or he might try to stop us. I would run away and live in the woods sooner than stay here with him."

"Why would you say such a thing?" Sofia asked, sitting up in bed again. "You act like he's an ogre or something."

Elin closed her eyes for a long moment. "Won't you at least think about going to America?" she asked when she opened them again. "Both of you? We have tickets . . ."

"No," Sofia said. "I won't go!" She flopped onto her stomach and tunneled beneath the covers again like a mouse scurrying into its hole.

Kirsten didn't have to think about it. She was going to marry Tor and live with him, not move to America. He would race to her rescue as soon as she told him about Elin's plans. He would confront his father, and finally declare his love. Tor would never allow Kirsten to move to America, where he'd never see her again. She could hardly stand waiting three more days to see him, much less leave him forever. But she would have to wait until Sunday to tell him Elin's news. She wouldn't have an excuse to walk into town before then.

When Sunday morning arrived, Tor sat dutifully with his family during the church service while Kirsten sat with her sisters. Afterward, while all of the other parishioners milled around outside, she signaled for him to meet her behind one of the outbuildings. When they were alone, he tried to pull her close for a kiss.

"No, wait, Tor, and listen to me," she said. "Elin wants me and Sofia to move to America with her. That's what was in that thick envelope the other day—tickets to America on an ocean liner. For all three of us."

She waited for his outraged protests, his declarations of love, but Tor simply stared at her as if he didn't comprehend.

"I told Elin I'm not going. I told her I'm staying here. I want to be with you."

"With me?"

"Yes!" Why was he being so thickheaded? She wanted to shake him. "We care about each other, don't we, Tor? Don't you want us to be together forever? We're going to get married someday."

His eyes widened in alarm. "Oh, Kirsten . . ." He stumbled backward. "We can't . . . we can't get married."

"Well, maybe not now, but when we're older."

"No . . . not even then."

"Why not? And don't tell me it's because of your father."

"No. It's because of yours."

Now it was Kirsten's turn to stare in disbelief. "Because of *mine?* But my papa is dead."

"Yes—and he killed himself."

"What?"

Tor's words tumbled out all at once, as if he wanted to throw them down on the ground and run. "My father won't let me marry you because suicide is a sin, and he says it would bring disgrace on our family and on our store if—"

"Papa did *not* kill himself! That's a lie! Suicide is for cowards, and he was never a coward. I don't know why your father would say such a terrible thing, but it isn't true, and I don't believe it! Papa made a mistake, that's all. The ice was too thin, and he fell through it and drowned."

Tor gave an embarrassed shrug and looked away.

"Don't tell me you believe that lie, too? It was an accident, Tor. Papa never would have left us all alone that way. He loved us."

"It doesn't matter what I think. What matters is what my father thinks. And a lot of other people in town think it's true, too."

"Well, they're wrong. I'll admit that Papa suffered from the winter sadness sometimes, but that's all it was. A lot of people feel that way right before spring comes. Tell your father he's wrong!"

Tor stared at his feet, kicking a pebble back and forth. "Your brother Nils thought it was suicide, too."

"He did not! That's a lie, and I hate you for saying it!"

Kirsten stormed away without looking back, hurrying down the road toward home. She expected to hear Tor's footsteps behind her, his pleas for her to wait, to listen to him. But he didn't run after her. He didn't try to stop her.

The accusation that her father had killed himself made Kirsten ache inside. But Tor had caused an even deeper wound by allowing anything to stand in the way of their love. It could only mean one thing: He didn't really love her. And that realization caused a pain she hadn't felt since her mother died. Kirsten managed to hold back her tears until she reached the edge of town, but at last they began to fall.

She had fallen in love with a man who didn't love her in return. And she had made a fool of herself with him, accepting his kisses and caresses, believing they meant something, believing he loved her and wanted to marry her.

By the time Kirsten's family caught up with her in the farm wagon, she was only half a mile from home. "What's the matter?" Elin whispered after Kirsten climbed onto the back of the flatbed wagon beside her and Sofia.

"Later," she mumbled. If she talked about Tor or even thought about him right now, she would burst into tears. Elin waited until they were alone in the barn that afternoon before asking her again what was wrong. Kirsten slammed down the empty milk pails with a clatter.

"Do you know what people in town are saying? They think that Papa's accident wasn't an accident. They think he died on purpose."

Elin rested her hand on Kirsten's shoulder. "Don't you remember how sad he was near the end? How much he mourned for Mama? He stopped living long before he stopped breathing."

"I know, I know. We were all sad after she died, but that doesn't mean—"

"I think Papa decided to join her in the grave."

"No! I don't believe it! It was an accident. The ice was too thin."

Elin gripped her arms. "Think about it, Kirsten. Papa knew how to test the ice better than anyone did. He taught all of us how to listen for exactly the right sound, remember? He left the cottage that morning and walked straight out onto the lake. He couldn't have made a mistake. He simply didn't want to live any longer."

Kirsten covered her face.

"That's why he wasn't buried beside Mama in the churchyard," Elin said. "They wouldn't allow it."

"He wouldn't leave us all alone!"

"But he did, Kirsten. And now all we have is each other."

Kirsten leaned against her sister and sobbed. Their father hadn't loved them. He hadn't wanted to be with them. And because of the disgraceful thing he'd done, Tor wouldn't marry her.

"What am I going to do?" she sobbed. She was in love with a man who didn't want her.

"We need to start all over again, far away from here," Elin said softly. "People will never forgive Papa for what he did, and they'll never forget it, either." She released Kirsten and held her at arm's length. "We need to go to America."

"All alone? All that way?"

Elin nodded. "Sofia will come with us once she gets used to the idea."

But Kirsten didn't want to leave home, either. She couldn't leave Tor. If she stayed, though, how could she face him in church and on the village streets, day after day, for the rest of her life?

Chapter Three

SOFIA CARLSON AWOKE at dawn on that fateful April morning to a fog so thick it shrouded their farmyard in a soggy gray blanket. She pushed aside the curtain to look out of the loft window for the last time. The barn's familiar silhouette looked smeared and misshapen. Beyond it, their tiny herd of cows had vanished from the pasture as if forest sprites had stolen them. This was the last morning she would ever peer from her dormer window. She would never see this view again. In time, the land's familiar contours would fade from memory, just as Mama's familiar face had.

Elin had told Sofia to dress nicely for traveling. As Sofia stepped into her petticoat and skirt and buttoned up her starched Sunday shirtwaist, she kept hoping that this was just a nightmare, that she wasn't leaving for good. *Please, Jesus, let this just be a dream.*

But it wasn't a dream. Elin and Kirsten had made up their minds to go to America, and they were making Sofia go with them. Their trunk was packed. Today they were leaving home, forever. She wondered what Elin and Kirsten would do if she decided to dig in her heels and grip the doorposts and refuse to go. Would they drag her away to America by force?

But no, Sofia would go with her sisters wherever they went. She had no other family except them. Elin and Kirsten had been by Sofia's side for as long as she could remember. No matter how frightening her circumstances or how dark the night, she could get through anything if they were beside her. Elin always seemed to know when Sofia needed her, and she would silently reach for her hand and take it in hers. Elin's fine-boned hands were no larger than Sofia's, but once they were joined she felt safe, protected.

Bring on the bullies, the barking dogs, the boogeymen in the dark of night. Elin would take care of her. Sofia's sisters were older and smarter than she was, and much more courageous. She wished she were more like them.

Nevertheless, Sofia was very angry with them for making her decide between two impossible choices. She didn't want to leave home, but she didn't want to be separated from her sisters, either. It was bad enough that Mama and Papa and Nils had all left her. She couldn't bear it if Elin and Kirsten left her, too.

Much too soon they were ready to go. Sofia's three little cousins scrambled onto the back of Uncle Sven's farm wagon for the trip to the train station, but he shooed them off again. "Why can't they come along?" she asked him.

"I'm afraid the roads might be muddy after all the rain we've had. Your trunk already makes a heavy load for the horses."

Sofia suspected that the real reason was because Uncle Sven was angry with them for leaving. Who would do all their chores from now on? He resembled their papa but he was nothing like him. He sat sternly on the wagon seat in Papa's place, a grim reminder that the three of them were orphans, passed from uncle to uncle like an unwelcome fever.

Sofia hugged Aunt Karin good-bye and felt the same breathtaking grief as on the day Mama had died. She hugged her three little cousins tightly, knowing she would never see them again. Kirsten was crying, too, but Elin strode toward the loaded farm wagon without even looking back.

"Why don't you climb up here, Sofia," Uncle Sven said, patting the wooden seat beside him.

"No," Elin replied before Sofia could. "I want her to ride back here with me." She offered Sofia her hand and pulled her up onto the wagon bed beside their trunk. Sofia rode facing backward, her eyes fixed on the faint, comforting light that glowed from the cottage windows. But the lights vanished in the fog before the wagon had traveled two hundred meters, as if Aunt Karin had doused all of the lamps.

The fog merged with Sofia's tears, blurring the journey into town, making everything seem unfamiliar and menacing. She had grown up in this forest, and the tall, silent fir trees had always seemed like friends. Now they towered in sullen silence, hiding behind a veil of gray mist as if mourning her departure. Invisible crows shrieked at her from the shrouded treetops.

No one spoke, and even Kirsten seemed unusually subdued, her legs dangling from the tailgate as the wagon traveled the familiar road into the village. She hadn't behaved in her usual bold, boisterous way since agreeing to move to America. In fact, Kirsten had acted as gloomy and nervous as Elin usually did. But suddenly, Kirsten slid forward and hopped off the wagon.

"What are you doing?" Elin demanded as the vehicle rolled away from her. "Get back here this minute!"

Sofia held her breath, hoping that Kirsten had changed her mind and had decided not to go to America after all. If Kirsten stayed behind in Sweden then Sofia could stay, too. She inched toward the edge of the wagon bed, ready to hop down and run home with her sister.

Please, Jesus, let her change her mind.

But Kirsten crouched beside a clump of spring wild flowers and began picking a bouquet of them. Uncle Sven didn't even slow down the wagon, as if not caring that he'd just lost a passenger. Kirsten had to race like a schoolgirl to catch up with them, lifting her skirts as she leaped back on.

"You'll break your leg someday doing that," Elin scolded.

"Who cares?" Kirsten brushed the loosened strands of hair off her face and handed Sofia the wispy flowers. "Here, I picked these for you. You can press them flat inside a book to remind you of home."

Sofia swallowed a lump of grief. "Aren't there any wild flowers in America?"

"Of course there are," Elin said. "Stop pouting, Sofia."

She gazed down at the delicate blossoms that had been ripped from the soil alongside the road, then lowered her face to her lap and cried.

Ever since Mama died five years ago, sorrow and fear had crouched in the shadows of Sofia's heart like wolves waiting to pounce. They had doubled in size when Papa followed Mama to the grave less than a year later, becoming huge, voracious animals that threatened to swallow Sofia alive, especially if she faced anything new. She had learned to hold the beasts at bay by doing everything exactly the same, day after day, never straying from the familiar.

The beasts had tamed down a bit after Aunt Karin and Uncle Sven had moved to the farm, but the moment Elin had shown her the tickets to America, Sofia felt her fear and sorrow growing into giant monsters that followed her everywhere with their bristling claws and jagged teeth. She wished she knew how to make them go away.

By the time the wagon reached the village, the sun had started to elbow through the clouds. Sofia longed to jump off as Kirsten had done and run to the cemetery behind the church to see her mother's grave one last time. Instead, she bid a silent good-bye to the church and the graveyard, to the wooden schoolhouse that she and her sisters had attended, to the tidy stores that lined the main street. It was market day, and the villagers went about their business as usual, setting up their booths in the square, laying out cheese and eggs for sale.

Kirsten slid off the wagon again before it came to a halt at the station. "I'll be right back," she called.

"No, come back here," Elin yelled. "You'll miss the train!"

"Don't worry, I'll hear the whistle."

Sofia jumped down from the wagon behind Kirsten. "Wait for me! I'm coming with you." If

Kirsten had suddenly decided to stay behind, then Sofia would stay, too. She lifted her hem above the mud and hurried to catch up with Kirsten, still clutching the bouquet of wild flowers, ignoring Elin's protests.

Kirsten looked annoyed to see Sofia running along behind her. "Why are you following me? Where do you think you're going?"

"I'm not getting on the train to America unless you do."

"Don't be stupid. Of course I'm getting on the train. We can't change our minds now. I . . . I just need to say good-bye to someone."

"Can we go to the cemetery afterward? I want to see Mama's grave one last time." With any luck, they would both miss the train.

"Fine," Kirsten said, grabbing Sofia's hand. "Come on."

She towed her down the walkway, hurrying through the market area without stopping to greet anyone. If Kirsten was heading toward the church, she was taking the long way around, passing the row of stores on the main street instead of taking the more direct route. She halted abruptly in front of Magnusson's General Store, where the owner's son, Tor, was sweeping the wooden sidewalk with a broom.

"Good-bye, Tor," Kirsten said primly. "We're leaving for America today, and you'll never see me again. Ever. As soon as the train comes we're leaving, and we're never coming back."

She whirled around before Tor could reply and strode away, walking so quickly that Sofia could barely keep up with her. She thought she saw Kirsten wiping her eyes. Tor returned to his task.

Kirsten didn't stop until they reached their mother's grave. "Hurry up and say good-bye," she told Sofia, "or we'll miss our train."

Tears filled Sofia's eyes as she knelt to place the wilting wild flowers on the grass. This was the last time she would ever be able to visit her mother. Sofia had come here to pray every week since Mama died and had spent the last month of Sundays—ever since the tickets had come—begging Mama to talk to Jesus and arrange a miracle so they could all stay in Sweden. His miracle had better come quickly.

She looked up at Kirsten, who was waiting with crossed arms. "How can we leave Mama?"

"She isn't here, you know," Kirsten said impatiently. "She's in heaven. She can't hear you talking to her."

Sofia's temper flared. "How do you know whether or not she can hear me?"

"Well, if she can, then I'm sure she'll hear you in America, too. Come on." She started walking back toward the cemetery gate.

"You have no feelings at all, Kirsten!" Sofia yelled as she struggled to her feet. "Your heart is just one big block of ice!"

They jogged back to the station, and by the time they arrived, panting from exertion, Elin was so angry she turned her back and refused to speak to them. When Kirsten sank down on a bench to wait, Sofia deliberately chose a different bench, staring up at Elin's turned back. It was Elin's fault that they were leaving. Kirsten's, too.

Uncle Sven roamed the platform as he waited for the train to arrive, raking his fingers through his hair and peering down the tracks as if eager to be rid of them and get on with his day. Sofia felt like a prisoner, banished into exile for a crime she didn't commit.

When the train whistle finally sounded in the distance, Sofia feared she might throw up. She looked over at Kirsten as the train rumbled to a stop and silently pleaded with her to change her mind and stay here. Kirsten's cheeks were very pink and her braids had already begun pulling loose from the pins, but she picked up her satchel and stood.

"Good-bye, girls," Uncle Sven said above the sound of the thundering train. "Godspeed."

He reached out to embrace them, but Elin walked away. Sofia went willingly into his arms.

"You can stay here with me, little one," he told her. "You don't have to leave." He had tried to convince her to stay with him from the moment Elin first told him about the tickets, but Elin had remained steadfast, insisting that Sofia come with her.

"Thank you," Sofia told her uncle now, "but I have to go with my sisters."

"Come on, Sofia," Elin called. She reached for her

38

hand and clutched it tightly as they walked toward the train. This was it. They were really, truly leaving home and never coming back.

"Good-bye," Sofia tried to say, but it came out in a whisper. "Good-bye . . ."

Chapter Four

THE TRAIN RUMBLED and hissed like a dragon as Elin walked toward it, clutching her sister's hand. Sofia wept aloud, and even Kirsten was sniffling and wiping her eyes. But Elin was so relieved to know that she would never see Uncle Sven again for as long as she lived that she didn't shed a single tear.

She helped Sofia climb aboard, then guided her down the aisle between the rows of seats. Kirsten had boarded ahead of them and had found a pair of seats that faced each other. "Ride backwards with me, Sofia," she said. "You'll be able to see more."

Sofia shook her head and leaned against Elin for comfort. When the whistle suddenly shrieked, Sofia yelped in fear. Elin hugged her close. None of them had traveled on a train before.

"We're going to be just fine," Elin soothed. "You'll see."

She did her best to put on a brave show for her sisters, but there was a cold place inside her that she didn't think would ever be warm again. It was too late to change her mind. She couldn't turn back. She wondered if Papa had felt this way as the ice had splintered beneath his feet and he'd plunged into the dark, bottomless lake.

Elin still couldn't believe she was leaving home. She loved their little farm, as poor and shabby as it was, loved the woods and streams and gentle hills that surrounded her family's land. They had worked so hard after Mama died to keep it running. Mama used to say that a woman's most precious treasures were her home and her family, and Elin believed it with all her heart. But she couldn't stay. She had to take Kirsten and Sofia someplace safe. They still didn't know the real reason they were leaving home. No one did.

Kirsten shoved open her window and leaned out, gazing behind them as the train steamed from the station, watching their village and neighboring farmland fade into the dwindling mist behind them. Tears trailed down her cheeks. Elin faced the opposite direction, toward their future, refusing to look back. "We'll be fine. Just fine," she said, although she doubted if Sofia believed her.

Grief numbed Elin—it probably numbed all of them. She watched the scenery race past, wanting to memorize her homeland. America might look very different.

"It's getting cold in here," Elin said as time passed. Sofia was rubbing her arms to warm herself. "You'd better close the window, Kirsten."

She tugged it shut and sat down again. They had been traveling for more than an hour, but tears still rolled slowly down Kirsten's cheeks.

"Are you all right? " Elin asked her.

Kirsten wiped her face with the heels of her hands. "I'm fine. The cool air made my eyes water."

"I hear there are a lot of unmarried men in America," Elin said, trying to make Kirsten smile. Instead, her temper flared.

"There were plenty of unmarried men in our village, too, but none of them would ever marry us. Not with everyone in town whispering about us the way they did and saying that—" Kirsten glanced at Sofia and stopped short. Sofia still didn't know that their father's death hadn't been an accident. But Kirsten had already said too much.

"What do you mean?" Sofia asked. "Why were people whispering about us? Tell me what you're talking about." Elin was trying to find a way to avoid Sofia's questions when Kirsten gave her a way out.

"I don't want to talk about getting married," she said.

"Later," Elin whispered to Sofia, holding a finger to her lips. Hopefully, Sofia would forget by then.

They lapsed into silence again, miles apart from each other even though they sat with their knees and shoulders touching. Elin had never traveled this far from home in her life. None of them had. As the hours slipped by and the train carried them farther and farther away, the landscape slowly began to change, looking more and more unfamiliar. Elin closed her eyes, wanting to remember home, afraid she would forget what it looked like.

"Are you sleeping?" Kirsten asked after a while.

"No, just resting." Elin straightened up and reached for the satchel of food they had packed. "Does anybody want lunch?"

Kirsten shook her head.

"No thank you," Sofia said.

Elin knew by Sofia's prim reply that she was still angry with them for not answering her questions. Sofia could nurse a grudge longer than anyone Elin knew.

Kirsten stood and moved into the aisle to stretch. "I think I'll go exploring. Come with me, Sofia."

"No thank you."

"I don't think you're supposed to roam around," Elin said.

"Why not? I can't get lost unless I fall off the train, can I?"

"That's not the point. We don't know what sorts of people are aboard. You'd better stay here."

Kirsten turned away and stalked down to the end of the aisle. Elin held her breath, hoping her sister wouldn't try to open the door and go into the next passenger car. But Kirsten turned around and paced the length of their car in the other direction before returning to her seat and sinking onto it with a huff.

Why did Kirsten and Sofia have to be so difficult—now, of all times? For months Elin had felt sick with worry, afraid to believe that they really would be able to escape. Protecting her sisters from Uncle Sven had been an exhausting ordeal requiring constant vigilance. But now she had exchanged a known fear for a host of unknown ones. What if Uncle Lars turned out to be even more of a monster than Uncle Sven had been?

But no, Uncle Lars had paid for all of their tickets and made all of the arrangements. He would lift this heavy burden from Elin's shoulders and provide a new home for all three of them. The promise of rest and relief and a roof above her head had kept Elin going. If only her sisters could understand this and be grateful for the choices she had made instead of sulking.

She handed Kirsten a chunk of *knäckebröd* from the food bag. Sofia shook her head when Elin offered her some. "At least eat a little bite," Elin insisted, pushing a small piece into Sofia's hands. "The mice will eat it if you don't."

Sofia reluctantly nibbled a piece. Elin didn't feel much like eating, either. The pain in her stomach made her feel as though she'd swallowed a pile of rocks.

"Will the bread taste the same in America?" Sofia asked after a moment.

"Of course, silly." Elin elbowed her gently in the ribs. "The person who bakes it determines the taste, not the place where it's baked."

Tears dropped onto Sofia's uneaten bread. "I'm going to hate America."

"Oh, don't be such a baby," Kirsten said. "If you're going to be this grouchy for the rest of your life, I'll pay to send you back to Sweden myself. Do you think this is easy for any of us?" Elin heard suppressed tears in Kirsten's voice.

"Listen, a few months from now we'll be glad we left this place," Elin said. "You didn't want to be Aunt Karin's servant for the rest of your life, did you? Wiping her children's runny noses and soggy bottoms?"

"At least Aunt Karin let us get up and walk around," Kirsten said. "Now we get to be your servant."

"Could we please stop fighting with each other?" Elin said with a sigh. "Please?"

Sofia sniffled in reply. Kirsten tore off another piece of the crusty bread and chewed it slowly.

"Who invited Uncle Sven and Aunt Karin to move in with us, anyway?" Kirsten asked with her mouth full. "We were doing just fine on our own but as soon as they moved in, everything changed. It's supposed to be Nils' farm, you know. They stole it from him."

"Nils said he didn't want it," Sofia said. "I heard him say it. I guess he didn't want to be bothered with us, either."

"Well, that's all in the past," Elin said, waving her hand. "We're going to look forward from now on, not over our shoulders. Uncle Lars must be very rich over there in America if he could buy all of these tickets for us. And he was Mama's favorite brother. He'll treat us like his very own daughters, not servants."

"I'll bet we'll never have to work another day in our lives," Kirsten said. "We won't have to milk the cows if we want a glass of milk, and we won't have to push the chickens off their nests whenever we want eggs. Everything will come from the shops."

"What will we do all day?" Sofia asked. Her soft voice reminded Elin of falling snowflakes.

"Nothing. We'll be just like Mrs. Olsson in the village, with serving girls to do all our work." Kirsten slouched languidly across the seat, pretending to lift a teacup with her pinkie finger extended.

"Kirsten! Your petticoats are showing," Elin said, tugging her skirt down over her ankles.

Kirsten ignored her. "Before long, we'll forget that we ever lived in a smoky old cottage on a run-down farm."

"It wasn't run-down!" Sofia said.

"Fine. Believe whatever you want." Kirsten sat up and rearranged her skirts with a huff. "Pretty soon we'll forget all of those stupid, ugly people in that stupid, ugly town."

The train reached the city of Gothenburg late in the afternoon. Elin gazed out of the window at a city so huge it seemed to take forever to travel from the outskirts to the station in the city's center. Kirsten had shoved open the window to lean out, but she quickly closed it again.

"Ew! Something stinks like rotten fish."

"Well, the city is on the ocean," Elin said. "Their fish market is very famous."

Papa had once visited Gothenburg, and he'd described it so beautifully to Elin—the call of the seabirds, the sigh of ocean waves, the flavor of salt that was so heavy in the air you could taste it on your lips. But the city must have changed since he'd visited it. Elin didn't hear any seabirds, only the shriek and rumble and hiss of the train. She couldn't taste the salt, only the stench of fish and soot and fumes.

Kirsten stood up before the train stopped, clutching her bag as if ready to bolt. Elin waited until the coach halted, but even then she felt as though she were still moving when she rose to her feet.

"The White Star Steamship Line sent a wagon to meet your train," the conductor told them as they got off. "They'll transport you to a boardinghouse near the pier for the night."

"See? Uncle Lars thought of everything," Elin said. "And it's all paid for, too." She hoped to reassure her sisters—and herself—that they would be well taken care of.

The platform shook beneath her feet as another train chuffed out of the depot. Baggage agents had heaped everyone's luggage on the platform, and travelers sorted through the pile for their belongings. Elin searched through the pile, too, but couldn't find their trunk. Even after the heap of baggage had disappeared, there was so sign of it.

Panic tightened her chest. She walked the entire length of the platform and back again, examining every box and packing crate, but none of them was hers. What would they do without their trunk? It contained everything they owned and all of their food for the journey. She hurried back to where her sisters stood waiting.

"Our trunk is missing! Help me find it!"

For several endless, heart-stopping minutes Elin and Kirsten ran around in a panic while Sofia sank down on a bench, hunched with self-pity.

"Why aren't you helping us?" Kirsten asked her.

"Because I hope we did leave it behind. Then we can get on the next train and go home."

Elin wondered if Uncle Sven had kept it on purpose to punish her and to make certain they would return home. The thought infuriated her.

"We aren't going back, Sofia. I'd rather leave everything behind and go without food for the next few weeks than turn back."

But could they really leave everything behind? Elin sorted through the trunk's contents in her mind, trying to recall what they had packed. They could replace their clothes and winter coats and bedding—although Elin had no idea where the money to buy new things would come from. She had also packed a few heirlooms from home, even though it meant sacrificing some other items to make space. The copper coffee kettle Mama had always used when they had guests was in the trunk, as was her book of hymns, along with linen towels and aprons and table runners that Mama had embroidered for her wedding chest. Elin had packed the wooden mortar and pestle that

Papa had carved, a bowl painted with rosemaling, and a white linen tablecloth that had been their grandmother's. There was nothing of great value, yet losing the trunk would mean one more loss after so many others.

"Here it is," Kirsten suddenly shouted. Elin hurried over to find their missing trunk, hidden behind one of the White Star wagons. Her shoulders slumped with relief. She motioned to Sofia, who was still sitting on the bench.

"Come on! We found it!"

Sofia stood and dragged herself to the waiting carriage. Night had fallen, and it was too dark to see very much of the city as they rode to the lodgings that the steamship line had provided. Elin felt drained. She closed her eyes and listened to Kirsten and Sofia talking quietly beside her.

"Why don't you want to move to America?" Kirsten asked Sofia.

"I just don't. Uncle Sven said I should let you and Elin go without me. He said I could stay with him."

Sofia's words made Elin's heart speed up. "He's not as nice as you think," she said in a shaking voice.

"He's the reason Nils left home, remember?" Kirsten added. "And I heard him saying that Elin was going to be next. He was going to make her move out and get a job in town."

"So instead, we *all* had to move out?" Sofia asked. "That makes no sense at all."

"I give up, Sofia," Kirsten said. "Be miserable if you want to." They rode the rest of the way without speaking.

Their room in the boardinghouse smelled like stale perspiration. Kirsten tried to open the tiny window, but it refused to budge. The three of them stripped into their undergarments and, after carefully laying out their good clothes so they wouldn't wrinkle, Sofia and Kirsten climbed into bed. But Elin was too upset to sleep. She turned off the gaslight and lit a candle.

"Do you mind if I write for awhile? I promise I won't be long."

"Just don't set the room on fire," Kirsten said before pulling the pillow over her head.

Elin opened her diary and began to write.

We are in a rooming house in Gothenburg after a long, exhausting day of travel. Our spare, narrow room with its barren walls and narrow beds seems fitting. Everything that once warmed and cushioned my life has been stripped away, and I've packed what remains of it into our trunk. I feel as naked and shivery as one of Papa's sheep after it has been shorn. I tell myself that I am lighter this way, freer. I'll recover everything I've lost someday, won't I? I'll have a home and a family again. Perhaps everything will take a different form, the way a lamb's shorn wool returns as a pair of mittens or a scarf or a warm winter sweater, but I am determined never to feel so naked and lost again.

Tomorrow we sail across the North Sea to a city called Hull, in England. Then we'll board another train and cross the English countryside to Liverpool. From there we'll board a steamship for the two-week voyage across the Atlantic Ocean to New York in America. But our journey won't end there. We must board yet another train and travel to Uncle Lars' home in Chicago. I remember meeting him once, when I was a very small girl, and he was leaving our village to make his fortune in America.

She paused, wondering what else to add. Kirsten was already asleep, but Sofia was only pretending. She had buried her face in the limp gray pillow to muffle the sound, but Elin knew that she was crying. Elin wanted to crawl beneath the covers and weep, too, but she needed to remain strong for her sisters' sakes. She drew a deep breath and slowly released it, trying to release her fear along with it.

Even though Sofia and Kirsten are with me, I feel lost and alone. If I'd had any other choice besides this long, inconceivable journey to a far-away land, I would have gladly taken it. But before Mama died she begged me to watch over my sisters, and the only way that was left to me, the only way that I knew how to do that, was to leave home and take them to America.

In some ways I feel like I've let her down, but I simply didn't know what else to do and I had to make a decision. I hope I've made the right one.

Elin closed her eyes. She wished she could pray the way Mama used to, but a deep pit stood between her and God, filled with guilt and regret. He knew all of the terrible things she had done. Anger filled the pit, as well. Why hadn't God protected her from Uncle Sven? Instead, Elin had been forced to find her own way to escape. If she hadn't written to Uncle Lars and begged him to let them come to America, they never would have been rescued. She was the one who'd had to figure out how to start a new life for her and her sisters. And now she would have to figure out how to find the courage to do it. She bent over her diary again.

I wish I wasn't the oldest sister. I wish someone would take care of me instead of being forced to take care of everyone else. If only I didn't have to make all of the decisions and take the first steps and be daring and brave and resourceful. I understand how Sofia feels, because I long to get back on the train tomorrow and go home, too— home to the way everything was five years ago. All I want to do is sit in our stuga and knit socks in front of the fire and listen to Mama reading aloud from her little Bible as the aroma of baking bread fills the room.

But that life is gone. I am the oldest sister. Sofia and Kirsten are depending on me. We can't turn back. Besides, I'm running away for my own safety as much as for theirs. I have no idea what we'll find at the end of our journey, but it can't possibly be any worse than what I left behind—can it?

She wiped a tear that had splashed onto her diary page, then closed the book and snuffed out the candle. She hoped that the bedcovers were warm, because she was so very cold. She couldn't seem to stop shaking.

Chapter Five

A CRASH OF THUNDER startled Kirsten awake. She sat up in bed, gazing around the unfamiliar room, unsure where she was. Then a flash of lightning illuminated the whitewashed walls and she remembered arriving at the boardinghouse last night after the long train trip to Gothenburg. She and her sisters had followed the sour-faced proprietor up the stairs to this barren room at the top.

Thunder rumbled like a steam locomotive in the distance. More lightning flashed. Kirsten remembered saying good-bye to Tor yesterday, seeing him for the very last time, and the pain she felt was as though someone had carved him out of her heart with a filet knife. She had hoped that the ache in her chest would fade as she traveled farther from home, but this morning the pain felt worse than it had yesterday. Tor had looked away as she'd told him good-bye, not at her.

Another flash of lightning, another peal of thunder, farther away this time. Kirsten wished that a bolt would strike her and end her misery. She climbed out of bed and parted the heavy curtains. Dawn had come, but the storm that had blown in from the sea obscured it. The tempest lashed the windowpanes with wind and rain and raised huge white waves in the harbor beyond.

"Is it morning?" Elin asked, her voice muffled beneath the bedcovers.

"*Ja.* But I don't think our ferry is going to leave today. You should see it outside!"

Kirsten had longed for adventure while growing up, envying her Viking ancestors who had bravely set sail to explore new lands. But even Erik the Red would have stayed in port on a day like today.

"Is it raining?" Elin asked.

"It's pouring! And you should see how huge the waves are!"

Heavy footsteps clumped up the stairs outside their room. A loud knock rattled their door. "The ferry leaves in one hour, ladies."

"Thank you. We're awake," Elin called back. She reached over to the other bed to rouse Sofia. "Did you hear that? Come on, Sofia. You need to get up and get dressed."

Sofia responded with a moan.

A gust of wind whipped against the wooden building, whistling its way into every crack and rattling the window glass. Kirsten could feel the room shaking.

"Listen to that wind! I don't even want to go outside in such weather, much less get into a boat."

"Well, we have to do what the tour people say. Uncle Lars sent instructions—"

"So what? Why does everyone else get to make decisions for me? When will I get to decide for myself?"

Elin stood with her hands on her hips, wearing that bossy look that Kirsten hated. "No one ever gets to do whatever they want all the time. Not even adults."

"Well, that stinks like dead fish!"

They got dressed, gathered their belongings, and ate a quick breakfast of bread and herring in the boardinghouse dining room downstairs. Kirsten wrapped a shawl around her shoulders and opened the door, bracing herself against the wind. Elin grabbed Sofia's hand and pulled her through the door, following the other passengers into the storm.

"Our boat is going to sink!" Sofia shouted above the wind.

"We'll be fine," Elin insisted. "Sailors and sea captains know all about the weather and how to navigate the seas. They wouldn't set sail if it wasn't perfectly safe."

"That's a bunch of nonsense," Kirsten said. "Ships sink all the time!"

The three of them linked arms, clinging to each other to keep from being blown away as they crossed the street from the rooming house and walked down the road to the dock. Ahead of them, seawater splashed across the pier and onto the walkway, reminding Kirsten of a cauldron of boiling water. Rows of wagons lined the harbor front, loaded with crates and barrels and trunks, all getting drenched in the cold, pelting rain. She wanted to sprint down the pier and board the ferry, but Elin stopped her.

"Wait here for me. I need to search for our trunk first and make sure it gets loaded. It contains everything we own. We can't lose sight of it again."

Kirsten huddled close to Sofia in the pouring rain while Elin consulted with the baggage porters. Ships of all shapes and sizes tossed and bobbed on the restless water until it made Kirsten sick to her stomach to watch them. The damp, fishy air was the foulest she'd ever smelled. Sofia pinched her nose closed.

The smell reminded Kirsten of the white-hot summer day when she had gone fishing with Nils and Tor in the lake where Papa had drowned. They had cleaned and gutted their catch afterward and tossed the remains on the compost pile, where they festered in the sun. Uncle Sven had been furious with them, swearing that the stench could reach all the way into town. Nils and Tor had laughed it off, imitating his tilting shoulders and crab-legged walk as soon as he'd turned his back to walk away.

The memory of Tor's laughter struck Kirsten like a kick in the stomach. She glanced around for Elin, who was still searching for the trunk, and spotted the overhanging roof of the baggage porter's shed nearby.

"Let's wait under there. We're getting soaked." She and Sofia hurried over to stand in the shelter of the ramshackle building. They were no longer getting drenched but still had to endure the brunt of the wind.

"Remember the stories we read in school about water *nacks*?" Kirsten asked as rain drummed on the eaves above them.

"No. What are *nacks*?"

"Come on, don't you remember? They're mysterious creatures who live in the sea and lure people to watery deaths in their kingdoms. They—"

"Stop it, Kirsten," Elin said. She had joined them in time to hear what Kirsten was saying. "You're not helping matters."

"All I'm saying is that if there is such a thing as a water *nack*, then the one in Gothenburg's harbor seems very angry this morning. I think he's determined to drown us all."

"Stop it."

"When are you going to realize what a mistake this stupid trip was," Sofia asked, "and take us home?"

"See what you've done, Kirsten? You've scared her."

"Well, I'm scared, too, in case you can't tell. You'd have to be crazy to get into a boat on a day like today."

"I'm sure the sailors know what they're doing."

"Right . . ." Kirsten mumbled under her breath, "but you sure don't."

The gangway onto the ship bobbed up and down, making it treacherous to board. Thrashing waves splattered Kirsten's skirt and soaked her shoes. The ship rocked from side to side and slammed against the dock as waves surged into the harbor. The motion made Kirsten feel dizzy as she tried to walk, as if she had a high fever. All three of them staggered and lurched across the deck like a village drunkard, hanging on to anything they could find along their path. Kirsten sank onto the first empty bench she came to. Sofia tumbled onto her lap.

"This ferry is going to sink before it ever leaves the harbor!" Sofia said.

Elin gave her a reassuring pat. "I'm sure the captain will wait for better weather before venturing from port."

But he didn't. The horn shrieked, the hull groaned, and the engines thrummed to life. The ship sailed out of the harbor and straight into the storm.

Sofia vomited three times in one of the buckets the sailors passed around. She cried inconsolably.

"Please, Elin, please. Can't we go home?" Of course the answer was no, but Elin stopped saying it.

"You won't want to go back home once you see

America," Kirsten told her. She was sorry that she had frightened Sofia by mentioning the water *nacks* and wanted to make amends. "It will be so wonderful there that we'll wish we had moved there sooner. Just look at all of these other travelers. I'm sure many of them will be continuing on to America, as we are. Do you think they would be going all the way to America if it wasn't a paradise?"

Sofia swiped at her tears. "What will it be like there?" she asked.

Kirsten didn't know how to describe a place she'd never seen, but the least she could do was make up tales to soothe her sister. "We'll all marry rich husbands and sit in the warm sunshine all day and eat strawberries and cream."

"Don't even talk about food!" Sofia begged. She hung her head over the bucket again.

Kirsten felt queasy at the mention of food, too. And she'd had an unexpected stab of pain the moment she'd mentioned husbands. She silently vowed never to give her heart away again after the way Tor had tossed it aside. Besides, Kirsten didn't think she could ever love anyone as much as she'd loved him.

"Take deep breaths," Elin told Sofia as she went through the dry heaves. Elin reminded Kirsten of their mother. Mama always used to tell them to take deep breaths whenever one of them felt sick. Kirsten missed her mother. She missed Papa and Nils, too, even though they both had abandoned them. Mama had had no choice whether she lived or died, but Papa and Nils had deliberately chosen to leave. They had rejected her as heartlessly as Tor had.

"Think of all the money we'll save on food if we're too sick to eat," Elin said. "Our bread and cheese will last much longer this way."

Sofia gripped the bucket like a life preserver and moaned. "I'm going to die. If the boat to America bounces and rolls like this, I will surely die of sea-sickness—unless we drown first."

Elin rubbed Sofia's back and smoothed her hair off her forehead. "Don't worry," she told her. "The ocean will be much calmer than the North Sea. Besides, we'll be sailing on a huge steamship, not a skimpy little boat like this one. The ocean liner will ride the waves much better. You'll see."

Kirsten caught Elin's eye above Sofia's bent head and mouthed the question, *"Is that true?"* Elin gave a helpless shrug.

A few hours after they set sail, Kirsten was as sick as Sofia, vomiting her breakfast into a bucket. When the bout ended, she lay down across the row of scarred wooden seats like Sofia was doing. Kirsten hadn't slept very well last night. Or the night before, for that matter.

Most of the other passengers became sick, too, as the ferry rolled and swayed, tossed like a toy on the towering waves. Kirsten watched one of the sailors cleaning the deck with a mop and thought of Tor, sweeping the sidewalk in front of his father's store. He had stopped sweeping as if surprised to see her, but after she'd said good-bye and had turned to walk away, she'd heard the shushing sound of his broom behind her as he'd resumed his work. She drew her knees up to her chest to ease the ache inside.

She and Tor and Nils had been friends for as long as Kirsten could remember. Then Nils had run away to Stockholm, leaving her and Tor behind. She had missed her brother every bit as much as she'd missed her mother and father—and that's how she'd found herself wrapped in Tor's arms one afternoon, weeping for everyone she had lost. He had comforted her, murmuring softly in her ear. *"I miss him, too, Kirsten."*

The next thing she knew, Tor's lips had found hers and they were kissing. A host of powerful sensations had surged through Kirsten as if she'd walked through a forbidden door and discovered a new land. She hadn't wanted Tor to stop kissing her. Even now the memory made her feel warm inside. Kissing him had been like tasting chocolate for the first time and longing for more.

Had he only pretended to love her in return?

Kirsten rolled over on the unyielding bench and hid her face in her folded arms. How was it possible to hate someone and still love him at the same time?

Chapter Six

WHEN SOFIA AWOKE, she knew they had been sailing for many hours. Someone had dimmed the gaslights in the ship's salon and people lay sleeping all around her, sprawled across benches and slouched in their seats. Rain no longer drummed against the cabin roof and the sea seemed much calmer, which was a good thing. Sofia's stomach felt like a herd of cattle had trampled it, but she dared to believe that she might not die after all.

She sat up and looked out of a window. The view outside had changed from dense gray storm clouds and churning seas to a blackness so complete it was as if the ship had sunk to the bottom of the ocean, where no light could reach it. The only thing visible in the darkened window frame was her own pale reflection.

Kirsten was asleep on the bench across from her, her knees drawn up to her chest. She had been sick all afternoon, too, and her cheeks, which usually glowed from the sun, looked milky white. Her lips were as colorless as a dead person's.

Elin had fallen asleep sitting up, and her face wore a worried expression, even at rest. Sofia knew she had caused some of that worry by arguing with her. She had wanted to punish Elin for ripping them away from their home, but now she was sorry, especially when she saw how pale and weary Elin looked.

Sofia pulled her satchel closer, careful not to disturb Elin. She dug through it until she found her mother's Bible, wrapped in one of Mama's nicest aprons for protection. The Bible was small enough for Sofia to hold in one hand and had a black velvet cover framed in brass, with a brass clasp to hold it closed. The swirling print was old-fashioned and very tiny. Papa had given it to Mama as a wedding present.

Their mother had read aloud from her Bible every evening when she was alive, and it seemed as though thrilling words and promises had leaped off the pages like spawning fish, landing right in Sofia's heart. But when Sofia tried to read the Bible herself, the words never seemed to make any sense. She couldn't find any comforting promises, only big words and alarming warnings like *every tree that does not produce good fruit will be cut down and thrown into the fire.*

Ever since Mama died, whenever Sofia had tried to pray in church or in her bed at night, her prayers seemed to fly around aimlessly like trapped pigeons beating their wings against the ceiling, unable to fly any higher. The only prayers that soared weightlessly toward heaven were the ones she murmured outside in the cemetery beside her mother's grave. Now, thanks to Elin, Sofia could no longer go there to pray.

The cabin gradually grew lighter as dawn approached. After sitting motionless for a very long time, Sofia made up her mind to close her eyes and open the little Bible at random and read whatever passage she pointed to first. She would not stop reading until she found words of comfort and assurance. She pried open the little book near the back, recalling that all of the stories about Jesus were near the end of the Bible. But when she opened her eyes, the alarming heading at the top of the page read *Paul Suffers Shipwreck.* She read the first sentence: *When neither sun nor stars appeared for many days and the storm continued raging, we finally gave up all hope of being saved.*

Sofia slapped the Bible shut. Where was the comfort in that?

Gradually, the view out of the porthole changed from black to gray. The other passengers began to stir. Sofia was still sitting with the closed Bible on her lap when Elin and Sofia woke up.

"What a night!" Kirsten said as she stretched and yawned. "It's a miracle we didn't sink to the bottom of the North Sea in that storm."

Elin moved over to sit beside Sofia. "How are you feeling?" she asked, smoothing Sofia's hair off her forehead.

"Still a little queasy." She rubbed her aching stomach.

"*Ja*, me too," Kirsten said. "But look at the bright side. At least the food we packed for the trip will last longer this way."

"Maybe the worst is behind us now," Elin said. "And at least one thing is certain: We'll never have to cross the North Sea again."

Sofia bit her lip. She would gladly recross that wind-ravaged sea and endure the storm all over again if it meant she could go home. But she didn't speak her thoughts; Elin was trying so hard to cheer her.

The three of them took turns washing and tidying themselves in the ladies' comfort room. Nearly all of the other passengers had been ill, and they had left the overused facilities trampled and foul-smelling. Sofia worked as quickly as she could, eager to flee the awful room.

Later that afternoon, she stood outside at the ferry rail with her sisters as their ship neared Hull, England. At first all they could see was a dark smudge on the horizon, but it slowly slid into focus and took shape as land formations and buildings and the masts and hulls of other ships. Piers stretched out like fingers to welcome them into port. The sky was the dull gray color of dead fish, and Sofia thought from the look of it that it was about to rain again. But when the dense cloud that hovered above the city never moved, she realized that it came from the soot and factory smoke that rose from dozens of tall smokestacks. The city's trees all looked as though someone had dipped their leaves into gray paint to match the water and the sky, and the gritty air stuck in the back of her throat as if she'd just swept out the fireplace back home.

Sofia could hardly wait to get off the rolling deck and step onto dry land again, but it seemed to take forever for the sailors to wrestle with the thick ropes and taut chains and secure the ship in place. "Finally!" she breathed as her feet touched the solid earth at last. "I don't ever want to get on another boat as long as I live!"

"Then I guess you'll be living here for the rest of your life," Kirsten said.

"What do you mean?"

"England is an island, silly. The only way you can get anywhere is to get on another boat. You don't want to live here instead of America, do you?"

"I want to go home," Sofia said. Kirsten rolled her eyes.

One of the sailors inspected their tickets and directed them to a row of wagons and carriages sent by the White Star Steamship Company. When their trunk was safely loaded, they rode through the city's swarming streets, moving so slowly that Sofia was certain she could have jumped off and walked there faster. Carriages and horses jammed the thorough-fares and people crowded into every space in between. Everyone seemed to be yelling. Sofia missed the lilting, musical sound of her own language. English sounded like a flock of fighting crows.

"This city must have been built by trolls," Kirsten said. "It's so dirty and loud! It even smells like trolls."

Sofia smiled in spite of herself, picturing lumpy rolls stumping down the sidewalks with bowler hats and canes.

It took an hour for their carriage to wedge its way through the city to Hull's train station. When they finally arrived, the confusion and noise unnerved Sofia. Trains rumbled into the station like summer thunderstorms, spilling torrents of passengers into the already flooded station, then rumbling away with shrieking whistles and clanging bells. Bewildering signs hung everywhere and Sofia knew they must be telling her important things, but she couldn't read any of them. She linked arms with Elin as the three of them scanned the place in confusion.

"How will we ever tell which train is ours?" Kirsten asked.

Elin straightened her shoulders as if drawing upon some inner reserve of courage. "I'll find out. You and Sofia find someplace to sit down," she told Kirsten. "And don't let our trunk out of your sight."

Sofia longed to be as brave as Elin, but the dogs of fear surrounded her, making her afraid to move. "What are you going to do?" she asked Elin.

"Uncle Lars gave me a letter in case anything went wrong," she said, digging through her bag. "It's written in English and explains all our travel arrangements and destinations and things. I'm going to get in line over there and show it to somebody."

"How will you understand what they're saying back to you?" Kirsten asked. Elin's mouth opened in surprise, then she closed it again.

66

"I'll figure something out." She hurried away, clutching their uncle's letter. Sofia sat down beside Kirsten and their trunk, watching as Elin got in line and slowly made her way to the clerk's window.

Sofia folded her hands in her lap to make them stop shaking. "Tell me the truth, Kirsten. Are you as scared as I am?"

"The truth?" Kirsten paused, looking all around as if someone might overhear her. "Sometimes it seems like we made a big mistake. Elin might as well be deaf and mute. She can't communicate with anyone or understand a word they're saying to her."

"Do you think . . . I mean . . . what if we just admitted we made a mistake and turned around and went home?"

"We can't, Sofia. We had to leave the village." Kirsten sounded as impatient with her as Elin usually did. It made Sofia furious to have both sisters turning against her and treating her like a child.

"I still don't understand why! Why did we have to leave? And I want to know what you meant the other day when you said that people in town were whispering about us."

Kirsten shook her head, refusing to answer. She stared down at the tiled floor, biting her lip.

Sofia looked over at the ticket window. It was finally Elin's turn, and she handed her letter to the clerk. A few other Swedes from the ferry had followed Elin, and they gathered around her, talking and gesturing. The frustration of not being understood, not being heard, boiled up inside Sofia until she wanted to scream.

"I think I have a right to know why we had to leave home!" she shouted at Kirsten.

"Because we're orphans!" Kirsten shouted back. "There—are you happy now?"

"What does being orphans have to do with leaving home? Or finding husbands?"

"We don't have a father or mother to speak up for us or to make a good match for us in the village. No one wants to marry an orphan."

"That's stupid. It's not our fault Mama and Papa died. Losing them isn't a disease or anything."

"But that's exactly how everyone treated us—as if their families might die, too, if their sons married one of us."

"So what? I don't even care if I get married or—"

"You'll care someday," Kirsten said sharply. "And then what?"

Elin returned. Her face looked haggard, but she smiled bravely. "Why is it that whenever people can't make you understand them, they shout at you—as if volume alone will solve the problem?"

Kirsten gestured impatiently, twirling her hands in the air as if winding a ball of yarn. "So? Did you find out about our train?"

"Yes. It took all of us Swedes putting our heads together to figure it out, but evidently the train left without us."

Fear rose up inside Sofia, and with it a wellspring

of tears. It was the same hollowed-out feeling she'd felt at her parents' funerals. Once again, she had been left behind.

"Why did the train leave without us?" she asked. "We had tickets!"

"The storm made our ferry late," Elin said, taking Sofia's hand, "but the train had to stick to its schedule."

"Well, what about one of these other trains? Can't we get on one of them?"

"England is a big place, Sofia. None of these other trains is going to Liverpool, where our ship is. We'll have to wait until tomorrow to catch the next one."

"Are we going to miss our boat to America, too?" Kirsten asked.

"Let's just go home," Sofia said.

"No, listen. Our ship doesn't sail until the day after tomorrow. But even if something does happen and we do miss it, one of the Swedish men said we could probably take the next ship—just like we're taking the next train. He says our tickets will probably still be valid."

"So we're stuck here for the night?" Kirsten asked. "With the trolls?"

"It seems so," Elin said. "Some of the other Swedes are going to leave the station and look for a place to eat and spend the night."

"Can we go, too?"

"We don't have money to spare for such luxuries, Kirsten. Besides, how would we find our way to a hotel and back? None of us can speak English or read any of the signs. What if we took a wrong turn and got lost? How would we ever find help?"

"You worry too much," Kirsten said. "Come on, I think we should go exploring."

"No," Sofia said. "I don't want to get lost." She could feel the pressure of tears building behind her eyes, and she wanted to run to a ladies' room and bawl her eyes out. But how would they ever find one? Who could they ask? How would they make themselves understood? "I need the washroom," she whimpered.

"Well, it shouldn't be hard to find," Kirsten said. She rose on her tiptoes, surveying the station. "I'll go have a look around."

"No, you stay with our trunk, Kirsten. I'll take Sofia."

Elin linked arms with her as they made a circuit of the perimeter, eventually finding the comfort facilities. The big echoing washroom was surprisingly nice for a public place, though the tile floor was scuffed and dirty.

"It doesn't even smell too bad," Elin said.

Sofia broke free and ran into one of the stalls, slamming the door behind her. She sat down on the stool and buried her face in her skirt as she finally released her grief and fear. She was an orphan. The villagers hadn't wanted them, and now she and her sister were lost and alone in a strange city. She felt as though she'd been pushed into a rapidly flowing river and left to drown as she drifted farther and farther downstream. She wept silently for a long time, keeping her sorrow to herself.

"Sofia? Are you all right?" Elin finally called to her.

"Yes," she sniffed. "I'll be right out."

She avoided her reflection in the mirror, staring at the floor. She and Elin made their way back to where they'd left Kirsten and found her sitting with two young Swedish men in their early twenties. Sofia had seen them last night on the ferry.

"Oh, here come my sisters," Kirsten said when she saw them approaching. "Elin and Sofia, I want you to meet Eric and Hjelmer. They're cousins from a village near Stockholm, and they're on their way to America, too."

"Pleased to meet you, ladies," Eric said, tipping his hat.

"Isn't it lucky that there are some other Swedes stranded here with us?" Kirsten asked. "At least we'll have someone to talk to besides the trolls."

The boys seemed very friendly and nice, but Sofia could tell by Elin's tight-lipped expression that she was angry. "Excuse me; I don't mean to be rude," Elin said, "but would you gentlemen mind sitting someplace else? There's something I need to discuss with my sisters. In private."

"*Ja*, sure . . . we can move." But they took their time doing it. The one named Eric looked offended.

"Nice meeting you," Hjelmer said as he slouched away.

Kirsten glared at Elin until the men were out of earshot, her body tensed as if waiting to lash out at her. "What is wrong with you, Elin? Why did you send them away?"

"Because we don't know anything about them. You have no idea what they're really like."

"So? That's why I was talking to them—to find out what they're like! They're far from home, too, just like we are. What can it hurt if we make friends with them and—"

"What can it *hurt?*" Elin said angrily. "We're all alone, Kirsten. It's dangerous to talk to strangers—"

"Eric and Hjelmer aren't dangerous! They're as nice as can be. If you'd stop being so suspicious of everyone and talk to them, you'd see."

"Sure, we'll make friends with these men and then we'll never see them again! Haven't we said enough good-byes?"

For a moment, Kirsten looked stunned, then hurt. "*Ja* . . . Thank you very much for reminding me," she said bitterly. She folded her arms as if hugging herself, and slumped back on the bench.

"I'm sorry," Elin said, "but we can't talk to strangers." She turned away and sat down on one of the benches across from them, leaving Kirsten and Sofia sitting side by side.

Sofia still felt dangerously close to tears, even after her bout of crying in the washroom. She didn't trust herself to talk. But Kirsten kept up an angry monologue, muttering alongside her.

"How does she think we're ever going to find husbands once we get to America? Won't they *all* be strangers? She's so stupid sometimes. We're all going to end up old maids because Elin will never let us talk to *anyone.*"

Sofia swallowed the lump in her throat. "Will being orphans make it hard to find husbands in America, too?"

"I don't know . . . but at least no one there will know how Papa died."

"What do you mean? Papa fell through the ice. What does that have to do with anything?"

"Um . . . nothing. Forget it." Kirsten quickly turned away, but not before Sofia glimpsed the guilty look on her face. She was hiding something.

"No, I won't forget it. You're not telling me the truth, Kirsten. Stop treating me like a baby."

"Stop acting like one."

"I have a right to know everything!"

She was surprised when Kirsten wiped a tear. "I can't, Sofia. I just found out myself, and . . . and it hurts too much."

Sofia waited. "Please tell me," she said softly.

Kirsten exhaled. She was quiet for such a long time that Sofia thought she would have to shake the truth out of her. But at last Kirsten spoke. "People . . . people were saying that Papa went out on the ice on purpose. That he wanted to die."

"That's not true!"

"*Ja,* Sofia. I think it is."

"Papa would never leave us all alone. . . . Not on purpose!"

"Don't you remember how sad he was all the time? How he hardly ever spoke to us? I think he wanted to die."

"No . . . no, no, no . . ." Sofia shook her head, unwilling to believe what Kirsten was saying. But somewhere deep inside she knew it was true. Kirsten pulled Sofia into her arms, hugging her fiercely.

"That's why he wasn't buried in the church cemetery. And that's why we had to leave town. Everyone thinks that what Papa did is a terrible sin, and his shame would have always hung over us."

Sofia thought she had exhausted all her tears, but the ugly truth made her cry even harder than before. Elin sprang from her bench across from them.

"What happened? What's wrong?"

"I told her about Papa."

"Kirsten!"

"She has a right to know, Elin."

At last Sofia drew back and wiped her cheeks. She pinned Elin with an accusing look. "What else haven't you told me?"

"Th-there's nothing else, Sofia." But Elin wouldn' meet her gaze.

They spent the night in the train station, forced to sleep on hard wooden benches for a second time Sofia and Kirsten both lay down, using their shawl; for pillows, but Elin sat on the bench between them writing in her diary.

Sofia tried to pray, but her prayers went nowhere, floating around the train station's high arched ceiling like smoke, unable to escape. She felt utterly alone, even with Elin and Kirsten right beside her.

Chapter Seven

EXHAUSTION NUMBED ELIN. They had only traveled for three days, but it felt like three years. The weight of responsibility she carried made it seem as though she had hauled her sisters on her back the entire way. She might as well have. Hadn't she dragged Sofia against her will every step of the way? And Kirsten had been uncooperative, too. They were both asleep on the long bench beside her, but Elin was afraid to close her eyes. Strangers surrounded them in the huge train station, and it must be obvious to anyone paying attention that she and her sisters were traveling alone.

She looked down at Sofia and brushed away the strands of fine golden hair that lay tangled across her cheek. Elin's earliest memory was of the day Sofia was born. Elin had been nearly four years old, and when she heard her mother suffering in childbirth she'd been angry with the new baby for causing so much pain. Afterward, Mama allowed Elin to come into the room. Tiny Sofia lay asleep in Mama's arms, and the love in her eyes as she gazed down at Sofia made Elin burn with jealousy. She wanted to push

Sofia onto the floor and take her place. Then Mama looked up at Elin.

"Would you like to hold your new baby sister?" she asked.

Mama hadn't waited for Elin's reply but quickly arranged a place for her to sit, leaning against the pillows. Elin still remembered the warm weight of her tiny sister and the sensation of Sofia's body against her own, alive and squirming. Elin stroked the pale-blond fuzz that covered Sofia's head. She looked vulnerable and fragile.

"You're her big sister, Elin," Mama said. "She will need you to look after her. Sofia and Kirsten both need you."

In an instant Elin felt strong. She didn't want to let Mama down. Elin and her sisters were bound together in that moment with invisible cords that had shrunk like new cotton cloth as the years passed, gripping them ever tighter. Even if Elin had wanted to break the bonds, she couldn't imagine her life without Sofia and Kirsten. They were part of her, part of Mama and Papa, and she had to stay strong for their sakes. She would protect them, watch over them, and find a safe home for all of them in America.

The train station grew gloomy as the night wore on, tempting Elin to sleep. Instead, she sifted through her memories in an effort to stay awake, remembering happier times on the farm when they had all been together. But in the darkest part of the night Elin's thoughts strayed to Uncle Sven. The things he had done seemed to belong to the realm of darkness and secrets. Shame shivered through her. She pushed away all thoughts of him—the way she should have pushed Uncle Sven away right from the beginning. She shouldn't have needed him. She should have known better.

As soon as the sun rose, the station began to fill with people rushing around like ants on spilled sugar as they raced to catch their trains. When her sisters woke up, they took turns guarding the trunk and going into the washroom to splash water on their faces. Then Elin got out the *knäckebröd* and cheese and potato sausage they had brought from home and fixed a quick breakfast. Tears filled Sofia's eyes as she looked at the food.

"Are you feeling sick again?" Elin asked her.

"No . . . That sausage was Papa's favorite, and . . . and . . . Oh, can't we please go home?"

Sofia had asked that question so many times that Elin was getting sick of hearing it. She wanted to shout *"No!"* and let the sound echo through the cavernous station. If only she could tell Sofia and Kirsten the truth about how their home had become a hell for her these past three years, the truth about how she had saved them both from suffering through that hell with her. But of course Elin would never yell in a public place. And she would never tell them the truth, either. She drew a long breath and slowly let it out, struggling with the effort to control her temper.

"No. We can't go back to Sweden, Sofia. So just make up your mind to look forward from now on, instead of always looking backward. I know we don't have a home right now, but we'll find one, I promise. We aren't leaving home; we're going home. Home is the place where we're loved and wanted, where we can laugh as we knit beside the fire every night and sing while we do our work every morning. We'll have a home like that again, I swear."

"How can you be sure?"

Elin hesitated for a fraction of a second, realizing how lost and homeless they really were at the moment. "Because I'm going to make certain of it. In fact, this train station is home for us right here, right now, because we have each other."

They ate in silence as trains rumbled in and out of the station, shaking the floor and the benches where they sat. The murmur of voices and the rush of feet all around them ebbed and flowed like a tide. With so many trains coming and going, Elin began to worry that they would miss theirs in all the confusion. She was about to go back to the ticket clerk for more information when one of the Swedish boys who had befriended Kirsten walked over to them, smiling as he waved a piece of paper in the air.

"Look at this, ladies. The Englishman explained the train schedule to me with these pictures." He showed them a sketch of two clock faces. "See? Our train will get here at 11:15 am and leave at 11:45. All we have to do is keep our eyes on the station clock." He pointed to the huge clock above the ticket windows.

It would be a few hours before their train arrived. Elin was so exhausted from staying awake all night that she decided to close her eyes for a minute. When she opened them again, two hours had passed. She had slept sitting up, right in the middle of the noisy train station. Kirsten had moved to the bench across from her and was talking and laughing with Eric, the young Swedish man who had showed them the drawings.

Elin could understand why he would be drawn to Kirsten. She had a happy, fun-loving nature that attracted people to her like cows to clover. She laughed and teased the young man the way she used to tease Nils and his friend Tor. Kirsten probably didn't know that she was flirting, but Eric would certainly interpret her playfulness that way.

Kirsten's golden hair was thick and beautiful. In the summer months she spent so much time outdoors that the sun would bleach her hair white, and she would glow with health and vitality. If Kirsten could have afforded a fancy gown instead of plain working clothes, she would have stopped the sun in its tracks. She was taller and shapelier than Elin was, with lovely womanly curves—even though she was still a young girl in so many ways. She and Kirsten were only eleven months apart in age, yet Elin felt old in comparison. Whenever she gazed in the mirror she saw a weary old woman, bent beneath a weight of shame—which is why Elin avoided mirrors.

If only she could explain to Kirsten what could happen to girls who were too trusting. But even if Elin had the courage to talk about Uncle Sven, Kirsten would never believe her.

Elin caught Kirsten's eye and beckoned to her. When she stood and walked over to Elin, the boy followed. "Thank you for helping us this morning," she told him, "but could you please let me talk to Kirsten alone?"

"Um . . . *ja* . . . See you later, Kirsten." He shuffled away.

Kirsten looked furious. "What did you do that for?"

"You're young and naïve, and much too trusting. The only boys you know are the ones from our village. You don't understand what can happen to a woman who is too friendly—and I don't know how to explain things like that to you."

"It isn't up to you to be my guard dog, Elin. You're not my mother."

"I know," she sighed. "Believe me, I wish Mama were still alive so that I wouldn't have to tell you what to do. But she asked me to take care of you and Sofia, and I promised her that I would."

"You're just trying to keep me from having fun."

"Listen, those men have their own lives to live and we have ours. America is a huge place, you know. It's ten times the size of Sweden. We'll probably never see them again once we arrive."

"We could ask them where they're going, couldn't we? Maybe—"

"No, Kirsten. I'd rather you didn't talk to them anymore."

She stomped her foot. "Why? Tell me why not!"

"I've told you my reasons," Elin said calmly. But she could tell that Kirsten wasn't listening.

"You're just jealous!" Kirsten gave their steamer trunk a kick.

Elin tried to keep her voice calm. "Those shoes are hand-me-downs, Kirsten, and they're nearly worn out as it is. If you keep scuffing and abusing them, they're going to fall apart and then you'll arrive in America with bare feet."

"I don't care!"

"Come on, let's work on our embroidery. It will help pass the time." Elin reached inside her satchel for their mother's sewing box, hoping to distract Kirsten. She would even let her sister use Mama's precious silver thimble. But Kirsten made a face.

"I'm tired of being bossed around. And I'm tired of sitting. I'm going to walk around and stretch my legs."

"Wait!" Elin grabbed her skirt to keep her from leaving. "You can't wander around all alone."

Kirsten pried away her fingers as if removing cockleburs. "I can do whatever I want, Elin."

"But . . . but we have to stay together. Sofia is asleep and we can't leave our belongings here—"

"Eric and Hjelmer could walk with me." The boys sat on a row of benches a short distance away. When Kirsten started to wave to them, Elin grabbed her hand and pulled it down.

81

"Be reasonable, Kirsten."

"Why should I be? You can sit here all morning if you want to, but I'm going for a walk." She freed her hand and strode away.

Elin didn't want to shout at her and cause a scene, yet she couldn't leave Sofia alone while she chased after her. She watched in frustration as Kirsten stalked around the perimeter of the train station, taking huge, angry, man-sized strides. She had such an angry expression on her face that Elin figured she would be safe—no stranger would dare to approach her.

Elin kept one eye on her sister and the other on the clock until half an hour had passed. Kirsten was going to wear out her shoes stomping and clomping around the building that way. She must have been watching the clock, too, because a few minutes before their train was due to arrive she finally came back and sank down on the bench beside Elin with a huff. Elin wanted to make peace.

"I'm sorry, Kirsten. I don't want to be bossy, but sometimes you want me to mother you and sometimes you resent it when I do. How am I supposed to know the difference?"

"You make it sound like I cause you so much trouble," she said sullenly. "In my opinion, you cause your own trouble by worrying so much. I can take care of myself, you know. And it's about time you stopped babying Sofia so much and let her take care of herself, too."

Sofia had awakened several minutes earlier, and Elin expected her to defend herself. She hated being called a baby. But Sofia stared at the floor without speaking. In fact, she had barely spoken all morning.

"Please, let's not fight," Elin said. She reached for Kirsten's hand, and to Elin's surprise, Kirsten's eyes flooded with tears. "What's wrong?"

"I miss Mama and Papa and . . . and Nils. If only they hadn't left us, then we wouldn't be here in this ugly train station and . . . and . . ."

Elin stood and drew her into her arms. Kirsten had always been close to their brother Nils and his friends, spending all of her free time with them. No wonder she needed to flirt with these new boys and win their attention. "I miss everyone, too," Elin told her as she hugged her tightly. "I'd like to wring Nils' neck like a chicken's for running away like he did. And the least he could have done is written to us and told us where he was."

Kirsten gave a little laugh as she pulled away and wiped her eyes. "I would gladly help you murder him."

Their train finally pulled into the station, right on time. They found seats in one of the cars and the two Swedish farm boys sat down across the aisle from them.

Elin tried to engage her sisters in conversation as the train began its sluggish journey across the English countryside, but Sofia turned her back on Elin to gaze sullenly out the window. Kirsten was much more interested in talking with the Swedish boys, and as much as Elin would have liked to stop her, she knew she couldn't. She took out her diary and began to write:

We are on the train again, a day later than we're supposed to be. The English countryside is lovely, much nicer than the city we just left, but I fear that the monotony of the train ride is going to put me to sleep. And I don't dare close my eyes.

Kirsten's new friend, Eric, is trying to work his charms on her and she is falling for it, getting friendlier and friendlier, telling him all about her life, which is none of his business. I don't know where those boys are going in America, but I hope it's far away from Chicago. I didn't turn our lives upside down and leave home so that Kirsten could fall into the hands of a stranger on the train. I left so that she would be safe—so that all of us would be safe.

This trip feels like it is taking forever. Every time the locomotive builds up a head of steam and starts going fast, it has to slow down again for the next station. We stop and go, stop and go. People get on and off, and I wonder where everyone is going. Some of their faces have that happy, hopeful look that tells me they are going home. I can almost see their hearts pounding with antici-pation as they gather their belongings and line up in the aisles to get off at one of the stations. As soon as the passengers step off the train, people rush forward to greet them and I hear cries of joy before the whistle drowns out everything and we steam out of the station again.

I try to imagine that Uncle Lars and Aunt Hilma will greet us that way when we finally reach Chicago. They will have warm smiles on their faces and a huge meal prepared for us in their home.

"Välkommen," Aunt Hilma will say as she opens her arms to us. "Welcome home." All of our sorrows and hardships will be forgotten.

Please, God, let it be so.

I'm feeling a little sleepy right now, so I think I'll rest awhile. We have many more hours to travel before we reach Liverpool. No harm can come to my sisters on a train—can it?

Chapter Eight

TRYING TO FORGET Tor Magnusson was proving to be impossible. Some days Kirsten found it easier than others, but today was one of the hard ones. Eric and Hjelmer had taken seats across the aisle from her on the train and Eric reminded her of Tor. He had the same high, wide forehead as Tor did, the same sandy hair and pale eyebrows. But Tor was taller and thinner . . . and he'd broken her heart.

Kirsten couldn't understand why Elin got mad every time she talked and laughed with these boys.

How could she explain to Elin that if it weren't for them, she would be crying all the time? Elin had never been in love.

If only Tor could see her talking with two good-looking men. Wouldn't he be jealous? Once again, tears filled her eyes at the knowledge that Tor hadn't loved her enough to beg her to stay.

Kirsten brought her mind back to the present and realized that Eric had asked her a question. "Sorry . . . what did you say?"

"I was wondering what we'll find to do for the next two weeks. We'll probably be on the same ship, you know."

"Oh . . . I'm sure we'll find something to amuse ourselves. At least we'll have more room to move around on the ship than on this train."

Eric leaned his elbow on the armrest and propped his chin on his hand, gazing at Kirsten the way Tor used to do. "So, where are you ladies heading to in America?"

"We have an uncle who lives in a place called Chicago. He's letting us live with him."

"I've heard that Chicago is a huge city—even bigger and more modern than Gothenburg, with lots of factories and things. I wouldn't like to live there myself. I prefer the countryside. That's why we're heading to Minnesota."

"Is that a big city, too?"

"No," he said, laughing, "Minnesota is a state, not a city. We're going to get jobs cutting timber this winter so we can earn some money, then we'll settle down and buy farms of our own. They say you can get a piece of farmland for next to nothing—forty or sixty or even a hundred acres if you want it. And it's good farmland, too."

"Why would they give away so much free land? What's the catch?"

"There's no catch. America is a huge place and they need lots of people to fill it up."

Once again, Kirsten thought of Tor. Maybe she should write to him and explain about all the free land. If he didn't want to be a farmer, maybe he could open his own store in America and . . . But no. She wouldn't write to him. She wouldn't humiliate herself any more than she already had.

"If you don't like Chicago," Eric said, "you can always move to Minnesota with me."

Kirsten rested her head against the seat, tilting her chin so her tears wouldn't fall. "I don't know if I want to live on a farm again," she said. "There's too much work to do on a farm. My sisters and I are going to be rich in Chicago and have servants to wait on us."

"Servants, eh? What will you do with yourself all day?"

"Anything I want—or nothing at all." But Kirsten couldn't imagine doing nothing. She had nothing to do on the train except look at the scenery or work on her stupid embroidery, and the inactivity bored her. She had loved to explore the woods back home

87

with Nils—and Tor. Once again, she battled her tears.

"Are you scared?" she asked Eric. "I mean, moving so far from home to a land you've never seen?"

"*Nej*, I think it's exciting. The place where we're going has already been settled by several families from our village back home in Sweden, so it's not like we'll be with strangers. We'll have friends and relatives there. They all say that it's just like home, only better because we'll each get our own piece of land—whether we're the oldest son or not."

"That sounds nice."

"Listen, I meant it when I said you should come up to Minnesota with us. Once I finish building my own house, I'll be looking for a pretty wife like you to marry."

Kirsten didn't know what to say. She wished Tor could hear Eric proposing marriage to her. Thinking about Tor, remembering how happy she once had been, made her stomach hurt.

Eric leaned a little closer to her. "I'll bet you had dozens of suitors knocking on your father's door back home. He must have been chasing them off with a broom."

The pain in Kirsten's stomach burned like hot coals as she shook her head. "*Nej*, I didn't have any suitors."

"That's hard to believe. A pretty girl like you?"

She waved away Eric's words with a shrug, pretending she didn't care. Tor had told her over and over how pretty she was as they'd kissed in the woods.

"Tell me everything you know about America," she said, desperate to change the subject. They talked about America all afternoon—what it would be like, how big the country was, how different it would be from home.

"There are places you can live in America where the weather is always warm," Eric told her, "and where it never snows, even in January."

Kirsten couldn't comprehend it. The more Eric talked about their new home, the more excited she became, catching his dream like a fever, as if his hope for the future was contagious. Kirsten knew she had fled from home unprepared, running away from her old life instead of journeying toward a new one the way Eric and his cousin were doing. If only Tor would stop intruding on her thoughts every few minutes, making her feel as though he had kicked her in the stomach.

Later that afternoon, Hjelmer unpacked his concertina and played folk songs to help pass the time. He was quite an accomplished player, and Kirsten and Eric soon joined in singing. Elin worked on her embroidery, barely glancing up, acting as cold and stiff as an iron post in January. Sofia wallowed in silent misery—which was surprising, since she had been the one who had loved to sing back home.

Kirsten ignored both of them as she stood in the aisle beside Eric, clapping in time to the music.

Singing these old, familiar songs helped make the endless train ride go faster. She could almost forget that she wasn't back home in Sweden with Tor.

"We'll start crossing the ocean tomorrow," Eric said when evening fell and Hjelmer finally put away the concertina.

"*Ja.* I'm very excited."

"Since we will be on the same ship," he said, lowering his voice, "do you think we could spend some more time together? Maybe we could go exploring—without your sisters?"

"Um . . ." Kirsten hesitated, glancing at Elin.

"I don't think your sister likes me," Eric whispered. "You will have to sneak away from her, I think."

The thought of doing something forbidden appealed to Kirsten. So did the chance to go exploring. Besides, Elin wasn't her boss. "I'll do my best to get away," she told him. "But if the ocean liner is as huge as you say it is and carries so many people, how will we ever find each other again?"

"Don't worry," he said with a grin. "I'll find you."

They arrived in Liverpool after nightfall. Once again, the steamship company had provided carriages and lodging for the night; the men were assigned to one boardinghouse, the women to another. Kirsten bid good-night to Eric and his cousin and climbed into the carriage with her sisters. It was too dark to see much of Liverpool, but it smelled even worse than the last city had.

"I hope Chicago doesn't stink like the cities in

England do," Kirsten said as the horses trotted down the narrow street. "And I hope it has lots of trees. I miss the forests and the giant fir trees back home, don't you?"

Too late, she realized that the mention of home might bring another rush of tears from Sofia. She glanced at her sister and saw that she was staring straight ahead into the darkness. Sofia had barely spoken a word all day. Kirsten nudged her with her elbow.

"Hey. Are you feeling all right? You're not sick again, are you?" Sofia shook her head in reply.

Their tiny room in the boardinghouse had only one bed. The landlady seemed to be offering them two identical rooms across the hallway from each other, but neither Kirsten nor her sisters wanted to split up and spend the night alone. They decided that all three of them would crowd into one room. Sofia undressed quickly and climbed into bed without saying goodnight.

"How can you possibly be tired?" Kirsten asked her. "You slept on the train most of the day."

"Well, I just am," she replied.

Kirsten watched her pull the covers over her head and felt a nudge of fear. Their father had slept all the time too, near the end. And he had also stopped talking. "Do you think she's all right?" she whispered to Elin.

She shrugged. Elin hadn't said very much all day, either. Her sisters might make Kirsten angry sometimes, but they were the only family she had left in the world and they shouldn't go to bed angry with one another. That had always been one of Mama's rules.

"Are you mad at me for talking to Eric and Hjelmer?" Kirsten asked as she pulled off her shoes.

"Of course I'm not mad."

"If you just took time to talk to Eric, you would see how nice he is. They're leaving home, too, just like we are. They could help us."

Elin was fiddling with the door as they talked, opening it and closing it and jiggling the knob. "What I find odd, Kirsten, is that you trust these strangers, yet you don't trust me, your own sister, to know what's best for you. I'm just trying to watch out for you."

"I know, I know . . ." Elin's fussing irritated Kirsten. "What are you doing with that doorknob?"

"I can't figure out how to lock this door. The landlady never gave us a key."

"Let me see." Kirsten stepped around the bed to look at it. "I don't think it has a lock. I'm sure it will be fine, though."

"But . . . but it's dangerous to sleep with the door unlocked. Anyone could just walk right in while we're asleep. How would we ever get help? I don't even know how to say *help* in English."

Kirsten stifled a sigh and turned away so Elin wouldn't see her roll her eyes. "Maybe *help* should be the first English word you learn since it's so important to you."

Kirsten finished undressing, folding her clothes neatly and laying them on top of Sofia's on the room's only chair. Elin continued to tinker with the door. "Why don't you just push the bed in front of the door if you're so worried?" Kirsten finally said.

"That's a good idea. Will you help me?"

"I was joking, Elin, but if it'll help you stop fussing and go to sleep, it'll be worth the effort." Sofia never stirred as Kirsten and Elin pushed the bed across the floor until it blocked the door. Since it was too heavy for them to lift, the legs scraped loudly on the wooden floor.

"Well, that's certain to bring the landlady running up the stairs," Kirsten said with a giggle. "Remember how Uncle Sven used to climb the ladder if we made even the slightest peep?" Elin didn't smile at the memory. She stared at Kirsten, her eyes wide with fright.

"Do you think this bed will keep someone out?"

"It should—unless they're thin as a stick. The door opens into the room, not out, and the headboard is blocking it like a gate."

But even after the door was secure, Elin didn't climb into bed. She lit a candle and sat on the floor beneath the window to write in her diary.

"Do you mind?" she asked. "Will the candle keep you awake?"

"No, I'm pretty tired," Kirsten said with a yawn. She climbed into bed beside Sofia, leaving a space near the edge for Elin. But it took Kirsten a long time to fall asleep. She missed Tor. There was nothing in the darkened room to distract her thoughts from him. She could only lie in the lumpy bed and allow her tears to fall, listening to the unfamiliar city noises outside her room and the sound of Elin writing in her diary, her pencil scratching across the page like mice feet.

Chapter Nine

SOFIA HAD NEVER SEEN anything as huge as the ocean liner that was docked at the wharf in Liverpool. How could it even float? Her entire village with all of its shops and houses and churches could fit inside that ship. And the people! More people than in all of Sweden, it seemed, were crowding onto the pier with their shabby clothes and tattered bundles and bags, chattering in an excited babble of languages.

The farther Sofia traveled from home, the more impossible it seemed that she could ever go back. They were about to cross an ocean that was so vast it would take two weeks to reach the other side. Her stomach ached at the thought of it. She had never imagined a world as big and as overwhelming as this one—and they weren't even to America yet. Elin had promised that they would have a home again someday. *Please, Jesus, let it be true.*

Sofia clutched her satchel with one hand and one of the trunk handles with the other as they waded into the throng and slowly inched their way forward to board. As usual, Kirsten had plowed ahead of them, going her own way.

"Kirsten, come back and wait for us," Elin called to her. "You're going to get lost."

"Stop worrying so much," she shouted back. "How can I get lost?" She stood on her tiptoes, scanning the faces as if searching for someone.

"I think she's looking for those boys she met," Elin said. "She's determined to make a fool of herself with them."

"I think she misses Nils and his friend Tor," Sofia said. "She was always with them, remember?"

"I suppose so," Elin said with a sigh. "But she also takes pleasure in annoying me. She's just flirting with them to make me mad."

"Maybe she's lonesome."

"She could talk to us, Sofia. And she could give us a hand with this trunk."

Everyone inched forward a few more feet. They were almost to the boarding ramp. Sofia hated being jammed together with so many strangers. They bumped into her on all sides, crowding so close that she couldn't breathe. She didn't hear anyone speaking Swedish. Her stomach knotted as she reached the end of the pier. They were about to walk up the gangway to board the ocean liner. Sofia set down her end of the trunk.

"What's wrong?" Elin asked.

"I hope this voyage isn't as rough as the one on the ferry."

"It won't be," Elin assured her. "Look up at that beautiful sky. See? No storms this time. There's hardly a cloud."

Sofia picked up her end again and started up the ramp. She was grateful not to feel the nauseating rocking motion this time as she stepped onto the ship. The mob funneled across a narrow deck, then through a doorway into the ship itself. The crush of passengers became much worse once they crowded inside. At least there had been open sky and fish-scented breezes outdoors, but the narrow, low-ceilinged corridors made Sofia feel claustrophobic as she followed the others through endless passage-ways, down steep metal stairs, down, down into the bowels of the ship.

"Do you see Kirsten anywhere?" Elin asked.

"She's up there. I see her red vest."

"I wish she would wait for us."

Sofia had lost track of how many stairs she had descended but she knew she must be well below the surface by now. "Are we under the water?" she asked. She hated the idea of the dark, icy sea sur-rounding her, pressing in on her from all sides.

"I don't know . . . I don't think we are," Elin said.

"You're lying."

They walked through still more corridors until Sofia feared they were all lost and would end up in some rat-infested storage hold. She longed to turn around and run back outside into the light and the fresh air, but the passageways were too tightly packed with people. She could barely move, let alone turn around. The other passengers were noisy and dirty, and the smell of body odor and unwashed hair made Sofia want to pinch her nose closed. If Kirsten thought the strangers in the train station were trolls, what must these people be?

Finally, the stream of traffic emptied into a huge open dormitory, filled with hundreds of bunk beds. Sofia wanted to weep when she realized she would have to live in this horrible place for the next two weeks. Porters directed the men to one side, the women and children to the other, but it seemed to Sofia that there were far too many people for the space—at least a thousand in a room meant to hold half as many. She felt like she was suffocating.

"I can't live here for two weeks," she told Elin. "There aren't any windows. . . . I-I can't breathe!"

"I'm sure we can go up on deck and walk around once we've settled in. We won't have to stay down here all the time." But even Elin looked shocked by the sight of the enormous room, in spite of her reassurances.

Kirsten had run ahead to lay claim to three beds, tossing her satchel and shawl on an upper and lower bunk, and sitting down on the bottom bunk of a third bed alongside it. A short olive-skinned woman wearing an embroidered headscarf dropped her belongings beside Kirsten. A hive of small children buzzed around the woman, and she frowned unhappily as she yelled a stream of orders at them, orders they largely ignored, behaving as if they didn't understand her any better than Sofia did. The mother turned to Kirsten, a question in her voice and in her eyes as she gestured and babbled, pointing to the beds. Kirsten could only shake her head in reply, clearly indicating which three beds were hers.

"Come on, hurry up," Kirsten said, beckoning to Sofia and Elin. "Sit down and claim your beds before someone else does."

"We could have used your help with this trunk," Elin said. "Do you want a bottom bunk or the top one?" she asked Sofia.

"The bottom, I guess."

"Good, I wanted the top," Kirsten said. She scrambled up as if climbing a tree, while Sofia and Elin sat down on the two lower beds, gripping their satchels.

Children swarmed all over the cramped space, bouncing on the bunks to test the mattresses, pushing and teasing each other. Sofia tried to count how many of them belonged to the woman in the scarf—at least five or six—but it was like trying to count minnows in a stream. One of the smallest boys fell down as he tried to climb onto a bed with his brothers, landing on the floor with a thud. Sofia reached instinctively to soothe him, but the woman quickly snatched him up.

Another one of the children, a little girl about four years old, started to climb onto Sofia's bed, but she shooed her away. "No, go away. This is my bed. Go find your own."

The girl flopped around on Sofia's mattress for a

few more seconds, then jumped onto another bed. All of the children except the oldest boy were making a game of tumbling across the beds, ignoring their mother. The boy, who Sofia guessed to be around eight years old, had a nagging cough and appeared unwell. Instead of jumping around with the other children, he lay down on the bottom bunk beside Elin's bed and draped his scrawny arm over his face to shield his eyes. Sofia instinctively covered her nose and mouth, wondering how she could possibly avoid catching whatever disease he had in such cramped living conditions.

"This is a terrible place," Sofia said. "These people are so dirty! Don't they ever bathe?"

"They can't help it that they're poor," Elin said. "That's why they're going to America—for a better life."

"Well, we aren't rich, either, but at least we use soap."

Kirsten leaned down from her bunk above Sofia's. "They wouldn't be so poor if they didn't have so many children. Look at them all. They're like a litter of piglets."

"Be nice, Kirsten," Elin said, frowning.

"Why? They can't understand a word I say."

The odors seemed to grow in strength as more and more passengers streamed into the room, milling around, heaving their bundles onto the beds. "This place smells worse than our barn!" Sofia said. She stood, fighting the urge to run outside.

"No, don't get off the bed yet," Elin said, waving her down. "Someone will steal it if you do."

Sofia sat down again, holding a corner of her shawl over her nose and mouth to block out the smell. Passengers continued to pour into the room, glancing all around as they searched for empty beds.

"There's no privacy at all," Elin said. "How will we ever sleep?"

"Never mind privacy; it's too noisy to sleep," Kirsten said.

"I can't breathe," Sofia said, her eyes filling with tears. "I want to get out of here! Please, let's go home."

Elin reached over from her bed and patted Sofia's knee. "Why don't you do something to take your mind off the smell. What about your embroidery?"

Sofia shook her head. Her hands were shaking too hard to manage a needle and thread. She considered reading from Mama's Bible, which she still carried in her bag, but the last time she had opened it and had read about a shipwreck it made her feel worse, not better. She knew there was also a story in the Bible about a man who was swallowed by a giant fish. No, she wouldn't try reading from it again. She listened to the children's voices and to their mother's constant yelling and wondered what language they were speaking.

Gradually, the flow of passengers slowed to a trickle, then halted. The porters helped several families shuffle around so they had beds close to one another until at last, everyone seemed to have found a bed and claimed their territory. Sofia wanted to stand up again but the deep ache in her stomach made her too sick to move.

The ship's engines made a deep, rumbling sound and she was aware of a steady tremor beneath her feet. She wondered how long it would take to get used to the incessant throbbing and if it would grow worse once the ship actually got underway. Elin had taken out her needlework, but Sofia's thoughts were too distracted to concentrate. She lay down on the bed and closed her eyes.

Please, Jesus, please . . .

She couldn't finish. She had no idea what to pray for. If only she would wake up and discover that this had all been a very bad dream.

Finally, the whistle blew.

"We're going to set sail," Kirsten said, sliding down from the top bunk. "Come on, let's go up on deck and watch."

"Why?" Elin asked. "It's not our homeland we're leaving. There's no one to wave good-bye to us, and besides, we can't leave our trunk."

Kirsten stomped her foot. "Don't tell me you're going to make us stay down here for the next two weeks guarding our stupid trunk. I'll go insane!"

"You and Sofia can go up if you want to. I'll stay here."

As much as Sofia longed for fresh air and open

space, she was afraid to move from the bed. "H-how will we find our way back? We'll get lost!"

Kirsten tugged on her hand. "Oh, come on. How hard can it be? We'll just keep climbing stairs until we reach the end of them, then turn around and go back the same way we came. This dormitory is so noisy, I'm sure we'll hear the racket a mile away."

Sofia let Kirsten lead her up through the maze of passageways until she was certain they would never find their way out again. But at last she felt cool, salty air blowing down the stairwell and saw blue sky and sunlight ahead. Passengers crowded the deck, especially along the rail, but at least Sofia could breathe fresh air and see billowing white clouds above her.

When she and Kirsten finally pushed their way forward and found a spot near the rail, Sofia made the mistake of looking down at the water. They were so high up that the water seemed miles below them. She felt as though she were falling. She gripped the rail and closed her eyes as a wave of vertigo rocked through her. When she opened them again, she decided to stare straight ahead at the horizon instead of down at the sea. The breeze felt wonderful against her face, the sun warm overhead. She watched the coastline slowly shrink into the distance as the expanse of water between her ship and the port of Liverpool grew wider and wider.

"Isn't this great?" Kirsten asked.

Sofia couldn't speak past the lump in her throat.

"Say something, Sofia."

"I-I miss our home. I miss walking down to the barn in the morning to milk the cows and then drinking the milk while it's still warm. I miss going to the chicken coop for eggs and eating them for breakfast, and eating the fish Nils used to catch for dinner. I miss going to church on Sunday and . . . and praying by Mama's grave . . ."

"I know, I know. But isn't this also fun, in a way? Sailing across the ocean and exploring new places? Everything was always the same back home. Every day the same."

"That's why I liked it."

"I give up," Kirsten said with a sigh. "Be miserable for the rest of your life, if you want to. I don't care. I didn't want to leave . . . um . . . my friends, either— but here we are and I'm going to make the best of it."

Sofia tried to make the best of it for the next couple of days, but no matter where she went there were always hordes of foul-smelling people reeking of perspiration packed tightly beside her like herring in a barrel. In good weather, everyone crowded up on deck and the men smoked pungent cigarettes, making it impossible to breathe the clean ocean air. Sofia had taken the aroma of sweet, fresh air for granted all her life, but now she hungered for just a tiny whiff of hay or pine trees or even the barnyard.

Down below in steerage, the smell of garlic and other foreign spices was so strong that Sofia had little appetite for the food they'd brought from home. The ship's water tasted like a rusty tin can, and she had to force herself to drink it. The latrines had stayed fresh for barely a day before they had begun to smell, too, forcing her to wash as quickly as possible every morning and evening. The foul, humid air down in steerage made her scalp feel itchy.

The smells in the dormitory were even worse at night, when the air turned damp and clammy from too many sweating people. Sofia tossed in her bed, barely able to sleep through the buzz of snoring men and the constant wail of babies. She didn't know what the lumpy burlap-covered mattress was stuffed with, but it smelled like hundreds of poor people had slept on it before she had. Elin had unpacked their own bedding from the trunk, and at first the thick linen sheets had smelled like sunlight and pine-scented breezes and the soap they'd always used back home. But it hadn't taken long for the smell of home to fade and for the stench of the mattress to work its way up through the bedding to Sofia's nostrils.

"Why does everyone talk so loudly?" Kirsten complained as they shared their meal the next evening. Elin always spread a cloth across the top of their trunk and set the food on it as if it were their kitchen table. She made them bow their heads and recite a blessing before they ate—although it was a mystery to Sofia why God would suddenly decide to bless their food after He had denied all of her other requests.

"Was it just our family that was so soft-spoken or was everyone in Sweden quieter than these people?" Kirsten asked. "I can barely remember."

"No, you're right," Elin said, breaking off a chunk of *knäckebröd*. "People back home never talked this loudly." She offered Sofia a piece, but she shook her head. She hadn't had any appetite at all since they'd boarded. "Yes, take it," Elin insisted. "You have to eat something."

"You can always tell the Germans—like that family over there," Kirsten continued, nodding in their direction. "They sound angry when they talk, even when they're not. And the Italians talk very rapidly, with everyone speaking at once. They're always gesturing with their hands, like this." She made wild, swooping motions in imitation until Elin pulled her hands down.

"Careful, you'll upset our dinner."

"I miss the deep silence of the woods at home," Kirsten said with a sigh. "It was so quiet sometimes you could hear the snowflakes falling from the tree branches and make that hissing sound when they landed on the ground, remember? I'm so tired of all this noise—people arguing and babies crying and women yelling at their children. I don't remember Mama yelling at us all the time, do you?"

She had addressed the question to Sofia, but she shrugged and shook her head in reply. Elin caressed Sofia's face, then lifted her chin, forcing her to look up.

"Talk to us, Sofia. You barely say a word anymore."

"I don't feel like it," she murmured. Talking made her cry, and if she started crying again she feared she would never stop. Besides, she had nothing to say except "I want to go home," and Elin got mad whenever she said it.

She saw Elin and Kirsten exchange glances. They finished their evening meal, and after Elin packed away the leftover food, she stood and reached for Sofia's hand, pulling her to her feet.

"Come on, let's all go up on deck for a walk." Her offer surprised Sofia. Elin usually chose to stay below whenever Kirsten and Sofia went outside for air. Kirsten looked surprised, too.

"You mean it?" she asked.

"Lead the way, Kirsten." Elin pushed Sofia forward, out of the crowded steerage hold and up the stairs.

Once they were outside, Sofia was glad she had come. The deck wasn't overcrowded for once, and millions of stars filled the night sky. The moon was nearly full, and it perched on the horizon like a huge broken dinner plate, casting a ribbon of light across the gently tossing waves. The water looked as though you could walk on it.

"Look up," Elin told Sofia. "Those are the same stars and the same moon that shone above our home in Sweden. They're following us to our new home."

"You know what tonight is?" Kirsten asked. "*Walpurgis* Eve."

106

"You're right," Elin said. "I've nearly lost track of what day it is, but tomorrow is the first of May."

"Everyone back home is probably gathering around the village bonfire," Kirsten said. She gazed at the horizon as if expecting to see a column of sparks swirling toward heaven in the distance.

Sofia used to love gathering with her friends and family on *Walpurgis* Eve to celebrate the return of the sun and warm weather. She loved singing the old familiar songs, saying farewell to winter's long, dark nights. The tears that filled her eyes at this reminder of home made the stars shimmer and whirl like snowflakes.

"So," Elin said after a long pause, "the past is behind us, just like the long, cold winter. It's time for us to make some new plans. Let's watch for a shooting star and everyone can make a wish. What would you wish for, Sofia?"

"She wants to go home," Kirsten said in a whining imitation.

"Be quiet and let her talk. Go on, Sofia."

"Let Kirsten go first," she mumbled.

"Fine," Kirsten sighed. "Let's see . . . I want . . . I want to marry the most wonderful man in the whole world and be as rich as a queen just to show all those stupid people back in the village that I don't need any of them. I wish they would all be sorry that they didn't think we were good enough to marry their ugly old sons—but by then it will be too late."

"That's it?" Elin asked. "You could have any wish in the world and you'd pick retribution?"

"Oh, you know what I mean," Kirsten said, waving her hand. "I wish this journey would make everything new for us, and that crossing this ocean would wash everything old away. I want a new home with Uncle Lars and Aunt Hilma, and a new village to live in. And new adventures!"

"That's better. Now it's your turn, Sofia. Forget about all the things we've had to endure and think ahead. Dream big dreams. What do you wish for in America?"

"I don't know," she said with a shrug.

"Come on, Sofia. You must long for something."

"I want things to be the way they were when Mama and—"

"No, Sofia. You can't live in the past. Even if we'd stayed in Sweden, we could never have Mama back and things could never be the way they were. Change is part of life, don't you see? Remember how quickly everything changed after Mama died? And then Papa gave up and the farm fell into ruin and everything changed again. Then Uncle Sven came and . . . and things were very different. Nothing ever stays the same. Try to remember what you used to dream of before Mama and Papa died."

Sofia thought hard and realized that she didn't have any dreams. It worried her that she didn't long for adventure like Kirsten or for a new start like Elin.

"All I want . . ." she said slowly, gazing up at the

stars, "all I want is what I left behind—a cottage on a farm with my own cows and chickens, and a little piece of land with a pasture and trees. I want to plant potatoes and grow flowers and eat dinner with my family around the table every evening. I want to smell soup cooking on the stove and bread baking in the oven and have freshly churned butter to spread on it. . . ." She had to stop as a wave of homesickness choked off her words. Elin wrapped her arm around Sofia's shoulder.

"You can have all of that someday, Sofia. You can meet a nice man and get married when you're ready and have a home and a family and cows again. And children. You would like children someday, wouldn't you?"

Sofia nodded and wiped her tears, remembering how she had cuddled her little cousins back home.

"What about you, Elin?" Kirsten asked. "What's your dream for America?"

"I would like to feel safe." Elin answered so quickly it was as if she had rehearsed it beforehand.

"To be *safe?*" Kirsten echoed. "We're safe right now, aren't we? What are you so afraid of?"

"I'm not afraid. I didn't mean it like that. I wouldn't have come on this journey if I felt afraid, would I? It's just that we need to be cautious traveling all alone. We have to use common sense when it comes to strangers."

Kirsten turned her head toward Sofia and rolled her eyes.

They fell silent, gazing up at the twinkling sky. The ocean beneath it seemed vast and dark and endless. The longer Sofia looked, the more she felt like a tiny speck, lost and alone in a fathomless universe. She closed her eyes, wishing she could go back inside.

"Remember that psalm Mama used to read to us?" Kirsten asked. "Something about looking up at the heavens at night and wondering about God and why He made us?"

"I think so," Elin said. "We should look for it in her Bible sometime."

Sofia remembered it, too. She longed to find it, but she was afraid to open the Bible again.

The depthless sky and bottomless ocean made her feel insignificant. They reminded her that God and everyone else had abandoned her—everyone except her sisters. She gripped Elin's hand a little tighter, afraid to imagine what would happen if she abandoned her, too.

"Say something, Sofia," Elin urged. "Tell us what you're thinking."

"It's cold out here," she replied. "I want to go back inside."

Chapter Ten

ELIN DIDN'T THINK the clammy odors in steerage could possibly get any worse—and then they did. The ship ran into a storm and seasick passengers taxed the overworked latrines to their limit. Everyone had to stay below deck or risk getting soaked by rain and sea. Down in steerage, the sickening motion of the rising and falling waves was even more apparent than it had been on the ferry. Elin hadn't needed a bucket yet, but if she didn't do something to take her mind off her terrible nausea, she would need it soon.

"I'm going up on deck," Kirsten said on the third day of the storm. She slid down from the top bunk with a thump.

"Kirsten, wait."

"Now what?" She swung around at Elin's words, hands on hips, a look of exasperation on her face. She had found her friends Eric and Hjelmer on their second day at sea and was spending too much time with them. Elin longed to tell her what could happen to girls who were too trusting, but she feared it would lead to awkward questions about her own experiences—questions she didn't want to answer. Instead, she searched for excuses to keep Kirsten away from them.

"I thought you said you weren't feeling well."

"I'm not. But Eric says seasickness is worse if you stay below. He worked on a fishing boat one summer and he says it helps to stay out in the open air, where you can keep your eyes on the horizon."

"But it's raining. You can't go outside in the rain."

"The deck has an overhang. I'll stay under the roof."

"What if the waves are rough and you get soaked? How will you ever dry your clothes?"

"Will you please stop worrying? You're driving me crazy!"

"I wish you wouldn't go up there—"

"Well, I wish you would! Why do you want to stay cooped up down here when there are so many interesting things to see on this ship?" When Elin didn't reply, Kirsten said, "You know, we've been so sheltered all of our lives. Our world was our farm and our family. A trip into the village was the most excitement we ever had. But now we're here with all these people on this enormous ship on this vast ocean, and I can't understand why you would want to stay in one place when there is so much to see. What are you so afraid of?"

"I'm not afraid—"

"You certainly act like it. And the more afraid you are of everyone and everything, the more fearless I want to be. I don't want to be like you, Elin."

"Well, you don't have to worry about that. You show no caution at all!"

Kirsten walked back to where Elin sat on the bed. The smile that usually graced Kirsten's pretty face was replaced with tight-lipped anger. "I don't understand how you could act so brave when we were back home in Sweden, telling us that this was going to be a great adventure and convincing us to sail halfway around the world to start a new life—and then act so wary of everyone we meet."

"These people are strangers. And those boys you're always hanging around with are bigger and stronger than you are."

"What difference does that make?"

"They could take advantage of you."

Kirsten shook her head in disbelief. "You're crazy!"

Her words made Elin shudder. What if she was crazy? She had hoped that by leaving home she would find peace and safety and rest, but her fears seemed to multiply with each passing day. Sometimes she worried that she was losing her mind.

"Why are you so suspicious of everyone?" Kirsten asked. "Who would want to go through life that way?" She turned to leave, but Elin grabbed her skirts.

"Wait—take Sofia with you."

"No," Sofia moaned. "I don't want to get wet."

"Sofia, please go up with her," Elin said, lowering her voice. "I'm worried that she's spending so much time alone with those boys. Please? For me?"

"What if I get sick again?"

"Why don't you go up and see if Kirsten is right? Maybe you'll feel better in the fresh air."

"You can come, too, you know," Kirsten told Elin. She shook her head. "Not this time."

"I don't understand why you stay down here in this awful place all the time. In fact, I don't understand you at all!"

"Well, I don't understand you, either," Elin shot back. She sometimes wondered how she and Kirsten could be sisters—born of the same flesh and blood, raised in the same home—and yet be so different. And she didn't understand Sofia, either, moping around like it was the end of the world. Elin recalled the way Papa had acted toward the end—sleeping a lot, refusing to eat, barely speaking to them—and saw the same behavior in Sofia. She shuddered.

"Go on, both of you," Elin said, shooing them away. "Come back and tell me how the weather is."

She watched them go, weaving between the bunks as they made their way to the stairwell. The enormous room seemed quieter than usual today with so many passengers ill. Elin had worried that the large, rambunctious family in the bunks beside her would be uncontrollable for the entire trip, but those children had all fallen ill, too. The oldest boy had been unwell since the day they'd left Liverpool, when the weather had still been sunny and the sailing smooth. But even before the ship had run into the storm, three more of his siblings had become sick, one after the other, with coughs and fevers. Now the remaining two lay sick and feverish.

For days, as Elin had watched the woman take care of them, she'd hoped that the children had nothing worse than croup or the measles, which Elin and her sisters had already had. She wished she knew how to break through the barrier of language and help the struggling mother, but most days Elin had been too preoccupied with her own sisters to be of any help to the woman.

Elin sighed and pulled out her diary. Writing in her journal transported her to a place where she could ignore her fears and the sickening motion of the

114

tossing sea. When her mother was alive, she had known exactly where to look in her little Bible to find all the right answers, all the right words to calm Elin's fears. But Mama was gone, her Bible useless. Elin's shame had sealed it shut more tightly than the cover's brass clasp. She had learned to set down her fears in her diary instead. She opened to a new page and began to write:

We are steaming into the Atlantic Ocean, far from land, our ship a tiny speck of wood and steel on a vast, featureless sea. I've never lived in a place without trees before, and I hate it. This is an alien, barren place without birds or animals— only endless gray water. Everything familiar has been stripped away, and when I go up on deck I feel as though I have died and am no longer on earth. I may have left hell behind, but I can't help wondering what lies ahead—and if I will be punished for my sins.

Kirsten begs me to come up and explore the ship with her, but I give her excuses. The truth is, I can't face the vast expanse of water. It stretches endlessly in every direction and I know that it is so deep I could sink down below the surface for an hour or more without ever reaching the bottom. Fear engulfs me whenever I go up on deck, and so I stay down here in order to keep my fear at bay. It is my means of survival, not a way to ignore my sisters.

Kirsten has found her friend Eric, and I know she is spending time with him whenever she's not down here. My fear for her is enormous, but my fear of the endless ocean is greater. I can't face the ocean. Besides, there are so many people crowded onto the deck along with Kirsten and the boys that she can scarcely move. I hope she will be all right.

During the day it is very noisy here in steerage, and the unending drumbeat of the engines pulses through me. At night I can hear the ship's hull groaning like an old man who is dying in his sleep. Sometimes I wake up with nightmares, and as I lie in the darkness I have the sensation that the ship is sinking to the ocean floor and I'm going to die in a cold, watery grave.

Everything about this journey seems like a picture of my life. I'm no longer standing on solid ground but have been cast adrift on changing, unstable water. When Mama and Papa were alive, it seemed like barely a day went by that the sun didn't shine and the heavens weren't blue. But the storms began to rage as we lowered Mama into her grave, and my life has been wind-tossed ever since.

Some of the sickness I feel is from the motion of the ship. But most of it is from the gnawing fear that I've made a terrible mistake. Maybe I'm like the foolish girl who ran away from a snake and encountered a bear. What if our lives become worse in America, not better? I believed that things would get better when Uncle Sven moved in with us, and look what happened. Maybe I should have found a different way to save all of us.

But no matter what, I can't let Kirsten and Sofia know how afraid I am of what lies ahead in America, afraid of what Uncle Lars will be like, afraid of what our new life will be like. I have to push aside my fear and stay strong—for their sakes. I have to . . .

Elin paused when she heard someone crying. She looked around and saw the olive-skinned woman in the bunk next to hers holding her youngest child, rocking him back and forth, weeping. The child lay limp and lifeless in her arms.

Was he dead? Horror shuddered through Elin.

She laid down her diary and moved to sit beside the woman. The boy's eyes fluttered open as the mattress shifted beneath her weight, then he closed them again. Elin felt a rush of relief. She brushed the baby's dark hair from his brow and felt the heat of his fever.

"I wish I knew what to say to you . . . how to help you," she murmured to his mother. "May I see . . . ?" She carefully lifted the baby's shirt to reveal a faint rose-colored rash on his chest. Elin had helped Aunt Karin nurse her three children through the measles, but this rash didn't resemble the measles.

The woman continued to weep, and Elin wrapped her arm around her shoulder in sympathy. As soon as she did, she felt the heat of the mother's own fever through her clothing.

"Oh, you poor woman. You're sick, too, aren't you? No wonder you're crying."

Elin pointed to the baby's chest, then to the woman's. She nodded in reply, weeping harder as she covered her eyes with one hand. Her body began to tremble with chills.

"Don't worry, I'll help you," Elin said. She lifted the baby from the woman's arms and motioned for her to lie down. Then she lay the baby beside her and covered both of them with a blanket. Within a few minutes, the woman and her child had fallen asleep.

For the next hour, Elin didn't have time to worry about her sisters as she bathed the mother and all six of her children with cool water to reduce their fevers and made sure they drank something. All of the children had rashes, the spots darker on the children who had become ill first, covering everything but the palms of their hands and soles of their feet. Some of the children had coughs, and all of them moaned and thrashed in delirium, including the mother.

Elin had just decided to move the children and their mattresses from the top bunks to the floor so they wouldn't fall out when Kirsten and Sofia returned.

"Oh good. You're back. Can you give me a hand? I've been trying to help this poor family. The mother is sick with whatever it is that the kids have, and—"

Kirsten took a step back. "I don't think you should go near them, Elin. What if you catch it, too?"

Elin waved away her concerns. "I've had all of the usual childhood diseases. So have you."

"What do you think they have?"

Elin hesitated, unwilling to admit that the rash didn't resemble anything she'd seen. "I don't know, but listen: Just help me move the children from the top bunks to the floor so they won't fall off. It will only take a minute."

When Kirsten and Sofia both hesitated, she added, "Come on. Please? We can't let them suffer. We have to help them. Suppose the three of us were sick and needed help?"

"All right," Kirsten said grudgingly. "You lift up the children and I'll pull down the mattresses. But let Sofia stay away so that at least one of us doesn't catch it."

"We're not going to catch it. I think this family was already getting sick before they boarded. Remember how droopy the oldest boy was?"

"Please be careful, Elin," Kirsten said.

"I will."

When they finished moving the children and their mattresses, Elin shooed Kirsten away and continued caring for them on her own. Days passed as Elin spent all of her time nursing the family. None of them showed signs of getting better. She began to grow weary, her sleep disturbed several times a night, but she refused to let Sofia and Kirsten help her, fearing that they would get sick, too. The task she dreaded the most was changing the baby's diapers, which had to be washed and hung up to dry every day. The odor in steerage had been foul enough without adding dirty diapers to it.

At first, most of the other steerage passengers were too seasick to notice the family's illness. But once the storm blew over and the sea became calm again, Elin saw everyone shying away from the family, keeping their distance from them—and her. Their fear was evident on their faces.

"I think you should get someone else to help them," Kirsten told her. "There must be a doctor aboard the ship, don't you think?"

"I don't know . . . I promised the woman that I would help her . . ."

"How could you promise her anything?" Kirsten asked. "She can't understand a word you say. Besides, if they do have something contagious, they need to be taken out of here before everyone else in this place gets sick."

"I don't know . . . what do you think I should do, Sofia?"

She shrugged. "I don't care if I do get sick and die," she mumbled.

"Stop it, Sofia! Don't talk that way, do you hear me?" Elin had been so preoccupied for the past few days that she hadn't noticed Sofia's darkening mood. But now, on top of everything else, it was one more thing to worry about.

In the end, Elin didn't have to decide whether or not to report the family's illness. Someone else must have told the ship's authorities about them, because the doctor came down to steerage one evening and examined the children himself. Elin couldn't understand a word he said, but he ordered the porters to carry the mother and her children away on stretchers and then collect all of their belongings and strip their beds.

When everything had been cleared away, the doctor turned to the passengers in the surrounding beds, including Elin and her sisters, and began examining them, feeling their foreheads for fever, asking questions that none of them could understand. Elin assured him that she felt fine, but fear made her heart race. The family obviously had a very serious illness for the doctor to go to all this trouble. What if he learned that she had been helping them? What if they took her away, too?

"I can't leave my sisters," she told the doctor, even though he couldn't understand her. "Please let me stay. We're all fine."

She breathed a sigh of relief when he left, but as the days passed, Elin couldn't shake the feeling that the other passengers were watching her. She had no doubt that they would report her to the authorities immediately if she or her sisters showed any signs of illness. Sofia acted so droopy most of the time that Elin feared her depression might be misinterpreted as illness. Every hour or so, she felt Sofia's forehead for signs of fever and tried to cheer her up.

"Talk to me, Sofia. Tell me what you're thinking. Why are you so quiet?"

"I don't have anything to say."

"Are you sure nothing's wrong? You're not getting sick, are you?" Elin reached to feel her forehead once again, but Sofia pushed her hand away.

"Leave me alone! I told you I'm not sick!"

"Then let's all go up on deck for a while." Elin stood, straightening her skirts, then reached for Sofia's hand. "Come on."

"This is a surprise," Kirsten said, swinging her feet to the floor. "Are you sure *you* feel all right?"

"Of course I do. Come on, show me around up there."

Together they pried Sofia off the bed and got her moving. And as weary as Elin was, and as much as she hated the sight of the open sea, her fear for Sofia outweighed everything else. She took her sister's hand and followed Kirsten up the stairs.

Chapter Eleven

WORD SPREAD ALL over the ship that this would be the last night at sea. Tomorrow Kirsten and her sisters would reach America. With so many languages spoken on board and so much confusion, Kirsten couldn't imagine how the news had been transmitted, but the excitement the passengers shared was contagious.

"Come up on deck with me tonight," she begged

her sisters after they'd eaten supper. "This will be our last night on the ship, and we need to celebrate together. Please?"

"I guess we could go," Elin said. Sofia followed wordlessly.

Numberless stars filled the canopy of sky above Kirsten's head, and the sound of music and laughter filled the cool night air. A spontaneous party had begun as people celebrated the beginning of their new lives. Kirsten longed to grab her sisters' hands and dance with joy, but she could barely move on the overcrowded deck, let alone dance.

"It looks like we're not the only ones who are happy to see our journey end," Kirsten said. "And tonight we don't even have to speak the same language. Joy is universal!"

Elin nodded. She seemed to be studying the deck planking instead of noticing how luminous the sea looked with moonlight gilding the waves. Sofia remained as somber and unenthusiastic as a fir tree. Kirsten wished they would share her happiness.

If only Tor were here—if only she could have shared this adventure with him. He would have loved this enormous party. But Kirsten refused to allow memories of Tor to dampen her joy. She spread her arms as wide as she could in the cramped space and twirled in a circle. "I'm going to miss the ocean. Isn't it magnificent? It's so powerful—almost as if it's alive! And we're crawling across the surface of it like a flea on a bear."

Her sisters looked at her blankly. She wanted to shake them. Maybe she should have come up on deck by herself. All around her, Kirsten heard the babbling conversations of the other passengers, gathering in their various ethnic groups. Many of them were celebrating with food and, judging by the raucous laughter, alcoholic drinks. Children jumped around like rabbits. Musical instruments appeared: a violin, an accordion, a mandolin. Some people sang, while others had cleared a tiny space to dance.

"Oh look. There's Eric and Hjelmer," she said, spotting her friends. "And Hjelmer brought his concertina. Come on, let's go talk to them."

She pulled Elin and Sofia through the melee to where the boys were conversing with the Lindahls, another Swedish family who were immigrating with their three small children. Kirsten had met them several days ago, and she introduced her sisters to them.

"I didn't realize there were other Swedes aboard," Elin said in surprise. Kirsten swallowed the temptation to remind Elin that if she had bothered to come up on deck more often, she could have met them. "Where are you staying?" Elin asked. "I didn't see you down in steerage."

"*Ja*, we are in steerage, too," Mr. Lindahl said. "I guess it's easy to get lost in such a huge place."

The conversation soon turned to talk of America—what it would be like, what everyone's relatives had written to say about it, what everyone's hopes and dreams were once they arrived. America's streets would be paved with gold, judging by the stories Kirsten heard. She would live like a queen. Anything was possible in America. As each person shared his own tiny sketch of the country, the finished picture resembled paradise.

"You ladies are very brave to travel to America all alone," Mrs. Lindahl told Elin.

"Well, we didn't have much choice. Our parents died, and it was too hard for us to keep the farm going all by ourselves."

"You had no other relatives to help you?" Mr. Lindahl asked.

"Our brother deserted us," Elin said. "He left home and never wrote to tell us where he is. Our uncle Sven and his family took over the farm, and so . . ." Her voice trailed off. She seemed to wither like a blossom in the sun, right before Kirsten's eyes.

"So we're going to Chicago to live with our other aunt and uncle," Kirsten finished. "What about you? Was it hard for you to leave home?"

"*Ja*, we left many, many friends and family members behind," Mr. Lindahl said. "But we also have family in America already. I was tired of being poor and struggling to make a living with thin soil and hard winters. They say the land in America is very good and that you can find a good job if you don't like to farm. Either way, we will soon be eating like kings."

"But it was very hard to leave," Mrs. Lindahl added. "We cried many, many tears. We will prob-

ably never see our loved ones again in this life—"
She stopped, her cheeks turning pink as if suddenly recalling that the sisters' parents were dead. "But you girls know how that is. Didn't you say that your mother is in heaven?"

"*Ja.* She died five years ago," Elin said.

"I'm so sorry. . . . I feel a little bit scared about coming to America," Mrs. Lindahl said, "but a little excited, too." She looked at Sofia, who hadn't spoken a word and asked, "How about you, dear? Are you eager to land tomorrow?"

"Elin said that our lives will never be the same," Sofia said morosely.

"No she didn't," Kirsten said. "Elin said that it's up to you, Sofia. Your life will be whatever you make of it."

She saw Eric and his cousin looking all around as if tired of the conversation and eager to join the party. Hjelmer lifted his concertina and squeezed out a few chords. "Look at all these people," he said, gesturing to the crowd. "We're all so different—different languages and clothing, different faces. But we're all the same in our hopes for the future."

"My brother in America says this is what it's like over there," Eric added. "People of all nations, becoming a new family."

"*Ja,* and we will all be Americans soon," Mr. Lindahl said. "Once we land, we won't be Swedish anymore."

His declaration gave Kirsten a strange feeling. She couldn't imagine not being Swedish.

They talked for awhile longer, until the Lindahl children grew tired. "I think it is time to put them to bed," Mrs. Lindahl said. "We have a big day tomorrow, and we must all look our best to pass the immigration inspection."

"You never said anything about an inspection," Kirsten whispered to Elin, but her words were lost in the confusion as the family bid everyone good-night and left. Eric and Hjelmer also drifted away.

"I'm getting cold," Sofia said, rubbing her arms. "I want to go inside."

"But don't you want to join the singing, Sofia? You used to love to sing." Sofia shook her head in reply. "Oh, come on," Kirsten begged. "The party is just getting started."

"I'm feeling pretty tired, too," Elin replied. "And as Mrs. Lindahl said, we need to be well rested for tomorrow."

"You're not getting sick, are you?" Kirsten asked.

"No. But I lost a lot of sleep when I was taking care of that family."

It still bothered Kirsten that the mother and her children had never returned. "What disease do you suppose they had?" she asked.

"It can't be anything too serious," Elin said, inching toward the door, "or the entire ship would be in an uproar. Aren't you coming with us?" she asked Kirsten.

"No. I want to stay longer. I'm not tired in the least." She could tell that Elin was searching for an excuse to make her come with them. Kirsten crossed her arms in defiance and waited. A hundred angry trolls couldn't force her to go back down to that dungeon on such a beautiful night. The sounds of laughter and singing filled the night air. Someone began playing a harmonica. Kirsten couldn't help tapping her feet in rhythm.

"Please let me stay," she begged.

Elin sighed. "Don't be too late."

As soon as Elin and Sofia were gone, Kirsten made her way over to Eric's side. A group had gathered around to hear Hjelmer play his concertina, and Kirsten listened and joined in on some of the songs. This was the happiest she'd felt since leaving Tor more than two weeks ago. She was thinking of him when Eric gently slipped his hand into hers.

"Want to explore the ship with me?" he whispered.

"I don't think we're allowed to explore, are we? Didn't they say that steerage passengers are supposed to stay on this deck?"

"How would I know?" he said with a sly smile. "I can't read the signs. We can plead ignorance if we get caught. After all, we don't understand English, right?"

Kirsten liked the idea of an adventure. She followed him willingly as he climbed over the gate into forbidden territory. "Where are we going?"

"Hjelmer and I have already done a little

exploring. That's how we found the secret route that leads to the first-class passenger deck. You should see how nice they have it up there with comfortable deck chairs to sit on and a real dining room with china and crystal. There's even a ballroom. Come on, I'll show you."

Kirsten let him lead the way. But as soon as she glimpsed the wealthy passengers in satin ball gowns and tuxedoes, she slowed to a halt, tugging on Eric's hand. "They'll know we don't belong here. Look at their clothes—and look at ours."

"So? They can hardly throw us overboard. Listen . . . hear the music from the ballroom? They have an entire orchestra playing."

Kirsten cocked her head as the strains of a waltz drifted toward them on the wind. "It's loud enough to dance to," she said.

"Shh—here comes somebody!" Eric pulled her into the shadows, ducking behind a lifeboat as a sailor hurried past. When the man was gone, she and Eric remained there, sitting side by side, concealed behind the lifeboat.

"Are you warm enough?" Eric didn't wait for her reply but draped his arm around her shoulder and pulled her close for warmth. Kirsten's heart began to race. She could feel the strength in Eric's grip and for a moment she felt a prickle of fear at being alone with him. She remembered Elin's warning: *"Those boys are bigger and stronger than you are. . . . They could take advantage of you."*

But her heart slowed again and her fear dissolved as they gazed out at the sea together. The water churned in the wake of the ship's propellers, the waves glowing in the light of the moon.

"The ocean is so beautiful," she murmured. "I'm going to miss it."

"And I'm going to miss you." Eric's voice sounded husky and breathless. "I've been wondering if you feel the same way I do."

"I . . . um . . . I don't know how I feel." She wanted to explain about Tor and tell Eric that she was still in love with him, but her pride wouldn't allow her to admit that Tor hadn't loved her in return. "We've only known each other for two weeks, Eric," she said instead.

His arm tightened around her shoulder. "It seems like much longer. I hate it that we might never see each other again."

"Never? . . . Are the places where we're going very far apart?"

Eric shifted his body around so that he could face her. His strong hands gripped her shoulders. "Come with me to Minnesota, Kirsten. You said you were tired of your bossy sister. You can tell her good-bye tomorrow and come with Hjelmer and me."

"How can I come with you? I have a train ticket to my uncle's house in Chicago."

"I'll bet the railroad company would let us trade it for a ticket to Minnesota."

"But Elin has all of our tickets in her bag."

130

"Wait until she's asleep and take yours out. You would have a lot more fun if you came with us."

"That's true, but . . . I don't know. Elin and I have our differences and I'm tired of Sofia's gloomy moods . . . but they're my only family, Eric. I don't think I could leave them."

"Come on, Kirsten. I can't stand the thought of leaving you tomorrow."

She looked at him and her heart speeded up. Tor hadn't wanted her, but Eric did. His hair looked like it was spun from gold in the moonlight, and she couldn't resist the urge to comb her fingers through it. The next thing she knew, Eric was kissing her. She closed her eyes and pretended that he was Tor.

But after a moment she realized that Eric's kisses were very different from Tor's. Eric held her too tightly and kissed her too possessively. She had known Tor all her life and Eric for only two weeks. She turned her face aside and pushed him away.

"We need to stop," she told him. "This isn't right."

She had been down this path before with Tor—she had even gone too far with him once—and that romance had ended with a broken heart.

But Eric wouldn't stop. He pulled Kirsten close again and crushed his lips against hers. She felt genuine fear. She pushed against his chest as hard as she could and twisted her face away from his, well aware that he could easily overpower her if he wanted to.

"Let me go," she said, loud enough for anyone nearby to hear. Thankfully, he didn't restrain her.

"Kirsten, what's wrong?"

"I have to go." She scrambled to her feet. He followed.

"Wait . . . What's the matter? Did I do something wrong?"

"Yes. Kissing me was wrong."

"I don't understand. I thought we liked each other."

"Is this all you wanted—to get me alone so we could kiss?"

It was what Tor had wanted, too, yet he obviously hadn't loved her. Maybe all men were alike. She looked at Eric with his golden hair and pale blue eyes and silently vowed never to trust a man's declarations of love again. He would have to prove his love with much more than words before she would believe him.

"Good-bye, Eric." She whirled around and hurried away from him, hoping he wouldn't follow, hoping she could find her way back to the steerage deck alone. She didn't look back.

"Come on, Kirsten . . . don't go." Eric followed her most of the way, begging her to be reasonable. He gave up when she reached their crowded steerage deck and plowed a path through the mob. People were still dancing and laughing, the party in full swing.

Kirsten longed to stay and join the fun, but she hurried through the doorway and down the stairs, her footsteps echoing on the hollow metal treads. She held her breath as she parted the privacy curtain that separated the men's sleeping area from the women's, hoping that Elin and Sofia were already in bed so she wouldn't have to talk to them. If Elin saw her face and noticed her tears, she would demand to know what was wrong.

Kirsten exhaled in relief when she saw that the lights had been extinguished and that her sisters both lay huddled beneath the covers. But she knew that Elin would never fall asleep until she returned.

"I'm back," she whispered, touching Elin's shoulder.

"Thanks for not staying too long," she murmured. *"God natt."*

Kirsten undressed as quietly as she could and climbed up to the top bunk. Only then, with her sobs muffled by her blanket and pillow, did she dare to release her sorrow. She had fallen hopelessly in love with Tor Magnusson—she loved him still. But he had been lying to her all along.

Chapter Twelve

ELIN LAY IN bed listening to the excitement all around her. The ship would land in America today. She should get up, fix breakfast, and put on her nicest clothes, but she felt too tired to move, too sick to eat. Her head throbbed to the beat of the engines, and she wished only for peace and quiet. The dormitory in steerage was as dark and dingy as always, but her eyes hurt every time she opened them, as though someone were shining a bright light in her face. Her

133

headache must be from all the excitement, she told herself. Or maybe a bad case of nerves.

She sat up and squinted at Sofia, surprised to see that she was already dressed and sitting on her bed with her hands folded in her lap. "How long have you been awake?" Elin asked her.

Sofia shrugged. "For awhile. I don't know how anyone can sleep with all this noise."

"I guess I was exhausted." Elin exhaled and slowly swung her feet out of bed, groping for the satchel with their food in it. She ached all over.

"You're not getting sick, are you?" Sofia asked as she watched Elin's sluggish movements.

"No, I'm just tired this morning. And I have a very bad headache. Do you want something to eat, Kirsten?" She gave the lump on the top bunk a gentle shake.

"No!" Kirsten answered much too quickly, too emphatically, pulling the blanket over her head as if for emphasis. Her behavior seemed odd to Elin.

"I'm surprised you're not the first one up today, Kirsten, ready for all the excitement. Are you feeling all right?" She stood on the bottom bunk and reached to feel Kirsten's brow for signs of a fever. Kirsten pushed her hand away.

"Would you please stop doing that? I'm not sick!"

"Then why don't you want any breakfast?"

"Because this place stinks worse than ever. Even a troll would lose his appetite down here."

"Well, you should try to eat something anyway. I

134

think this is going to be a very long day, and who knows when we'll get a chance to eat again."

Elin sat down on the bunk beside Sofia and smoothed the hair off her sister's face, using the gesture as an excuse to feel her brow for fever. Sofia pushed her hand away, too.

"I wonder what happened to them," Elin said, nodding toward their neighbors' empty beds. "They never came back."

"I hope they didn't die," Sofia said.

Elin's stomach churned at the thought. She recalled how the woman had shielded her eyes with her hand as if the room had seemed too bright for her, too, and felt a ripple of fear. She could *not* get sick—not today of all days.

"Well, let's eat some breakfast," Elin said, attempting to be cheerful. "Then we'll put on our Sunday best and go up in the fresh air for our first glimpse of America. Come on, Sofia. Help me spread out the food. Kirsten, you need to 'eat for the hunger that's coming,' as Mama used to say."

"We're all going up on deck?" Sofia asked.

"Yes, I think we should, don't you? This is one of the biggest days of our lives and we need to enjoy it." Elin would fight this aching, dragging feeling. Nothing was going to keep her from landing in America today. And she would do everything she could to keep her sisters from getting sick, too. Fortifying them with food was a good start.

Elin did feel better once she was outside in the sunshine, breathing the fresh salty air. Kirsten and Sofia seemed to revive, as well. The sky was a clear, cloudless blue, and the ocean looked calm and serene for once. But so many excited passengers jammed the deck that Elin could barely move. Most of the other people crowded forward, trying to be the first ones to see America, stranding Elin and her sisters in the rear. They peered at the horizon over a multitude of bobbing heads. Elin kept her eyes fastened on the sky, not the endlessly churning waves. She felt tense with excitement as everyone waited for the first sign of land.

"Eric says we'll be able to tell when we're near land because we'll start seeing birds," Kirsten told them.

Elin glanced around, wondering where Eric and Hjelmer were this morning, and why Kirsten hadn't gone in search of them as usual. But she decided not to mention them.

"I've missed hearing the birds sing every morning," Elin said.

"I know what you mean," Kirsten said. "I've even missed hearing our rooster crow in the morning. Do you suppose Uncle Lars and Aunt Hilma will have a rooster?"

"And I miss Sofia's songs," Elin said. "Why don't you sing for us anymore, Sofia?"

She shrugged.

A murmur of excitement suddenly spread through the crowd. "Look!" Kirsten shouted, pointing to the sky. "I think those are birds!"

Elin shaded her eyes against the glare, her headache worsening as she focused on the bright western sky. "You're right," she said after a moment. "Look at them all! And the air feels different somehow, doesn't it?"

Kirsten hopped up and down with excitement. "Isn't this great? As soon as our feet touch the ground in America, it will be a new beginning for us."

"It feels like the end, not the beginning," Sofia said gloomily.

Elin wrapped her arm around her sister's waist. "Come on, Sofia. Cheer up. Our journey is almost over. And to tell you the truth, I'll be glad when it ends, too. By this afternoon we'll be on the train to Chicago, where our new home is waiting for us." Only then would Elin finally be able to relax and find true rest.

"We'll never see Sweden again," Sofia murmured.

Elin decided to ignore her moodiness. She looked away from the bright sunlit sky and saw the Swedish family they had met last night approaching them. "*God morgon*, Mr. and Mrs. Lindahl. This is going to be a big day for all of us, isn't it?"

"*Ja*, it will be a very big day," Mrs. Lindahl replied. Elin thought she detected more fear in the woman's voice than excitement. She wondered if immigrating had been Mr. Lindahl's idea and not hers.

"I'm so excited I can hardly stand still," Kirsten said. "See those specks in the sky? They're birds. That means we're approaching land."

Mr. Lindahl nodded without looking up. He didn't seem to share Kirsten's enthusiasm, either. "I will feel more excited once we have successfully passed through immigration," he said.

"What do you mean?" Kirsten asked. "What do we have to do? Can't we just get off the boat when we land?"

"*Nej*. We have to go through the immigration center on Ellis Island first and pass inspection before they will let us into America."

"Inspection?" Kirsten echoed. "You're making that up."

"No, it's true. My relatives who came earlier told me all about it. There are doctors on Ellis Island who check to see if you are well. They look at your eyes and at your scalp, and they watch to see if you are lame or have some other deformity or maybe a bad heart. They give everyone a medical inspection card, and if they find anything wrong with you—phutt!" He gestured over his shoulder with his thumb. "You're not allowed into America."

"Well, we're all healthy," Elin said, "so I guess we have nothing to worry about."

"After the medical inspection," Mr. Lindahl continued, "you must wait in line to present your papers and be questioned by an immigration official. He will make you read something to see if you are literate."

"Uncle Lars never told me any of this," Elin said. "I hope we don't have to read in English."

"*Nej*, they will give us a passage in Swedish."

"Well, that's good. . . . What kinds of questions will they ask?"

"I'm not sure, but my friends say it's important to convince them that you are able to work and to support yourselves. And if they ask how much money you have, tell them twenty-five dollars."

"But—but we don't have that much money," Elin said. Mr. Lindahl's fears were starting to rub off on her.

"It doesn't matter. They won't make you show them the money or anything. The best thing to say is that you have relatives waiting for you."

"We do," Elin said. "We're going to our uncle's house in Chicago. We have train tickets and everything."

"Then as long as you pass the medical exam," he said with a shrug, "you should be fine."

"Thanks for the information." Elin felt reassured. Her head still throbbed, but surely she wouldn't fail the health exam because of a headache. How would they even know?

They stood out on the deck late into the morning, until Elin could no longer tolerate the pain of the sun's glare. She moved beneath the deck's overhang and shaded her eyes, but it still didn't ease the pain.

"Does your head still hurt?" Kirsten asked.

"It's so bright out here, I'm surprised we don't all have headaches. I don't know if I'll be able to stay outdoors much longer."

"Don't tell the immigration people," Mr. Lindahl warned. "Don't give them any excuse to detain you."

Elin decided to stay a little longer for her sisters' sakes. Then, just when she was starting to feel nauseous from the unending pain, a cheer went up from the passengers on the other side of the deck. Land! Someone had spotted land. Everyone crowded forward, straining for a look. Elin saw a dark smudge on the horizon that might have been a bank of clouds.

"That's it!" Kirsten cheered. "That's America!"

Elin hugged both of her sisters. Everyone had tears in their eyes, but she suspected that Sofia's were not tears of joy. As time passed, the smudge of land grew larger and clearer, sliding into focus and taking shape. More and more ships appeared on the horizon, too. The cheering grew louder, until Elin feared that her head would burst.

"I'm going down below to gather our belongings," she said. "Come and get me when we're almost there. I'll need your help with the trunk."

Elin staggered down the stairs with her eyes closed, gripping the railing to guide her way, grateful that the passageways were dimly lit and deserted. The dormitory in steerage was nearly deserted, too. She lay down on her bunk and closed her eyes, desperate for relief. It didn't come.

She couldn't get sick, not when they were this close to their goal. She had to get through the next few hours and pass inspection and board the train to Chicago. She wondered what would happen if she didn't pass inspection. She had been afraid to ask Mr. Lindahl that question.

Elin awoke to a buzz of excited voices. She sat up, disoriented. She hadn't meant to fall asleep. She looked around and saw the other passengers packing their belongings, preparing to haul them up the stairs to the deck. That's what she should be doing. She climbed slowly out of bed and finished stuffing everything into their trunk just as Kirsten and Sofia came downstairs to help her.

"Hurry up, Elin," Kirsten said. "We're almost to America. We're supposed to see that famous statue from France any minute."

It took a great deal of tugging and pushing and grunting to maneuver their trunk up the many flights of stairs, especially with Elin's body aching the way it did. "Going down was definitely easier," she said.

Outside, the sunlight seemed even more blinding than before. But ahead of them, visible in the steamy haze, was the city of New York. It sprawled into the distance as far as Elin could see, with buildings that seemed to soar into the sky. She had never seen so many ships in her life, lying at anchor, and sailing up and down on the wide river. And trees! She was relieved to see that America had trees. The horizon was green with them.

"Look! There's the statue," Kirsten said, pointing above everyone's heads. "The Statue of Liberty."

Passengers rushed to the left side of the boat to view it, forcing Elin to stand on her toes, craning around people's bobbing heads to see it. At first, it looked like a coppery shadow pointing up into the air above the trees, but as they neared Liberty Island, the statue grew larger and larger. Elin gazed at the huge stone pedestal and graceful figure in awe. Men removed their hats in respect.

Lady Liberty wore a starlike crown on her head and her long, elegant robe hung in beautifully draped folds. She held a tablet in one hand and a torch in the other, high above her head as if to light the way into the harbor.

"She's beautiful," Elin murmured.

At first the crowd stared in near silence. Then someone began to clap. Others quickly joined in, and the sound swelled in strength until it was deafening. Joy and hope sounded the same in every language.

"I feel like I'm dreaming," Kirsten said. "We're in America! We're finally in America!"

Elin glanced at Sofia to see her reaction, but her sister wasn't cheering. Instead, Sofia stared at the statue with a frown on her face. Elin was afraid to ask what she was thinking. She had given up trying to lift Sofia's spirits. Time would have to heal her sorrow. Until then, Elin comforted herself with the knowledge that she had rescued her sister from a future too horrible for words.

The ship sailed past the monument. Lady Liberty was so close, so enormous that she seemed to fill the sky. For the first time, Elin dared to hope for freedom—from her past and from Uncle Sven. She was really here in America, and she would never have to see him again. Tears of joy flowed down her face.

"Why are you crying?" Sofia asked.

"I don't know . . . she's Lady Liberty. And she's welcoming us. I can't explain it."

"It is a beautiful sight," Kirsten breathed. "I've never seen anything that huge and that lovely before. America must be a very rich place. . . . What do you think of her, Sofia?"

Sofia said nothing. Elin glanced at her again and saw her staring morosely into the distance.

"I know I didn't want to come with you at first," Kirsten told Elin, "but I'm so glad I did. This is so exciting! I don't think I could bear living on our little farm ever again, so far away from town. Oh, if only—" She stopped.

"If only what?" Elin asked.

"Nothing. I can't believe we're finally here. I'm so excited I feel dizzy! What do you think of the statue, Mrs. Lindahl?" Kirsten asked. The family had moved up to stand beside them again.

"It truly is a wonder. I've never seen anything like it in my life—and probably never will again."

"I've heard there is an inscription on the pedestal," Mr. Lindahl said, "that tells how the statue welcomes all of the poor, suffering people in the world to America. She is holding up her lamp to light their path."

Elin still couldn't stop her tears. She felt so weak

and shaky all of a sudden that she had to sit down on their trunk and rest. Probably from all of the excitement.

Their ship slowly sailed away from the statue, steaming across the river to the port of New York City. America looked so big and beautiful to Elin, the sky and water so blue—like something from a dream. It seemed like paradise. And best of all, she and her sisters would be safe.

Chapter Thirteen

"I CAN'T WAIT to get off this boat," Kirsten said, kicking the bulwark with her foot. "I know it has only been two weeks, but it seems like we've been living down in steerage for a hundred years."

All of the other passengers seemed eager to get off, too, crowding forward with their belongings, pushing against the railings and each other. But even after the ship was safely docked at the pier in New York and all of the ropes and anchors and gangways were secured, the barrier that confined the mob to the steerage deck remained closed. The wait was maddening.

"It figures they would let all the rich people with first-class tickets get off first," Kirsten grumbled as they watched throngs of well-dressed passengers disembark. "I wish they would hurry up."

"But we will not be getting off here at all," Mr. Lindahl told them.

"We won't?"

"*Nej.* They send all the steerage passengers to the immigration station on Ellis Island."

The news made Kirsten angry. Elin was looking weaker and more ill by the moment, and judging by the way she shaded her eyes with her hand, her headache must be excruciating. If they didn't pass the health inspection soon, Elin would no longer be able to pretend that she was well.

Kirsten knew it must be close to noon, for the sun felt like a fire above their heads. She was beginning to feel a little dizzy. She wished she had eaten breakfast.

"Where is Ellis Island?" Kirsten asked. "How far away?"

Mr. Lindahl shrugged. "I'm not sure. But they will begin calling the roll of passengers soon and giving us landing cards with our numbers on it. We must listen very carefully for our names. The Americans do not know how to pronounce them correctly."

The flow of first- and second-class passengers finally tapered off until only the steerage passengers remained aboard the ship. Roll call took a very long time as, one by one, the ship's officials called out everyone's name. Men and women in workmen's caps and kerchiefs came forward, trailing their children behind them, waiting to have their landing papers pinned to the front of their clothing. Kirsten could barely control her impatience.

The officials called the Lindahl family forward,

then Eric and Hjelmer. Kirsten looked away to avoid meeting Eric's gaze. He had successfully avoided her all morning, and that was fine with her.

"Carlson!" the official called out. "Elin Carlson . . . Kirsten Carlson . . . Sofia Carlson . . ." Kirsten helped Elin stand up, linking arms with her as they went forward.

"I feel like an item for sale in Magnusson's store," Kirsten said as the officials pinned tags to her clothing. She had hoped that her joke would make Elin smile, but it didn't. She looked more unwell by the minute, her face deathly pale. "Are you all right?" Kirsten whispered.

"Just nervous. This is the last stream to jump."

"Well, pinch your cheeks, for goodness' sake. You look like you've seen a ghost."

Finally the barrier opened, but instead of allowing the passengers to step onto American soil at last, the officials herded everyone onto ferryboats. "Help me with the trunk," Kirsten told Sofia. Elin usually took charge of it, but she looked too weak to help wrestle it on board. Sofia didn't look ill, just sulky and stubborn. She could pout all she wanted to; it wasn't Kirsten's job to cheer her up.

The ferry was small and unbelievably crowded. It felt very unstable in the water, rocking back and forth and banging against the dock every time another ship sailed up or down the river, leaving a wake. When every inch had been packed with passengers and baggage, the engines fired up and the boat slowly chugged away from the dock, heading downstream again, back across the wide river toward the statue. The water was so choppy it was nearly impossible to remain standing without holding on to something.

"Oh no," Kirsten groaned. "Not another wild ride. I hope we don't have to go too far."

She started feeling sick before they were halfway across the river. She couldn't get ill now, not when they had to pass inspection. She glanced around and saw that the rocking motion was affecting everyone. She fastened her eyes on the horizon, the way Eric had advised. The ferry seemed to be heading straight toward the statue.

Then Kirsten saw a cluster of small ships waiting to dock at another island not far from the statue. As they drew closer, a huge three-story wooden structure came into view. It looked like a castle from a fairy tale, with a blue slate roof and four magnificent towers topped with pointed spires. Dozens of mullioned windows decorated the façades. Kirsten nudged Elin.

"Look at that place. It's like a palace or a grand hotel or something."

"America must be a very rich country," Elin said, "if this is how they welcome poor people like us—first with a giant statue and now this."

The engines slowed, then halted. The ferry lined up behind several others and the ship became a floating waiting room. Except for the crying babies, the other passengers were unusually quiet. Everyone else must be nervous, too. Kirsten wished she could talk to the other immigrants and ask them why they had left their homelands and what they wished for in America. If someone had asked for her story, she would have confessed that she had fled from small town gossip and a faithless lover. And what future did she wish for? Her wish was impossible to fulfill. She still loved Tor, in spite of everything.

The sun grew hotter and hotter by the minute. Kirsten's vision began to blur. If they had to wait here much longer she feared she might faint. She dug through her bag for something to use as a fan. Elin sat on their trunk with her eyes closed.

Finally their ferry moved forward to dock. The sailors slammed the gangway into place and everyone crowded toward the ramp, struggling with cumbersome luggage and restless children. Fear and excitement and hope filled each face. Kirsten wanted to be the first person off the boat, the first person to pass through the inspection lines. But Elin seemed to be having trouble standing, much less walking across the ferry's bobbing deck.

"Sit down," she told Elin. "No sense being in a rush. We'll have to wait for our turn anyway." Elin sank onto the trunk again. She looked relieved. "That ride across the river made me woozy," Kirsten said. "And after hearing everything that Mr. Lindahl said, I think I'm a little nervous, too." Once again she wished she had eaten breakfast. Too late now.

When they finally stepped onto dry land, Kirsten felt as though she had forgotten how to walk. Her head reeled and her knees felt rubbery after being at sea for so long. She struggled to recover her balance, teetering like a drunken woman. Good thing everyone else moved as slowly as she did or the Americans would think something was wrong with her. She longed to close her eyes, but she and Sofia had to lug their trunk into the building. They staggered up the pier with it and joined the long line of people waiting beneath the entrance canopy.

Kirsten saw several uniformed men standing between the dock and the building's entrance and she hoped they were porters who would help them with their luggage. But the men never moved from their posts as they carefully surveyed the crowd, and she remembered what Mr. Lindahl had said about the inspection process. Evidently it had already begun. She and Sofia hoisted the trunk between them, dragging it along the ground half of the time, pushing and shoving it up the ramp.

"Don't scowl," Kirsten whispered to Sofia. "Try to look strong and healthy."

"I am healthy," she grumbled. "You and Elin are the ones who look sick."

It was true. Elin did not look well at all. And she was much too quiet. She clung to Sofia's arm, her eyes squeezed shut to block out the sun's glare.

"Are we almost there?" Elin murmured.

"We're almost to the building," Kirsten said, "and

then it will only be another hour or so until we're on the train to Chicago."

Inside, an enormous baggage room took up most of the building's main floor. Piles and piles of steamer trunks and suitcases and wicker baskets and crates of all shapes and sizes filled most of the space, while more men in uniform directed the flow of immigrants up a long, steep flight of stairs in the center of the room. Kirsten saw some people checking their luggage, while others dragged their bags with them up the steps. She knew it would take all three of them pushing and tugging to get their trunk to the top, and she dreaded the thought of it. But she also knew that ever since the first day of their journey, Elin had refused to let the trunk out of her sight.

"I think we should leave the trunk here," Elin said wearily. Kirsten and Sofia gaped at her in surprise.

"Are you sure?" Kirsten asked.

"Yes, I'm sure. We can't possibly haul it up all those stairs by ourselves." When they continued to stare at her, she added, "Look, I know I've been a fanatic about keeping my eye on that stupid thing, but I don't see how we can push it any farther. Look how steep those stairs are."

"Thank goodness." Sofia dropped her end of the box to the floor.

"Plenty of other people are leaving their things here, so it must be safe," Elin said.

Kirsten gladly handed the cumbersome trunk over to one of the baggage agents and got a claim check for it in return. Then she rejoined the line and followed the others toward the stairs. More uniformed officials were stopping people to look at the tags pinned to their clothing.

"I think I know how the cattle used to feel, going to auction on market day," Kirsten said when the man checked hers.

"Kirsten . . . shh . . ." Elin warned.

"No one can understand me," she said. "Although I wish they could. I'd like to stand up and say, 'Hey! I'm a person, you know. I have feelings!'"

"Hush! They'll think you're crazy and send you back home."

"Good," Sofia mumbled under her breath.

"Why do they make this so degrading?" Kirsten asked. "They push you here and there, shouting at you if you do something wrong—as if getting angry will help us figure out what they're saying. And why is everyone wearing a uniform? It's like we're all in prison or something."

"It's not a prison," Elin said. "But with so many people I suppose there's a chance someone might get lost. I think the tags are to help us as much as them."

"Besides, it stinks in here," Kirsten complained. "I'll bet most of these people never took a bath in their lives." The smell of hundreds of unwashed bodies, magnified by the heat, was making her nauseous again. She looked around at all the worried faces and thought she could smell their fear, too.

Kirsten knew the officials were inspecting people

on their way up the stairs. They pulled aside an elderly woman who paused to catch her breath partway up. Kirsten and her sisters made it past the inspectors on the stairs, but a row of physicians in white medical coats stood waiting for them to reach the top. The first doctor studied them from head to toe, then directed them to the next doctor. He was making people remove their hats or kerchiefs to check their scalps. Most people were directed to the next doctor, but one woman had a chalk mark scribbled on her lapel and was taken to a side room. The third doctor had an instrument that resembled a buttonhook and he used it to pry back each person's eyelids to inspect her eyes.

"I still haven't seen the sick family from the ship anywhere, have you?" Kirsten asked as they waited their turn.

"Poor things," Elin murmured. "I wonder what happened to them?" She was leaning heavily on Sofia's arm, still squeezing her eyes closed.

"Try to act well, Elin. Please," Kirsten begged. "We're almost there."

The man checked Kirsten's eyes first. The hooklike instrument pinched for a brief, painful moment, then it was over. She turned around and watched as he inspected Sofia's eyes, and then Elin's turn came. The moment he touched her eyes, Elin gasped in pain. She reeled back, doubling over and covering her face.

"No, Elin, no . . ." Kirsten whispered under her

breath. "Just get through it . . . don't let him know you're sick. . . ."

But Elin's pain was obvious. She covered her eyes and wept. The man made her lift her head as he asked her a question. None of them knew what he was saying. He reached to examine her eyes again, but Elin pushed his hand away. She had been trying so hard to act well, but she wasn't. She shivered with chills in the overheated building, and Kirsten knew she was getting a fever. The inspector would know it, too.

He marked something on Elin's shoulder with chalk and waved her to the room on the left, not straight ahead with everyone else. Sofia and Kirsten followed her. For the first time since entering the building, Kirsten felt real fear.

"What's going on? How come everyone else went the other way?" Sofia asked.

"I'm sorry. I'm so sorry," Elin said. "I just need to sit down somewhere." She had been pale all morning, but now two feverish spots brightened her cheeks. Kirsten took her hand as she guided her to a seat in the small waiting room. The place reeked of strong soap. Kirsten could feel the unnatural warmth of Elin's body, even though she shivered with chills. "I'm sorry," she repeated.

"Don't worry. . . . We're going to be fine," Kirsten soothed.

Eventually a nurse came and took Elin's arm, leading her into another room. Sofia and Kirsten both stood to go with her, but the nurse babbled at them and motioned for them to sit down.

"I'm sure I'll be right back," Elin said. "Wait right here for me."

Sofia could no longer hold back her tears. "Elin, no!" she cried. "I want to go with you!" She looked terrified.

"You'll be fine, Sofia," Elin said. "Kirsten will take care of you."

Kirsten watched Elin stumble down the long hallway and disappear into another room. Then Kirsten collapsed onto a chair in shock. Elin was the strong one, the wise one. She knew what to do and where to go. How would they get through this ordeal without her?

"I don't want to go to America without Elin," Sofia whimpered.

"It's going to be all right, you'll see. They'll bring her right back." Kirsten wished she believed her own words.

"If they do send her back to Sweden, I'm going with her."

"Shh, stop talking like that. Nobody is going back to Sweden."

They waited and waited for Elin to return, but she never did. Other immigrants came and went, sitting in the waiting room for awhile until the nurses called for them, but no one came for Sofia and Kirsten. And no one told them what had happened to Elin.

"What are we going to do?" Sofia asked when several hours had passed. Kirsten didn't reply. She didn't know the answer. They clung to each other's hands and waited. Sofia looked so young and helpless. She was only sixteen, and even though Kirsten was only two years older, she was in charge now. The weight of that responsibility terrified her. Poor Elin. She had been carrying everyone's weight for the entire trip, and she was only eleven months older than Kirsten.

"Don't worry. She'll be back soon," Kirsten murmured, trying to reassure herself. She didn't believe it. And she suspected that Sofia didn't, either.

The room seemed to grow hotter by the hour, the smell of soap stronger and stronger. Kirsten looked around for a window that opened. The longer she sat, the more nauseated she felt as the combination of the heat, the soapy smell, and her rising fear began to overwhelm her.

"It's so stuffy in here," she said, fanning her face with her hand. "Do you suppose they'd let us open the window?"

"It feels fine to me," Sofia said. "Are you all right? You're not getting sick, too, are you?"

"Of course not. I'm fine." But she wasn't. The heat was sapping her strength.

"You look white, Kirsten. Maybe you should eat something."

The mention of food did it. Kirsten clapped her hand over her mouth and stood. "I'm going to be sick. . . ." But when she tried to walk, the floor jumped up to meet her.

Then everything went black.

• • •

The next thing Kirsten knew, she was lying on a cot in a different room. Everything in the room was white, including the uniform on the nurse who bent over her bed to hold a cool cloth to her forehead. The smell of that terrible soap was even stronger in here. Kirsten covered her mouth again as her stomach turned inside out. But there was nothing in her stomach to vomit. She told herself to take deep breaths.

When the nausea passed, Kirsten tried to sit up. "What happened to Sofia? Where is she?" But the nurse shook her head, forcing her to stay down. "I'm fine. I'm not sick. I need to go back to the other room with my sister. I can't leave Sofia all alone!"

The woman's reply sounded soothing, yet her firm grip made it clear that Kirsten had to remain lying down. She wondered if Sofia was close enough to hear her.

"Sofia? Are you out there?" she called. The woman grew upset at Kirsten's shouts. She shook her head and made shushing sounds, refusing to let Kirsten rise, insisting she lie still.

Kirsten told herself not to panic. She knew she wasn't sick; she didn't have a fever or a headache like Elin did. It was just a bad case of nerves and too much excitement on an empty stomach. Or maybe the awful rocking motion of the ferry had done it. If she remained calm, the doctors would find out that

156

she was fine and let her go back to the waiting room with Sofia.

Poor Sofia. She must be terrified.

After a very long wait, a doctor arrived. He listened to Kirsten's heart and took her pulse. She knew it must be racing, but why wouldn't it be? She was upset about Elin and trapped in this room and worried about Sofia. She wished she could explain it to him. He stuck a thermometer under her arm to take her temperature. There. He would know she didn't have a fever. He examined her skin while he waited, probably to look for a rash. According to Elin, the sick woman and her children had been covered with rashes from head to toe. Kirsten wished she knew if Elin had one. She closed her eyes, pleading with God to let Elin be all right.

When the doctor finished he looked at Kirsten's landing tag, said something to the nurse, and they both left. Kirsten stood up and smoothed down her skirts. But she must have stood up too fast, because another wave of dizziness swept over her. She collapsed onto the bed again and closed her eyes, willing herself not to be sick. She waited some more. It seemed like a very long time.

At last a different woman entered the room, wearing street clothes instead of a white uniform. Kirsten stood up, careful to do it slowly this time. "Kirsten Carlson?" the woman asked.

"That's right."

"You speak Swedish, yes?"

Relief flooded through Kirsten. "Yes! Yes! Thank heaven they sent someone who could understand me!"

"I'm sorry it took so long. There were several other Swedish immigrants arriving on your ship, and they needed me to interpret for them in the Registry Room. I'm Mrs. Bjork from the Swedish Immigrant Aid Society. How can I help you?"

Kirsten's words poured out in a torrent. "You have to tell them that I'm not sick! Please, tell them that I feel fine now. I just got a little dizzy from the boat ride and the heat, but that's all it was. I need to go back out to the waiting room and find my sister Sofia. They took our sister Elin away to one of these rooms, and then they stuck me in here, and they left Sofia out there all alone. She'll be so frightened and—"

"I understand. It is frightening when you're so far from home and don't know what's going on."

"So you'll tell them that I'm not sick? I can go now?"

"Not yet. The immigration officials wanted me to explain to you that a family aboard your ship became ill with typhus."

Kirsten's skin prickled. *Please, not Elin.*

"But I'm fine! I don't have that disease and neither does Elin."

"That may be true, but the immigration officials need to be very cautious about letting any further typhus patients into the country. It is a very serious disease, and they don't want an epidemic on their

158

hands. That's why they took your sister to the hospital building."

"The hospital? Will she be all right?"

"I'm sorry, but it's too soon to know."

Kirsten's fear for Elin soared, but she told herself to remain calm. "I have another sister, Sofia. She's out in the waiting room and she's only sixteen and—"

"Unless she became ill, too, she'll still be in the waiting room. I'll talk to her and explain what's going on when we're finished."

"Why can't I go talk to her? I'm fine, really."

"The nurse said that you fainted, Miss Carlson. Because of the threat of a typhus outbreak, they've decided to take you to the hospital, as well."

Kirsten's panic soared. "No, no, please! They can't separate us!"

"Just listen. Don't make yourself upset. The doctors will examine you in the hospital and keep you under observation, and if they discover that you are fine, you'll be brought back here to rejoin your sister."

"Can't you convince them that I'm fine? I don't even have a fever—"

"I'm so sorry, but it isn't up to me. All I can do is explain to you what's going to happen. There is nothing I can do to change the doctor's mind. I'm sorry."

Kirsten covered her face. If only this nightmare would end and she would wake up. After a moment the woman touched Kirsten's shoulder.

"I will go and talk to your other sister now."

Kirsten wiped her cheeks. "Please, tell her that I'm fine . . . and tell her not to be scared."

"I will."

In spite of all her efforts, Kirsten couldn't stop crying. They wouldn't let her walk, carrying her instead down the stairs on a stretcher, out of the immigration building through a rear door, and across the tiny island to a smaller two-story building. Kirsten had never been inside a hospital before.

This living nightmare was growing worse by the hour. *Typhus?* Kirsten had heard of the disease but didn't know anything about it. Did people die from it? She was frightened half to death for Elin.

Once inside the hospital, Kirsten waited in a cubicle behind white curtains for a long time. A nurse made her undress and put on a nightgown. She waited some more, trying to convince herself to stop crying. It would only make her eyes puffy and her nose run, and they would think that she was sick.

At last a doctor came in to examine her. She made up her mind to talk to him, whether he understood her or not.

"There is really nothing wrong with me at all—as you'll soon see. I grew up on a farm, so I've always been strong and healthy. All of us are. I've never even been to a hospital before. We had a doctor in town, of course, and he would come out to the farm when we had the measles or something, but—"

The doctor put his fingers to his lips to shush her,

then listened to her chest with his stethoscope. The entire examination was humiliating, but Kirsten would willingly endure anything if only they would let her return to Sofia. When he finished, she looked around for her clothes. Someone had taken them away. She had no choice but to sit on the examination table and wait. It must be close to suppertime by now. Kirsten hadn't eaten all day. And what would Sofia do? Their food was in their trunk in the baggage room.

Eventually, Kirsten heard a noise outside her cubicle that sounded like a very wobbly cart being wheeled down the hallway. It must be food, she decided, because the smell of boiled potatoes and meat grew stronger by the minute. She was very hungry. But when the curtain parted and a small dark-haired man offered her a tray of food, she took one whiff of it and her stomach tried to empty itself. The man called out and two nurses rushed into her room.

"I'm not sick! I'm just upset and worried." Kirsten's protests were useless. She couldn't make them understand her, nor could she understand them. But she couldn't even look at the tray of food without wanting to vomit, much less take a bite of it.

The nurses wheeled Kirsten out of the cubicle in a wheelchair and into a big ward with three rows of beds, all filled with sick women. "Elin?" she called as they wheeled her down the aisle between the rows. "Elin, are you in here?"

The nurse shushed her.

"I'm looking for my sister, Elin Carlson. I think they brought her here." She spoke loudly enough for Elin to hear if she was in the room, but no one replied.

The nurses helped Kirsten climb into one of the white iron beds near a window. She could see from a small patch of sky outside that the sun was going down. They were going to keep her here all night. What in the world would happen to Sofia? What would she eat? Where would she sleep? Kirsten pictured her sister all alone and lost in that huge building with all of those strangers, and she burst into tears. Poor Sofia. She was so timid and shy, afraid of everyone and everything. She must be terrified by now. Elin had entrusted Kirsten to take care of her, and she had let both of her sisters down.

Oh, Lord, please let them see that I'm not sick, she prayed. It was the only thing she could think of to do. *Please send someone to help Sofia . . . and please, please let Elin be all right. Please bring us all together again.*

Kirsten was sorry for giving Elin a hard time, sorry for running off to flirt with Eric and his cousin. She wished she could tell Elin that she had been right about not trusting Eric, but it was too late. What a horrible, horrible mess this had turned into.

Poor Elin. What if she did have typhus?

What if she died?

Chapter Fourteen

OH, DEAR GOD, please don't do this to me.

The very thing Sofia feared had happened. Everyone she loved had abandoned her and now she was alone. *Alone.* The fact that her sisters hadn't abandoned her on purpose made no difference at all. Mama hadn't died on purpose, either.

How could God do this to her? How could He take away everyone she loved? Sofia's heart raced as she sat in the waiting room. She couldn't stop crying. What if Elin and Kirsten didn't get well? What if they died, too?

Please, Jesus, please don't let Elin and Kirsten die. I don't know what I would do without them.

Sofia shivered as if she stood naked in a snow-storm. She couldn't help it. She had never felt so alone. She had no idea where to go or what to do, no one to watch out for her, no one to talk to. She couldn't understand a word anyone said.

She remembered a summer day back home when she had picked berries in the woods with her family. They had found dozens of bushes filled with berries, and without realizing it, Sofia had wandered farther and farther away from the others as she'd filled her pail. When she finally looked up, she was alone. No one was in sight. Only the forest and numberless trees surrounded her. The only sounds were the lonely cry of birds and the rustling of branches in the wind.

And now the same numbing panic filled her. She was abandoned and alone in a strange place. Back home on that summer day she had cried out, *"Mama! Mama, where are you?"* and within minutes her mother had rescued her. But even though Sofia sat in a building filled with thousands of people, no one heard her cries this time. No one could understand her. No one could tell her what would happen next.

As she waited in vain for Elin and Kirsten to return, the beasts of fear and sorrow that had hounded Sofia for most of her life circled her, waiting to tear her to pieces. She longed to run but had no place to go. They would follow her wherever she fled, just as they had followed her to America. She stood and peered out of the open doorway, looking for one of the nurses or a uniformed official she could talk to. When a nurse passed by in the hallway, Sofia called to her.

"Excuse me . . . I need to know where my sisters are. I need to know if they're all right. Won't someone please help me?"

The woman's blank expression told Sofia that she hadn't understood her. The nurse babbled an incomprehensible reply and steered Sofia back into the room, motioning to a chair, making it very clear that she wanted her to sit down and stay there.

"Can't somebody please tell me what's going on?" she begged. "Please, I don't know where to go or what I'm supposed to do!"

All she got for her pleas was another reply that

clearly meant, *Sit down and wait.* Sofia didn't want to cry, but she couldn't help it. She wondered if she should pretend to be sick, too, so she could join her sisters. Or would that make matters worse? She remembered the woman and her six little children in the beds next to theirs on the boat. The doctors had carried them all away and the family had never returned. What if Elin and Kirsten vanished, too? *Please, Jesus . . . Please don't let anything happen to them! And please, please help me!*

For a moment, Sofia thought she heard Kirsten's voice calling to her from far away. Sofia sprang to her feet, shouting, "Kirsten? Kirsten, is that you? . . . Where are you?" There was no reply. Sofia peered out of the door, looking in all directions, calling, "Kirsten?"

Eventually, Sofia sat down again. She needed to remain calm. They couldn't leave her in this room forever, could they? They would have to do some-thing with her when they found out she wasn't sick. But if her sisters never came back, would the officials make her go to Chicago without them? Sofia would much rather go home to Sweden. But where would she get the money for a ticket?

Maybe if she just sat here and prayed as hard as she could, Jesus would help her. She pulled out her mother's Bible and held it on her lap, stroking the velvet cover for comfort. If only she could open it and hear God speaking to her, telling her what to do. But she was terrified to try. The last words she had read had spoken of death. She still remembered them: . . . *we finally gave up all hope of being saved.*

Sofia had no idea how much time had passed when a nurse finally came to the doorway and beckoned to her. She gathered up all three satchels—Kirsten and Elin had left theirs behind—and followed the woman into a smaller room. A few minutes later the nurse returned with a doctor who began to examine Sofia, taking her temperature, listening to her heart, peering into her eyes and down her throat. She flushed with embarrassment when he made her unbutton her blouse so he could look at her chest, but she guessed that he was looking to see if she had a rash, like the family aboard the ship.

She wished she would start to feel sick. Then they would take her to wherever they had taken her sisters. But when the doctor finished, the nurse took Sofia back to the waiting room and motioned for her to sit down again. An older woman with a small baby on her lap now waited there, too.

The day dragged on as Sofia sat waiting and worrying, wondering what to do. She could hear the rumble of voices like the never-ending roar of a waterfall in the huge main room beyond the door. She thought surely her tears would be exhausted by now, but they continued to fall.

The waiting room filled and emptied countless times. One woman sat with her eyes closed, fingering rosary beads as her lips moved in prayer. Sofia tried to pray, too, but the only words she could think of were, *Please, Jesus, please.* She repeated them over and over in her mind.

Every time a nurse walked into the room, Sofia stood up. But each time, as the nurses brought in more worried-looking people or took them out again, they would shake their heads and motion for Sofia to sit down. Sofia studied the strangers waiting with her. They were dressed differently than she was and spoke different languages, but they were very much like her in their fear and solitude and silence. Did she look as fearful as they did? Did she sound like them, muttering words that no one could understand?

After a while, Sofia's fear transformed into anger. She silently raged at her sisters for dragging her so far from her home, forcing her to endure this terrible journey, and then abandoning her. And why did Elin have to help that sick family in the first place? What business was it of hers if they were sick? Elin never should have interfered. She should have considered her own sisters' welfare first.

But slowly the rage turned to sorrow again. It wasn't Elin's fault for getting sick. In fact, maybe it was Sofia's own fault that she was alone. Maybe God was punishing her for being so moody and disagreeable. "I'm sorry, Jesus . . ." she murmured, just in case He was still listening to her.

She was sorry she had given Elin such a hard time, sorry for not speaking to her sisters for days and days. She would give anything to be able to talk to them now, anything to hear her own language spoken again. If only God would bring them back to her, safe and sound, she would be cheerful from now on. She still may not like it here in America, but she needed her sisters!

Please, Jesus . . . please . . .

Hours later, a fair-haired woman who looked as though she belonged in Sofia's village back home came into the waiting area. "Sofia Carlson?" she asked.

Sofia sprang to her feet. "Yes? Yes, I'm Sofia."

"I'm Mrs. Bjork from the Swedish Immigrant Aid Society. I just spoke with your sister Kirsten and she wanted you to know that she is concerned about you being in here all alone."

The soothing sound of the woman's voice, speaking in a language Sofia could understand, made her start crying all over again. She had the urge to hug the woman.

"Can I go see her?" Sofia begged. "Where is she? And where's Elin?"

"Let's sit down, shall we? And take one question at a time?" Sofia sat on the very edge of her seat, bracing herself for bad news. "I'm afraid you can't see either one of your sisters at the moment, Miss Carlson. The immigration officials explained to me that there were some confirmed cases of typhus on your ship. They are worried that your sisters might have contracted the disease, and so they will have to be isolated."

"Typhus?" Sofia repeated. She had heard of the disease, usually whispered in hushed tones, but she had no idea how serious it was. She was afraid to ask.

"Both of your sisters have been admitted to the island's hospital. Once the doctors have had a chance to examine them, I will be able to give you more information about their condition. But for now, you will have to remain separated from one another."

Sofia covered her face and wept. The woman waited, making no move to comfort her. Perhaps she was fearful of catching the disease, too.

"What am I supposed to do?" Sofia asked when she finally looked up.

"You will be detained here on Ellis Island for the next few days."

"All alone?" The snarling beasts inched closer, threatening to devour Sofia.

The woman smiled faintly. "There are always several hundred detainees here at any given time. You won't be alone."

"I meant without my sisters. Could . . . could you please ask the doctors if I may go over to the hospital and wait there with them? Please?"

"I'm afraid not. Typhus is a very serious disease, and patients who have it must be isolated. If you'll come with me," she said, rising to her feet, "I'll show you where you will be staying."

"Can't I talk to Kirsten first? Is she still in the next room?"

"She is already on her way to the hospital where they took your other sister."

Sofia picked up all three of their satchels and followed the woman out of the waiting area and down a long hall. She tried very hard to be brave, but it was nearly impossible, as fear dogged her heels. They climbed up a set of stairs and emerged on a narrow balcony that overlooked the main room. Below were rows and rows of people seated on wooden benches, waiting with their bundles strewn at their feet. A line of tall desks stood at one end of the room beneath an enormous American flag, and a uniformed man stood behind each desk. It could have been a picture of Judgment Day, with the officials deciding who would be admitted to heaven and who would be kept out.

Sofia and her sisters should be down there, waiting in line with everyone else. The inspection process was supposed to take only a few hours, and then they would be on their way to Chicago. Why was this happening? She felt another surge of anger at Elin. If only she hadn't helped those sick people on the boat.

Mrs. Bjork halted in front of an open door and gestured for Sofia to go inside. "This is the women's dormitory, where you will be staying while you are detained," she explained.

It was worse than their accommodations in steerage had been—a prison cell where she would be forced to sleep with a hundred strangers. The room was stacked with cots made of pipes and canvas, suspended by chains from the ceiling. The three tiers of bunks hung so close together that there was barely room for a person to lie down in the narrow space, much less sit up. The cots had no mattresses, only a piece of canvas stretched across the frame and one thin blanket. Sofia's blanket was in her trunk in the baggage room. So was most of their food. Three white porcelain sinks stood against one wall—three sinks, for all these beds.

"It looks like a jail," she murmured.

"Well, it is called a detention center, but no one here is being punished. It's simply a place to wait. You will be free to leave Ellis Island as soon as you and your sisters receive medical clearance. Now come this way and I'll show you the dining hall. You'll receive three meals a day while you're waiting."

It was a large, sunny room with plenty of windows and row after row of long tables and benches. Workers passed up and down the rows, setting out china plates and bowls and cups. Sofia could smell food cooking somewhere and her stomach rumbled with hunger. She hadn't eaten anything since breakfast.

"I believe that dinner will be served around six o'clock," Mrs. Bjork said.

"H-how will I pay for all of this?"

"Oh, you don't have to pay. Everything is provided for you, free of charge. In fact, the cost is billed to the shipping company that transported you here. It's up to them to make sure that all of the passengers they transport to America are in good health. If someone is refused admission to the country, then the steamship line has to pay for their transportation home."

"Could that happen? Could they send us home again?"

"If you or your sisters fail the health inspection, then yes. You will be sent home on the next available ship."

Sofia stared at Mrs. Bjork, uncertain how she felt about this news. Hadn't she been begging to go home? But the thought of traveling back all that way made her feel exhausted. Fear chased through her when she recalled how sick Elin had looked. What if she and Kirsten died? What would Sofia do then? Everyone else in her family had died except Nils— and he may as well be dead, too, for all anyone knew. He had never written to tell them where he was or what had happened to him.

"Will my sisters get well?" she asked Mrs. Bjork. She was afraid to ask if they might die. "How bad is this disease they might have?"

"I'm not a physician, Miss Carlson, but I will find out for you. I'll come back in a day or two, when I have more information. Is there someone we should notify about the delay? Someone here in America who is waiting for you to arrive?"

"Yes—my Uncle Lars in Chicago."

"If you have his address, I can help you send a telegram to him."

Sofia had to stop and think. Elin had been taking care of them all this time, making all of the decisions and arrangements. Sofia had paid no attention to any of the details and had no idea where Chicago even was, much less where their uncle lived. But she suddenly remembered that Elin had left her bag behind when the nurses took her away. In fact, the bag was growing very heavy in her arms. She set all three bags on the floor and crouched down to search through Elin's. She found her uncle's name and address in the packet with their tickets.

"Here it is . . . but I don't know how to send a telegram."

"I will send it for you."

"How much does it cost?" Again Sofia realized how dependent she had been on Elin. She had behaved like a child when she was nearly an adult.

"The Swedish Immigrant Aid Society will cover the cost of the telegram for you. That's our job—to help travelers like you."

"Thank you," Sofia said as the woman copied down the information. "And tell the society thank you, too."

"You're welcome. Now, since it is such a lovely spring day, I'll show you where you can get some fresh air and a little exercise."

Sofia followed her through a doorway to an outdoor courtyard. She could see the river beyond a retaining wall and the city of New York in the haze on the other side.

Mrs. Bjork turned to Sofia to say good-bye. "I must leave you now, Miss Carlson. I know that waiting is difficult, but you will be safe here, and all your needs will be provided for. I'll see you again in a day or two."

She left Sofia standing all alone.

The three satchels were growing heavy in Sofia's arms. She walked across the courtyard to an empty bench and sank down, dropping the bags at her feet. Hundreds of strangers surrounded Sofia, but as she studied them for several minutes, she saw that they looked frightened and bewildered and lonely, too. Only a few of them had someone to talk to who understood their language.

Sofia couldn't bear the thought of spending the rest of her life all alone this way. If Elin and Kirsten did die, then maybe she should just jump into the river and die, too. Wasn't that what Papa had done? Maybe he had felt this aching loneliness after Mama died. And maybe he'd felt this relentless fear. Maybe it had hounded him, too.

Please, Jesus, I don't know what to do. I'm so scared, and I need your help.

She drew a deep breath and decided to open Mama's Bible at random again. If it talked about dying again, then that would be her answer: She would jump into the river and end her life. She pulled out the Bible, closed her eyes, and pushed her finger between the pages. For a long moment, she was afraid to look. But when she finally opened her eyes, her finger was pointing to Psalm 66: *Shout with joy to God, all the earth! Sing the glory of his name; make his praise glorious!*

174

Tears blurred Sofia's vision. She had loved to sing back home in Sweden. People in church had raved about her beautiful voice and had begged her to sing for them. Hadn't Elin said just this morning that she'd missed Sofia's songs?

Sing the glory of his name. . . .

Sofia hadn't felt joyful for a long, long time. How did God expect her to sing?

She read a little more of the psalm: *For you, O God, tested us . . . you brought us into prison and laid burdens on our backs.* That was where Sofia was now—in prison, held captive on this island all alone. *You let men ride over our heads; we went through fire and water, but you brought us to a place of abundance.* She read the last phrase a second time. Was that a promise? Would God really lead her to a place of abundance where she would sing for joy again?

She closed the Bible, then closed her eyes, numbed by all the emotions she had endured. *Please help me, Jesus,* she prayed. *Please, please help me. . . .*

Chapter Fifteen

A SUDDEN MOVEMENT awakened Sofia. She hadn't meant to fall asleep, and now a man was sitting on the bench beside her. She gasped and sprang to her feet, but the stranger stood, too, spreading his hands and shaking his head as he babbled in another language. She could see that he was apologizing for disturbing her and telling her to sit down again. He

175

would go away. Sofia glanced around at the crowded courtyard. All of the other benches were taken.

Elin would not want her to sit beside a strange man. She had worried endlessly whenever Kirsten spent time alone with strangers on the boat. But Sofia felt so desolate that she didn't care what happened to her. Hadn't she just contemplated jumping into the river?

"No, it's all right," she told the man. "You may sit here with me." She moved to the far side of the bench, making room for him, then patted the seat, gesturing for him to sit.

He nodded and sank down wearily, sweeping off his hat and holding it on his lap. *"Danke, Fraulein,"* he said. Sofia thought he might be speaking German. His deep-set eyes were an unusual shade of golden brown, but they looked kind. He began talking to her in a low, soothing voice as if pouring out his story.

"I'm sorry," Sofia said when he finally paused. "I don't understand you. My sisters and I are from Sweden. We were on our way to Chicago, but Elin and Kirsten got sick and had to go to the hospital, and—"

She stopped. Should she tell this stranger all about her family? But what difference did it make? He probably couldn't understand a word she said, either. And it did feel good to talk to someone. She had barely spoken to Elin and Kirsten for days, and now she was sorry for acting so moody and sullen. "I would give anything to have my sisters back and to be able to talk to them," she said aloud.

He started speaking again as if they could understand each other perfectly, and his soft deep voice soothed her. She looked up at him, wanting him to know how much she appreciated his company, wishing she could make him understand what she was saying.

"Thank you for sitting with me," she said.

Sofia couldn't judge people's ages very well, but she thought the man was about the same age as Nils, who was twenty-one. She knew the man was tall like Nils, too, because she had to look up to see his face as he sat beside her. He was clean-shaven and strong-jawed, yet his expression was gentle at the same time.

His long legs stretched out straight in front of him, and he was clothed in a shabby brown suit that looked as though it had seen a lot of wear. He had thick dark hair and brows, the same color as the strong coffee that Papa used to drink. His hair was a little too long and could have used a trim, curling over the top of his ears and touching his shirt collar in back. Maybe the Americans had detained him here for such a long time that he couldn't get a haircut.

He pointed to the Bible on her lap and asked her a question. She heard a word that sounded like *Bible*.

"Yes, it's my mother's Bible," she said, handing it to him. He leafed through it, nodding, then he reached into a tattered leather satchel lying at his feet and pulled out a book, handing it to her in return.

"Die Bibel," he said, pointing to his, then hers.

"Yes, they are the same." Sofia sighed. "I wish we

could understand each other. I wish you could help me find all of the promises my mama used to read to me. But my Bible may as well be written in German or French or some other language, for all the good it does me."

He watched her closely as she talked, his head cocked to one side as if wishing he could understand her, too. She could confess her fear and her frustration to him and he wouldn't condemn her. He wouldn't understand a word she said.

"My mama loved Jesus and always read to us from this Bible," she told him. "This belonged to her. We used to go to church back home, and we'd sing hymns to God, and the music and the minister's words were always so beautiful. But I can't find any of those beautiful words in the Bible now that Mama is gone—none of the promises she used to show me."

He looked at her very intently as her tears began to fall. She saw compassion in his eyes and it made her tears fall faster. Then he talked for awhile, his voice soft and soothing. Suddenly he stopped and his face brightened with excitement, as if he'd just had an idea. He opened both of their Bibles on his lap, comparing their tables of contents, then turned to the New Testament gospel of John in each one. He rummaged in his bag again for a pencil and a piece of paper and wrote down 20:15. Sofia realized that he wanted her to look up the same passage in her Bible that he had found in his.

She dried her eyes and read the verse: *"Woman,"*

he said, "*why are you crying? Who is it you are looking for?*" She couldn't help smiling at the humor of it, and at his ingenuity, even if the passage had reminded her of her plight.

"My sisters," she said. "I'm crying because my sisters are in the hospital and—" She wished she could find a verse that would explain it, but she didn't know the Bible well enough. Her ignorance shamed her. The only biblical sisters she could remember reading about were Mary and Martha, but she didn't know where to find them. She leafed back a few pages, reading all of the headings at the top of each page, and stopped when she came to chapter 11 and Lazarus. *Now a man named Lazarus was sick. . . .* She pointed to the chapter and verse numbers and waited for him to find it in his Bible. A little further down the verse read, *Mary and her sister Martha . . .*

How could she explain that her sisters were the ones who were sick? Sofia gestured uselessly. She could tell by his expression that he was baffled.

"Never mind," she mumbled.

She closed the book and hung her head, but the stranger continued to page through his own Bible, stopping when he came to the book of Psalms. He wrote down the numbers 22:1–2 and nudged her with his elbow. She looked up the verses: *My God, my God, why have you forsaken me? Why are you so far from saving me, so far from the words of my groaning? O my God, I cry out by day, but you do not answer, by night, and am not silent.*

She stared at him, then nodded, laying her hand over her heart. "Yes, that's exactly how I feel. How did you know?"

He pointed to himself, to the verse, talking and nodding. He must feel forsaken, too. She wondered why he was being detained there and wished she could ask him. But then he led her to another verse, Joshua 1:9: *Be strong and courageous. Do not be terrified; do not be discouraged, for the Lord your God will be with you wherever you go.*

When she looked up at him again, he was smiling.

"That was one of the promises my mother taught me," she said, smiling in return. And as she wiped away her tears, she suddenly thought of a way she might be able to communicate with him. She took the piece of paper and pencil from him and began to draw a picture of six stick figures. She had never been much of an artist, but she drew her mama and papa at the top, then Nils, Elin, Kirsten, and herself beneath them. She gave beards to the stick figures of Papa and Nils and long skirts and coils of hair to all of the women. He watched her closely, straining forward to try to understand.

"Mama," she said, pointing to the first figure. She marked an *X* through it. "Papa," she said, making another *X*. "My brother, Nils . . . my sister Elin . . . my sister Kirsten . . . and me." She pointed to her stick figure, then to herself. When she finished, hers was the only one without an *X* through it. "So, you see? I'm all alone."

She pointed to the three satchels lying on the ground at her feet. "Mine," she said, lifting hers. "Kirsten's . . . and Elin's." She pointed to their bags, then to the crossed out drawings. She held up three fingers, pointed again to the three drawings, then slowly lowered two fingers. He finally seemed to understand, and once again, she saw compassion in his eyes.

He began talking rapidly as if needing to get something off his chest, gesturing to the immigration building behind them and to the city across the river. Then he drew a dark, bold line beneath her pictures and began drawing. He, too, drew figures of a man and a woman at the top. *"Mutter . . . und Vater,"* he told her. Then he drew five stick-figure men below them. He rattled off four names, pointing to each one. But when he got to the last figure—the one he'd drawn smaller than the others—he pointed to himself. He was the youngest of five brothers.

He took a minute to find another verse, Matthew 13:3, and waited for Sofia to find it: *A farmer went out to sow his seed.* . . . He drew a big circle around the figures and pointed to the verse. He hadn't included himself in the circle. She thought he was telling her that his family members were all farmers and that for whatever reason, he couldn't or didn't want to be one.

He stared at her for a long moment as if deciding whether or not to say more, then slowly lifted up his pant leg to reveal a long, ugly scar. The muscle in his calf looked withered. Was that why he had been detained? Mr. Lindahl had said that no one would be allowed into America if he was lame or deformed and couldn't work.

The stranger paged through his Bible again, stopping at the story of the Prodigal Son in Luke 15:13: *Not long after that, the younger son got together all he had, set off for a distant country . . .* He pointed to himself. He had left home.

"America!" he said, gesturing to the city across the river. Then he spread his hands and shook his head. He pointed to his leg. They wouldn't let him in because of it.

"Oh, I'm so sorry," she said. "Does that mean you'll have to go all the way back home? What will you do?"

Almost as if he'd understood her, he pantomimed swimming then gave a wide grin. She laughed. It felt so good to laugh instead of cry.

"But it's much too far to swim all the way across the river," she said. "Maybe you'd better think of another plan."

He babbled something in return, then lifted his hands hopelessly. Sofia wondered if he would ever set foot in America. And for that matter, if she would.

He smiled and pointed to his chest. "Ludwig Schneider."

"Hello, Ludwig Schneider. My name is Sofia Carlson."

"Sofia Carlson," he repeated.

"It's so nice to meet you, Ludwig." They smiled at each other, then leaned back on the bench again and watched the boats traveling slowly up and down the river.

"Before you sat down," Sofia told him, "I felt so alone. I was desperate for help. Everyone left me and I still don't know if I'll ever see my sisters again. I'm so afraid that they might die, and I don't know what I'll do if that happens. We have train tickets to go to my uncle's home in Chicago, but I would rather go back home to Sweden . . . except that it's so far, and . . . and I don't have any money to go back. I miss my sisters so much. And it's so hard to wait."

He began paging through his Bible again, searching for another verse as she spoke. When he showed her Psalm 27:14 and she read it in her own Bible, she could only gaze at him in astonishment. It said: *Wait for the Lord; be strong and take heart and wait for the Lord.* How had he known? Had he read her thoughts?

He showed her another verse, Isaiah 40:27 and 31: *Why do you say, O Jacob, and complain, O Israel, "My way is hidden from the Lord; my cause is disregarded by my God?" . . . those who hope in the Lord will renew their strength. They will soar on wings like eagles; they will run and not grow weary, they will walk and not be faint.*

"Thank you," Sofia murmured. She was certain that he understood her, even though he didn't speak her language. He smiled and pointed to their two Bibles, asking a question. Did she want more? "Yes! Yes, please show me more." She took the paper and pencil and began writing down the references he gave her so she could read them again on her own.

He showed her Psalm 42:11: *Why are you downcast, O my soul? Why so disturbed within me? Put your hope in God, for I will yet praise him, my Savior and my God.*

And Psalm 46:1–2: *God is our refuge and strength, an ever-present help in trouble. Therefore we will not fear, though the earth give way and the mountains fall into the heart of the sea.* . . . He pointed to verse 11: *The Lord Almighty is with us; the God of Jacob is our fortress.*

For the next hour or more, Ludwig shared Scripture verses with Sofia, each one promising her that she wasn't alone, that God was with her. Her fear and loneliness began to recede until she was ashamed that she had considered jumping into the river.

Elin had warned her and Kirsten repeatedly to stay away from strangers, but Ludwig didn't seem like a stranger at all. Besides, Sofia felt as though Jesus were sitting right on this bench with the two of them. She used to feel His nearness this same way when her mother was alive. Sofia had prayed for help when she first sat down here, and God had sent this stranger.

"How do you know all these verses?" she asked, gesturing to him and to his Bible, then to his forehead. "You seem to know the Bible so well."

He sighed and made a sweeping motion with his

arm, to indicate the entire island. He pointed to the sun, which was now slowly setting in the west, then to the east, where it would rise tomorrow. He traced the sun's arc with his finger, winding it faster and faster. He was telling her that he had been detained here for a long time. He sighed again and held up the Bible, slowly turning the pages. He'd had plenty of time to read it.

"Oh," she said. "I'm so sorry. I've only been here for one day and I've been behaving like such a baby. . . . But it's just that I'm so worried about Elin and Kirsten. If only I knew for sure that they were all right. . . ." Tears filled her eyes.

"*Nein . . . nein,* Sofia," Ludwig said, shaking his head. He held up his hand for her to wait while he rummaged in his large leather bag again. She wondered if he was going to offer her a handkerchief, but instead he pulled out a long object wrapped in a soft gray cloth. He unwound the cloth to reveal a violin and a bow.

Ludwig took a moment to tighten the bowstrings, then placed the instrument beneath his chin. He played a few tentative notes, adjusting the tuning pegs, then lowered the violin to his lap while he thought for a moment. When he raised it to his chin again, he closed his eyes and began to play.

A tender, poignant melody poured from the instrument like tears, bathing Sofia in its beauty. She was enraptured. Music and song had once filled her life before God began taking everyone away from her.

She had loved listening to the soaring organ music in church, loved singing to the Lord with all her heart. But the song inside her had faded after her mother died and was silenced altogether when she and her sisters left home.

Now all of the emotions she had felt for the past few months—sorrow, loss, fear, and loneliness—poured from Ludwig's violin. He understood exactly how she felt, better than anyone else did, even her sisters. A wounded place inside her began to heal as he played. She didn't want him to stop. When he finally did, she rested her hand on his arm, feeling the warmth of the sun on his shirt.

"That was beautiful, Ludwig. Thank you."

He pointed to the heavens, played a few notes, then pointed up again. He was playing for God. Sofia remembered the verse she had found at random, moments before Ludwig sat down beside her: *Sing the glory of his name; make his praise glorious!*

She paged through her Bible to Psalm 66 and pointed to it. He read the verse in his own Bible and a smile spread across his face.

"More," she said, pantomiming playing. "Please, play more." He smiled shyly and lifted the violin again. He played a variety of melodies for the next thirty minutes, fast and slow, happy and sad. Sofia listened and felt the Lord's presence in Ludwig's songs, just as she had felt His presence in church when Mama was still alive. Sofia's heart silently sang with him.

"Thank you, Ludwig," she said when at last he seemed to run out of melodies. He looked up at the lowering sun and asked her a question, gesturing as if he were eating. Sofia shook her head. "I don't feel much like eating." The few minutes of joy had faded along with the music, leaving her stomach in turmoil once again.

Ludwig wrapped his violin and returned it to his bag, then stood and beckoned to her to join him, again making motions as if eating. Maybe he was as lonely as she was. He had been so kind to her. She shouldn't refuse him.

"All right," she said, standing and smoothing her skirts. "I'll go with you." She lifted her sisters' satchels along with her own, but he quickly took two of them from her, helping her carry them. She followed him through the building's maze of hallways, realizing that she never would have found the dining hall on her own. She had been too upset to pay attention when Mrs. Bjork had given her the tour earlier. She noticed a slight limp in Ludwig's step and how one shoulder seemed to dip a little lower than the other as he walked beside her. No doubt the immigration officials had noticed it, too.

A crowd had already gathered around the entrance to the dining room, and as soon as the doors opened, the people stampeded inside. Ludwig held Sofia out of the way so she wouldn't get trampled, waiting until the surge ebbed. Then he found two empty places for them at one of the tables.

The light supper consisted of baked beans, stewed prunes, rye bread, and tea. The waiters also served the small children crackers and milk. Many of the other immigrants reached and grabbed for their food and seemed to have no idea what to do with the white napkins at each place, but Ludwig ate with impeccable manners.

They went outside again after eating and enjoyed the slightly cooler air. As the evening progressed, they watched the moon rise and the stars light up the sky one by one. The lights of New York City twinkled faintly in the distance across the river. America seemed a long way off. Sofia convinced Ludwig to take out his violin and play it again. Other detainees gathered around as he did, applauding each time he finished a song. Everyone seemed to draw comfort from his music.

Later, Ludwig walked Sofia to her dormitory, carrying her two extra satchels for her. She glimpsed the room where the men slept as they passed the open door, and it seemed even more crowded than the women's quarters. Both rooms were so noisy that Sofia wondered how she would ever fall asleep among so many strangers. At least in steerage she'd had the comfort of her sisters nearby.

Ludwig must have seen her hesitation. He laid all of their belongings down and began talking to her in a soothing voice, trying to reassure her. He rested his hands on her shoulders as he looked directly into her eyes, and his own eyes grew very soft. No man had ever stood so close to her or looked at Sofia that way. She liked the shivery feeling it gave her. Elin would reprimand her for trusting a stranger, but Elin wasn't there.

When Ludwig finished his monologue, he pulled out his Bible again and urged her to open hers, turning to Psalm 4:8. Tears filled her eyes as she read the words: *I will lie down and sleep in peace, for you alone, O Lord, make me dwell in safety.*

"Thank you, Ludwig," she murmured. "You are the kindest man I've ever met . . . a godsend."

He smiled as if he'd understood and said, "*Gute Nacht*, Sofia." He started to leave, then turned back and asked for her Bible again. He opened it to the book of Ruth and laid the book in the palm of her hand, then placed her other hand on top of it. He was telling her to read it. His own hand, with his long, tapered fingers, covered hers completely.

"Thank you. I will read it. *God natt.*"

The only empty bed Sofia could find was a bottom bunk. She wondered how she would ever sleep with two women suspended on top of her mere inches away. She laid her satchels on the bed, but it was impossible to sit down on it. The bunk hanging above it was much too close. She loosened the buttons of her dress but decided not to take it off. She wanted to be able to run out of this airless room if she had to.

Lines of women took turns washing at the three sinks. The women sleeping in the beds near Sofia smelled as though they had never bathed in their lives.

189

She wondered how long they had been detained there, and if she would smell as bad as they did, in time.

She sat down on the floor, leaning against her bunk, and opened her Bible to the place that Ludwig had shown her. At first, she couldn't understand why he wanted her to read the book of Ruth. She couldn't find any promises from God in it—only tragedy. But as she continued to read, she slowly began to see that Ruth had also lost many of the people she had loved—her husband, her parents, her family in Moab—everyone except her mother-in-law, Naomi. And Naomi admitted that she was angry and bitter from all of her losses.

Like Sofia, Ruth also had left her country to start all over again in a new land. Her life proved very difficult at first, but then Ruth's story turned into a love story. A kind, gracious man named Boaz watched over Ruth and later married her. They had a baby. The last verses of the book revealed that Ruth's baby was an ancestor of King David, the composer of so many beautiful psalms. God had been with Ruth, turning her losses into joy. And hope.

"Thank you, Ludwig," she whispered.

A matron turned off the lights for the night. As Sofia climbed onto her narrow bunk, groping in the dark, she felt utterly alone. Everything in her life had been stripped away—her parents, her home, her country—and now she'd lost her sisters, as well. But when she closed her eyes to pray, she knew that God was with her in the darkness.

Chapter Sixteen

KIRSTEN AWOKE THE next morning in the hospital ward, dismayed to see that the room was real and not simply a bad dream. Her stomach seethed with nausea the way it had aboard the ferry during the height of the storm. Worry was doing this to her—and who wouldn't be upset? She had awakened to a nightmare. She was alone and afraid—afraid for Sofia and for Elin and for herself. She had no one to talk to. No one could understand a word she said.

The nurses passed around trays of food, setting one in front of Kirsten. But as the aroma of boiled eggs rose to her nostrils, the smell made her gag. She pushed the plate away, covering her mouth to avoid throwing up. A nurse rushed over to her. The woman held the plate of eggs out to Kirsten as if insisting that she eat them. Kirsten's stomach turned inside out. She couldn't help retching.

"I can't eat," she said when the sickness passed. "Please, I just want to get out of here and go back to my sisters."

They took away the food and sent in a doctor to examine her. He probed her abdomen, pressing down on it in several places, then listened with a special instrument. When he finished, Kirsten lay in bed, trying to pray. She remembered the Lord's Prayer from church and recited it over and over as the long morning passed.

191

Finally, the interpreter from the Swedish Immigrant Aid Society came to speak with her again. "How are you today, Miss Carlson?" she asked.

Tears filled Kirsten's eyes at the familiar sound of her own language. "I'm fine. Please tell the doctors that I'm fine. I just need to find my sisters. Sofia must be frantic by now. She has always been so fearful and shy. She needs me! Can you please ask the nurses where my clothes are?" She tried to swing her feet out of bed, but Mrs. Bjork held up her hand, stopping her.

"Wait. They want you to remain in bed, please."

"Why? Did they tell you why I have to stay here?"

The woman looked down at the sheaf of papers in her hand, then said, "Yesterday you told me you have another sister, Elin Carlson?"

"Yes. Is she all right? Where is she?"

"She's here in this hospital in another ward. They've determined that she is ill with typhus."

"Typhus! Oh no!" Fear for Elin made Kirsten's stomach twist into knots.

"As I mentioned yesterday, there were several confirmed cases of typhus on your ship."

"Is-is she going to be all right?"

"She's young and strong and otherwise healthy. The doctors are confident that she will recover, but it will take some time. They want to make certain that you don't contract it, too."

"But I have to get back to Sofia. Please . . . where are my clothes?"

"They are being fumigated. Typhus is transmitted by lice, which can inhabit your clothing."

"Oh no . . . please . . ." Kirsten groaned. She didn't want to start crying, but she couldn't help it. She felt like a prisoner. There was nothing wrong with her. "When they finish checking my clothes, then will they let me go? My sister Sofia is all alone and she needs me. She's only sixteen."

"I explained the situation to Sofia yesterday. I'm sure she'll be fine. She is staying in the dormitory in the immigration center and will be fed in the dining room."

"This is a nightmare," Kirsten groaned. "We're so far from home, and we need to get to our uncle's house in Chicago. Why is this happening?" She couldn't stop crying. She was aware that the interpreter was watching her, waiting for her to control her tears. She dried them with her fists. "I'm sorry, I'm sorry . . . but I need to know how long it's going to be until can I leave."

"They've decided to keep you for a few more days—"

"No!" she wailed. "No, they can't!"

The hospital ward grew very quiet at her outburst. Several of the nurses shushed her.

"The doctors are very concerned that you can't keep down any food," Mrs. Bjork said softly.

"Well, it's their fault! They're making me upset by keeping me here. It's no wonder I can't eat. And I'm worried sick about my sisters. Can't you tell the doctors that? Tell them if they let me leave here I'll be fine."

"I'll tell them," she promised, "but I doubt if it will do any good. Maybe if you tried to eat something . . ."

Kirsten did her best to eat all her meals that day, to look healthy, to show them that she was fine. It did no good. The doctors kept her in the hospital for another long day, and an even longer night.

Poor Elin. And poor Sofia. She must be frantic by now. *Please, God, let them be all right.*

Kirsten still felt nauseated the next morning, and the doctor examined her again. If only he would return her clothes and let her go back to Sofia. She waited all day, and by the time the interpreter came to speak to her, it was late in the day. Kirsten felt like screaming.

"The doctors say that your sister Elin is doing much better," Mrs. Bjork told Kirsten. "And your sister Sofia is fine. I spoke with her this morning. She is being well taken care of at the detention center."

"When are the doctors going to let me out of here?"

"Most likely in a few days. They need to make sure you're getting adequate nourishment and feeling stronger. But, Miss Carlson, there's something else we need to talk about." She lowered her voice, even though they both knew that no one else in the hospital ward could understand a word they said. Kirsten's stomach clenched in dread.

"What's wrong?"

"The doctor who examined you believes . . . um . . . that you are expecting a child."

"*What?*" Kirsten went cold all over. It was the same shocked reaction she'd felt when Elin first told her that their father had fallen through the ice and drowned. A child? They must be mistaken. "No . . . no, that can't be true. . . ."

The woman waited patiently as Kirsten continued to shake her head in denial. She refused to believe it. The doctors had confused her with another patient. Married people had babies—not unmarried girls like herself.

"It's not possible," she insisted. But as the woman calmly waited, the truth slowly penetrated Kirsten's shock. One time when she had been alone in the woods with Tor they had been swept away. Just once . . . or maybe twice . . . but that was all. They loved each other. Tor had assured her that it was all right for them to be together because they loved each other. He had said they would be married someday.

"It-it can't be true," Kirsten murmured.

But it was.

In an instant her body went from cold to hot. She felt her face flush with shame. The interpreter looked away, as if embarrassed for her. She cleared her throat.

"I know it's hard, Miss Carlson, and I'm not passing judgment on you. Neither is the doctor. But I'm afraid you need to accept the truth."

Kirsten covered her face and wept. The woman

waited in silence until Kirsten finally controlled her sobbing. "I don't know what to do," she mumbled. "Are you sure that I'm . . . ? Oh, what in the world am I going to do?"

"I can't advise you what to do, Miss Carlson, but here is the situation, and please listen carefully: An unmarried woman who is expecting a baby won't be allowed into the country. The immigration officials will declare her 'LPC'—likely to become a public charge—since she has no husband to support her. She will be sent back to her homeland. Do you understand?"

Kirsten nodded as her tears continued to fall. She didn't know if that was good news or bad. Tor would have to marry her if she returned home to Sweden carrying his child. But she couldn't face the thought of traveling all the way back there. And what about Elin and Sofia? What would she tell them? Elin wouldn't want to go back to Sweden, but Sofia would—and then the three of them would be separated. They would all be punished for Kirsten's sin.

"W-will my sisters have to return home, too?"

"That depends. Single women and unaccompanied married women aren't allowed to leave Ellis Island unless a male family member comes to claim them. That's true in all cases, not just under these circumstances. I'm surprised this wasn't explained to you."

"My uncle Lars paid our way and made all of the arrangements. He lives in Chicago. My sisters and I have train tickets from here to Chicago, and we plan to go there as soon as we leave New York. Everything is paid for. We're going to live with him. Our uncle is going to take care of us."

"I see. That's good. Once your sister receives medical clearance, she will be allowed to take a train directly there."

"But I won't be?"

"Well, again, that depends. For instance, if the baby's father is waiting in Chicago, I'm sure you would be cleared." Kirsten started to speak, but the woman stopped her. "No, just listen. It's up to you to decide what you would like me to tell the doctors and other officials. I'm only the interpreter, you see. I don't need to know your personal information. But if the baby's father comes forward to support you, that would be different."

Kirsten knew that lying was wrong. She also knew that what she and Tor had done was wrong. She had no excuse for getting carried away with him except that she had loved him—and she had believed that he loved her in return. But now what should she do?

The only solution was to return to Sweden. Elin and Sofia could decide for themselves what they would do. Kirsten had to write a letter to Tor and explain her circumstances and tell him to quickly arrange for their marriage. He needed to take care of her and their baby.

Their baby. Kirsten couldn't believe it.

"If we aren't allowed into America, how quickly will we be sent home?"

"Right away. If you are refused for medical reasons, you will be put on the next ship from the White Star Line that is returning to Europe."

Kirsten's baby couldn't be more than a month along. People in the village would never have to know that it was conceived out of wedlock. Tor wouldn't even have to tell his father.

"You don't have to decide right now," the woman said when Kirsten hesitated. "I'll be back in a few days, when the doctors are ready to release you, and you can tell me then what your plans are."

"Could you . . . I mean . . . I need to send a letter to Sweden right away and explain about . . . you know . . ." She still couldn't comprehend that she was going to have Tor's baby. It didn't seem real.

"Would you like to send a telegram? It's much faster."

The arrival of a telegram from America would be big news in their tiny village. Kirsten imagined everyone in Magnusson's store gathering around to read it, and she blushed with shame.

"No, I think a letter is better. Do you know where I can get postage stamps and things?"

"I'll tell the nurses to find you some paper and a pen. And I'll bring an overseas stamp the next time I come."

"Thank you."

"I'll be back when they are ready to release you."

Kirsten lay back against the pillows. The ordeal had exhausted her. Could she really be expecting a child?

What would she tell her sisters? She wanted to bury her face in her pillow in humiliation at the thought of how she had disgraced them. First Papa had dishonored their family by killing himself, and now this. Kirsten had not only ruined her own life, but she probably had ruined Elin's and Sofia's lives, too.

She couldn't tell them the truth. She couldn't. She would make up a reason why she couldn't get medical clearance.

In the meantime, she would contact Tor and tell him that she was returning home. *I'm going to have your baby, Tor, and I don't know what to do,* she would write.

She imagined him receiving her letter in his father's store, tearing open the envelope, reading the news. He would stand up to his father and explain why he had to marry Kirsten. He would do the right thing—wouldn't he?

Chapter Seventeen

SOFIA FOLLOWED THE other women out of the dormitory and down to the dining hall for breakfast, hoping she would see her new friend, Ludwig Schneider, again. When she recalled meeting him the day before her heart began to speed up—not with fear, for once, but with anticipation. And there he was, standing outside the door, waiting for her—a head taller than most of the other immigrants. He smiled when he saw her.

"*Guten Morgen*, Sofia."

She couldn't help smiling in return. "*God morgon.* I hope you haven't been waiting a long time. And I hope there is plenty of food left. I'm very hungry this morning."

He babbled a reply and led her into the crowded dining room. The other immigrants snatched and grabbed for their food again, as if they might never have another meal, but Ludwig seemed to know the best places to sit and what to do to get served, and he made sure they both had plenty to eat. She guessed from the way Ludwig handled himself and the friendly way that he and the waiters got along that he must have been detained here for quite some time. She wished she could ask him how long.

After breakfast Sofia followed Ludwig upstairs, and he showed her a crowded rooftop where detainees were allowed to go for fresh air. A few minutes later she saw the interpreter she had talked to yesterday walking toward her. Sofia's stomach rolled over in dread, but Mrs. Bjork smiled pleasantly, relieving some of Sofia's fear.

"Do you have good news about my sisters, I hope?"

"Your sisters must remain hospitalized, I am sorry to say. But their condition seems to be stable."

"Thank God. I've been praying for them to get well. How much longer will they be in the hospital?"

"The doctors aren't certain. But I'll let you know as soon as I find out."

It seemed strange to hear Swedish again after listening to the babble of incomprehensible languages all around her—even stranger to speak it herself to someone who could understand.

"If I wrote a letter to Elin, would you be able to deliver it for me? I know that she must be very worried about me being here all alone, and I want her to know that I'm all right."

"I could make sure that it gets delivered. I have to go downstairs to the Registry Room to translate this morning. They are expecting more Swedish passengers to arrive today." She nodded her head toward the river, where the first of countless ferries had already lined up with boatloads of immigrants. "But I will find you before I leave the island this afternoon and take your letter to her if it's ready."

"Thank you so much. I know it will relieve Elin's mind. She worries about Kirsten and me so much."

"If there is any other way that the Aid Society can help you," Mrs. Bjork said as she walked slowly toward the stairs again, "please be sure to let me know."

"I-I do have a question," Sofia said, following behind her. "I met someone who has been kept here in detention for a long time, and I'm wondering what's going to happen to him."

"People who are refused entrance can take their case to the Board of Appeals, which meets periodically. Perhaps he is waiting to do that. Or, if his plea has been refused already, he is probably waiting for the next ship that is returning to his home country."

"He has been very kind to me, helping me and making everything easier for me. I want to thank him but I think he is speaking German. Could you—"

"I'm sorry, but I only speak Swedish and English."

"Could I write him a note and maybe you could translate it into English, and then he could give it to another translator, who could change it into German and—"

Mrs. Bjork smiled but shook her head. "I'm sorry, but that would be a long, laborious process. And I'm not really authorized to do things like that."

Sofia glanced over her shoulder to where Ludwig waited for her. She wanted to tell him so many things, and she saw the same eagerness in his eyes whenever they tried to converse. "But . . . isn't there some way—"

"I'm sorry, but I'm afraid I can't help you. I need to go now, but I'll come by later for the letter to your sister."

"Yes. Thank you." She watched the woman turn away, already missing the sound of her own language, and found Ludwig gazing at the Statue of Liberty a short distance away on a nearby island. Everyone arriving in America had cheered for joy when they'd first spotted the statue welcoming them to this country, lighting their way to a brand-new life. Now everyone on this rooftop waited to learn if they would be allowed to enter or be sent back to their old countries.

"My sisters are getting better," she told Ludwig,

smiling as she held up their two bags. "Maybe we will be able to leave here soon."

Ludwig answered her in German. She couldn't understand what he said, but she loved the sound of his deep, soothing voice. She would miss him. Sofia looked up at his gentle face in surprise as she realized just how much. She had made a friend. He had helped her through a difficult time—and once she left Ellis Island, she would never see him again.

"Why am I always saying good-bye to people?" she murmured. "Why does life have to be so hard?"

He turned to her with a look of concern as if detecting the sadness in her voice. She smiled to reassure him and made a fiddling motion with her arms, begging him to play for her. "I won't spoil the time we have today by worrying about tomorrow," she said.

He found a place to sit down and pulled out his instrument. At first, he played scales and exercises without melodies, as if warming up his fingers. Then his violin began to sing again—sad, poignant tunes; happy, spirited ones; hymns and folk songs and dances. Everyone on the rooftop seemed to enjoy his performance, applauding after each song, shaking his hand and thanking him in countless languages. When he grew tired and laid down his violin, Sofia joined him on the bench. She pulled out her Bible and handed it to him. "Would you show me where to find more verses in the Bible?"

He nodded in understanding, answering her in

German as he got out his own Bible. They had nothing else to do. And it would help pass the time, which seemed to stand still on Ellis Island.

The first verse he showed her was John 14:23: *Jesus replied, "If anyone loves me, he will obey my teaching. My Father will love him, and we will come to him and make our home with him."*

Sofia had kept the piece of paper from yesterday so she could look up the verses later, but Ludwig gently took it from her and began drawing on it again. Beneath the sketches of their families he drew a picture of a simple square house with windows and a peaked roof and smoke curling from the chimney.

"Ein Haus," he told her, pointing to the picture and then the verse. He sighed, gesturing to the city across the river, then to himself.

"I want a home, too," she told him, "more than anything else. Elin asked me what I wished for in America, and that's really all I want—a home. Do you think we will ever have one, Ludwig?"

Again, he must have detected the sorrow in her voice. He turned back one page in his Bible to the beginning of the chapter and pointed to John 14:1: *"Do not let your hearts be troubled. Trust in God; trust also in me. In my Father's house are many rooms; if it were not so, I would have told you."*

"So you believe that God does have a place for us—not just in heaven someday, but now, on earth?" She could tell by his expression that he hadn't understood her, but he turned to another place in his Bible, Romans 8:28: *And we know that in all things God works for the good of those who love him, who have been called according to his purpose.*

"Is that true?" she murmured, more to herself than to Ludwig. Could God really be working for her own good in the midst of all the losses she'd faced? She wanted so much to believe it, but what about her mother's death? How had that worked anything good?

Sofia drew a circle around the verse on her piece of paper. She would have to think about it some more before she was willing to believe it was true. She looked up at Ludwig, wanting to ask him for more verses that might help her understand, but he had spotted someone he knew near the stairs and was waving to her. He slid his Bible onto Sofia's lap and stood, gesturing for Sofia to watch his bag with his violin.

The round, plain-looking woman was clutching a sheaf of papers just like Sofia's translator, Mrs. Bjork, had carried. Perhaps this was Ludwig's German translator.

He talked with her for awhile, and when he came back he showed Sofia a verse from Acts 17:31: *For he has set a day when he will judge the world with justice by the man he has appointed.*

Ludwig must be referring to the Board of Appeals that Mrs. Bjork had mentioned. Maybe Ludwig's case would be decided soon. "I'll pray for you,

Ludwig," she told him. She folded her hands and bowed her head to explain what she meant. He nodded and folded his hands in prayer, too.

Days passed, and Sofia found that she didn't mind waiting at all. Her sisters were getting well, and in the meantime, she spent every day with Ludwig, listening to his violin music, eating with him, walking around the detainees' courtyards with him as far as they were allowed to go. They watched the ships passing up and down the river, and the immigrants coming ashore looking frightened and forlorn, filing into the huge Registry Room downstairs. The fortunate ones left on ferries to the mainland a few hours later to begin their new lives. The unfortunate ones joined her and Ludwig in the detention pens.

Sofia and Ludwig were on the roof one morning when he spotted his translator again and hurried over to speak with her. Sofia watched as the woman explained something to him, and the longer Ludwig listened the more agitated he became, running his hands through his dark hair and pacing in front of her. When the woman finished, Ludwig began pleading with her, shaking his head, gesturing to the city across the river, his voice growing louder and louder until Sofia could hear him, even at a distance. At last the woman left and Ludwig returned to sink down onto the bench beside Sofia. She saw his disappointment turn to despair.

"I'm so sorry, Ludwig," she said, touching his arm.

"I can tell that she brought you bad news. I wish I could do something for you. You've helped me so much."

They sat in silence that way for several long minutes as he wrestled with his emotions. His bag lay open at his feet, the violin on top of it, but when he looked down and saw it, he shoved the violin deep inside the bag. Then he took his Bible from Sofia and stuffed it in beside the violin, shutting the clasp on the valise with a snap. She waited, and when he was finally ready to talk, his words came out in a rapid burst.

She heard sorrow and anger in his voice as he gestured to America on the other side of the river, then shook his head, pointing to himself. He sighed, then pointed emphatically down the river toward the Atlantic Ocean and waved farewell. They weren't going to let him into America. They were sending him back home.

"No . . . oh, Ludwig, no. I'm so sorry. It's so unfair. Isn't there anything you can do?"

He talked for a long time, slower now, unburdening all of his sorrow, just as she had done on their first day together. She couldn't understand his words, but she knew what they meant—and she knew that his heart was breaking. When he finally stopped talking, he glanced all around as if looking to see if anyone was watching him, then pantomimed swimming across the river once again.

"You can't swim that far. You'll drown."

He shook his head and spread his hands wide as if to say, *"I have no choice,"* then pretended to swim again. Sofia wondered how he would ever make it that far with his lame leg. The river looked too wide for even a strong swimmer to cross. Ludwig folded his hands and put them under his face like a pillow, closing his eyes to mimic sleeping. Then he made swimming motions again.

"No . . . You can't go at night! It will be even more dangerous! Ludwig, please don't do it." But she saw the determination in his eyes and knew that he wasn't listening to her pleas—even though she was certain he understood them.

"America," he said firmly, pointing to the city. "Ludwig Schneider," he said, nodding his head decisively. She saw how much America meant to him, how badly he wanted to stay, and Sofia was sorry for not appreciating everything that Elin had gone through to bring them this far.

Sofia opened her Bible to the book of Romans and to the verse he had shown her the other day. "It says that God will make everything work together for your good, Ludwig. Don't you believe that?"

He reached over to her lap and gently closed her Bible, shaking his head. She wished she knew how to encourage him. She scanned through the list of verses he had shown her, searching for one that would encourage him, and pointed to Psalm 27:14: *Wait for the Lord; be strong and take heart and wait for the Lord.*

Ludwig glanced at her, then shook his head, unwilling to open his own Bible. She longed to help him the way he had helped her, but she didn't know what to do. He had blessed her with his violin music, but the only thing she possibly could do in return was sing. What would he think of her voice? He was a gifted musician and she a mere amateur who sang to her cows and chickens back home.

She was about to give up the idea when she remembered the verse she had opened to on the first day: *Sing the glory of his name; make his praise glorious.* Ludwig had given her hope with his music and had helped her find God's promises again. If the only thing she could give him in return was a song, then she would offer one to him. She rested her hand on his arm and looked in his eyes.

"Ludwig? I want to sing something for you. It was my mother's favorite hymn; that's why I memorized it. It's called, 'Children of the Heavenly Father.' I-I haven't been able to sing it since she died, but . . . but I want it to be my gift to you."

She cleared her throat, staring down at the ground for a moment, wondering if she would be able to get through it. Then she lifted her chin and looked into his eyes again as she began to sing.

" 'Children of the heavenly Father safely in His bosom gather; nestling bird nor star in heaven such a refuge e'er was given.' " Ludwig listened intently, never taking his gaze off her face. She had to look away or she would start to cry and be unable to sing.

She could tell he was still watching her, though, as she started the second verse.

"'God His own doth tend and nourish; in His holy courts they flourish. From all evil things He spares them; in His loving arms He bears them.'" She swallowed, struggling to continue singing as she remembered the feeling of God's arms around her as she'd slept in that terrible dormitory the first night. Ludwig had helped her find that comfort, and now he needed it himself.

"'Neither life nor death can ever from the Lord His children sever; unto them His grace He showeth and their sorrows all He knoweth.'" Tears rolled down her cheeks. Sofia understood sorrow and loss, but for the first time in her life she truly comprehended the strength of God's love for her. God was with her there on Ellis Island, so far from home. She and Ludwig were both in His hands. No matter what happened, she could trust God.

She turned back to face Ludwig and sang the last verse to herself as well as to him. "'Though He giveth or He taketh, God His children ne'er forsaketh; His the loving purpose solely to preserve them pure and holy.'"

Ludwig had not taken his eyes off her the entire time, but when she finished, he closed them. She could tell by the way his strong, square chin quivered that he was battling his emotions. When he opened his eyes again, he reached for Sofia's hand and lifted it to his lips for a kiss.

"*Danke*, Sofia," he whispered. "*Danke.*"

He pointed to a bird sitting atop a nearby railing, then to her. He smiled. Ludwig Schneider had a magnificent smile, even though grief still lingered in his eyes.

"You're welcome," she said. And she realized with surprise—and joy—that she had just sung her first song in America.

Chapter Eighteen

ELIN HAD NO idea where she was or how she'd gotten there. She lay in a white iron bed in a stark white room while death held her body in its grip, trying to shake the life out of her. Her head ached. Her entire body ached. She was out of her mind with fever. White-clad men and women peered at her from time to time. The people in the beds all around her were as sick as she was.

Every once in a while she would remember Sofia and Kirsten, and she would try to call out their names. Her efforts would lead to fits of coughing, and a nurse would hurry to her side to quiet her. What had happened to her sisters? Where were they? Were they as ill as she was? No one could understand her or answer her questions.

She had made a huge mistake in coming to America. She had wanted to save her sisters from Uncle Sven, but she had made their lives worse, not better. Elin had promised Mama that she would take care of Kirsten and Sofia, but instead she had lost them. As she lay helplessly in bed, Elin could only trust her sisters to God's care—and realized that she should have done that from the very beginning.

At times Elin wondered if she was going to die. She deserved to die in punishment for seeking comfort from Uncle Sven, for allowing him to do what he did. He inhabited some of her feverish dreams, taking her to such horrible, fear-filled places that she was certain she had entered hell. Other times, her dreams took her to such beautiful places that she wondered if she was in heaven and would soon see her mother.

As the grip of her fever slowly loosened, Elin became more and more aware of her surroundings in the hospital room and how kindly the nurses treated her. She couldn't understand a word they said, but their voices were soothing, their gestures gentle as they offered her sips of water and bathed her brow with cool water and tried to make her comfortable. Now and then she would attempt to talk to them, hoping that one of them would be able to understand her.

"Can you find out where my sisters are?" she begged. "Sofia is too young to be all alone. She has never been separated from me before. She must be terrified."

⋅ Each time, the nurses spoke gibberish in reply—soothing gibberish, but incomprehensible just the same.

She had no idea how many days had passed, but she thought it must be many. Several times she tried to sit up and look around at the other beds to see if her sisters were there, too. When she didn't see them, she comforted herself with the knowledge that it must mean they weren't sick. They hadn't caught whatever disease she had. But what had become of them?

Please, God, let them be all right. Punish me, not them.

At last the day finally came when the fever broke for good and Elin could think clearly again. She pulled herself up in bed and was able to eat a little food. "I need to find my sisters," Elin told the nurse. "I need to know what's going on, and where they are, and if they have been ill, too."

The nurse smiled and held up her hand, asking her to wait. An hour later, an interpreter from the Swedish Immigrant Aid Society came to talk with Elin.

"Your sisters are both fine," the woman told her. "They are waiting for you here on Ellis Island. The officials in the detention center provide them with three meals a day and a place to sleep at night."

"Is it safe there?"

"Yes, of course it is. One of your sisters wrote you a note a few days ago, but you haven't been well enough to read it. It's here by your bed if you would like to see it."

"Oh yes! Please!" Elin recognized Sofia's writing as soon as she saw it. She unfolded the paper.

Dear Elin,

I have been very worried about you and I'm praying every day that you will get well. I am fine, not sick at all, but I miss you. The days are very long and always the same as I wait and wait. I know they must be long for you, too. But the food is good and the beds are clean, and the room where I'm sleeping has sinks where I can wash, so everything is fine.

I'm praying that you will get better so we can continue our journey. We are almost there now. I want you to know how sorry I am for the way I acted during our trip. And I want you to know that if you just hurry up and get well, I promise not to be sulky or to mope around anymore. We are sisters. We're a family. And we are going to start a brand-new life together in America.

Every day I see thousands of people coming in and out of Ellis Island and they all want to live in America so badly that they are willing to do anything to stay. Even though I didn't want to come at first, I want you to know that I'm glad you found a way for all three of us to move here. And I promise not to give you a hard time about being homesick anymore.

Please get well soon and don't worry about me. I'm fine.

Love,
Sofia

Elin wept with relief, then read the letter a second time. Sofia was all right. She was safe. She didn't even sound frightened to death, as Elin had expected her to be. All Elin had to do was get better so she could rejoin her. Best of all, Sofia had finally accepted the fact that America would be their home from now on.

It was only after Elin read the letter for a third time that she realized that Sofia had never mentioned Kirsten. And why hadn't Kirsten written a letter, too? Elin felt a ripple of fear until she remembered what the interpreter had said: *"Your sisters are both fine. They are waiting for you on Ellis Island."* She would have to trust that all was well with Kirsten until the doctors allowed her to join them.

Elin soon grew tired of living in this bleak white room. It was so large and impersonal that she felt swallowed up in a blizzard of white. She longed to see trees again and hear the birds singing and feel the breeze on her face. Her bed was too far away from a window to get even a glimpse of what was outside. But she noticed that whenever one of the nurses walked between the rows of beds to tend to her patients, the room seemed transformed. The nurses reminded her of Mama. Elin's mother had had the same effect on her patients, transforming any sickroom from glum to cheerful simply by entering it. She had entertained Elin and her sisters for hours whenever they were sick.

Mama also had worked as a midwife, traveling to

neighboring women's homes to help them through their labor and caring for the new mothers and their babies afterward. For two years before she died, Mama had taken Elin with her. The work had fascinated Elin, and she had begged to stay home from school when she knew that a baby was on the way.

"God has given you the gift of healing, too," Mama had told her. "Maybe you would like to be a midwife someday?"

Elin had believed so. She'd never experienced a joy like that of delivering a new life into this world. But then Mama had become sick, and no amount of medicine or loving care had been able to save her. Afterward, Elin had sought refuge in the wrong place, with the wrong person—Uncle Sven. Now the idea of having "the gift of healing" seemed ridiculous.

But Elin wanted the nurses in this hospital to know how much she appreciated their loving care. The next time the woman from the Swedish Immigrant Aid Society came, Elin asked her to thank all of the nurses for her.

"They are saying that no thanks is necessary," Mrs. Bjork told her after she'd interpreted Elin's words. "They are insisting that they enjoy their work and are simply doing their job."

"How does someone get a job like theirs here in America?"

"Many hospitals in big cities like New York have nursing schools where women can be specially trained."

"Nursing schools? Are there some in Chicago, too?"

"It's a very large city, so I'm sure there must be. Do you think you would like to be a nurse, Miss Carlson?"

"Me? It's probably impossible. . . ." Elin didn't dare to dream of something so far out of her reach. She was a poor village girl with no money and no family. She couldn't even speak English.

"How do the nurses keep from getting sick?" Elin asked her. "When we were on the boat, I took care of a sick woman and her children. That's probably how I caught typhus."

"I'm told that typhus is spread through lice that people can carry in their clothing if they don't wash very often. I suppose nurses learn in school how to be careful and keep everything clean."

Again, Elin thought of her mother. She had known so much about caring for people and bringing babies into the world. She had started to pass that knowledge along to Elin before she became sick. Years of wisdom and experience had been lost when Mama died.

"I need to be going," Mrs. Bjork said, "but I'll be back when you're well enough to be released. I hope you and your sisters can continue on your journey then."

"Thank you. We will be going on to Chicago, and—Oh no! I just remembered! My uncle was expecting us to arrive days and days ago. He must be wondering what happened to us."

"Don't worry, I helped your sister send a telegram to let him know you would be delayed. We will send another one to let him know your new arrival time."

"How can I ever thank you?"

"It isn't necessary. I was once a frightened immigrant just like you and some very kind people helped me. You can thank me by helping someone else in need someday."

"Yes . . . I would like to do that." But Elin wondered if the time would ever come when she wasn't helpless and dependent on others, a time when she could help someone else.

Chapter Nineteen

"MY CLOTHES! OH, thank goodness." Kirsten couldn't recall ever being happier to see her own homemade skirt and shirtwaist. It felt wonderful to stand up and put them on instead of lying in bed all day wearing a thin hospital gown. She assumed, as soon as the nurse handed back her clothing, that she was being discharged from the hospital. The translator, Mrs. Bjork, confirmed it when she arrived.

"The doctors gave you a clean bill of health on your medical card," she said, "but the card also states that you are pregnant. It will be up to the immigration officials on Ellis Island to decide whether or not you will be allowed into the country. You can tell me whatever you would like me to say about the baby's father, and it may have some bearing on their decision. But if they declare that you are 'likely to become a public charge,' you will be sent home at the steamship company's expense."

"I-I don't know—"

Mrs. Bjork held up her hand. "You still have time to think about your reply while you wait for your other sister to get well."

"Are my sisters going to find out about the baby?"

"That's entirely up to you. I will be translating for you, so they won't know what I'm telling the officials in English—or what they are saying to you. I won't mention the baby in front of your sisters unless you want me to."

"I don't want you to—for now. But if I'm sent home, will my sisters have to go with me?"

"That's up to them. Their medical clearance is determined separately from yours. Now, if you're ready, I'll walk back to the immigration building with you."

Outside, the May afternoon was sunny and cool, the kind of spring day that Kirsten had loved back home. She remembered exploring the woods with her brother, reveling in the new life budding all around her. Now she was on a tiny barren island in a strange foreign land.

"I'm needed in the Registry Room this afternoon to do some translating," Mrs. Bjork told her. "I'll show you where you can find me if you have any more questions. And your sister can show you where to sleep and take your meals."

The thought of food made Kirsten feel nauseated again. She knew it was common among pregnant women to feel sick, and she wondered how she would ever bear another long ocean journey back to Sweden, stuck in steerage with all of its foul smells. And what would she eat on the trip if she did feel hungry? The food they had packed in Sweden must be long gone.

As soon as she neared the main building, Kirsten saw Sofia waiting for her behind a fence, waving her arms above her head and hopping up and down. They both had tears in their eyes as they hugged each other.

"Oh, it's so good to see you!" Sofia said. "How are you feeling? Are you all better now? They said you didn't have typhus, but did they ever find out what was wrong with you? It feels like you've been gone for a hundred years!"

Kirsten laughed. "That's the most I've heard you say since we left Sweden. But believe me, I know how good it feels to have someone to talk to. I'm fine now—the picture of health." She deliberately avoided Sofia's question about what had been wrong with her, hoping she wouldn't notice, hoping a lie wouldn't be necessary.

"Come on. I'll show you where I've been staying." Sofia picked up their three satchels and handed one to Kirsten. "You can help me carry these bags from now on. I'm getting tired of dragging them around with me everywhere I go, but I knew Elin wouldn't want me to leave them unattended."

Kirsten smiled at her sister. She had expected timid little Sofia to be nervous and panicky after being stranded in a foreign country with all these strangers for days and days. But Sofia seemed amazingly happy and more content than she had been since leaving home.

"Lead the way," Kirsten told her.

Sofia gave Kirsten a tour of the outdoor areas, the dining hall, and finally the women's dormitory, talking nearly nonstop. "Why do they have so many rules and guards everywhere?" Kirsten asked her. "I feel like we're being held prisoner. This is an island. We couldn't escape even if we wanted to."

"I don't know. Maybe it's for our own safety."

Kirsten dropped her bag onto one of the empty bunks. "Phew, they've kept me in bed too long. I'm not used to all this exercise, climbing up three flights of stairs. Do you mind if we rest here for awhile?"

"All right. But it's nicer outside. . . ." Sofia slid to the floor, leaning against the wall. Kirsten looked around and realized that the floor was the only place to sit down. It was impossible to sit comfortably on the beds with the ones above them hanging so low. She joined Sofia on the floor, sitting cross-legged.

"Listen, Sofia. I want to ask you something. . . . Do you still want to go home to Sweden?"

"What difference does it make what I want? We're already here, aren't we?"

"Well, suppose something happened and one of us

changed our mind. Suppose Elin or I decided to go home."

"Elin doesn't ever want to go back."

"Well, suppose I wanted to go back. Would you want to stay here or come with me?"

"I don't want to split up. We've come this far together, and I think we should stay together. If one of us decides to stay or go, we should all do the same thing."

Kirsten quickly lost her patience. "Suppose I got sent back. Suppose they didn't allow me to immigrate, for some reason, but they accepted you and Elin. Would you want to stay with her or come home with me?"

"Why are you asking such stupid questions? Did the doctors find something wrong with you?"

"Nothing's wrong with me. It's just that I know you didn't want to come to America in the first place, and you've been complaining and moping the entire trip. I just wondered if—"

"I promise not to mope and complain anymore, but we need to stay together."

"Fine. We'll stay together," Kirsten said with a sigh. "Listen, are we allowed to lie down and take a nap? I didn't sleep very well in the hospital. Would you mind?" She crawled onto a lower bunk without waiting for Sofia's reply.

"I don't mind. But I'd like to go outside while you're napping. It's a beautiful day. And if you're going to stay here, can you watch our bags?"

Once again, it amazed Kirsten that timid Sofia would want to wander around alone on an island full of strangers. She wondered what had caused this sudden change in her. But before she could ask, Sofia slipped out the door.

Kirsten did manage to nap for a little while, but she dreamed of Tor and woke up crying. She wished she could predict what his reaction would be when she arrived home with the news of their baby. She wished he loved her as much as she loved him.

She rolled off the bunk, pushing Tor from her thoughts. She felt surprisingly hungry for once. Maybe she could find something to eat in Elin's bag. She knelt on the floor to rummage through it—and pulled out Elin's diary instead.

Elin had carried the tattered old journal everywhere, even before they'd left Sweden. The plain unlined notebook looked like something a child might take to school. Kirsten couldn't remember how long ago Elin had first started writing in it, but she thought it was after Papa died.

She ruffled the edges of the swollen pages with her thumb and saw coffee rings and water stains and places where Elin had erased so fanatically that the paper had torn. She always used a pencil, yet her tiny, precise letters looked neat and prim—like Elin herself. Her handwriting reminded Kirsten of exquisite embroidery—gray thread on white linen. Words filled every page from top to bottom, with barely a pencil's width of space for margins.

Elin wrote endlessly in this book, often ignoring everyone as she scribbled away.

Sometimes, after they argued, saying hurtful things and throwing harsh words at each other like stones, Kirsten would sit across their attic bedroom from Elin with her back turned, wondering what terrible things Elin was saying about her in these pages. If Kirsten turned her head, Elin would pause and glance up at her with a frown, then bend over her page again, scribbling faster.

Even on their way to America, Kirsten remembered lying in bed in the boardinghouse trying to sleep while Elin stayed awake, writing by candlelight, her pencil scratching across the page. Aboard the ship, Kirsten had begged Elin to come outside on the deck with her for fresh air, but she had waved her hand in that impatient way of hers and remained below, writing.

Now Kirsten held Elin's notebook in her hands. Elin wasn't here to stop her from reading it, yet even so, it felt wrong to trespass among her private thoughts. She had always been so careful to keep this diary out of everyone's reach. But maybe Kirsten would understand Elin better if she read it. Maybe she could finally figure out what made her do the things she did, and how she made the choices she had, and why she was so rigid and unbending at times. Kirsten didn't understand her sister; that much was certain. They had endured so much together, and she was closer to Elin than to anyone else on earth, yet she felt as though she didn't know her at all.

She stared at the notebook, unsure why she hesitated. She recalled one winter night back home when they'd sat by the fireplace and Elin had been writing in her stupid diary, as usual. Kirsten got up to poke the smoldering logs, and as sparks leaped up the chimney like wood sprites, Elin looked up at her and said, "Kirsten! Promise me you'll throw this notebook into the fire if anything happens to me—without reading it! Promise?"

Kirsten had smiled at the drama and urgency in her voice and asked, "Why? What are you writing in there that's so important?"

"Never mind. You owe me, Kirsten. . . . Now, promise!"

"*Ja*, sure. I promise." But Kirsten had winked at Sofia and crossed her fingers behind her back, where Elin couldn't see them.

Kirsten smoothed her hand over the tattered cover. She knew it was wrong to read Elin's diary . . . but maybe it would help Kirsten understand why Elin had decided to come to America in the first place. And maybe it would help her decide whether or not to tell Elin the truth about the baby and why she needed to return to Sweden.

She opened to the first page.

An hour later, Kirsten slowly closed the diary without finishing it. Her hands trembled as she placed it back inside Elin's bag. The truth about their uncle Sven astounded her. She didn't want to believe it, didn't want to imagine Elin suffering in silence for so long. How could Uncle Sven do such a terrible thing, ensnaring her and deceiving her that way?

But hadn't Tor Magnusson done a similar thing, saying he loved Kirsten and that he wanted to marry her, just to get his own way?

Kirsten was sorry she had read the diary, not only because she had violated Elin's privacy but because the weight of Elin's secret felt much too heavy on her shoulders. No wonder Elin looked so old and tired and crippled. No wonder she worried so much. No wonder she was so fearful. If Uncle Sven, a trusted family member, could do such evil things, then Elin had a good reason to distrust strangers.

But what brought tears to Kirsten's eyes was the knowledge that Elin had loved her and Sofia so much that she had found a way to save them, too, instead of merely running away from Uncle Sven and deserting them the way Nils had. She wished she could thank Elin and explain how grateful she was, but she could never confess that she had discovered the truth. If Elin knew her secret had been uncovered, it would destroy her. The shame and guilt that Elin felt were evident on every page of the diary.

No, Kirsten would now carry the burden of Elin's secret along with the weight of her own. And one thing was certain: She could never ask Elin to go back to Sweden. Or Sofia, either. But what if Kirsten returned home to marry Tor, and Sofia insisted on going with her? Sofia had no place to live in Sweden except with Uncle Sven.

Kirsten groaned at the complexity of her dilemma. She needed to go home and marry Tor; Elin and Sofia needed to stay here. But what if Tor's father still refused to allow them to marry? Then what? She couldn't possibly stand up to Tor's father on her own. She had been counting on Uncle Sven to support her and to insist that Tor do the right thing. But now she wanted nothing to do with her uncle.

The only solution that she could see was for Tor to break away from his father and come to America to marry her. She needed to write a letter and explain her circumstances to him. He needed to come over right away. Maybe by now he had missed her so much that he was sorry he had let her go. Once Tor learned about the baby, he would surely do the right thing. She was almost certain of it.

Kirsten needed to find the translator and tell her what she had decided. She knew it was wrong to lie, just as it had been wrong to read Elin's diary and to have a baby with Tor. She would compound her sins by lying to the immigration officials, but she was desperate. Somehow she had to untangle the mess she had created. She would try to keep her story as close to the truth as possible.

"I know what I want you to tell the immigration officials," Kirsten said when she found Mrs. Bjork downstairs, outside the Registry Room. "Tell them . . . I-I do have a husband. His name is Tor Magnusson. Tell the officials that we were secretly married in Sweden and that Tor is planning to come to Chicago as soon as he can. We couldn't afford both of our fares, so I came with my sisters. That way my uncle in America would pay for mine. As soon as Tor earns enough money, he's going to come over, too, and then we'll be together."

"Do you have a copy of the marriage certificate? The officials might want to see it."

"Tor has it with him. In Sweden."

The woman didn't look at Kirsten, as if unwilling to see the lies written all over her face. "I'll tell the officials about your husband, Miss . . . I mean . . ." She paused, looking embarrassed.

"It's Magnusson. Mrs. Tor Magnusson."

"The fact that you and your sisters have tickets to Chicago and a sponsor waiting for you should help matters. I'll see what I can do."

Kirsten had committed herself to that decision. Once the immigration officials allowed her into the country, she would have no way to return to Sweden. But what if she stayed here and Tor didn't come? The baby would have no father. She and the child would both be outcasts. Surely Tor wouldn't want that to happen.

"Stay well," Mrs. Bjork said as she turned to go. "I trust that you and your husband will raise your baby to be a fine American."

Mrs. Bjork's words surprised Kirsten. Her baby would be American, not Swedish.

She had not only chosen her own future but her child's, as well.

"Thank you," she murmured. "We will—God willing."

Chapter Twenty

SOFIA SAT ON THE GROUND at Ludwig's feet, listening to him play his violin. Ever since Ludwig had learned that he would be deported, he had expressed his sorrow through his violin, pouring his very soul into each mournful song. Sofia had never realized that tragedy could produce such beauty nor that music had such healing power. She listened to each piece with her eyes closed, allowing the sound to envelop her. But when Ludwig finished and she opened her eyes, she saw Kirsten come out of the building.

"Oh no," she murmured. "Here comes my sister." She and Ludwig had grown accustomed to talking out loud in their own languages, even though they couldn't understand each other. She watched Kirsten scan the hundreds of faces in the crowd, looking all around for Sofia.

"Is it wrong to be sorry that my sister is back?" she asked. "I mean, I'm glad that she and Elin are getting well, but that means I will have to leave you." She sighed and rose to her feet to beckon to Kirsten.

Ludwig rose from the bench as Kirsten approached and bowed slightly in greeting.

"Kirsten, this is my new friend, Ludwig Schneider. Ludwig . . . my sister Kirsten." She pulled the stick-figure drawing from her Bible and pointed to one of the figures, then to her sister.

"What's this picture for?" Kirsten asked, snatching it from her hand. "And what are all these numbers?"

"Ludwig doesn't understand Swedish. I drew the picture to try to explain my family to him."

"Nice of you to cross me off," Kirsten said with a frown.

"You were in the hospital. I was trying to explain to him that you and Elin were gone and I was all alone."

"Sofia! Why would you tell a stranger that you were all alone? Didn't Elin teach you anything?"

"Ludwig wouldn't hurt a soul. He plays the violin and—"

"Yes, so I see. Hey, when is lunch served? I'm starving."

Sofia looked up at the sun. "In a few more minutes. Would you mind if Ludwig ate with us? He's been here for a while and he's very helpful in the dining hall. The biggest meal is always served at the noon hour, and most of these other people have never learned any table manners."

"I don't know, Sofia. I don't think it's wise to get too friendly with strangers."

"Well, you've certainly changed your attitude! You

sound just like Elin. What about those Swedish men you spent all your time with on the boat?"

"It so happens that I have changed my mind. I saw another side of those fellows that I didn't like at all. And you might see a different side of this man, too, if you spent enough time with him. People aren't always what they seem."

"And sometimes they are exactly as they seem. Ludwig has helped me more than any other person ever has. I can't explain it to you, but I was alone and scared and he became my friend. He showed me God's promises in the Bible." Sofia waved the paper with the drawings and Bible verses in front of Kirsten. "That's what these numbers are, Kirsten. They're Bible verses."

"That doesn't mean you should—"

"Don't tell me what to do. I'm going to continue to eat my meals with him and listen to him practice his violin, and you can join us—or not."

Kirsten stared at her for a long moment as if sizing her up. "You've changed, Sofia."

"Well, maybe it was time I did."

Sofia did exactly as she pleased. She continued to eat her meals with Ludwig and spent the afternoon and evening hours with him, even though Kirsten stayed close to her side most of the time. When they were in the women's dormitory that night getting ready for bed, Kirsten turned to Sofia and said, "You're falling in love with that man, aren't you."

Sofia's heart began to race. She stared at her sister with her mouth open, unable to reply. It had never occurred to her that she was in love with Ludwig until Kirsten said the word—but she knew in an instant that she was right. She couldn't reply.

"I saw the way you look at him," Kirsten continued. "And the way he looks at you."

Again, Sofia knew exactly what Kirsten meant. She had seen the soft, tender look in Ludwig's eyes whenever he gazed at her. "It's because we can't speak to each other with words," she said. "All we have is our eyes."

"How did it happen, Sofia?"

"I-I don't know. . . ." She leaned against the wall, suddenly feeling weak-kneed, wishing she had a chair. "We've been together since my first day on this island. Ludwig is so kind and gentle, and when he plays his violin for me . . ." She couldn't finish. She had no words to describe how she felt about him. The word *love* seemed inadequate.

"Oh, Sofia," Kirsten said softly. "What are you going to do?"

"Well . . . I mean . . . I'm sure we'll see each other again when we get off this island and—"

She stopped. Ludwig wasn't getting off this island. He was being sent back to Germany. He had threatened to swim across the river rather than go back, but how could he swim that far? How could anyone?

To Sofia's surprise, Kirsten's eyes filled with tears.

She quickly pulled Sofia into her arms as if she didn't want her to see them. "I should have warned you not to fall in love, Sofia. I should have told you that love always ends in heartbreak."

How did Kirsten know about love and heartbreak? Had she fallen in love with one of those men on the boat? Sofia was about to ask her when she suddenly recalled a string of events back home that hadn't made sense to her at the time. She remembered how Kirsten would neglect her chores or convince Sofia to do them for her so she could spend time exploring the woods with Tor Magnusson. She remembered how Kirsten's cheeks would flush with pleasure whenever Tor walked out to their farm with a letter, how she and Tor always managed to find each other after church on Sunday. And she remembered how Kirsten had leaped off the farm wagon on their last day in the village just to bid Tor good-bye—and it had been such an odd farewell. Sofia pulled free from her sister's embrace to look at her.

"You were in love with Tor Magnusson, weren't you?" The pain in Kirsten's eyes gave her away. "Tor must have broken your heart or you never would have left him."

"What difference does it make?" Kirsten said, turning away. "I just don't want the same thing to happen to you. Don't believe this man's promises, Sofia, even if he says he loves you. America is a big country, and you might never see each other again."

"Don't say that!" Sofia covered her mouth to try to

hold back her tears. She couldn't bear the thought of never seeing Ludwig Schneider again.

"Listen, Sofia. You have to face the truth. It's nice that you made a friend, but Mrs. Bjork says Elin will be getting out of the hospital soon, and we'll be leaving this island. You'll probably never see him again."

"I know," she murmured, "I know . . . But Kirsten . . . is it better not to fall in love at all, or to love someone for a little while, even if you have to say good-bye?"

"It's better not to love," she answered quickly. "Good-byes are terrible. Papa couldn't bear to say good-bye to Mama, remember? He couldn't live without her. I don't want you to go through that much pain or to feel the way I feel, loving Tor and having to leave him."

Kirsten's admission surprised Sofia. And so did the strength of her own feelings for Ludwig Schneider.

"It's too late, Kirsten. I already love Ludwig." She knew it was true the moment she spoke the words. And she also knew the answer to her own question. "I may never see him again, but the gifts of joy and hope that he has already given me are worth any pain that might come."

"You say that now, but you don't know . . ."

Sofia pulled Kirsten into her arms and they held each other again. When Sofia could speak, she said, "No matter when I have to say good-bye to Ludwig, it's going to hurt. But until then, I want to be with

234

him as much as I can. Please let me do that, Kirsten. We'll be in plain sight all the time. There's no place to go on this island to be alone. There are always thousands of people here. Besides, we can't even talk to each other properly. I just . . . I just want to be with him while I can."

Kirsten slowly shook her head. "Don't say I didn't warn you. I hope you're not sorry . . ."

"I know. I hope I'm not, either."

For the next few days, Sofia spent every waking minute with Ludwig as she waited for Elin to get well. The days passed much too quickly, each one bittersweet. Now that Sofia knew she was in love, she suddenly understood the meaning of all the love songs she'd ever sung and all the love stories she'd ever read. She saw her love for Ludwig mirrored in his eyes and heard it in the music he played for her and felt it in his touch when he reached to caress her golden hair or brush his fingers across her cheek. As the moment when they would have to part drew closer and closer, their time together became more and more precious.

"I have some very good news," Mrs. Bjork told Sofia and Kirsten one afternoon. "Your sister Elin is going to be discharged from the hospital tomorrow morning. I'm sure you'll be happy to get off this island and be on your way, *ja*?"

Nej. Grief welled up inside Sofia at the thought of leaving Ludwig. God had answered her prayers and restored Elin's health—but that meant she and Ludwig would have to say good-bye. How would she tell him?

"I'll be in the Registry Room tomorrow to translate for you," Mrs. Bjork promised.

In the end, Sofia didn't have to tell Ludwig that tomorrow would be their last day together. He must have read the news in her sorrowful expression, because he pulled out the picture she had drawn on their first day together and pointed to the stick figure of Elin. She nodded. She had already erased the *X* she'd drawn through Kirsten's picture; now she took out the pencil and began to erase Elin's *X*. Her tears dropped onto the page as she worked.

Ludwig reached for her hand to stop her, holding it tightly in his own, as if by preventing her from changing the picture he could prevent her from leaving.

"Sofia . . ." he whispered. "Oh, Sofia . . ." He finally released her hand and pulled out his Bible, paging quickly through it to find what he wanted to say. He stopped at the Song of Songs—a book Sofia had never read before—and waited for her to find it, too. He pointed to chapter one, verse fifteen: *How beautiful you are, my darling! Oh, how beautiful!*

She looked up at him again. No one had ever told her she was beautiful before.

He flipped ahead a few pages and pointed to chapter four, verse nine: *You have stolen my heart, my sister, my bride; you have stolen my heart. . . .*

Sofia laid her palm over her own heart for a moment, then rested her hand on his chest, leaving it there. She could feel the strong beat of his heart beneath his shirt. "My heart is yours, Ludwig," she murmured. "I can't bear the thought that we may never see each other again. Please tell me that we aren't saying good-bye forever. . . ." She wished she could understand what he said to her in return as he placed his hand over hers.

Sadness permeated their final day together. Kirsten gave them the gift of privacy, and Sofia and Ludwig remained side by side until it was time to return to their own dormitories for lights-out. In the morning, Sofia and Kirsten dressed in their Sunday clothes and pinned all of their immigration tags and cards to their dresses as they prepared to meet with the American officials. Sofia knew she should be happy to leave Ellis Island and grateful that Elin was finally well, but sorrow filled her at the prospect of leaving Ludwig.

Ludwig sat with Sofia and Kirsten at breakfast, but Sofia didn't feel like eating. Afterward, Kirsten looked at the two of them and said, "I'll go by myself to wait for Elin. We'll come and find you when she arrives."

"Thank you," Sofia said.

As soon as she and Ludwig were alone, her tears began to fall. She saw Ludwig's grief in his tear-filled eyes, and in the way his shoulders slumped, and in the deep sigh he uttered. He reached into Sofia's bag, which lay at her feet, and pulled out her Bible, opening it to a verse. He didn't open his own, so she knew that he must have stayed up last night searching for the right verse to leave with her. Once again, he turned to the Song of Songs. She read the words through a shimmer of tears: *Many waters cannot quench love; rivers cannot wash it away. If one were to give all the wealth of his house for love, it would be utterly scorned.*

He took the Bible from her and gathered both of her hands in his, speaking urgently, as if begging her to understand what he was saying. When he finished speaking, he pulled his violin and bow from his bag. She thought he was going to play one final song for her, but he didn't unwrap them. Instead, he pointed to the violin, then to her as he placed the bundle in her hands.

"No, Ludwig. You can't give this to me." She tried to hand it back, but he shook his head, holding up his hands, refusing to take it. He pointed to New York City and once again pantomimed swimming across the river. "No . . . oh, please don't try to swim. You'll never make it! Nobody can swim that far. Isn't there any other way?"

He picked up her Bible and pointed to another verse from Song of Songs: *I will get up now and go about the city, through its streets and squares; I will search for the one my heart loves.* He pointed to her, to himself, to the verse.

"And you want me to keep your violin for you? Until you find me?"

He nodded as if he had understood her words and took the instrument from her. He knelt down and carefully tucked it inside Sofia's satchel, then placed his German Bible inside, as well. He was giving her his violin as a promise of his love, a promise that he would search for her and find her. Sofia wanted to believe that he would be able to swim all the way across the river, but she was filled with fear for him.

Ludwig stood again and folded Sofia's hands inside his own, then he bowed his head to pray. She couldn't understand his prayer, but she prayed silently along with him, begging God to keep him safe and to bring them together again.

When he finished, Ludwig exhaled as if preparing himself for the long swim. Then he pointed to her many tags and gestured as if writing something down. Of course, he wanted the name and address of Sofia's uncle in Chicago. She wrote it out for him on a piece of paper.

Sofia still wasn't ready to say good-bye to him, but when she looked up, she saw Elin and Kirsten emerge from the building, looking all around for her. She and Ludwig were out of time. Ludwig followed her gaze and when he saw Kirsten, he suddenly reached for Sofia and folded her into his arms. He was so tall that he could rest his cheek on the top of her head. Sofia clung to him, not caring if it was proper or not, not caring who saw them. She loved this man and she didn't want to let him go.

"Promise me that we'll see each other again," she

wept. "Promise me that you won't try to swim that far, that you'll find another way. . . ."

"Sofia," he murmured. "Oh, Sofia . . ."

When he finally released her, his cheeks were wet. He pushed a folded piece of paper into her hand, then turned and hurried away, as if unwilling to watch her go. Sofia didn't take her eyes off him until he disappeared into the crowd. She couldn't seem to move. She wanted to sink down on the ground and weep, but Elin and Kirsten were approaching. She pulled Elin into her arms, pretending that her tears were for her.

"I've missed you so much, Sofia," Elin said. "I feel like I've let you down—that I wasn't here to take care of you like I promised I would."

"You couldn't help being sick," Sofia said hoarsely. "Besides, God took good care of me while you were away."

"I see that. You look wonderful, Sofia."

"And you look . . . like you could use a good home-cooked meal," Sofia said, trying to smile. It was true. Her sister looked very thin and pale. "But thank God He spared your life."

"Come on," Kirsten said. "Let's get through this immigration ordeal and get on that train to Chicago."

Sofia felt hollow inside as she followed her sisters into the Registry Room and joined the long lines of waiting people. She and her sisters slowly progressed from one official to the next, each one peering at their many tags, then directing them to the next official.

The last one motioned for them to sit down on one of the long wooden benches to wait for their names to be called.

Sofia had watched the procedure from afar for almost two weeks and knew that getting the stamp of approval from the men standing behind the tall desks was the last step. But all she could think about was Ludwig. Leaving Ellis Island meant she might never see him again. She looked all around the room for him, and up in the balcony where the dormitories were, desperate for one last glimpse of him.

"What are you doing?" Elin finally asked her. "Who are you looking for?"

"For—for a friend I met while I was waiting for you."

"Was she Swedish? Why didn't you introduce me to her?"

"Not Swedish, German."

"You don't speak German, Sofia. Did she understand Swedish?"

"No. We talked without words. . . . I can't explain it, but we became good friends. I told him that—"

"*Him?* You spent time alone with a strange man? Are you crazy, Sofia?"

She didn't trust herself to reply. She was going to burst into tears and then the immigration officials would think there was something wrong with her, and all three of them would be refused entrance into America. Just in time, Kirsten rescued her.

"I met him, Elin, and he's really very nice. Besides,

from now on we'll have Uncle Lars to protect us, right?"

"I guess so." Elin still looked doubtful, but again, Kirsten distracted her.

"Sofia told me that she's been watching this whole procedure while you and I were in the hospital— right, Sofia? And she says it's just like the Day of Judgment in the Bible, where we have to stand before St. Peter and he looks in his book and decides whether or not he's going to let us through the pearly gates into heaven. America is like heaven, right?"

Kirsten babbled on and on, fidgeting so nervously that Sofia wondered what was wrong with her. She seemed afraid for some reason—and that wasn't like Kirsten. Elin finally shushed her.

"If you don't be quiet, we won't hear our names being called and we'll be stuck in this place forever."

The wait seemed endless. Sofia still clutched the scrap of paper that Ludwig had given her, but she didn't dare rummage in her bag for her Bible. Ludwig's violin and German Bible were on top and she was afraid to let Elin see them. Finally Mrs. Bjork from the Immigrant Aid Society arrived, and after talking to one of the immigration officials for a few minutes, she called them over to his desk, one at a time. Sofia went first. The official examined her tags and paged through his ledger book until he found her name, then asked several rapid-fire questions, which Mrs. Bjork translated: "Where were you born? Are you married or single? Where are you going?

242

How much money do you have? Have you ever been in jail? Are you able to work?"

Finally, he handed Sofia a card and asked her to read it. "It's to prove that you're literate," Mrs. Bjork explained.

Sofia was surprised to see that it was a Bible passage, taken from Job 1:19: *"Suddenly a mighty wind swept in from the desert and struck the four corners of the house. It collapsed on them and they are dead, and I am the only one who has escaped to tell you!"*

The verse seemed fitting to Sofia considering all the losses that she and her sisters had endured. Like the biblical Job, they also had lost everything, yet they had survived.

Kirsten was the last one to appear before the official, and even from a distance, Sofia could see that she was nervous. She wondered if it had something to do with Tor—if Kirsten felt reluctant to take this final step and sever all ties to their homeland. But the official passed Kirsten through, as well, and Mrs. Bjork escorted them downstairs to find their trunk, which had been sitting in the baggage room all this time. Finally, Mrs. Bjork waited in line with them at the railroad ticket office and helped them book passage on the next train to Chicago. Sofia looked around in vain for Ludwig.

"I'll help you send a telegram to your family in Chicago, and then you are free to go," Mrs. Bjork told them. "All you have to do is take the ferry from here to Hoboken, New Jersey, then show them your railroad tickets and they'll put you on the train to Chicago."

"I feel like a bird being let out of a cage," Elin said. "How can we ever thank you?"

"It's my job to help you, and I'm happy to do it. Good luck to you all." She waved as she strode away.

Sofia was still searching for Ludwig as Elin led the way to the pier. They joined the long line of people waiting for the ferry to arrive. "Just one more boat ride," Elin said, "then one more train ride and our journey will be over."

"I wish I could wake up back home and find out that this was all just a dream," Kirsten said.

Elin looked at her in surprise. "I would expect a comment like that from Sofia, but not from you. What's wrong?"

"I heard someone say that from now on we'll be Americans, not Swedes, and it made me feel . . . lost."

"At least we're together," Elin said. "And we will have a home again, I promise. When we get to Chicago, we can finally settle into our brand-new life."

Sofia heard the conviction in Elin's voice and believed her. But she battled her tears as she watched the ferry approach. She had been looking everywhere, but there was still no sign of Ludwig. The sailors lowered the gangway. They inspected everyone's ticket, then herded Sofia and her sisters onto the ship.

"So, this is it," Elin said. "Take one last look at Lady Liberty over there. From now on we're not going to shed another tear—promise?"

"I promise," Kirsten said softly. Sofia nodded, but she didn't know how she would ever be able to keep such a promise.

"We have each other," Elin said, "and that's all we need."

As soon as she boarded the ferry, Sofia pushed her way to the rail for one last look at Ellis Island—and there was Ludwig standing alone on shore. He lifted his hand to her in a wave, and she waved in return. She forced herself not to cry, afraid her tears would blur her last vision of him. She kept her eyes pinned to him until the island grew so small she could no longer see him.

At last she went inside and found a place to sit down. She wanted to be alone when she read the slip of paper Ludwig had given her. On it was a verse from Genesis. She opened her satchel to retrieve her Bible and slid her fingers beneath the violin's wrappings to feel the warm, smooth wood. Ludwig would find her again. The violin was his promise to her.

She opened her Bible and read the final verse Ludwig had given her: *May the Lord keep watch between you and me when we are away from each other.*

PART II

Chicago

MAY 1897

"There is only one journey.
Going inside yourself."

RAINER MARIA RILKE

Chapter Twenty-One

ELIN'S HEART SPED up as the train's momentum slowed. They were reaching the end of their journey. They had left the farmland behind and had entered the outskirts of the city of Chicago several minutes ago. The buildings were becoming larger and more densely packed; streetcars and wagons and carriages filled the roads. Little children gathered at the railroad crossings to watch the train steam past and wave at the passengers.

Kirsten knelt on the seat and slid open the window to lean out, just as she had when they'd begun this journey back home in Sweden. "Be careful," Elin warned. "You shouldn't lean out so far." Kirsten ignored her, of course. Her hair blew wildly as it came loose from its pins.

They passed through a desolate area of factories and warehouses. Boxcars sat on side rails waiting to be emptied and filled. They were evidently getting very close.

"I think I see the train station up ahead," Kirsten said. "It looks like a huge whale with its mouth open. We're about to be swallowed any minute." Some of the other passengers stood up in the aisles, gathering their belongings as the brakes hissed and the train slowed.

Elin tugged on Kirsten's skirt. "Please, sit down and be ladylike. And you need to tidy your hair. We want to make a good first impression on Uncle Lars."

"Why?"

It took Elin a moment to formulate a reply. She longed for her aunt and uncle to embrace them as their own daughters, to love them and take care of them. But she had wanted the same thing from Uncle Sven—and look where that had led. She wouldn't make that mistake again.

"Because we're Mama's daughters," she finally replied. "Uncle Lars was her favorite brother. The way we behave reflects on her and how she raised us."

Kirsten turned around and slid into her seat with a sigh. A moment later the train entered the station, plunging them into semidarkness.

"Look around and make sure we have everything," Elin said, even though she and her sisters had been ready for the past hour, their needlework and books stowed in their bags. Sofia sat with her satchel on her lap, cradling it as if it contained a sleeping infant.

She had seemed happier and less fearful after their ordeal at Ellis Island. Kirsten had been quieter and more subdued than usual, too. The change in both of them reminded Elin of the transformation new mothers underwent after enduring the pain and exhaustion of childbirth. The moment they held their baby in their arms, dreams of the future erased the sorrows of the past. This journey had birthed a new life in all three of them, and although the future was still unformed, Elin hoped that with time and patience, their lives would grow into something miraculous.

"We're here," Kirsten said when the train halted.

Elin stood and felt her knees trembling. Part of it was the lingering weakness from her bout with typhus, but most of her shakiness was emotional. They had arrived at their destination at last: Chicago, their new home. Elin could rest and be a sister again after trying to be a mother to Kirsten and Sofia for so long. She wouldn't have to be strong and decisive anymore. She had brought her sisters to safety.

As they stepped off the train, Elin saw many of her fellow passengers rushing forward to greet waiting loved ones. She looked around hopefully, studying the strangers' faces, searching for their uncle.

"Do you remember what Uncle Lars looks like?" Kirsten asked.

"Not really. I was a child when he left. But it seems to me he was tall and thin and looked a lot like Nils— or I guess Nils resembled him."

They continued walking, surveying the area. Minutes passed, and when no one came forward to greet them, Elin could see the disappointment on her sisters' faces. She smiled to mask her own.

"Come on, we'd better find our trunk." Carts piled high with luggage were being wheeled past them from the baggage car. Elin beckoned to her sisters to follow her to the baggage claim area. They quickly found their trunk, but Elin couldn't spare the money to hire a porter to carry it for them, as many other people were doing. Kirsten and Sofia would have to haul it a little farther.

"I'll be so glad to get rid of this behemoth," Kirsten said, grunting as she lifted one end of it. "It's like dragging around a dead troll with handles on his sides."

The crowds diminished, the platform emptied, and still no one came forward to meet them. They went inside the cavernous station—deeper into the belly of the whale, as Kirsten had called it—and sat down on a bench to wait.

"We sent a telegram," Kirsten said. "Uncle Lars must know we're arriving today."

"Be patient, Kirsten. There's nothing we can do but wait." Kirsten wasn't patient, of course. And Elin had to admit, after the first hour passed, that she was losing patience, too, as her anxiety increased.

Kirsten stood and set her satchel down on the bench. "I'm tired of sitting. I'm going for a walk."

Elin opened her mouth to caution her, then closed it again. Kirsten and Sofia had already proven that they could get along fine without her warnings and admonitions. She watched as Kirsten circled the perimeter of the room, searching the huge, high-ceilinged station as if their relatives were hiding and would spring out like children playing a game.

"How are they supposed to recognize us?" Kirsten asked when she returned to the bench and sank down again with a sigh.

"Look at us," Sofia said, gesturing to her coarse cotton skirt and embroidered vest. "Do you see anyone else in the station dressed in Swedish clothes?"

"She's right," Elin said, trying to remain cheerful. "We do stick out like goats in a sheep pen."

"I'd prefer to think we're lilies among thorns," Sofia corrected.

"No, I think Elin is closer to the truth," Kirsten said. "We do look like misfits. I hope Uncle Lars lets us buy some American clothes." She leaned back on the bench, but her impatience showed in her jiggling foot and drumming fingers.

Another hour passed. People continued to stream in and out of the station, and every time someone approached them Elin would look up, feeling hopeful, only to be disappointed again.

"We have Uncle Lars' address. Can't we just go there?" Kirsten asked when they were well into their third hour of waiting.

"How would we get there? On foot? We don't know how far away he lives."

"And I'm not dragging this trunk another inch," Sofia added.

Kirsten exhaled her frustration. "Well, that stinks like dead fish!"

Elin was frustrated, too, but she remained convinced that eventually Uncle Lars would arrive if they were patient. They waited another half hour, and the sound of Kirsten's fingers drumming on the armrest became so irritating that Elin laid her hand on top of Kirsten's to make her stop.

"See that line of carriages out there by the curb?" Kirsten asked. "I'll bet they're for hire. Want me to go ask?"

Elin winced. "I don't think we should get into a wagon with a stranger. We don't know our way around the city. He could take us anywhere. We would be at his mercy."

"Why must you always believe the worst about people?" Kirsten asked. "I'm sure there are honest, God-fearing wagon drivers in America."

Her naïveté made Elin angry. But the realization that Uncle Sven's treachery had caused her to lose faith in people made Elin angrier still. "I'm sure you're right, Kirsten, but how are we going to find a God-fearing one? No one speaks Swedish, and we don't speak English."

"There must be something we can do besides sit here."

"Well, you'll have to think of it, then. I'm tired of solving every problem."

"I did think of a solution—hire a wagon!"

"Listen to the two of you," Sofia said. "A few days ago we promised we would work together from now on, and you're already snapping at each other."

Elin remembered how happy they all had been after being reunited, and she made up her mind to try to compromise with her sisters. She waited until her anger diffused and she was certain she could speak in a calm voice, then said, "What do you think we should do, Sofia?"

"I think . . . I think Uncle Lars would have been here by now if he was coming. Maybe he never got our telegram. I think Kirsten is right. We should see how much a wagon costs and how far away Uncle Lars lives."

"How are we going to do that?" Elin asked. "We don't speak English."

"Well . . . I got pretty good at sign language when I was waiting on Ellis Island," Sofia said. "I could try talking to one of the drivers."

Kirsten sprang from the bench and lifted one end of the trunk. Sofia lifted the other end. Once again, the change in her sisters surprised Elin.

The line of wagons was indeed for hire and several of the drivers raced over to assist them, babbling loudly and pointing to their wagons as soon as the sisters emerged through the door with their trunk. Sofia paused and seemed to be sizing up each man in her mind, finally choosing a friendly looking middle-aged driver who had the cleanest clothes and, Elin noticed, a kind smile. He was the only one who had removed his hat in respect. His wagon was clean, too, his horse alert and well fed. Sofia's discernment surprised Elin.

Sofia made a sweeping motion with her arm, taking in the three of them and their baggage, then showed the driver Uncle Lars' address on one of the letters he'd sent. The man nodded and pointed in the direction his carriage faced, speaking with confidence as if he did indeed know the way.

He pulled out a handful of coins from his pocket and jingled them in his palm. "He wants to negotiate the price," Sofia said. "How much money do we have?"

"Uncle Lars sent me some American money, but I don't know how much it's worth."

"Well, give me some of it—but don't let him see how much more we have." They huddled together as Elin shook out some coins into Sofia's palm. Then Sofia turned and held out her open hand to the driver. He winced and shook his head, chattering away as if they could understand him perfectly and motioning as if their destination was well beyond the station. Sofia turned around and picked out a few more coins. After two or three tries, they finally agreed on a price.

"Come on, he's going to take us," Sofia said. The man hoisted their trunk onto his shoulder and stowed it in the back of his wagon. Then he helped them onto the seat behind his and snapped the reins.

"Finally!" Kirsten said as the wagon merged into the stream of traffic. "That wasn't so hard, was it?"

"I hate being at the mercy of a stranger," Elin said. "He could take us anywhere." *And do anything,* she wanted to add, but didn't.

The farther they drove from the station, the more fascinating and exciting the city appeared. Elin perched on the edge of her seat as she tried to take it all in, and she noticed that her heart was beating faster again. Tall brick buildings lined both sides of the streets as if the wagon were driving through the bottom of a canyon. Striped awnings and brightly painted signs decorated many of the buildings, along with elaborate carvings and fancy stonework over the windows and doors. Elin saw more horses and carriages than she'd ever seen in one place, and pedestrians wearing the most unusual clothes she'd ever seen. The streetcars ran on rails and carried dozens of passengers at one time, driving right down the center of the street. The pace of life seemed to have speeded up in Chicago as if the world turned faster here than it did in Sweden.

"This is amazing," Kirsten said.

Elin heard the same awe in her voice that she was feeling. "I never imagined that America would be like this."

"It's very different from home," Sofia said. "There are hardly any trees. And the ones I do see aren't very tall."

"I think that's because most of the city burned down about twenty-five years ago," Elin said. "Uncle Lars told me all about it in his letters. Chicago's trees haven't had time to grow as tall as the ones in Sweden."

"Are we near the ocean?" Sofia asked.

"No, but Uncle Lars says that the city is built near a big lake—so big that you can't see the other side of it."

"I hope it has fish in it, and that they're good to

eat," Kirsten said. "I've missed eating fresh fish like we always had back home."

"Me, too," Sofia said. "The food on Ellis Island wasn't very good."

"At least it was free," Kirsten said.

Eventually, the wagon carried them away from the busy center of the city. They began to see fewer and fewer tall buildings and more and more homes. The driver turned off the main thoroughfare and onto a side street, then made a few more turns until they were on a street filled with large two-story houses. They stood all in a row, side by side, with barely any land between them. Elin checked the address on the envelope in her hand and compared the number with the ones painted on the houses. When the driver drew to a halt, the two numbers matched.

"Are we there?" Kirsten asked.

"I think that's it." Elin pointed to the house. "The numbers are the same."

"Oh my!" Sofia said. "You could fit four cottages like ours back home inside of it."

"It's bigger than our barn," Kirsten added.

"Now you're exaggerating," Elin said. But Uncle Lars' house did look very large after what they were used to in Sweden. It stood two stories tall with a castlelike tower, a wide front porch, and lots of large windows. A sign in Swedish hung on the porch railing: *Boardinghouse. Rooms for Rent.*

"Are you sure this is it?" Kirsten asked.

Elin checked the house number again. "I'm pretty sure. . . ."

"Let's go see." Kirsten jumped down and led the way up the front steps while the driver unloaded their trunk, carrying it on his shoulder.

Elin knocked on the door. Nothing happened. She knocked a second time. She was preparing to knock again when a woman finally opened it. She looked hot and sweaty and red-faced, with her sleeves rolled up and her hair falling loose from its pins. And she looked very annoyed at them for bothering her.

"Are you Hilma Larson?" Elin asked.

"Yes, but we only accept gentlemen boarders," she said in Swedish. "No women. I'm sorry—"

"No, wait!" Kirsten said before she could close the door. "We're your nieces—the Carlson sisters, from Sweden."

Aunt Hilma frowned. "How did you end up here?"

"We hired a wagon from the train station."

Elin's hopes for a warm welcome faded quickly as their aunt continued to scowl at them. For an embarrassingly long moment, Aunt Hilma couldn't seem to find her voice. Elin turned to the driver, who still balanced the trunk on his shoulder, and nodded to him that this was indeed the right address. He set the trunk down on the porch, tipped his hat to them, and returned to his wagon.

"Lars will be surprised to see you, that's for certain," Hilma said. She remained in the doorway, glaring at them.

"Didn't he get our telegram?" Elin asked. "We sent one two days ago telling him when we would arrive."

"Oh, he got it, alright. But he can't take time off from work whenever he feels like it, you know."

"Yes, of course. We understand." Elin forced herself to smile, battling her disappointment at this ungracious reception.

"He won't be home until suppertime."

Kirsten sat down on their trunk and crossed her arms. "Should we wait out here on the porch until then?" Elin could tell by her tone of voice that she was annoyed, too—and hinting that they had yet to be invited inside.

"You could have left the trunk at the station until later," Hilma said. "And you probably paid way too much for that wagon. They'll cheat you every time if they know you can't speak English. But never mind. Come in."

"Finally," Kirsten mumbled, sliding off the trunk. Elin elbowed her in the ribs in warning. Sofia and Kirsten hefted the crate and followed their aunt through the door.

The home was very clean and orderly inside, with polished wooden floors in the front hallway and a graceful staircase leading to the second floor. Elin glimpsed a comfortable parlor on the right with a fireplace and soft, cushioned chairs, and a dining room on the left with a long wooden table. There were too many chairs gathered around it to count as

Hilma herded them quickly down the hallway toward the rear of the house.

"Did any mail arrive for me?" Kirsten asked as they passed a hall table with several letters laid out on top. "I'm expecting a letter from Sweden any day, and I gave them this address."

"There have been no letters," Hilma said. "You can take your trunk upstairs, I suppose. I'll show you where you'll be sleeping." But she bypassed the wide front staircase and rushed them through a swinging door into the kitchen.

"What's wrong with the other stairs?" Kirsten grumbled as she and Sofia strained to carry the trunk.

"Shh . . ." Elin whispered. "Let's not get off on the wrong foot with her."

"Too late," Kirsten said.

As soon as they entered the kitchen, Elin understood why Aunt Hilma had been so sweaty and red-faced. It was as warm as a steam bath, the windows so foggy she couldn't see outside. A sweating girl who was about the same age as Sofia was kneading a lump of bread dough on the kitchen table. She looked as wilted as a bowl of butter in August. Mist was billowing from a line of pots boiling on the cast-iron range. Elin smelled turnips cooking and her stomach growled in hunger.

"You'll need to use this back door from now on," Aunt Hilma said, pointing to it. "The front door and the parlor are for boarders only. Follow me up these steps, girls."

They were narrow and steep, boxed in with paneled walls on both sides. Aunt Hilma's lips pursed and a worried frown creased her face as she watched the three of them wrestle the trunk up the stairs behind her.

"Careful, girls! Will it fit? Don't scuff my walls."

She led them to a room that was tinier than their attic bedroom back home—only now they would have to share it with Aunt Hilma's two daughters. "I know it's crowded," Hilma said, "but it's only for a short time, after all."

"A short time?" Kirsten asked. "And then what happens?"

"We take in boarders to make ends meet, but the boarders are all men. And we have five children, you know."

"Yes, I know, but—"

Elin poked Kirsten in the ribs again to shut her up. "Thank you for taking us in, Aunt Hilma," she said. "We are very grateful."

"There's hot water in the kitchen boiler if you want to freshen up. But you'll have to come down and get it and carry it upstairs yourselves. I have a meal to prepare."

"We will. Thank you," Elin said.

As soon as she was gone, Kirsten opened her arms wide to Sofia and pantomimed the greeting they all had been expecting, smiling and saying, "*Välkommen*, my dears! It's so wonderful to see you! Oh, but you must be tired and thirsty. . . . Can I fix you a cool drink? A little bite to eat?"

"Kirsten, shhh. What if she hears you?"

"Good. I hope she does. Maybe she'll realize how rude she was just now."

"What did she mean when she said we won't be here for very long?" Sofia asked.

"I honestly don't know—but I suppose she'll tell us when she's good and ready. Let's wash up and see if we can help with supper."

"Oh yes! Let's help her!" Kirsten said. "After all, she went to all this trouble to kill the fattened calf for us."

"Be nice, Kirsten."

"Why?"

"It's called 'turning the other cheek,'" Sofia said. Elin looked at her in surprise. It was something their mother would have said.

"You mean, like this?" Kirsten asked, pantomiming again. "Here you are, Aunt Hilma. That was a nice slap you gave us the first time—now slap us on the other cheek. See if you can hit us harder this time." But in the end, Kirsten joined Elin and Sofia as they washed in the basin of water they hauled upstairs from the kitchen, then changed into work clothes to help their aunt with the evening meal.

"What can we do to help you, Aunt Hilma?" Elin asked her.

"Do you know how to knead bread? Help Inge with that dough before she makes a mess of it. The table needs to be set and the potatoes peeled. Can you manage that?"

"Yes, I'm sure we can."

"Go outside and get more firewood," she told Inge. The girl hadn't been introduced to them, but Elin assumed she was a hired girl, not Hilma's daughter— at least she hoped she wasn't.

Later that afternoon, the Larson children arrived home from school: three boys, Carl, Gustave, and Waldemar, and two daughters, Anna and Dagmar. Aunt Hilma didn't seem to have time to tell their ages or make elaborate introductions, but Elin guessed the oldest to be about fourteen, the youngest eight or nine.

"These are your cousins from Sweden," Hilma said. The children nodded shyly and disappeared upstairs to change out of their school clothes. When they returned, they went to work immediately on their chores.

As the supper hour neared, Elin heard the front door opening and closing and the sound of men's boots clomping up and down the stairs as the boarders arrived home from work. But the kitchen door separating the boarders from the family remained firmly closed. Just when the dinner preparations seemed to reach a frenetic pace, Uncle Lars arrived home from his job as a bricklayer, tired and dusty. He stopped short the moment he stepped through the back door and saw the three of them in the kitchen, a look of surprise on his face—but also a smile.

"Well, for goodness' sakes! You must be my sister's girls."

"Yes, Uncle Lars. I'm Elin and this is Kirsten and Sofia." Elin didn't go forward to greet him. He was too sweaty and dirty to offer them a hug—and Elin would have been too wary to accept one, even if he had. But at least he had greeted them with a huge grin.

"Your telegram said you would arrive today," Lars said. "I was going to go pick you up at the station as soon as I got cleaned up. Well, never mind. Here you are. *Välkommen!*"

He resembled their brother, Nils, but with a sandy, brushlike mustache and darker hair. Unlike his wife, he seemed very happy to see them—but Uncle Sven had been friendly, too. Elin pushed away a flood of memories. "Thank you, Uncle Lars. And thank you for paying our way and for taking us in, and—" She had to stop or risk dissolving in tears.

"I could only imagine you as the children I knew in Sweden," Lars said. "But of course I knew you would be all grown up. You look like your mother, Elin. In fact, you gave me a start when I first saw you. I thought for a moment that you were her."

"Save your talking for later," Hilma said. "Dinner is nearly ready, and you need to get cleaned up, Lars. And you'd better not let the girls eat in there with the boarders. There isn't enough room, and besides, some of them can be pretty rough."

Elin managed to peek into the dining room as Hilma pushed through the door with bowls of turnips and potatoes. Elin could see the men gathering around the table and hear snatches of conversation in Swedish. She didn't realize how hungry she had been for food from home until she'd smelled it cooking. She and her sisters crowded around the kitchen table to eat with their young cousins, who all seemed too shy to speak.

"Are your school lessons in English or Swedish?" Kirsten asked the oldest boy.

"A little of both."

"I want to learn to speak English," Sofia said to one of the little girls beside her. "Will you help me learn?" The girl nodded shyly.

Elin was still trying to get used to the change in Sofia. She didn't understand how it had happened, but she was grateful for it.

After supper, they helped Inge clear the table and wash all of the dishes and cooking pots while Aunt Hilma tended to the children. The kitchen was finally cooling off, and it seemed to be the place where the family lived, allowing the boarders to occupy the other rooms. Uncle Lars settled into his chair near the back door with a sigh and propped up his feet.

"We are so grateful to you for sending the tickets to us, Uncle Lars," Elin began as she helped dry a stack of dinner plates. She had already sensed a lot of tension between Aunt Hilma and Uncle Lars, and she guessed that they had not been in agreement about helping her and her sisters come to America. She wanted to explain their situation to him and let him know that he had made the right decision.

"Things fell apart back home after Mama died. We tried our best to hold everything together, but it was very hard. For one thing, Papa left us."

"Left you? Where did he go?"

"Well, he still lived in the cottage with us, but it was as if he had buried his heart in the ground with Mama. He simply stopped living. If the cows got fed and milked, it was because Kirsten and I milked them. If the potatoes got planted, it was because Nils decided it was time to plow and plant. We wouldn't have had enough wood to last through the winter if Nils hadn't hauled it all home and chopped it. Papa spoke so seldom that at times we wondered if he even remembered how to talk."

"She was a wonderful woman, your mother," Lars said with a sigh. "I have no doubt that he missed her."

"We kept things going as best we could, hoping and praying that Papa's grief would thaw when spring arrived, but it never did. Pieces of our life began tumbling down around us like boulders. For every step forward we made—a new litter of hogs, a good season of rainfall—we seemed to take three steps backward. The roof leaked. Foxes killed half of our chickens. A late spring frost destroyed the apple blossoms. Life became very hard, and we couldn't keep up with everything.

"Mama always made sure that we attended church every Sunday, but Papa wouldn't go with us anymore, and Nils didn't want to overwork the horses, and we couldn't walk that far to the village and back

267

every week. The journey was too cold in the winter, the roads too wet in the spring, our legs too weary in the summer after working so hard. I know this sounds like a pile of excuses, Uncle Lars, but you have to understand how hard everything was for us after Mama died." To Elin, it had seemed as though God was punishing them for something, but she didn't know what they had done.

"Then Papa decided to join Mama in the grave," she continued. "I-I think I told you in my letters what he did."

"Yes, yes . . . It was a terrible thing to do. Terrible."

"He had stopped living long before he stopped breathing, so it seemed inevitable that he would finally choose to end his own life, but I still wasn't prepared for it. He left the cottage one morning without saying good-bye and walked straight out onto the lake, even though the ice was too thin. Everyone in town knew it wasn't an accident. Papa knew how to test the ice better than anyone did. He taught all of us how to listen for exactly the right sound. He wouldn't have made a mistake. He simply didn't want to live any longer. People in town said it was a sin and a disgrace, and the minister wouldn't let us bury him in the church cemetery beside Mama."

"And the villagers didn't want us to marry their sons," Kirsten added. Elin looked at her in surprise, wondering if there was more to her words than she was saying.

"Now, listen," Uncle Lars said. "There is no reason at all to tell the people here in our community how your father died. Your parents are both gone. That's all they need to know."

"I understand." There were a lot of other things that no one ever needed to know. Elin cleared her throat. She felt as though she were walking on thin ice herself as she prepared to tell the next part of her story.

"We all hoped that things would be better once Uncle Sven and Aunt Karin moved in to help with the farm, but things got worse. Sven and Nils fought all the time, until Nils finally left. He's the one who should inherit the farm, but he said he was sick of it and he was never coming back. He's never written to tell us where he is. I loved our home and I never imagined leaving it, but after Uncle Sven took over, it didn't feel like our home anymore. For one thing, our cottage was too small for everyone."

"And for another thing," Kirsten added, "Aunt Karin made us do all the work while she gave all the orders."

"I promised Mama before she died that I would take care of Kirsten and Sofia, and I intend to keep that promise. I had to do something . . . so I decided to write to you. I can't even begin to tell you how grateful we are that you brought us all here."

"Yes . . . well . . . but you see—"

"It's time to call it a night," Aunt Hilma interrupted. "The workday begins very early around here, and the children need their sleep. I'm sure you girls are tired, too, after your long trip."

Elin felt a ripple of fear, wondering what Uncle Lars had been about to say and why Aunt Hilma had interrupted him. It was obvious that unless some changes were made, there wasn't room for Elin and her sisters to live here as part of the family.

"We will talk more on Sunday," Uncle Lars said, "when we have a day of rest. I'm sorry that your bedroom is so crowded—"

"I already explained that we can't afford to turn away any of our boarders in order to make room," Hilma said.

Elin felt like an orphan all over again as she trudged up the stairs to their room. She felt even worse when she saw that her two little cousins, Anna and Dagmar, had to sleep on pallets on the floor after giving up their beds.

"This isn't fair," she told them. "Maybe we can take turns sleeping in the beds."

"Mama says it's only for a short time," Dagmar said.

"And then what happens?" Kirsten asked. The girl shrugged.

"I have the feeling that Aunt Hilma doesn't want us," Kirsten whispered, as she and Elin lay side-by-side in one of the beds. "She's probably going to make us pay back the money for our tickets, too."

"Well, that's only fair," Elin replied, although she didn't know how they would ever be able to do that.

"What are we going to do now, Elin?"

"I have no idea."

Chapter Twenty-Two

"WE LOOK LIKE a family of ducks heading to the pond," Kirsten said as she and her sisters followed Uncle Lars and his brood of children to church on Sunday. Walking through the busy city streets was very different from walking through forestland and past neighboring farms back home. The city was exciting, but Kirsten missed the stillness of the forest, where the silence was so deep she could almost hear the trees breathe. She and Tor had often stood in wonder, gazing up at the towering firs and sensing that the trees were living things, creations of God.

As always, thinking about Tor brought an ache to her stomach. Sunday had been the one day she was certain to see him, even if they hadn't been able to meet during the week.

"Don't lag behind, Kirsten," Elin called. "You're going to make us late."

She looked up and realized that everyone was walking faster than she was, her steps slowed by her memories.

Kirsten passed a row of shops, their colorful wares displayed behind huge glass windows. Aunt Hilma and Uncle Lars had hurried past the windows as if it were a sin to even think about buying and selling on Sunday, but Kirsten lagged behind again, wishing she could go inside. It took her a moment to realize that she was able to read all of the signs, even though she was in America now. Everything had been written in Swedish, as if an entire Swedish town had been plucked up by its roots and transplanted here. But Chicago's Swedish neighborhood was much bigger and more modern than their village at home had been. Streetcars rolled past on the main thoroughfare. Rich people, dressed in their Sunday best, hurried to church in fine carriages.

Elin grabbed Kirsten's arm, pulling her forward again. "Come on. We'd better keep up or Aunt Hilma is going to be upset."

"So? Everything we do irritates her anyway, so what's the difference?"

"Please, Kirsten. Can't you do what Sofia says and turn the other cheek? It is Sunday, you know."

"Oh, I suppose so." She would hurry, but she wouldn't stop looking in the windows.

"These stores certainly are different from Magnusson's store back home, aren't they?" she asked Elin. "Instead of carrying a little bit of every-thing, there are stores just for groceries and some for clothing, and I saw one that had nothing but jewelry."

Elin nodded in reply. She'd seemed distracted and worried ever since they'd arrived in Chicago. Kirsten had been worried, too, especially when she remem-bered that she was carrying a baby. What would Tor think when he read her letter? What would he do? She wished she would hear from him.

"How long does it take for a letter to get to Sweden?" she asked Elin.

"Well, our ship took two weeks to cross the ocean and that was just from England to New York."

Kirsten groaned. That meant that the soonest she would hear back from Tor would be a month! That was much too long.

"What's wrong?" Elin asked.

"I miss Nils. I wish we would hear from him, don't you?" She hadn't lied; she did miss her brother.

They turned the corner and there was the church. It resembled the rich older sister of the one back home— grander and more elaborately dressed. Inside, the people who had gathered for worship looked so familiar with their light hair and fair skin that Kirsten almost expected to meet someone she knew from her village. The minister conducted the service in Swedish. The songs and hymnbooks were in Swedish, too. To be among so many people, all talking her language, made Kirsten feel as though she had never left home.

"We could live here and do everything in our language and never have to learn English at all," she whispered to Sofia.

"But I really want to learn English," she said.

"Are you still hoping that man from Ellis Island will find you?"

"I'm not hoping," Sofia said. "I know he will."

Sofia was going to have her heart broken. Kirsten longed to warn her to be careful, to explain to her that what looked like love sometimes could be deceiving. But if someone had warned her about Tor, Kirsten doubted she would have listened.

On the way home, Kirsten caught up with Uncle Lars and walked beside him. "What's that terrible smell? Does Chicago always smell this way?" She had noticed the odor the moment she'd arrived in the city—and she'd also noticed that her pregnancy made her more sensitive to smells, touching off bouts of nausea.

"It's the stockyards," Lars explained. "Cattle and hogs get shipped here from all over the Midwest to be slaughtered. There is a huge meat packing company here, too, and tanning the hides adds to the stench."

"So the smell never goes away?"

"You'll get used to it," he said with a shrug. "I did."

Aunt Hilma had begun preparations for their huge Sunday dinner on Saturday night and had left her hired girl home to watch over the meal during the Sunday service. Hilma pounced on Inge the moment she walked through the door, peppering her with questions, lifting lids, and peering into the oven.

"You didn't let the potatoes burn, did you? Have you been watching the fire? Is the meat overcooked? Did you press the butter?"

Kirsten and her sisters hurried to change their clothes so they could go to work in the kitchen. Aunt Hilma seemed grateful but didn't offer any thanks. Perhaps she considered their labor as payment for their room and board.

Everyone sat down to a good meal. Kirsten and her sisters ate in the kitchen with the children once again. But the food was so good and it reminded Kirsten so much of home that she didn't care where they ate it—although her curiosity tempted her to peek into the dining room whenever she had a chance in order to get a look at the mysterious boarders.

"Where do all the boarders come from?" she asked her uncle when the meal ended. "Are they all Swedish?"

"*Ja*, they are. Some are men with families back home in Sweden, trying to earn enough to send for them. Others are single men. We don't know most of them very well, which is why Hilma thinks you should stay in the kitchen. We don't know their character."

"How did they find jobs here? I mean . . . suppose Nils were to come over, for instance." Kirsten asked about her brother, but she was thinking of Tor. "Could he find work?"

"I suppose he could—"

"If someone paid his fare," Hilma added firmly.

Kirsten would write to Tor right away and tell him about the boardinghouse and the young men with good jobs and their new life in America, where everyone in the neighborhood spoke Swedish. She would plead with him to come, writing letter after letter to him every single day, until he was forced to answer her.

Sunday was a day of rest, when no work was done. In the afternoon, Kirsten walked with her cousins and sisters to a pleasant little park to spend some time outdoors. The park's few trees, planted in orderly rows, reminded her of domesticated lap dogs compared to the wild, untamed forests back home. But it reassured Kirsten to know that Chicago did have trees.

They returned home to a light supper of cold leftovers. Afterward, she could tell by the tense glances that passed between her aunt and uncle, and the fact that they had sent the children upstairs to their rooms, that something was going on. She didn't know what, but it was obvious that Hilma wanted Lars to speak to her and her sisters. Kirsten waited, certain it was bad news, feeling sick inside.

"I wanted to spend a few days visiting with you girls," Uncle Lars said, "but I think that tomorrow I'd better arrange for tickets to Wisconsin for the three of you."

"Tickets for . . . what?" Elin asked. She wore a brave smile, as if she hoped the tickets might be to a play or a concert or something fun. Kirsten's first thought was that they would have to travel again.

"Train tickets," Uncle Lars said, as if it pained him to say it. "Wisconsin is a state north of here, where there is wonderful farmland, and the weather is very much like home."

"I don't understand," Elin said. "Why are we going there? Don't you live here?"

His cheeks reddened a bit, and Kirsten saw him cast a worried glance at Hilma. She stood listening with her arms crossed.

"You must understand," he said, "that I didn't have

the money for your passage to America—especially for all three of you. You see how my family lives, how difficult it is to make ends meet. But I have a friend who is homesteading up in Wisconsin with a larger group of Swedes. They have their farms all set up and some houses built, and it's turning into a very nice little community. He happened to mention that the young men outnumbered the women up there and he asked if I knew any girls who could come up and become their wives."

"No . . ." Kirsten whispered. For a moment, she thought her heart had stopped beating. She glanced at her sisters and saw that all the color had drained from Elin's face. Sofia sat very still, her mouth open in shock.

"I told these young men about the three of you and how desperate you were to come to America. So they pooled their money together to buy your tickets. The men had planned to come down and meet you themselves, but when you were delayed, they had to stay home. They're right in the middle of spring planting now, so of course they can't get away. You'll have to go up there to meet them."

Kirsten finally found her voice. "You mean they expect us to *marry* them—in return for our *tickets?*"

"You said you wanted to start all over again. And I know that the life you'll have up there will be very much like home."

"You *sold* us?" Elin asked.

"Come, now, what did you expect?" Hilma asked.

"You begged us to help you come to America. We have all of your letters if you've forgotten how you pleaded with us. You said you were desperate to leave. That you would do anything to come to America. What did you expect? As you can see, we have no money to spare for tickets."

"You sold us," Elin repeated.

"Not at all," Uncle Lars said. "These young men are starting a wonderful new life. They have land—forty, sixty, a hundred acres and more. More land than we could ever dream of owning back home. And they want the same things you girls want—a home of your own, a family. They are good, decent, hard-working men."

Kirsten saw the look of panic in Sofia's eyes—as if the house were on fire and she wanted to run out of it. Kirsten wondered if she had the same look on her face. Sofia was in love with the man she had met on the island, just as Kirsten was in love with Tor. Neither one of them wanted to marry a stranger.

"Can we have some time to think about this?" Kirsten asked. She knew it would take time for her letters to reach Tor and for him to make arrangements to come to America. She had to stall until she heard from him.

"We can't afford to feed the three of you," Hilma said. "We have five children of our own."

"But we don't even know what these men are like," Elin said. "Suppose we don't like them—or they don't like us?"

"Oh, you'll have a choice," Lars explained. "There are five young men, you see, and only three of you. Once you arrive, you will have time to get to know each other and then everyone can decide who is compatible and so forth. The three fortunate bachelors have agreed to pay back the two who are left out."

Kirsten felt numb. Her sisters looked shocked, as well. No one seemed capable of voicing her outrage. Besides, there didn't seem to be any way out of this arrangement.

"The day begins before sunrise," Hilma announced, "so we all need to get to bed." She must have timed this discussion so that she wouldn't have to deal with all of their questions.

"Yes, let's sleep on it," Lars said, "and we can talk some more tomorrow."

Kirsten wondered how in the world she was supposed to fall asleep. They said good-night and went upstairs to their room, but after the lights were turned out, Kirsten and her sisters all gathered on the same bed, tenting the covers over their heads and whispering so their cousins wouldn't hear them.

"I'm so sorry," Elin said. She hadn't cried in front of Uncle Lars, but now the tears poured down her cheeks. "Writing to him was a huge mistake. I don't know what we're going to do, but I wouldn't blame either of you if you hate me. I just wanted to leave home so badly because—"

She stopped. Kirsten didn't ask her to finish. She understood Elin's secret and reached for her hand.

"It's not your fault, Elin. Uncle Lars wasn't honest with us. He should have told us the truth right from the start. I don't blame you for this."

"And neither do I," Sofia added. "He should have told us the truth and given us a choice."

Elin wiped her cheeks with the hem of her nightgown. "I don't know what to do. It's obvious that we can't stay here—Aunt Hilma doesn't want us and there's no room."

"It's true. We aren't really welcome here," Sofia said. "I wouldn't want to stay very long."

"I promised you that we would stay together and that we'd have a home again, and I've let both of you down."

Kirsten pulled Elin into her arms. "Listen, we don't blame you. It's not your fault. We'll figure a way out of this mess together."

"But I don't know what to do," Elin said again. "We can't live here. Do you think we should go up there and see what those men are like? What the village is like? Maybe it is the home we're looking for. . . . Oh, I just don't know! And it isn't up to me to decide, anyway. I'm willing to do whatever the two of you want to do."

Kirsten knew her pregnancy was another complication to this decision that Elin wasn't aware of, but she couldn't bring herself to confess. What she'd done with Tor was disgraceful.

But what if Tor wouldn't marry her, even after he learned about the baby? If she knew for certain that he wasn't coming, then the best thing to do would be to go to Wisconsin and marry one of the men right away so he would think the baby was his. But Kirsten didn't know how she could bear to make a vow before God to live with a strange man for the rest of her life when she still loved Tor.

Tor deserved to know that he had fathered a child. She had to give him a chance to do the right thing and marry her. If only she would hear from him. If only it was safe to send him a telegram. Kirsten was trying to think of how to reply to Elin when Sofia spoke first.

"I don't want to get married right now. I'm not even seventeen yet. And when I do get married, I want to choose the man myself. I want to marry someone I love. Please don't make me live in the middle of nowhere and marry a stranger."

"This has turned out to be a disaster," Elin said. "I was so hopeful when we left home. We were going to have a new life in a big new land where the streets were paved with gold."

"And I thought we would be ladies of leisure with servants of our own," Kirsten said, trying to lighten the mood. Neither sister saw any humor in the situation.

"Uncle Lars didn't tell me the truth," Elin said. "If he had . . . I'm so sorry. I'll let the two of you decide. If you don't want to go—"

"I don't," Sofia said.

Kirsten had to stay in Chicago until she heard from

Tor. How would his letters ever reach her if she moved that far away? But how long could she stall before everyone noticed that she was pregnant?

"I don't want to go, either," she finally said. "But now what should we do? There isn't enough room for us here. And we owe money to those men for our tickets to America."

"Maybe we could try to find jobs here in the city," Sofia said, "and pay them their money back. Aunt Hilma pays Inge to help her; maybe we can get a job like hers."

"Inge sleeps on a bed behind the stove," Kirsten said, "like a dog. And Aunt Hilma treats her like one, too."

"How can we get jobs?" Elin asked. "We don't even speak English. Besides, I don't like living in the city. I would prefer to work on a farm that was like home."

"I think Sofia is right," Kirsten said. "If we could just get jobs here in Chicago and earn some money, maybe by the time we paid the money back we would be more familiar with America. We'd have a better idea what to do next."

"I know one thing we need to do," Sofia said. "We need to pray and ask God to help us." Kirsten and Elin both stared at her. "Remember how Mama used to pray whenever she needed help with something?" Sofia continued. "When I was alone on Ellis Island, I was so scared that all I could do was pray and pray. I asked God to help me—and He did. He sent a friend to keep me company and show me God's promises in the Bible. I also prayed that both of you would get better, and you did."

"You're right," Elin said. "We should pray."

"How?" Kirsten asked. "Out loud . . . or what? I'm not very good at praying."

"It doesn't have to be out loud," Sofia said. "We can pray on our own, by ourselves. But we need to ask God what to do. He can help us find jobs."

Kirsten climbed back into her own bed and lay down beneath the covers. She closed her eyes and tried to pray. The minister had done all of the praying in church, so the only prayer she knew was the Lord's Prayer. She decided to try it.

She got as far as *Give us this day our daily bread* . . . and realized that it was a genuine plea. They needed God to take care of them and provide for them. Aunt Hilma resented every morsel of food they ate. But when she got to *Lead us not into temptation,* Kirsten's eyes filled with tears. She had fallen into temptation and had sinned. Having Tor's baby was a huge sin in God's eyes.

She rolled over and buried her face in the pillow. She couldn't pray. She had no right to ask God for anything. Instead, she cried herself to sleep.

In the morning they helped Aunt Hilma with the cooking and washing. Once the boarders left for work, Hilma allowed the three of them to go into the front of the house to clean and sweep. Kirsten was dusting the stair balusters when a man in a uniform brought the mail right to the front door and pushed it through a narrow slot. Aunt Hilma swooped up the letters before Kirsten could descend the stairs.

"I'm expecting a letter from Sweden," she told her aunt once again. "I gave everybody back home this address."

"Well, there is nothing here for you," she replied as she sifted through the letters.

At lunchtime Kirsten took her plate outside and sat down on the back steps to eat. The tiny yard was barren except for a chicken coop, a few scraggly bushes, and clotheslines full of bed linens and dish-towels.

"I can't believe we gave up our home and forests full of trees for this," she said when Sofia sat down beside her.

"We're all disappointed, but we're here now, and we have to make the best of it. Did you get any answers when you prayed?"

Kirsten shook her head.

Elin joined them a moment later. "What are we going to tell Uncle Lars?" she asked. "I'll do what-ever the two of you decide."

"I still don't want to marry one of those men," Sofia said. "I think we should ask God to help us find jobs here and pay the money back."

"What do you think, Kirsten?" Elin asked.

"Um . . . I . . . ." Maybe a letter would come tomorrow. Maybe Tor would ask her to marry him. "I

. . . I don't want to go to Wisconsin, either," she finally said. She hoped she wasn't making a huge mistake.

They had to wait until after supper to tell Uncle Lars their decision. Kirsten wished they could talk to him without Aunt Hilma hovering in the background. He seemed much more sympathetic to their plight than she did. But Hilma obviously knew all about his soft heart, and she listened to their every word.

"We're really sorry," Elin began, "but we've talked it over and decided that we don't want to go to this Wisconsin place and marry strangers."

"But Lars gave those young men his word," Hilma said. "They trusted us with all that money. It's our reputation that's on the line."

"We'll explain everything to them," Elin said, "and we'll tell them that it isn't your fault."

"And then we will work very hard," Sofia added, "and pay back all of the money that the men gave you for our tickets. Maybe they can use it to send for new brides."

"I don't want to be sold that way," Elin said, "and I don't want my sisters to be sold, either. I don't think Mama would approve. Thank you for all your help. I'm sorry if we let you down, but you should have told me the truth."

"Would you have come if I had?" Lars asked quietly.

"I . . . I think I would have tried to find another way."

285

Kirsten remembered why Elin had run away and knew that if Lars had told her the truth, Elin would have faced an impossible choice.

"You look around," Uncle Lars said, "and you'll see some terrible living conditions here in the city and very few opportunities for young, unmarried women, especially if they don't speak the language. It's easy for people to take advantage of you."

"People like us have to work very hard for a living," Hilma added.

"I might be able to find you a job in a factory," Lars continued, "or scrubbing laundry at a hotel. But I would be letting your mother down for certain. Factories and sweatshops are terrible places to work, with long days and very little money."

"And there are very few decent places where young, unmarried women can live," Hilma said.

Her husband nodded in agreement. "These boys in Wisconsin are honorable, God-fearing young men. Your mother would approve of them, I'm sure. And the countryside is like home. Your life on their farms would be just like home. Believe me, what they're offering you is much better than working ten hours a day, six days a week, for a few measly dollars pay."

"But we don't want to go," Sofia said.

Uncle Lars exhaled in frustration. "I don't understand why you won't at least go up there and meet these men. See what the place is like before you decide. You might like it."

"If we went there, we would have even more expectations placed on us," Elin said.

"And we would owe them even more money for our train tickets," Kirsten added.

They had reached a dead end. In the strained interval that followed, it was clear that none of them was happy with the situation. Surprisingly, Aunt Hilma broke the impasse, coming to their defense.

"They do know how to work hard," she said. "I suppose they could find jobs as domestics. We could ask Pastor Johnson if he knows of a family from church who needs servants."

"You would rather work hard all day long for some rich lady instead of your own husband and family?" Lars asked. "You'd rather clean someone else's home when you could be tending your own?"

"If we have to," Elin said, "then that's what we'll do."

Kirsten wondered how Elin really felt. She had never told them her opinion, but had let Kirsten and Sofia decide. Would Elin choose to go to Wisconsin?

"I want you to know," Elin continued, "that I feel very bad for the young men who paid our way. I would like to write to them and tell them that we're sorry."

"Apologies won't replace their money," Hilma said. "They had to work hard for those dollars. You'll see just how hard when you try to earn enough to pay them back."

"Even so, I would like to have their addresses, if

you don't mind. I would like to explain our decision and tell them that it isn't your fault."

"I suppose it wouldn't hurt," Lars said.

"And we want to pay you back, too, Aunt Hilma," Elin continued. "Once we find jobs, we'll pay back what we owe you for our room and board."

Hilma waved her hand as if the money didn't matter, but Kirsten suspected that she wouldn't turn away any money if it was offered. As soon as Lars gave Elin the address in Wisconsin, she herded Kirsten and Sofia upstairs to their room.

"Why are you banishing us to our room?" Kirsten asked as she sank down on the bed. "It's too early to go to sleep."

"I know. But I think Uncle Lars is disappointed in us, so we probably should stay out of his way. I'm going to try to write a letter of apology to our would-be husbands." She got out several sheets of writing paper, while Sofia opened their mother's Bible and began reading silently.

Kirsten decided to write another letter to Tor. He needed to come over and marry her immediately. He had to rescue her. But where would he get the money? His father had been against their marriage, so she doubted if he would pay for Tor's ticket. That stingy old grouch used to have a fit if someone stole a penny candy from his store. Kirsten should have remembered that. And she should have remembered that Tor already chose his father's store over her.

Maybe she had made a mistake. Maybe she should

have let the doctors deport her back to Sweden. But after reading Elin's diary, the thought of returning to Uncle Sven had terrified her. And now she might have made a second mistake in not going to Wisconsin. If Tor didn't come, she would need to get married very soon to give her baby a name. Who else would take care of them?

"If I had decided to go to Wisconsin," she asked Elin, "would you have wanted to go, too?"

Elin didn't look up from her writing. "We can't keep changing our minds, Kirsten."

She sighed. "I keep thinking about all those people on the ship and at Ellis Island. They were so hopeful, so happy to be starting all over again. I wonder if they're as disappointed as we are."

When it was time to turn off the lights, Sofia reminded them once again to pray. Kirsten wished she could ask God what to do and that He would send a neatly printed reply in an envelope. But He seemed as far away as Tor did, His answers just as slow in coming.

If only the doctors had made a mistake about the baby. If only something would happen and the baby would go away. Was wishing for such a thing an even worse sin?

Kirsten had made a mess of her life. No wonder God wouldn't listen to her prayers.

Chapter Twenty-Three

SOFIA THOUGHT ABOUT Ludwig Schneider all day as she and her sisters labored in their aunt's boarding-house. Whenever her longing for him threatened to overwhelm her, Sofia would pause from her task of dusting or sweeping and close her eyes. She would picture him sitting on the bench near the river, bending and swaying in time to the music as he played his violin. She would hear in her mind the melodies he had played and see the tender smile he'd given her each time he finished a song.

"Sofia? Why are you smiling like that?" Kirsten asked her.

"I was just thinking . . ."

"Well, you'd better come back to earth. Aunt Hilma is out in the backyard wringing the necks of two spent laying hens for our supper, and she wants us to pluck them for her."

"I like working outside," Sofia said as she followed Kirsten through the kitchen door. "I miss working in the garden and taking care of the animals, don't you?" Her sister didn't reply.

The chickens lay on the outdoor worktable beside the pot of scalding water. "Save the feathers," Hilma said, handing Sofia a sack. "We can't afford to waste a thing."

"This is no different than slaving for Aunt Karin all day," Kirsten grumbled after their aunt went inside, "except that there aren't any beautiful woods to explore and no cows to give fresh milk. I would love a glassful right now, wouldn't you?"

"Yes," Sofia admitted, "but let's try not to talk about home in front of Elin. She feels responsible for getting us into this situation."

"I know. But, Sofia? I'm really sorry for making you leave Sweden. You would have stayed behind if I had stayed, so it's really my fault that you're here."

Sofia looked up at her sister in surprise. Tears filled Kirsten's eyes. She seemed more emotional than usual, and Sofia wondered why. Kirsten had always been the least sentimental of the three of them. "You miss Tor, don't you?"

Kirsten nodded.

"I miss my friend Ludwig, too," Sofia said. "I pray every night that I'll see him again. I'll pray for you and Tor, too."

"Thanks," Kirsten sniffed. Then she grimaced and covered her nose and mouth with her hand. "The smell of these chickens is making me sick. Could you finish them by yourself?"

"I guess so." This was more like the Kirsten that Sofia remembered—always conniving to get someone else to do her chores. Kirsten thanked her and hurried inside. A few minutes later their cousin Dagmar returned home from school and offered to help Sofia.

"Would you teach me some English words?" Sofia asked while they worked.

"You don't need to learn English," Dagmar said. "Mama doesn't speak it."

"I know, but I would like to learn." If she and Ludwig both spoke English, they could talk to each other. "Let's start with the words for everyday things, like chicken and tree and house."

They made a game of it, and Sofia penned a list of all the words Dagmar taught her, writing their Swedish meanings beside them. When they collected the eggs at the end of the day, Dagmar taught her how to count in English. Sofia made up her mind to practice speaking English every day.

After the supper dishes were done, Uncle Lars walked with Sofia and her sisters to the parsonage to speak with the pastor about finding work. "These are my three nieces," he told Pastor Johnson. "Their parents died tragically, and they've just arrived in America to look for work. Do you know of anyone needing help?"

The pastor appraised them with a stern expression. "Are they willing to work as domestic servants? I've been told that unmarried Swedish women make up the majority of Chicago's servants. Our girls have earned a good reputation for being clean, honest, and hardworking."

"We're willing to do whatever we can," Elin said.

"They know their way around hard work, that's for certain," Lars told him. "If you hear of a reputable family that would hire them, please let me know."

"I'll do that."

"I hope he doesn't get the wrong idea and sell us as wives, too," Sofia whispered to Kirsten on the way home.

"I hope we don't end up sleeping behind someone's stove like poor Inge does," she whispered back.

Two days later Aunt Hilma and Uncle Lars received word that the pastor and his wife were coming to call on them after dinner. Sofia and her sisters would be allowed to go into the front parlor to receive the guests. Aunt Hilma brewed a pot of coffee and even baked a batch of *pepparkakor*. "But the cookies are for Pastor and Mrs. Johnson," Hilma warned. "I can't afford enough for the three of you, too."

"Has he found work for us?" Sofia asked her.

"He didn't say—and don't be nosy and start asking rude questions, either. He'll tell us the reason for his visit in his own time."

"Yes, ma'am." Sofia carried the serving tray into the parlor and set it on the coffee table. Two boarders sat beneath the gas lamps she had cleaned that afternoon, reading Swedish language newspapers. Three more boarders sat around a small parlor table in the corner, talking softly. Sofia didn't see any boarders who matched Aunt Hilma's description of "coarse and rough." But the moment she entered the room, every one of the men eyed her as if she were a Yuletide present, wrapped in fancy paper and ribbons. No wonder Aunt Hilma kept her and her sisters confined to the kitchen.

When the pastor and his wife arrived, all but one of the boarders discreetly left the room. The guests settled down on the sofa as if they had come for nothing more than a pleasant visit. Sofia could see Kirsten growing impatient as Pastor Johnson and Uncle Lars sipped their coffee and discussed the weather, and Mrs. Johnson and Aunt Hilma tasted the cookies. Sofia hoped that at least one of the gingery *pepparkakor* would be left over so that she and her sisters could share a taste, but Mrs. Johnson was swallowing the little treats as if in a race to clean the plate.

Finally, Pastor Johnson came to the point of their visit. "I have learned of someone who is looking for temporary help with her spring cleaning," he said.

"Oh? Isn't spring cleaning usually begun in March?" Hilma asked.

"*Ja*, but the family wants to offer the house for sale, so they would like to have it thoroughly cleaned. They've had trouble with their hired help lately, so now they are behind on the work."

"Do I know this family?" Uncle Lars asked.

"I'm sure you do." The pastor hesitated. It seemed like a very long pause to Sofia. "Your nieces would be working for Silvia Anderson—Gustav Anderson's widow."

Sofia waited, wondering again why there was such a long pause and why she saw her aunt and uncle exchange looks. But Hilma had warned her not to ask questions.

"Mrs. Anderson will pay them four dollars a week plus room and board. She told me that she is only looking for two girls, but it wouldn't hurt to ask her if she'll take all three. The work will get done faster that way, and as you know, her home is quite large."

"I don't think I've seen Silvia Anderson in church these past few months," Aunt Hilma said, pouring Mrs. Johnson another cup of coffee.

"She hasn't been well." Mrs. Johnson added cream and three teaspoonfuls of sugar. Sofia could tell by her aunt's expression that she noticed the large quantity of sugar, too. "Mrs. Anderson is in poor health, which is why her son and daughter-in-law would like to sell the house. They want Silvia to move in with them. At the moment, Mrs. Anderson employs a cook and she has a nurse taking care of her. But I understand that very little cleaning is being done."

"We would be willing to go and meet her," Kirsten said.

"It's more important that she meets you," Aunt Hilma said, giving Kirsten her customary frown. "It will be up to Silvia Anderson to decide if she wants to hire you, not the other way around."

The pastor gave them a letter of reference before he left. When Sofia carried the tray back to the kitchen, she was disappointed to see that not a single *pepparkakor* remained.

"Silvia Anderson," Hilma said, grunting the name. "She's so rich she thinks she owns everyone and everything."

"She does own everything, Hilma," Uncle Lars said, smiling wryly.

"Oh, you know what I mean. And I shouldn't wonder that she needs help. From what I hear, she goes through serving girls like rinse water."

"Don't be a gossip, Hilma."

"It's not gossip, it's the truth. She is notoriously difficult to get along with."

"We have plenty of experience with that," Kirsten whispered to Sofia, nodding her head in their aunt's direction.

"What's that?" Hilma asked, pinning Kirsten with a stare.

"I said we have plenty of experience with cleaning houses. And we won't be burdening you with our room and board anymore."

"Exactly how much do we owe the men for our trip?" Elin asked as she washed the coffee cups.

"Well, let's see . . ." Lars said. "There was the train across Sweden, the ferry, then another train across England, then the ship's passage . . . Altogether, I believe it cost more than thirty-five dollars."

"For *each* of us?" Kirsten blurted.

He nodded. "Then add the trip from New York to Chicago on top of that, some traveling money, and the fare to take you up to Wisconsin—"

"We didn't go to Wisconsin," Elin said.

"*Ja*, that's true, but I think you should plan on at least forty dollars apiece."

"That means," Kirsten said, "that we would have to

work for at least ten weeks at four dollars a week. By then, it will be the middle of August."

"At least," Hilma agreed. "And I wouldn't blame the young men in Wisconsin if they charged you interest on their money, since it turned out to be a loan."

Forty dollars felt like a million. They would never get out of debt. Sofia thought of Ludwig, and how he had spent all that money for his boat fare to America, only to be sent back. No wonder he planned to swim off the island. Worry shuddered through her each time she pictured him jumping into the cold gray water and trying to swim across that impossibly wide river. But each time she began to worry, she made up her mind to say a silent prayer for Ludwig. She would picture God's hands beneath him, holding him afloat.

"I think we should call on Silvia Anderson first thing in the morning and ask her for the jobs," Sofia told her sisters in their bedroom that night.

"We can find out how mean she really is," Kirsten added.

"Aunt Hilma says the choice is up to Mrs. Anderson," Elin said, "but there's no reason why we can't quit if we don't like her."

"It will buy us some time," Sofia agreed. She held on to the hope that Ludwig would find her in the meantime and come to her rescue.

Before they turned out the lamp, Sofia read silently from the Bible, returning to some of the verses that Ludwig had shown her. Each one reassured her that

God was with them. He would watch over them and help them out of this situation if they trusted Him. She also found a few new verses of her own, such as the promise from Psalms that said, *Then they cried out to the Lord in their trouble, and he delivered them from their distress.*

She always finished her nightly reading with the verses from Song of Songs that Ludwig had shown her on their last day together: *Many waters cannot quench love; rivers cannot wash it away. If one were to give all the wealth of his house for love, it would be utterly scorned.*

She reached into her satchel to feel the smooth wood of his violin as she read his last promise: *I will get up now and go about the city, through its streets and squares; I will search for the one my heart loves.* Ludwig would find her again. She would wait for him, no matter what.

Sofia and her sisters rose early the next morning and dressed in their Sunday clothes to make a good impression. "I'll draw you a map so you'll know how to find the Anderson house," Uncle Lars said. "It's a long way to walk—"

"But we can't spare the trolley fare for all three of you," Hilma finished.

Sofia had never met anyone who worried about money as much as their aunt did. "We used to walk all the way into the village when we had to," she told her aunt. "We're used to walking."

"Don't use the front door," Hilma warned. "The hired help is supposed to go around to the rear."

It was a long walk, but only a quarter as far as the trip from their farm to the village had been. They followed Uncle Lars' map as if it would lead to buried treasure, and the closer they got to the address, the larger the homes and surrounding gardens became. But they all stopped short when they saw Silvia Anderson's enormous three-story stone mansion for the first time. Sofia thought it was nearly as imposing as the building on Ellis Island.

"I've never seen a house that huge," Elin said.

"She must be as rich as a queen!" Kirsten said.

"How will we ever clean all those rooms?" Sofia asked.

"Listen, the longer it takes," Elin said, "the more money we'll make, and the sooner we can get out of debt."

They went around to the back door as they'd been told to do and were greeted by a woman who was so tiny and gnarled with arthritis that she reminded Sofia of a gnome; all she needed was a pointed red hat. She appeared to be in her sixties, her golden hair fading to gray and worn in braided coils. But the warmth in her smiling gray eyes assured Sofia that she would be a friend.

"God morgon," Elin said. "Pastor Johnson sent us here to apply for jobs as domestic servants. We're the Carlson sisters, nieces of Lars and Hilma Larson." She showed the woman the letter.

The woman introduced herself as Mrs. Olafson and told them she was the cook. But then her pale eyebrows knitted in worry. "Oh, but you look like such nice girls. Take my advice and look for jobs someplace else."

"Is Mrs. Anderson really that hard to work for?" Kirsten asked.

"She's impossible. And there is a great deal of work to do. This house has more than twenty rooms. She is playing a game of tug-of-war with her son, you see. He wants to sell the house and she doesn't, so she fires anyone who works too hard. She would fire me, too, if she didn't have to eat. She doesn't want to move in with him, you see. And . . ." she added in a stage whisper, "when you meet her daughter-in-law, Bettina, you'll understand why. They are two of a kind, and they get along like cats and rats."

"We really need the money, Mrs. Olafson," Elin said. "Even if she only lets us work here for a week or two, that's still better than nothing."

"Yes, yes, I understand. I need the money, too, you see. And believe me, she is paying me more than I could get anywhere else, because no one else can get along with her. As I say, she has to eat. Well, come in. I'll show you around."

Mrs. Olafson even hobbled like a little gnome as she led Sofia and her sisters into the house. The kitchen was very large but as tidy as a cottage kitchen. Sofia smelled fish chowder bubbling on the stove and rye bread baking in the oven.

"Mrs. Anderson is awake. I already sent up her breakfast tray—"

"Oh, then we'd better not disturb her," Elin said.

"You won't disturb her. She has nothing else to occupy her time. Now, most of the time you will use these back kitchen stairs, you see, but I'll take you up the main staircase so you can see all the work you'll be getting yourselves into."

She opened a service door that led into an enormous paneled dining room. Sofia counted fourteen chairs around the table, but the dust on top of it was thick enough to draw pictures in. The mirror hanging above the ornately carved sideboard was so murky with dust and grime Sofia could barely see her reflection. Dozens of silver serving pieces cluttered the top of the buffet, and all of the silver, including a pair of candelabra on the table and a second pair on the fireplace, was black with tarnish. Cobwebs draped the carved plaster ceiling and hung from the chandelier.

"Oh my," Sofia whispered. "I wouldn't know where to begin."

"This is only the first room, you see. And this one has been in use recently. When I show you some of the others, you may change your minds."

The dining room led to the main foyer with a massive fireplace and a carved walnut staircase that looked wide enough to drive a team of horses up it. The ceiling soared two stories above Sofia's head.

"A family of giants could live in this house," Kirsten said.

"That's the formal parlor, across from the dining room," Mrs. Olafson continued, pointing to a dusky room filled with upholstered furniture and shelves full of bric-a-brac. "It's been shuttered for quite some time. Mrs. Anderson prefers the smaller morning room, which I'll show you later."

From the window on the first landing, Sofia glimpsed what might have once been a sunny conservatory, with plants long withered from lack of care and so many grime-covered windows it would take a month to wash them all. At the top of the stairs, a U-shaped balcony looked down on the foyer, and another set of wide stairs led to the third floor.

"I'll take you through one of the cleaner bedroom suites," Mrs. Olafson said, opening a door off the hallway. "Each bedroom has its own sitting room and dressing room, you see. And each suite has one of these . . ." She pointed to a magnificent *kakelugnar*—a Swedish porcelain tile stove. Even with the drapes closed and the lamps turned off, Sofia could see that the room's elegant plasterwork ceiling had been carefully painted with flowers and vines to match the stove's hand-painted tiles.

"This is amazing," Kirsten murmured.

"Gustav Anderson had this house built and decorated for his wife and family. I understand that it took two years to build, you see. And now his widow lives here, all alone."

"Why don't her son and his wife move in here," Kirsten asked, "instead of selling it?"

"Oh, you don't know Bettina Anderson. She wants everything modern and built the American way. This place is much too Swedish for her tastes."

There seemed to be a great deal more of the house that they hadn't seen, but the brief tour ended with Mrs. Anderson's suite. The cook knocked on the door, and a woman wearing a white uniform and a peaked nurse's cap answered it. If Mrs. Olafson was a gnome, then the nurse was surely a witch. She was thin and pointy-looking, with glistening black hair and a severe face.

"What is it?" she asked.

"Pastor Johnson sent these three nice young ladies over to fill the servants' positions."

"Send them in," a voice thundered from inside the room.

"Good luck to you," Mrs. Olafson whispered. "And watch out, she hears everything."

Silvia Anderson sat propped up by pillows in an enormous four-poster bed. Sofia had expected to see an ogre, but she was much too wispy and fine-boned to be an ogre. Instead, she resembled a fairy queen with her corona of white braided hair and her pale blue ruffled nightgown. Sofia wouldn't have been surprised to see gossamer wings sprouting from Mrs. Anderson's shoulders. Sofia felt as though she'd wandered into a bedtime story, complete with a haunted castle, a gnome, a witch, and now a fairy queen.

"Don't huddle near the door," she bellowed. "Come

in here so I can see you." Her voice was loud enough for a body twice her size and as imperious as an empress'. An enormous gray cat that had been asleep on her lap lifted its head to examine Sofia and her sisters along with its mistress. The cat was as large as a raccoon with blue-gray fur and an oddly flattened face, as if it had run headfirst into a brick wall.

"Why are there three of you? I only asked for two girls."

"We are sisters, Mrs. Anderson," Elin said, stepping forward to explain. Sofia remained a step behind her with Kirsten. "We just arrived in America. We need jobs in order to pay back the people who loaned us the money for our tickets. Pastor Johnson sent you this letter." She held it out to her, but when Mrs. Anderson didn't reach to take it, Elin lowered her arm again. "Our parents died, so we came here to live with our uncle."

"Who's your uncle?"

"Lars Larson."

"Oh yes. And his wife, Hilma. Biggest gossip in the community and as tight-fisted as a miser."

Sofia glanced around the room while Elin was speaking and saw another magnificent porcelain stove, painted with pink and blue flowers. Everything in the room matched the tiles, from the delicately painted border around the ceiling to the drapery and bed linens—even the vase of fresh flowers on the bedside table. All of the furnishings looked as though they belonged in a Swedish castle.

"What are your names?"

"I'm Elin Carlson. This is Kirsten and Sofia—"

"You look like children. I don't believe in hiring children. How old are you? And I want the truth."

"I'm nineteen," Elin said. "Kirsten is eighteen and Sofia—"

"I'm sixteen. But my birthday is in a few weeks and I'll be seventeen." Elin was being so strong and brave that Sofia suddenly decided to step forward and stand beside her.

"I know what comes after sixteen, Miss Carlson." She gave Sofia a look that made her heart race and was probably intended to silence her. The cat stared at her, as well, its yellow eyes blinking slowly.

"Well, I only need two girls," Mrs. Anderson said.

Sofia saw Elin swallow. But she lifted her chin and bravely held her head high. "Which two would you like to hire, ma'am?" Elin asked.

Sofia waited, holding her breath. At first she wondered why Elin hadn't pleaded with her to take all three of them, but then she saw the wisdom in Elin's reply. Instead of lowering herself to beg, she would give the old ogre the task of rejecting one of them, face-to-face.

"Well, that one looks like she can work," Mrs. Anderson said, pointing to Kirsten, "but the two of you are scrawny little beggars. I don't see how much good you'll be."

Elin didn't respond. Sofia knew that if Mrs. Anderson rejected her because she was the youngest, she likely would end up working for someone like Aunt Hilma and sleeping behind the kitchen stove. But Elin looked calm and determined, and Sofia made up her mind to be calm, too.

Please, Jesus, please, she prayed.

"Well . . . I guess I'll keep all three of you—for now. But it will be on a trial basis, you understand."

"Yes, ma'am. We understand."

"You'll get room and board and three dollars each per week."

"Excuse me," Kirsten said, "but Pastor Johnson told us it was four dollars."

"That was before I knew there were three of you."

"Then we can't accept," Kirsten said after glancing at Elin and Sofia. "You would be receiving more work from us for less money. That isn't fair."

The fairy queen stroked her gray cat's fur as she looked them up and down, forcing them to wait. Her tiny fingers glittered with rings. Diamond and emerald earrings dangled from her ears. Sofia had never seen anyone so elaborately arrayed just to lie in bed.

"Very well," Mrs. Anderson finally replied. "This is what I will expect from you in exchange for your room and board and four dollars each per week: You will arise in the morning to begin working before I'm awake, and you will not retire to your beds at night until after I'm asleep. I will give you one morning, afternoon, or evening off per week—I'll choose the times, depending on my schedule for that week.

These times will be staggered, of course, so that you don't all disappear at once."

She paused, looking them up and down, her eyes narrowed. "You'll need decent clothing. You look like a bunch of Swedish peasant girls, fresh off the boat."

"Excuse me, ma'am," Kirsten said, "but that's exactly what we are."

Mrs. Anderson barked out a laugh that roused the cat. It stretched its bloated body, claws extended, then sat up, blinking at them in disapproval. As quickly as Mrs. Anderson's laughter began, it abruptly changed into a coughing spell. The nurse leaped up to offer her a glass of water, but Mrs. Anderson swatted her hand away.

"Stop treating me like an invalid, Agne, and go sit down."

"But you hired me to take care of you."

"No, it was my dim-witted son's idea to hire you, not mine."

"He cares about you."

"Hmmph. The truth is, the sooner I'm gone, the sooner that harpy he married will get her hands on my money. How do I know she isn't paying you to poison me?"

The nurse appeared outraged. "Really, Mrs. Anderson, I don't know how you can—"

"Oh, go sit down. In fact, you shouldn't even be in here listening. The arrangements I make with these girls are none of your business. How much extra is Bettina paying you to report all of my goings-on?"

"I'm not . . . I mean . . . I wouldn't . . . I—"

"You're a very poor liar, Agne. Take my advice and just sit down and shut up."

The nurse slunk back to her chair by the window. Sofia saw the wisdom in respectfully standing their ground, as Kirsten and Elin had done, instead of allowing Mrs. Anderson to walk all over them.

The fairy queen turned her attention back to Elin. "I will give you three *used* maids' uniforms—unless you would like new clothing, in which case I will deduct it from your earnings?"

"No thank you," Elin said. "We don't mind hand-me-downs."

"You will sleep in the servants' quarters on the third floor. There will be no visitors and *absolutely* no suitors. Don't expect any holidays off. Don't help yourself to my larder. You will be fed, of course, but you'll eat the leftovers in the kitchen after my guests and I have dined. . . . Mrs. Olafson!" she suddenly called out. The cook hobbled into the room. "Show the Carlson sisters their rooms. They will start work today, as soon as they've moved in and changed their clothes. Give them three of the old staff uniforms. That's all. You're dismissed." She waved her hand as if flourishing a magic wand to make them disappear.

Sofia and her sisters followed Mrs. Olafson from the room and down the hall toward the rear of the house. "Well, I see you passed the first test," Mrs. Olafson said. She opened a door that looked as though it might be a closet. Instead, it led to a narrow set of stairs. "I hope you aren't sorry for accepting the jobs."

She motioned for them to follow her up to the third floor. "Your bedroom is up here, you see. But I may as well show you this as long as we're up here. . . ." She opened another door and led them into an enormous ballroom.

"Oh my!" Sofia breathed. "It's like something from a fairy tale!"

"You mean an *ancient* fairy tale," Kirsten said. "This place hasn't been cleaned since the Vikings sailed the seas."

A pile of furniture littered one corner of the room, covered with yellowing sheets. Cobwebs hung from the gilded chandeliers and wall sconces. A pair of moth-eaten maroon velvet curtains draped across a raised wooden stage on the far end of the room. Dust balls skittered across the floor on the breeze from the open door, and Kirsten left a trail of footprints in the dust as she walked into the room. Sofia could see the splendor beneath it all and could imagine magnificent music playing while women in ball gowns whirled across the polished floor with their partners.

"Look at the center of this ceiling!" Kirsten said, halting in the middle of the ballroom. "It's made of glass!"

Sofia looked up and saw blue sky and white clouds floating past. "You could dance beneath the stars," she murmured. She pictured herself in Ludwig's arms, waltzing in the moonlight beneath the glass dome.

"Well, we certainly have a lot of work to do," Elin said with a sigh. "Come on. We'd better get started."

The servants' quarters were at the end of the hallway, behind the ballroom and two floors above the kitchen. They were sparsely furnished, with bare wooden floors and narrow beds and a chest of drawers. These rooms would need to be thoroughly cleaned, too. Sofia parted the curtains for a glimpse of the view outside, and the cloud of dust she raised made her sneeze.

"It's such a shame to see this beautiful home so run down," Elin said. "How could she let it get this way?"

"The truth is, Mrs. Anderson doesn't want to sell the house and move," Mrs. Olafson said. "She wants everything to look cluttered and shabby and dusty, you see, so that no one will buy it. If you do too good of a job, she'll find a reason to fire you. And if you're lazy and don't work, she'll fire you for that, too. You're really in a difficult place, you see."

"But she'll pay us for the days we do work, won't she?"

"Yes . . . but . . ." Mrs. Olafson stared at the floor, wringing her gnomelike hands.

"Please tell us," Elin said.

"You seem like such nice girls . . . so I must warn you to be careful. Mrs. Anderson accused the last maid of stealing from her, you see. She made a terrible scene, and of course the poor girl will never be able to get another job as a domestic. She'll be off to the sweatshops for certain—or maybe someplace worse. And so will you if the old lady manages to destroy your reputation."

"Thank you for warning us," Elin said.

"Why does she need a nurse?" Kirsten asked. "What's wrong with her?"

"From what I've observed—nothing. She is sick when it's convenient to be sick and well when it's convenient to be well. Likewise, she speaks perfect English when it's convenient and not a word of it when it isn't. . . . Anyway, I'll show you where the uniforms are—although they're such shabby old things I can't imagine anyone wanting to wear them. Then I need to get back to my kitchen."

Sofia noticed that her sisters were quiet as they walked back to the boardinghouse to get their trunk. Elin paused before going inside. "Do you think we should take the job?" she asked.

"We don't really have a choice, do we?" Kirsten asked. "Everyone keeps telling us not to work in a factory. What do you think, Sofia?"

There was no doubt at all in Sofia's mind. "I think this job is an answer to our prayers. God found it for us—and He will be with us."

Elin gently cupped Sofia's cheek in her hand. "You sound so much like Mama."

It didn't take Sofia long to gather her belongings, but she had one very important thing she needed to do before leaving the boardinghouse for good. While her sisters were still upstairs, Sofia carried her satchel down and went outside to talk to Aunt Hilma, who was pinning clothes on the line. She pulled out Ludwig's Bible and showed it to her.

"Aunt Hilma, a friend will be coming here to get this Bible. He gave it to me for safekeeping. His name is Ludwig Schneider, and—"

"A German man?"

"Yes. He doesn't speak Swedish, but he will be asking for me by name, so will you please tell him where I am so I can return this to him?" She held up the Bible, then quickly stuffed it back into her bag. Her sisters would be coming downstairs any minute. "It's very important that he finds me and gets his Bible back. Please?"

"I don't like the idea of a strange man—"

"He isn't a stranger. He's a friend. And a good Christian man." The back door opened and Elin and Kirsten came out, carrying the trunk.

"Thank you, Aunt Hilma," Sofia said. "Thank you for everything."

Chapter Twenty-Four

"I'M SORRY, BUT I need to rest again." Elin set down hcr cnd of the heavy trunk and leaned against it for support. Her illness had left her feeling weak and wrung out. She and her sisters had decided to take turns carrying the trunk on the walk back to the mansion, and it bothered her that she was unable to carry her fair share of the load. "I wish I didn't tire so easily."

"I don't mind stopping," Sofia said, flexing her fingers. "My hand keeps cramping around the leather handle."

"I thought we were finished lugging this thing around," Kirsten said, giving it a kick. "Too bad it didn't fall overboard in the middle of the ocean. Do we really need all the stuff that's inside?"

"Maybe not now," Elin said, "but someday we'll have our own home again."

She thought of all the items she had carried for so many miles. The copper coffee kettle brought back memories of Mama. So did the book of hymns. Mama's fingers had embroidered the linens, every stitch a labor of love. Papa's carved wooden utensils helped her picture his work-hardened hands. The silver candlesticks had belonged to their grandmother, and Elin had fought with Aunt Karin over who would keep them. The items in the trunk were not very costly. Their value was only in the memories they evoked.

Elin had stopped to rest in front of a shop on one of the Swedish neighborhood's main thoroughfares, and she saw Kirsten gazing longingly at the items on display in the window. "Wouldn't you love to go inside and look around?" Kirsten murmured.

"Go ahead," Elin told her. "I'll stay out here with the trunk."

Kirsten looked at her in surprise. "Do you really mean it?"

"Yes. You can go inside, too, Sofia."

The three of them were about to begin a life of hard work in a difficult situation, and Elin wanted to give her sisters a few moments of pleasure. Sofia and Kirsten had changed since beginning their journey, so perhaps it was time for Elin to change a little, too. After all, she wasn't their mother. The giddy excitement she saw on her sisters' faces as they opened the door and disappeared inside made Elin smile.

She sat down on the trunk to wait, watching the traffic go by. Once again she was struck by the city's energy and vitality, almost as if it were a living thing. Life here in Chicago was so different from the life she'd left behind—and so different from the one she had imagined.

"You should see all the things they have for sale!" Sofia said when she and Kirsten came out of the shop a few minutes later. "And the variety! In one display alone, they had a dozen different styles of hair combs."

"And they have an entire counter full of things that only cost five cents," Kirsten said. "The shop girl says that the five-cent coin is called a nickel. And since there are 100 cents in a dollar and we earn four dollars a week, I figure we can buy—"

"We can't spend any money until we pay back what we owe," Elin said.

"Not even a little bit?"

"We can't take a chance, Kirsten. We don't know how long we will be able to keep this job."

"But we're going to need some spending money, Elin," Sofia said. "We'll need to buy things like soap and—"

"Writing paper and stamps," Kirsten added.

"You're right. I'm sorry. I don't want to end up like Aunt Hilma, worrying about money all the time." She lifted one end of the trunk and waited for Sofia to lift the other. They started walking again.

"The women in America dress so beautifully, don't they?" Sofia said as they made their way through the crowds. "Everyone looks like one of the rich ladies back home."

"And the gowns are so colorful," Kirsten said. "You should see the ones that were for sale in that store back there. You can buy them already made. Nobody has to sew it for you."

"But if it isn't sewn for you, how do you know it will fit?" Elin asked. "People come in all different sizes—look how different the three of us are."

"Small . . . medium . . . and large," Kirsten said, smiling as she pointed first to Sofia, then to Elin, then to herself.

"You aren't large," Elin said, laughing. "You're . . . buxom. I could use a few more curves like yours."

"I love all the fancy hats the women wear," Sofia said. "I wish I could buy one with flowers on it."

"I hate wearing a hat," Kirsten said, making a face. "But I do wish we could dress like the American women do. We look so old-fashioned!"

"Mrs. Anderson said she's going to give us clothes to work in, remember?" Sofia said.

"Don't get your hopes up. They won't be like the pretty ones in these windows, I'm sure."

Elin felt exhausted by the time they returned to the mansion, and she still hadn't even done an hour's work yet. She dreaded the prospect of dragging the trunk all the way up to the third floor. But just as they reached the back door, a bedraggled-looking man who had been digging weeds out of one of the flowerbeds hurried over to them.

"Here, let me help you with that. It looks heavy." Like nearly everyone else Elin had met in Chicago, he spoke Swedish. With his raggedy clothes and shaggy beard, it was difficult to tell how old he was, but Elin guessed he was in his fifties.

"We could use some help," she said, "but you may change your mind when you find out that this trunk has to go all the way up to the third floor."

"Oh, that's no problem," he said, tipping his cap to all three of them. And it wasn't. He hefted it onto his shoulder with ease and followed Elin up the back staircase to their room.

"I'm Mr. Lund," he said after he'd set it down.

"And we're the new servants. I'm Kirsten Carlson, and these are my sisters, Elin and Sofia. We're so grateful for your help."

"Nice to meet you. Young Mr. Anderson hired me to clean up the yard. It's very overgrown, as you can see, but I can tell that it was beautiful once. I'm afraid it's going to take more than one man to make it look that way again, but I'll do my best. So, I guess I'll get back to work now."

"We should start working, too," Elin said as Mr. Lund clomped down the back stairs.

Kirsten collapsed on one of the narrow beds and pulled off her shoes. "Why? What's the big hurry? I think we should take our time so we can stay here longer."

"Isn't that deceitful?" Sofia asked. "We'll be cheating Mrs. Anderson if we don't work as hard as we can every day."

"But if she doesn't want to move, then the longer we take to finish, the longer she can stay here. We'll actually be helping her."

"But she is paying us to work, and—"

"Listen," Elin said, stepping between them, "this house is so big and there's so much work to do, it's going to take us forever no matter how hard we work. Let's change into our uniforms and get started."

The closet that Mrs. Olafson had shown them smelled strongly of camphor—as did the men's and women's uniforms hanging inside it.

"The Andersons must have had a lot of servants at one time," Sofia said. "Look at all these clothes."

Kirsten pulled out one of the long, gray gabardine

skirts and held it up in front of her to test the length. She wrinkled her nose. "Ugh! They smell old. I don't want to smell like this."

"With all the cleaning and dusting we have to do," Elin said, "we'll smell worse than this once we start working. We can launder them on the next wash day, but we'd better change into them for now. Mrs. Anderson told us to."

They took a few minutes to sort through the closet, looking for skirts and bodices that might fit them. The wrinkled aprons that were worn on top might have once been white but were now limp and yellow with age. When Elin and her sisters had each found garments in their sizes, they went back into their room to change.

Elin grabbed her satchel to look for a kerchief to tie over her hair, but when she opened her bag she found a book lying on top. She had never seen it before. She lifted it out and saw another strange shape beneath it, wrapped in a gray flannel cloth. She pulled out the wooden lump and, much to her surprise, found a violin and bow beneath the cloth.

"Where did this come from?" she asked.

Sofia's eyes grew wide. "Be careful! That's mine! That's my bag." She took the violin and bow from Elin, then snatched up the book.

"*Yours?*" Elin asked in disbelief. "But—but where did it come from?" She knew that Sofia hadn't brought a violin with her from Sweden.

Kirsten stopped buttoning her blouse and came

over to look. "Sofia! That belongs to the German man. Why did you take his violin?"

"What German man?" Elin asked. Fear raced through her.

"I didn't take it, Kirsten. He gave it to me. He asked me to take care of it for him." The tender way Sofia handled the instrument baffled Elin.

"Why did he give it to you?" Kirsten asked. "That doesn't make any sense."

Elin was standing right beside her sisters, but they were both ignoring her. "Sofia! Whose violin is that?" she asked, raising her voice.

Sofia seemed reluctant to answer. "It belongs to a friend of mine named Ludwig Schneider. I met him on Ellis Island and he . . . we . . . we became friends." She carefully rewrapped it in the flannel cloth, handling it like an infant.

"But why do you have it?"

Sofia took a moment to reply, and when she did her chin jutted stubbornly. "The immigration officials weren't going to let him into the country because he has a crippled leg, so he decided he would swim—"

"Oh, Sofia," Kirsten said. "He can't be serious. It's much too far to swim. Besides, there are so many ships on that river that it would be dangerous—"

"That's why he asked me to take care of it for him. I gave him Uncle Lars' address, and he's going to find me when he gets to Chicago to get his things back."

"You trusted a stranger with our address?"

"It's the other way around, Elin. He trusted me with his violin. I wish you could have heard him play. He's a very gifted musician. But America has a stupid rule that you can't immigrate if you're crippled, and Ludwig has an injured leg. It isn't fair, because there are plenty of jobs he could do if they would just give him a chance. I'm sure he could make lots of money playing his violin."

Elin stared at her, wondering what to think. Sofia held up the strange book. "He also asked me to take care of this. It's his Bible. He's a good man, Elin. And besides, you had no business looking in my bag in the first place."

"It was an accident; I mistook it for mine. I'm sorry." Elin was surprised to see tears in Sofia's eyes as she tucked the Bible back into her satchel and set it on her own bed.

Elin was keeping a secret from her sisters, so why should it surprise her if her sisters kept secrets from her? But what if this German man was scheming to take advantage of Sofia's innocence and vulnerability? Maybe she and her sisters weren't safe here in America after all. She hoped Sofia's chance meeting wouldn't end in disaster.

"I think we'd better get to work," Elin said, summoning her strength. "We don't want to give Mrs. Anderson an excuse to fire us."

"Especially on our first day," Kirsten added.

They finished dressing and went downstairs to the kitchen, where Mrs. Olafson was fixing a lunch tray.

"Don't you girls look lovely in your new outfits—or should I say *old* outfits? Would one of you like to carry this tray upstairs to Mrs. Anderson when it's ready?"

"I will," Kirsten said.

"I didn't realize that it was noon already," Elin said. "All we've accomplished is moving in."

"How big did you say this house is?" Kirsten asked.

"It has more than twenty rooms—not counting the servants' rooms on the third floor."

"Let's see . . ." Kirsten said, counting on her fingers, "if we spent two days cleaning each room, it would take us only forty days—no, that's not long enough. We need to work for at least ten weeks to pay back the money we owe."

"Longer if you count spending money," Elin added.

"Did you see all of that woodwork in the dining room?" Sofia asked. "We could never clean and polish all that wood in two days—not to mention the furniture and the silver and—"

"Where do you think we should begin, Mrs. Olafson?" Elin asked.

"Well, first you should eat your noon meal. I fixed enough for the three of you, you see. After that I would start with the rooms she is most likely to use. The morning room behind the stairs, where the sun comes in. She likes to sit in there. And the dining room. She does use it for guests from time to time, but right now the silver is a mess and the dishes need to be washed and the rugs hung out and beaten and . . ."

The little woman paused to take another breath, then gestured to the kitchen table. "But sit—eat, eat."

Mrs. Olafson's fish chowder was the best Elin had ever tasted. The rye bread was still warm from the oven. Elin hadn't felt so full or so satisfied since leaving home.

"I'd like to start with the dining room," Sofia said after they'd finished. "I think it must look beautiful beneath all that dust. If you show me where to find the silver polish, Mrs. Olafson, I'll be glad to start with that."

After lunch, Elin dragged herself into the dining room behind Sofia and Kirsten. Sterling silver serving pieces covered the top of the sideboard—chafing dishes and a coffee set; dishes for condiments and fruit and butter; salt and pepper shakers, a pickle caster, a mustard pot, and even a silver toothpick holder—all black with tarnish. Elin opened the cupboard doors and found even more silver pieces, along with a set of bone china dishes and enough silverware to serve twenty people. She covered a corner of the table with an old cloth to protect it and helped Sofia pile all of the pieces in one place so she could begin.

Kirsten hauled in a bucket of warm soapy water and began washing the mahogany-paneled walls. Elin followed behind her with a rag and furniture polish. As she worked, Elin couldn't stop thinking about Sofia and the mysterious owner of the violin and Bible. It was so unlike her sister to befriend a stranger. She had always been so timid and shy. What had brought about this change in her? Sofia had been reading Mama's Bible every night, too, and reminding them to pray before they went to sleep. Was this the reason for the change, or the result of it?

Elin suddenly realized that Sofia was humming while she worked. She used to love to sing and had a beautiful voice, but Elin hadn't heard her sing since everything started falling apart back home.

The humming turned spontaneously into song. Sofia chose their mother's favorite hymn, "Children of the Heavenly Father." Elin stopped polishing and closed her eyes to listen.

" 'Though He giveth or He taketh, God His children ne'er forsaketh; His the loving purpose solely to preserve them pure and holy.' "

Tears blurred Elin's vision from the beauty of Sofia's voice. It seemed like a miracle that she was singing at all. Elin was afraid to speak, afraid to make Sofia self-conscious. But she longed to hear more.

"That was beautiful, Sofia," Kirsten said when she stopped. "It's so good to hear you sing again."

Sofia smiled shyly, her cheeks turning pink. "When my friend Ludwig played his violin for me, his music gave me hope and courage."

Kirsten dipped her rag in the bucket and wrung it out. "We sure could use a lot of each," she said softly. "I don't think our new life in America is what any of us had hoped for or expected, is it?"

"But in spite of everything," Sofia said, "I'm happy."

"Then sing some more," Kirsten coaxed. "Maybe we'll sing with you."

It took them four days to clean the dining room. They had to ask the gardener for a ladder so they could wash the cobwebs off the crown molding and clean the chandelier and wall sconces. Mr. Lund also helped them move the table and chairs aside and carry the rug outside so they could beat it. Then they put everything back into place again.

When they were finished, the dishes and silver serving pieces gleamed. Elin could see her reflection on the polished tabletop. With the chandelier and sconces lit, the room sparkled. She and her sisters stood back to admire their work.

"I knew there was a beautiful room beneath all that dirt," Sofia said.

"And now we have only nineteen more rooms to clean," Elin said.

"By the time we get to the last one, the first one will be dirty all over again," Kirsten said. "At least we'll never be out of a job."

"Yes we will," Sofia said. "Her son wants to sell the house, remember?"

The sound of the front door chimes echoed through the hallway. Elin hurried to open the door, and the moment she did, the woman on the doorstep pushed past her and breezed inside, talking loudly and rapidly in English. She was beautifully dressed and appeared to be in her forties, with the fair hair and skin coloring of a Swede, but her colorful clothing and elegant hat were those of an American woman.

Elin held up her hand to interrupt the stream of chatter. "Excuse me, ma'am, but I just arrived in America a short time ago and I haven't learned English yet."

"Oh. I see," the woman said, switching to Swedish. She was only a few inches taller than Elin, but the way she scrutinized her with narrowed eyes and upturned nose made Elin feel very small.

"Well. I'm Bettina Anderson. And as I was saying, I heard that Mother Anderson had hired some new girls and that they were very young—and it seems I heard correctly."

Elin realized that their employer's suspicions were true: The nurse, Agne, was an informant. Kirsten and Sofia, who had joined Elin in the foyer, also came under Bettina Anderson's sharp scrutiny.

"I hope that you prove to be more trustworthy than the last maid we hired. What sort of experience have you had as domestics? Who else have you worked for?"

"No one, ma'am. Our experience comes from growing up on a farm, tending to all of the usual household chores."

"But we do know how to scrub and dust and mop," Kirsten said, stepping forward. "Those aren't diffi-cult skills."

Elin could tell that the woman's condescending

tone was making Kirsten's temper rise. Bettina Anderson talked to them as if they were feeble-minded.

"If you would like to look at the dining room, you'll see what kind of work we do," Kirsten said, gesturing to the doorway.

"I can smell the silver polish—and the ammonia," Bettina said, wrinkling her nose. "Don't use too much of either. It makes the house stink."

She strode across the foyer and halted in the archway that led to the dining room. Elin expected to see a look of pleasure at the transformation they had accomplished. Instead, Bettina frowned, then turned to look at the shuttered salon across the hall.

"You've been here a week and you've gotten only this far?"

"We've only worked three and a half days, ma'am," Kirsten said. "And there was a great deal to do. All of that silver needed—"

"Forget the silver. Your priorities are all wrong. Just take care of the worst of things and hide the dishes and silver away. In fact, you could have packed it all up. It will all have to be moved anyway."

"We were told that Mrs. Anderson sometimes entertains dinner guests, and—"

"That's nonsense. Now follow me," she said, marching across the hall, "and I'll give you your orders for the remainder of the week."

Elin didn't move. "I don't mean to be disrespectful, ma'am, but Mrs. Anderson is the one who hired us, and I believe that she should be the one to give the orders."

Bettina whirled around to face her. "You are nothing but an inexperienced little farm girl. If it were up to me, I would fire you on the spot!"

"Then I'm glad it isn't up to you," a voice boomed from the balcony above them. Their employer, Mrs. Anderson, was up and dressed and floating down the stairs with her cat and her cane. The animal walked regally by her side like a royal attendant. It was the first time, as far as Elin knew, that Mrs. Anderson had been out of her room since they'd been hired.

Bettina's frown quickly changed to a smile as she strode across the foyer to greet her. "You're looking much better, Mother Anderson."

"That's because there was absolutely nothing wrong with me. In fact, you can take that sorry excuse for a nurse back home with you when you leave—which I hope is very soon."

"You'll have to talk to Gustav about the nurse, not me. He's the one who hired her for you, Mother Anderson."

"I would be happy to talk to my nitwitted son if he ever bothered to come over and visit me. Instead, he sends you over here to plague me."

"Gustav is very busy. He has a newspaper to run."

"He's busy running it into the ground, if you ask me."

Mrs. Anderson made her way across the foyer, forcing Bettina to jump aside, then halted as she surveyed the dining room. Elin held her breath, wondering what her reaction would be and if she would find fault with their work and fire them. The flat-faced cat wandered into the room, stopping to sniff some of the chair legs. Elin hoped it didn't do its business on their handiwork. When Mrs. Anderson finished taking it all in, she turned on her daughter-in-law.

"What did you think you were doing, criticizing my servants and ordering them around? They've done a splendid job on my dining room. I think I'll throw a dinner party to show it off."

"When?" Bettina asked.

"None of your business when. You won't be invited." She gave Kirsten a poke in the arm with her cane. "Go tell Mrs. Olafson to fix some coffee. I'll be in the morning room." She turned to Elin next. "Now that the dining room is finished, I would like you girls to clean the main salon next, so it's presentable for my guests." She pointed to the enormous parlor with her cane, then limped away. Bettina Anderson and the cat trailed behind her.

"She certainly has a huge voice for such a delicate little woman," Sofia whispered.

"I noticed that, too." Elin went into the parlor to assess the work, and what she saw dismayed her. The room was larger and filthier than the dining room had been. There were twice as many windows to wash, along with twice as many draperies to take down, wash, press, and rehang. The curtains were all drawn shut, making the darkened room feel even grimier. Yellowing sheets draped the furniture. Elin was glad that the remnants of her illness were finally fading and that she was regaining her strength. She was going to need it.

"Look . . . a grand piano," Sofia said. She had lifted a corner of one of the sheets to uncover the beautiful ebony instrument. She tested a few of the keys, playing part of a scale, then lowered the cover again.

"Let's get the ladder and take down these drapes first," Elin said. "Then we can at least see what we're doing."

By the time they had taken down the last curtain an hour later, the cloud of dust in the room was making all three of them sneeze. Elin could see particles floating in the sunbeams that managed to stream through the smeared windows.

"Help me carry these out to the washhouse," she said, pointing to the mountain of curtains, "and I'll start washing the windows."

She was bending to scoop up the first armful when Bettina Anderson strode into the room. The woman kept her voice low, but her face and tone were very stern as she shook her finger at Elin.

"Now, you listen to me. There is a potential buyer coming to view the house next Saturday, and I want to see some progress by then. Get some work done, do you understand? And don't pay any attention to my mother-in-law if she tries to fire you. Keep working! I'll pay you the same wages that she's giving you."

"But, ma'am, there are twenty rooms in this house and only three of us—"

"Don't give me any excuses. This is a good prospective buyer, and I want this place sold!"

Elin waited until the front door slammed behind Bettina, then huddled with her sisters to talk. "What do you think we should do? I don't know which woman to obey!"

"I want to stay here for as long as we can," Kirsten said. "We're being well fed and we have a very nice roof over our head. I say we should ignore the young Mrs. Anderson."

"I don't blame our Mrs. Anderson for not wanting to live with that woman," Sofia said. "She isn't very nice."

"No, but our Mrs. Anderson isn't very nice to her, either," Elin said. "So are we in agreement? Should we help her stay here as long as she can?"

Everyone nodded. Elin was bending to pick up a pile of drapes for the second time when she heard her employer shouting upstairs. She hurried out to the foyer and saw Mrs. Anderson on the balcony outside her bedroom, throwing armfuls of clothing over the railing and shouting at the nurse, Agne.

"This is my house, not Bettina's! Now get out before I throw you out!"

"You don't have to fire me," Agne said, "because I quit!" She rushed down the stairs and scooped up her belongings from the foyer floor, then scurried out the front door with the bundle in her arms.

"Good riddance!" Mrs. Anderson called after her. "And don't come back!"

Elin stared up at her employer in surprise.

"She was a spy," Mrs. Anderson said, wagging her tiny finger at Elin. "So, you'd better remember who you're working for, young lady."

Chapter Twenty-Five

KIRSTEN TIED A handkerchief over her mouth and nose and gave the carpet, draped over the sagging clothesline, a hefty whack with the beater. Pounding several years' worth of dust and dirt out of the rug was a filthy job, but she had volunteered to do it, hoping to release some of her anger and frustration through hard work.

No letters had arrived from Tor. *Whack!* Not a single one. *Whack!* Kirsten was growing desperate. Enough time had passed for her first letter to reach Sweden and for his reply to arrive by return mail, providing he had written to her right away. She had pleaded with him to help her. Why didn't he reply? Surely he had received at least one of the many letters she'd written to him since finding out about the baby.

Whenever Kirsten and her sisters had an afternoon or evening off from work, they would walk to Aunt Hilma's boardinghouse to check for mail. Sofia still expected her German friend to come looking for her any day, but so far she had been disappointed. Kirsten had tried to warn Sofia about the dangers of falling in love. Now she would have her heart broken, too.

Kirsten gave the carpet another whack, squinting her eyes to keep out the dust. She longed to close her eyes against the reality that a child was growing inside her, as if by not thinking about it, it would go away. She still looked the same as usual. She felt the same. And she did manage to forget, at times—until a foul smell touched off her nausea.

She felt a sprinkle of raindrops on her arms and looked up at the threatening sky. She had better beat faster before the sprinkle became a downpour. She carried on an imaginary conversation with Tor as she worked, wishing she could send a message across the ocean from her mind to his: *Please, Tor. We have to do something! Your baby is going to be born without a name. It will be an outcast. This child is your fault as much as it is mine, so please don't make me take all of the punishment. It isn't fair! Besides, your child—who is innocent of any wrongdoing—will be the one who suffers the most. You have to help me!*

"Do you want help with that?"

The voice behind her made her jump. She turned and saw the gardener hurrying toward her, pulling his cap down to keep the rain off his face.

"It's going to start pouring any minute," he said, "so

we'd better take that rug inside. I'm on my way home for the day. Can't work in the rain, you know. . . . Are you all right, miss?"

Kirsten pulled the kerchief down to uncover her mouth. "Yes. I'm fine." But the gardener must have been able to tell that her face was wet from tears, not rain. "You're just in time, Mr. Lund. I could use your help."

He carried the carpet inside to the salon, where Elin and Sofia were hard at work. Elin was on her hands and knees, putting the final coat of wax on the parquet floor. Sofia was polishing the grand piano that took up one corner of the enormous room. Mr. Lund helped Kirsten roll out the rug and move the furniture back into place on top of it. They were nearly finished cleaning this room.

Bettina Anderson had sent them a note reminding them that she was bringing a potential buyer to look at the house at two o'clock today. Kirsten and her sisters had all risen early this morning to finish working on the salon. It looked sparkling clean, even on a dreary day such as this. But they had done no work at all on the rest of the house, aside from keeping the foyer looking nice and tidying the morning room and Mrs. Anderson's bedroom. Scrubbing laundry had taken an entire day, and they'd had the living room draperies to wash and press besides their usual work.

"Is that rain I hear?" Sofia asked.

Kirsten went to the window. The clouds had burst

333

open and the wind was blowing the rain against the front of the house, lashing the windowpanes. "It's pouring!" she said. "We got this rug inside just in time. Maybe these mysterious buyers will change their minds and stay away on a day like today."

Elin leaned against the sofa as she pulled herself to her feet. "No, it's more likely that they'll come and track mud all over our nice clean floors."

Every day, Kirsten and her sisters discussed how they should balance their labor. They wanted to work hard enough to earn their pay, yet make sure they didn't finish too soon and lose their jobs. Kirsten worried that she would be forced to move to Wisconsin if they couldn't pay back the money they owed. If they were no longer employed here, there didn't seem to be anyone else who wanted them or anyplace else they could go besides Wisconsin.

She heard the thump of Mrs. Anderson's cane in the hallway and went to see what she wanted. Their employer always seemed to choose Kirsten to wait on her, for some reason. "Did you need something, ma'am?" she asked.

"What is that disgusting thing around your neck?"

Kirsten quickly untied the kerchief and hid it behind her back. "Sorry, ma'am. I was beating the carpet, so I tied this cloth over my mouth."

"I am going up to my room," Mrs. Anderson said. "Kindly inform that woman my son married that I do not wish to be disturbed. Nor do I appreciate strangers in my bedroom. I wish Bettina would get it through her wooden head that she is not welcome here." She turned and limped away, muttering to herself.

Kirsten watched her ascend the stairs, concerned that she might fall. Mrs. Anderson seemed so brittle and frail that Kirsten had to resist the urge to carry her up to her room in her arms.

Sofia had come out into the hallway and stood watching with her. "I can understand why her family is worried about her," Sofia whispered. "If she fell down those stairs it would kill her."

"I know. But she doesn't want to move out of her house." A few moments later, Kirsten heard a waltz playing faintly in the distance. "There's that music again. Where do you suppose it's coming from?"

She and Sofia tiptoed upstairs, stopping in front of Mrs. Anderson's bedroom door to listen. "It's coming from in there," Sofia whispered.

"I know. But how can she be making music in her bedroom?" Kirsten asked. "It sounds like an entire orchestra." Sofia held her finger to her lips and tiptoed back downstairs.

"We have to do something to discourage people from buying her house," Kirsten told her on the way down.

"What do you mean?"

"Well, if the buyers thought the house was falling apart, for instance, then they might be afraid to buy it and . . . Wait! I have an idea. Come and help me, Sofia."

Kirsten hurried into the salon and gathered up all of the towels and cleaning rags she could find. "Take these out to the kitchen, Sofia, and get them soaking wet. Don't wring them out. I'm going to lay them on all of the windowsills in the front of the house and pretend the windows are leaking."

Sofia looked shocked. "Isn't that deceptive?"

"Yes, of course it is—but so what? Look, if you don't want to help me, I'll do it myself."

"I'll help you," Elin said.

While they were stuffing the windowsills with wet rags, Kirsten had another idea. "I need to ask Mrs. Olafson for some old pots and pans. Elin, get our scrub bucket and fill it with water. Sofia, I'm going to need a couple of brooms."

Sofia stared at her. "Now what are you going to do?"

"I told you, I'm trying to keep these people from buying the house. Bring everything up to the first two bedrooms at the top of the stairs."

Tiny Mrs. Olafson seemed very worried about the fate of her cooking pots, but Kirsten gathered a towering armful of them—as many as she could carry—and scattered them around the bedroom floors.

"Put a little water in each one," she told Elin when she arrived with the pail of water. "We're going to pretend that the roof leaks." Kirsten soaked a rag with water and threw it up at the ceiling so it would leave a dripping wet spot, then positioned one of the pots beneath the place where it fell.

"You have a devious mind, Kirsten," Elin said. But she smiled as she said it.

"What are the brooms for?" Sofia asked.

"We're going to use them to scare away the rats. Like this . . ." Kirsten took one of the brooms and demonstrated, chasing an imaginary rodent around the room.

"There aren't any rats in this house."

"I know there aren't, Sofia. But the people who are coming don't know it."

"I can't lie."

"You don't have to. Just run around the room beating the floor with your broom. If they ask what you're doing just say something like, 'I hate rats.' That's not a lie, is it?" Sofia looked doubtful. "Please, Sofia. You don't want to move out of this house, do you? How will your German friend ever find you again?"

Sofia finally agreed, and as two o'clock approached, Kirsten sent her into the second bedroom to wait. Kirsten waited outside the first bedroom door, watching and listening from the upstairs balcony while Elin let in the visitors. Bettina charged through the door, brushing Elin aside as she led her guests, who were also Swedes, on a tour of the downstairs rooms.

"I'm certain you'll agree that this is a magnificent foyer," Bettina said in a phony, fawning voice. "Of course it could use some work, but you'll see what the servants already have accomplished in the dining room."

She pointed the way and they disappeared beneath the arch. Kirsten couldn't hear their conversation until they came out of the dining room and followed Bettina across the hall to the living room.

"This is a lovely home beneath the surface," Bettina said. "Unfortunately, the girls are slow and very inexperienced. I don't know why Mother even hired them. If they had a little more time and a little more gumption, you would see the potential in this home more clearly."

Kirsten watched from the balcony as Bettina toured the rooms at the front of the house. As the visitors emerged from the morning room Kirsten heard the man say, "It appears as though the windows will all need to be replaced."

Bettina looked worried. "That's odd. They seemed fine the last time I visited."

"It's pouring rain, Bettina," the woman said. "And they are obviously leaking like sieves."

As soon as they approached the staircase, Kirsten ran into the bedroom, leaving the door open. She waited until she heard voices outside in the hallway, then began chasing imaginary rats around the room, beating the floor with her broom.

"What in the world are you doing?" Bettina asked. Kirsten looked up. The three intruders stood in the doorway.

"Oh! I'm so sorry," Kirsten said. "I didn't know you would be coming upstairs so soon. I-I meant to get these pots moved before . . . but here you are and . . ." Kirsten gave a little curtsy. "Good afternoon, ma'am." She let her gaze stray to the corner behind the bed as if worried about something.

"Does the roof leak?" the man asked, surveying the ceiling and the scattered pots.

"Oh! Did you want us to leave all these pans of water, ma'am?" Kirsten asked, "or just let the floors get soaked? I didn't think you would want the wood or the carpets to get ruined, so—"

"I wasn't told there was a problem with leakage," Bettina said, smiling fiercely. "I'll have Gustav look into it. But you didn't answer my question. What are you doing with that broom?"

"Don't worry, I think we've found most of their nests—and that's the most important thing. If you get rid of the rats' nests and all of their young, the problem is mostly licked."

"Did she say *rats?*" the woman asked, clearly appalled.

"With a house this old it's hard to keep them out," Kirsten said.

"Don't listen to her," Bettina said. "I'm certain this is a joke. Come in and I'll show you the lovely sitting room and dressing room. Each bedroom has one of each." Bettina tried to usher them inside, but the woman wouldn't budge from the doorway.

Kirsten glanced into the corner behind the bed again, then gave the floor another whack with her broom. "Sorry. I'll try to keep them out of your way. . . ."

When she looked up again, the buyers and Bettina had fled. Kirsten heard thumps in the next room a moment later as Sofia did her part with the broom.

"Don't tell me there is a problem in this bedroom, too?" Bettina said. Sofia gave a few more impressive thumps.

"I believe this house needs more work than we care to take on," the man said. From the sound of his voice, he was heading down the stairs. Kirsten covered her mouth to stifle her laughter. In no time at all, the front door banged closed behind the three visitors.

Elin raced up the stairs. "They're gone!"

Kirsten was laughing out loud by the time Sofia joined them. "Good job, Sofia. Very convincing."

They all hurried to the bedroom window, watching as the carriage pulled away. Suddenly Kirsten felt something brush against her leg and she gasped in surprise. The fat gray cat sat at her feet. Kirsten whirled around. Its owner, Silvia Anderson, stood in the doorway.

"What in the world is going on in here?" She looked down at the pans of water, then up at the wet splotches on the ceiling, then at the three of them. "Would you be kind enough to tell me how in the world the roof could be leaking on the second floor when there is an entire third floor above it?"

"It can't be leaking, ma'am," Kirsten replied. "But those people never made it upstairs to the third floor, so I don't suppose they realized the impossibility."

"And why are you talking about rats? My home does *not* have rats."

"No, ma'am, it certainly doesn't. But as your daughter-in-law said, I'm just an ignorant farm girl."

Mrs. Anderson pinned Kirsten with her stern eyes, making her wait. Kirsten's heart raced as she wondered what would happen.

"Why did you do this?" Mrs. Anderson finally asked, motioning to the pots.

"Because I don't want you to sell your house, ma'am. My sisters and I want to stay here. We need a home."

Mrs. Anderson didn't reply. She seemed to be studying the three of them as her cat inspected the pans of water, sniffing each one, a look of disapproval on its pushed-in face.

"We have to keep working here until our passage is paid for," Kirsten continued. "We each owe about forty dollars. After that, we will need a little extra money to live on until we can find another job and someplace to live."

"Why did you leave Sweden in the first place if you had such poor prospects here in America?"

"Our parents both died," Elin said.

"Have you no relatives?"

"Our relatives in Sweden were trying to push us out of our home," Kirsten said. "They made our brother, Nils, leave and they took over our farm. Uncle Lars and Aunt Hilma are our only relatives here in America, and they don't have any room for us."

"That's ridiculous. Hilma has plenty of room. She could take you in if she wasn't such a miser."

"We thought they would take us in," Elin said, "seeing as they sent us the tickets. But when we arrived, it turned out that some men up in Wisconsin whom we never met had paid for our tickets and we were supposed to go up there and marry them."

"There's nothing so unusual about arranged marriages."

"I want to choose my own husband," Sofia said.

Kirsten waited, hoping for words of sympathy from the fairy queen. They didn't come. She couldn't tell what her employer was thinking. Kirsten gestured to one of the pots of water. "I did this because I know what it's like to have to leave your home. I know how you feel—"

"I doubt that! This home was a gift to me from my husband. He had it designed and built just for me. We planned every room together, chose every color. It has been our home for more than thirty years. We raised our son here, gave lavish parties here, entertained the cream of Chicago society here. Every room is filled with memories."

Kirsten looked down at the floor. "Then I'm very sorry for making those people think your home had rats. I'm sorry if it reflected badly on you and your husband."

"Hmmph," she snorted. She bent to stroke her cat, which had finished its circuit of the room and was looking up at her as if to report that its inspection was complete. "I know I'm disagreeable," Mrs. Anderson said when she straightened again. "You would be disagreeable, too, if you had a shrew like my daughter-in-law trying to dictate your life, making plans for you, telling you where you should live and how you should feel. I may be old, but I'm not dead yet!"

She thumped her cane against the floor and the cat gave a tiny, high-pitched *meow*. The noise sounded as though it had come from a kitten instead of this obese pillow-sized cat. Its voice was as mismatched to its body as its owner's was.

Mrs. Anderson shook her finger at Kirsten. "What you did was very deceitful, young lady. Nevertheless . . . I appreciate it." A tiny hint of a smile twitched on her lips. "If you continue to help me stay in my home, I'll make certain you have a job here until your passage is paid for."

Kirsten smiled with relief. "It's a deal, ma'am."

That evening Mrs. Anderson's son arrived, looking thoroughly drenched and very annoyed. Kirsten let him in the front door and watched in frustration as he shook rainwater from his umbrella and tracked mud all over the clean floor. He was a small, prim man with fair hair and skin so pale he looked as though he never stepped outside in the sunlight. He reminded Kirsten of a baby mouse.

"I would like to speak with my mother. Is she upstairs?"

"I'm right here, Gustav."

Kirsten marveled at her employer's acute hearing and the way she could sneak quietly into a room without thumping her cane when it suited her. During the day, the only warning they had of her arrival sometimes was the sudden appearance of her cat.

"What's this I hear about the roof leaking, Mother?"

"How would I know what you've heard?"

"Bettina told me there were pails and buckets everywhere," he said, glancing all around. "And that water was pouring in around the windows."

Silvia Anderson gazed steadily at her son. "I was in my bedroom the entire time."

"And I told Bettina that I'm quite certain there are no rats in this house. Have you seen any rats, Mother?"

"Yes, two of them: that woman you married and that nurse you sent over here to plague me."

"Now, Mother . . . why did you ignore Bettina today?"

"She brought strangers into my home, Gustav. I see no reason why I should be civil to strangers, seeing as I didn't invite them here in the first place."

He rolled his eyes then turned to Kirsten. "What about you? What's your name?"

"Kirsten Carlson, sir." She gave a little curtsy.

"If you have found any evidence of rats, I should like to know where."

"I've never seen a rat in this house, sir."

He turned to his mother again. "Bettina said—"

"I really don't care to know anything that woman said. Look, did you come over here to drip water all over my house, or are you going to stay and visit?"

"Yes, Mother."

"Yes *what,* Gustav—the dripping or the visiting?"

"I came for a visit. Shall we go into the morning room?"

Kirsten waited until they disappeared through the door, then tiptoed down the hall and stood outside to listen. She knew eavesdropping was wrong, but her life was already so scarred with sin that one more wouldn't matter.

"Now, Mother, be reasonable," she heard Gustav say.

"Why should I be? I've told you countless times that I don't want to sell this house, yet that is exactly what your wife is trying to do behind my back."

"We don't like the idea of you living here all alone. This house is too big for you. And there are too many stairs. We worry about you."

"I have three very capable girls taking care of me now."

"That's the other thing we need to talk about. Why did you fire Agne?"

"I don't need a nurse hovering over me—especially one who is a spy for your wife."

"She isn't a spy. And the doctor said—"

"The doctor is a nitwit."

"If you don't need a nurse, then why were you in bed today when Bettina came?"

"Because I can't stand your wife, Gustav. I told you that *before* you married her, I told you that on the *day* you married her, and I've been telling you every day *since*. You can't seem to remember anything I say, so perhaps you are the one who is in need of a physician, not me."

Kirsten covered her mouth to stifle her laughter.

"I wish the two of you would get along. . . ."

"And I wish you would listen to me and take my wishes into consideration. I don't want to sell my home. Period. I don't want to live with that woman. Period. Perhaps you'll get your wish when I get mine."

"This home is very expensive to maintain, Mother. The country has fallen on hard economic times."

"Then why don't you ask your wife to sell her home? Why are you selling your mother's home? If your father were alive, which home do you suppose he would tell you to sell?"

Kirsten heard Gustav exhale. "We're getting nowhere."

"That's the first sensible thing you've said all evening."

"So. Now that your health is better, shall I pick you up for church tomorrow? You can join Bettina and me for dinner afterward."

"No thank you. I don't need dinner or a ride to church."

"How will you get there if we don't come for you? You no longer have a carriage driver. Or horses."

"I'm well aware that I no longer have a driver or horses. But as it happens, I don't need them. I don't care to attend church."

"But . . . you and Father have been members of that congregation for a long time, and—"

"Why do you insist on telling me things I already know? 'You don't have a carriage driver,'" she mimicked. "'You've been a long-time church member.' I'm not senile, Gustav. I simply don't care to attend services. If you need to know why, then I'll tell you, even though it's none of your business. Pastor Johnson is a nitwit."

"Really, Mother!"

"Yes, really."

They were quiet for such a long time that Kirsten tiptoed away from the door, worried that they would come out of the room and catch her. She had heard enough to get a sense of the man, and that's all she needed for now. She was very relieved to learn that Gustav Anderson wasn't going to fire her for her deception. And content to know that he was not strong enough to bully his mother.

Two days later, on her afternoon off, Kirsten walked to the boardinghouse, hoping for a letter from Tor. She went around to the rear door and found her aunt outside, pinning sheets to the clothesline. Kirsten knew from experience that doing laundry in the boardinghouse was an endless job.

"*Hej*, Aunt Hilma. Has any mail come for us?"

"A letter came for one of you—I don't remember who. It's on the hall table." She frowned, as if carrying a letter from the mail slot to the hall table had been a huge imposition.

Kirsten hurried inside and pushed through the swinging door from the kitchen to the front hallway. Maybe the letter was for her. Maybe it was from Tor. She snatched up the envelope and saw that it had her name on it! And it bore a Swedish stamp! But the handwriting didn't resemble Tor's, and the contents of the envelope seemed very thin. She turned it over and read the return address on the flap.

It was from Tor's father.

Kirsten's hands trembled as she ripped it open. Inside was one page of inexpensive paper, folded in half. There was no date, no greeting—only a few lines of writing scrawled in dark ink:

Stop writing to my son. You are a liar and a harlot. If you are with child, it is certainly not my son's baby. Therefore, I see no reason at all to allow him to read your letters. If you continue to write to him, I will continue to throw every letter you send into the fire, unopened.
Carl Magnusson

"No . . ." Kirsten's knees buckled. She leaned against the hall table, rocking it and sending a metal ashtray clattering to the floor.

Tor hadn't even seen her letters. He didn't know

348

about their baby. He wasn't coming to rescue her. She had waited all this time in vain. She covered her face and sobbed.

"Is something wrong? Can I assist you?"

The man's voice startled her. She looked up to see one of the boarders standing in the parlor doorway with a newspaper in his hand. She struggled to control her tears.

"I'm sorry for disturbing you," she said, bending to retrieve the ashtray. "I-I didn't know you were here. I'm sorry. . . ."

He continued to stare at her, his brow furrowed in concern. "Are you ill?"

"No . . ." She lifted the envelope to show him. "I've received some terrible news from home, and—"

She couldn't finish. The thought of Carl Magnusson burning her letters without ever showing them to Tor made her start weeping all over again. Her grief overflowed until she couldn't stop. She forgot all about the boarder until he gently took her elbow and guided her forward.

"Perhaps you need to sit down to absorb the shock." He led her to a chair in the parlor.

"Wait—my aunt doesn't allow me to sit in here."

"Please, I insist. You look quite pale."

He made her sit down, then took his handkerchief from his pocket and pushed it into her hand. His kindness after the cruelty of Tor's father brought more tears. She bent over in pain, her face buried in her hands.

"Are you certain there is nothing I can do, miss?" he asked after a long moment. "I can see how distressed you are. Shall I summon your aunt?"

"No! No, please don't tell my aunt!" Kirsten struggled to regain control, sitting upright and wiping her eyes. "I-I'm all right. . . . I'm all right. . . ." She stood, using the arms of the chair for support. The man towered over her, standing several inches taller than her. His high, broad forehead made him appear even taller.

"Wouldn't Mrs. Larson want to know if there was bad news from home?"

"No . . . it's . . ."

Kirsten couldn't let her aunt know the truth. The entire family would be disgraced. Her cousins Dagmar and Anna would never find suitable husbands—not to mention the shame that would fall on Elin and Sofia. Oh, what a terrible mess she had made. What should she do?

Tor doesn't know about our baby. Kirsten began crying all over again.

"Please, Miss Larson. I insist that you sit down again." His newspaper rustled like leaves as he laid it down. He put his hands on her shoulders and forced her to sit.

"My name is Carlson, not Larson," she said when she could speak. "My Aunt Hilma isn't . . . I mean, this letter . . . it has nothing to do with her."

"Shall I fetch you some water?"

"No! I mean, no thank you. Aunt Hilma would

350

probably complain about the cost." Kirsten tried to smile as she blotted her tears with his handkerchief.

What might have passed for a smile flickered briefly across his face. "I understand."

Kirsten took a deep breath. She had to get her grief under control before her aunt came inside and began asking questions. Besides, her sisters were certain to notice her swollen eyes and blotchy face if she returned home this upset. Kirsten had planned to browse in all of the shops on the way home and find something special to buy with her nickel, but she no longer felt like shopping. Nothing could distract her from the terrible truth that she was pregnant—and Tor didn't even know.

"I don't know what to do," she mumbled.

"Pardon me?"

"I'm sorry. I didn't mean to speak out loud. Listen, Mr.—"

"It's Lindquist. Knute Lindquist."

"Thank you for your kindness, Mr. Lindquist. But I should be going." She had to get out of there. She stood and made her way toward the front door, leaning against the furniture and doorframes to support herself on shaking knees.

"Miss Carlson, I really don't think you should—"

"I apologize for disturbing you. I won't take up any more of your time." Kirsten staggered through the front door without closing it and ran blindly down the street.

Chapter Twenty-Six

"THIS IS PROBABLY a lovely piece of furniture, but how would anyone know?" Sofia stared at the massive library desk in dismay. Mounds of papers, books, ledgers, and letters lay heaped like snowdrifts on the polished mahogany surface, concealing what lay beneath. "What should I do with all of this stuff?" she asked her sisters.

"I don't think you should throw anything away," Elin said. "It might be important."

"You're right. I guess I'll just try to stack everything into piles. . . . God bless you," she said when Kirsten sneezed. Sofia expected one of Kirsten's wry comments about how they had raised enough dust to start their own desert, but her sister had been very solemn and moody for the past few days. Sofia thought she'd heard her crying in the middle of the night. Kirsten had insisted it was only a bad dream.

They had decided to clean the library next. Elin chose to dust all of the leather-bound books, wash the shelves, and then arrange the books on them again. Kirsten decided to scrub and wax the woodwork. One entire wall had built-in cabinets with ornately carved paneled doors. The contents of those locked cupboards was a mystery.

Sofia had tackled the huge desk that must have once belonged to Mr. Anderson. She sang while she worked, neatly stacking all of the papers and placing the ledgers and books on the shelves where she thought they might belong. She would have hidden the papers in one of the desk drawers, but they were all locked, too.

"You can tell this was a man's room," she said, pausing in the middle of her song. "It still smells like cigars. And look—a bottle of brandy." She held up the crystal decanter for Elin to see. "I found it buried under all this stuff. Do you suppose it's any good?"

"I don't know. Does anyone know how long ago Mr. Anderson died?" Elin asked.

"Mrs. Olafson thought he died about two years ago. Maybe I'll ask her what to do with it."

Sofia set the decanter to one side and resumed her song. Suddenly something bumped against Sofia's leg, startling her. She looked down at the big gray cat, then turned around to find Mrs. Anderson standing in the doorway. The cat rubbed against Sofia's other leg, and she bent to lift him in her arms. He felt as heavy as a sack of grain.

"I don't think we ever asked you what your cat's name is, ma'am," Sofia said.

"His name is Tomte."

Sofia smiled, remembering folktales from her childhood about the benevolent sprites he was named after. "I've never seen a cat this big."

"I would like to speak with you in the morning room, please."

"Me?" Sofia asked in a squeaky voice. Mrs. Anderson nodded and thumped away with her cane.

The cat jumped down from Sofia's arms to follow her.

"What do you think she wants?" Elin whispered.

"I don't know. Please come with me, Kirsten. I-I'm afraid of her. She yells at people, and I don't like to be yelled at. But she likes you."

"You don't have to be afraid," Kirsten said. "I think she likes all of us now that we saved her house from being sold."

"Come with me anyway."

But when they walked into the morning room, Mrs. Anderson waved Kirsten away. "Not you. Just the little one—and stop your blasted curtsying," she told Kirsten. "I'm not the queen. Come in and sit down," she told Sofia. "What's your name again?"

"Sofia." She perched on the edge of the chair, twisting her hands.

She could understand why Mrs. Anderson preferred this sunny, light-filled room. It was the plainest room in the house, the furnishings the simplest, the windows unadorned with curtains or drapes. Unlike the rest of the mansion, which had dark parquet floors and heavy ornate furniture, the morning room had pale wide-planked floors covered with striped-woven rugs. The white-washed tables and chairs looked well-worn, with faded blue-and-white upholstery the color of Sweden's winter sky. Everything in the room reminded Sofia of home.

Mrs. Anderson sat on a white-painted divan near the window, the enormous cat on her lap. Sofia could hear the animal purring all the way across the room.

"I heard you singing," Mrs. Anderson said. "You have a beautiful voice."

"Thank you, ma'am."

"It cheers me to hear you sing."

Sofia smiled nervously. "Singing cheers me, too. When I was all alone on Ellis Island, I felt very frightened until a kind gentleman played his violin for me. The music comforted me."

"Why do you always sing hymns?"

Sofia hesitated, unsure how to explain her reasons. She offered her songs as prayers, pleading with God not to let Ludwig drown in the river or to be sent back to Germany. Hymns seemed appropriate.

"They're the songs I like best," she finally said.

"Don't you know any folk songs or popular songs?"

"Yes, I know some folk songs."

"Yet you don't sing them. You're religious, aren't you?"

"I'm not sure what you mean. My mother was religious, but I'm nothing like her. I wish I could be."

"Go on."

"She always read to us from the Bible and talked about God's promises. But after she died, I had trouble finding those promises in her Bible. Then the man with the violin helped me find God again."

Mrs. Anderson frowned. "I wasn't aware that God could get lost."

"He wasn't lost. I-I think I was mad at Him." Sofia

realized the truth for the first time as she spoke. "Have you ever been mad at God, Mrs. Anderson? I was mad at Him for making my sisters and me suffer."

"You're a child. What do you know about suffering?"

"Quite a bit, I think. I was only twelve when my mama died. I never had a chance to know her very well or to ask her all the things I'll need to know about being a woman. I didn't understand why God allowed her to die. Then my father killed himself. He didn't love his own children enough to stay with us and take care of us. He left us all alone in the world. And God didn't help us then, either."

Sofia remembered, too late, that she wasn't supposed to tell people about the disgraceful thing her father had done. She wished she could take back her words. She stumbled on, hoping Mrs. Anderson wouldn't hold it against them.

"My sisters and I are orphans, Mrs. Anderson. We have nobody in the world who cares about us or wants to take care of us—except each other. And we don't have a home. You told us how much this home means to you and how you don't want to leave it. Well, we used to have a home, not nearly as big or as fancy as this one, but it was ours. I didn't want to leave it and come to America. But I didn't want to leave my sisters, either, because they're the only family I have left. So I came with them."

"And that's why you were mad at God, as you put it?"

"Yes, ma'am. I thought the Bible promised that we would always be happy and that bad things would never happen to us. And when God didn't keep those promises, I got mad at Him. But now I see that what God really promises is to always be with us, even in the bad times. He promises to love us and always do what's best for us, even when it doesn't seem like it. So that's why I sing—to help me remember that I'm not alone."

"You find all this when you read the Bible?"

"Yes, ma'am. I haven't been reading it for very long, but I already noticed that most of the people in the Bible didn't have a very easy life, either. But God was always with them, using the hard times in their lives to change them. I don't think the Bible is just supposed to say nice things to comfort me. It's supposed to tell me how to live. So now I've been reading it to find out how to live my life."

Mrs. Anderson abruptly dumped the cat from her lap and stood. She began pacing in front of the window, her cane thumping with each step. "I didn't ask you here to preach a sermon."

Sofia felt as though she were made of wax and melting beneath the little woman's fiery glare. "Oh. I'm so sorry, ma'am. I—"

"I asked you here because I'm planning a dinner party on Midsummer's Eve, and I would like you to sing for my guests."

"Me?" Her voice squeaked again.

"Do you see anyone else?" Mrs. Anderson asked,

gesturing to the room with a sweep of her arm. Sofia shook her head. "Do you or your sisters play the piano?"

"No, ma'am. None of us do."

Mrs. Anderson continued to stare at her, waiting. Sofia realized that she hadn't answered her question about singing for her dinner guests. "I used to sing in church back home. And for my family, of course. But I-I've never sung for people before."

"Aren't your family members *people?* Was your church back home filled with *cats* rather than people?"

"No, ma'am. Of course it wasn't. But I knew all of those people. I-I would be much too frightened to sing for strangers."

"You just told me how someone's violin playing cheered you. Aren't you interested in cheering me and my guests?"

"I-I wouldn't know what to sing."

"So you are refusing my request?"

"I . . . I . . ." She could barely speak. How could she sing?

"Fine. Go back to your cleaning, then." The fairy queen pointed to the door. Sofia feared that she had made her angry.

"I'm sorry. I didn't mean to offend you."

"Go. And take that tray with you."

"Yes, ma'am."

Mrs. Anderson's breakfast tray lay on the small table near her chair. Sofia hurried to do as she was told. But as she picked up the tray she glimpsed the headline on the Swedish language newspaper lying on the table beside it: *Scenes of Terror at Ellis Island.* Sofia set the tray down on the table with a clatter.

"What in the world are you doing?"

"Excuse me, ma'am. I didn't mean to be nosy . . . but I couldn't help seeing this headline about Ellis Island." Sofia set a fallen cup back in its saucer and mopped up the spilled cream with a napkin. "Please, could you tell me what happened on Ellis Island to cause scenes of terror?"

"The place caught on fire last night. Every building on the island burned to the ground."

"What?" Sofia backed onto a chair. She had to sit down before her knees gave way. "Was . . . was anyone hurt?"

"The paper didn't say. The story went to press before all of the details became clear. What difference does it make to you? Why should you be so upset?"

"I stayed on Ellis Island just a short time ago. My sisters and I had to live there for two weeks until Elin got better. I'm worried about all the people who worked there and who were being detained there—"

"The gentleman with the violin?"

"Yes. He was still on the island when I left. I can't believe it caught on fire! D-did you say that all of the buildings burned to the ground?"

"Apparently. Look, what's done is done and there's

nothing you can do about it now. How will it help to worry about a fire that took place last night?"

"I need to find out if anyone died."

"It will be in tomorrow's news."

"Tomorrow?"

"The English language papers might have something in their evening editions."

"But I can't read English."

"Then I guess you'll just have to wait. Please leave now. Take the paper with you and read it for yourself."

"Thank you." Sofia laid the folded newspaper on the tray and hurried from the room into the hallway. She was so distraught that it took her a moment to recall what she was supposed to be doing. She carried the tray out to the kitchen and set it on the kitchen table without a word of greeting or explanation to Mrs. Olafson, then snatched up the newspaper and hurried away with it. Her sisters were still cleaning the library.

"Elin! Kirsten! You have to see this!" She waved the paper in the air. "There was a fire on Ellis Island last night and the entire place burned to the ground!" Sofia sank onto the desk chair as her sisters put down their rags and came to peer over her shoulder.

"A fire? What happened to all the people?" Kirsten asked.

"Did the hospital burn, too?" Elin asked. "What about all the patients and the nurses?"

"I don't know yet. Let me read it to you: 'Ellis

Island is a waste of smoking ashes today, after last night's conflagration, with here and there a heap of timbers not yet fully conquered by the flames. There is little left in the way of walls or any sort of erect structure on the eleven-acre island to break the desolate expanse of what was formerly a busy immigration station.' "

"Remember that passage from the Bible that we had to read to prove we were literate?" Kirsten asked. "Something about the four corners of the house collapsing, 'and I am the only one who has escaped to tell you'? It seems prophetic under the circumstances, doesn't it?"

"Don't say that!" Sofia begged. "I still don't know if anyone was killed." She continued to read the article aloud: " 'Survivors describe scenes of terror in the middle of the night, as they were awakened from their sleep and forced to flee the dense smoke and fast-moving flames. The immigrants who were lucky enough to escape are thankful to be alive, even though they have been deprived of all of their belongings. There was no word this morning on how many survived or the number of fatalities.' "

"You're worried about your friend, aren't you?" Kirsten asked.

Sofia could only nod. She felt numb with fear.

"Is that all it says about the fire?" Elin asked. "Let me see it." She took the newspaper from Sofia and scanned it from front to back before saying, "I guess that's all there is."

"Mrs. Anderson says there might be more about the fire in tomorrow's paper—or maybe in the English papers, if we could read them."

"It's hard to wait for news, isn't it?" Kirsten said.

"Come on, the best cure for bad news is hard work," Elin said. "You'll be so tired tonight you'll fall right to sleep."

But Sofia couldn't sleep that night. When she tried to pray, she realized the bitter truth of Mrs. Anderson's words: The fire was over and done with. It was too late for prayers to do any good. Sofia slipped out of bed and tiptoed from the room, taking her Bible with her.

The house had gas lines and gas lamps in every room, but Sofia was unfamiliar with the layout of the third floor beyond their bedroom. She wandered down the inky passageway and felt her way through a door and into the ballroom. Light bathed the center of the enormous dance floor almost as if a chandelier were lit, and it took her a moment to realize that the light was coming through the window in the center of the ceiling. She stood beneath it and looked up at a full moon and millions of stars.

"It's so beautiful," she murmured. She remembered how Elin had pointed to the star-filled sky when they were at sea, telling her that they were the same stars that had shone above their home in Sweden. And at this very moment, those stars and this brilliant moon were shining above New York

362

City, too. Ludwig might be looking up at them and thinking of her.

She tried to find comfort in that thought as she sat cross-legged on the floor and opened her Bible. The moonlight was bright enough to read by. But when a piece of paper fell out of her Bible with Ludwig's handwriting and the drawing he had made of his family, she began to cry.

God promised never to leave her or forsake her, but what would she do if something happened to Ludwig? What if she never saw him again? If Ludwig died, if she suffered yet another loss in her life, would she still be able to trust in a loving God? Sofia realized how shaky her newfound faith really was, in spite of the confident "sermon" she had preached to Mrs. Anderson. She bent forward until her forehead rested on the dusty floor. *Hang on to me, Lord,* she prayed. *Please, please hang on to me.*

The next morning Sofia was washed and dressed and waiting downstairs in the kitchen when Mrs. Olafson arrived. The cook always bought the morning newspaper for Mrs. Anderson on her way to work. Sofia saw it tucked under her arm.

"May I please read the newspaper before you take it upstairs?"

"Oh dear, no. You don't want to do that. Mrs. Anderson will know if it's been opened, you see."

"How can she possibly know?" Kirsten asked as she emerged from the back stairwell into the kitchen.

"That woman doesn't miss a thing," Mrs. Olafson said. "If you know what's good for you, you'll leave the paper just the way it is." She set it on the kitchen table and began stoking the coals in the cast-iron range, adding kindling.

"But I need to find out if—"

"Don't do it, Sofia." Kirsten snatched up the paper before Sofia could. "We don't want to make her angry."

"Then will you at least let me take Mrs. Anderson's breakfast tray upstairs to her so I can ask her myself?"

"Certainly," Mrs. Olafson replied, tying on her apron. "You'll save me a trip up those steps." It seemed to take forever for Mrs. Anderson's breakfast to finish cooking, but when it was finally ready, Sofia carried it up to her.

"You'll be wanting to know what's in the newspaper, I suppose," the fairy queen said the moment Sofia walked into the room.

"Yes, ma'am. If you don't mind, ma'am."

"I'll tell you what. If you agree to sing for my dinner guests, I'll let you read it right now."

Two fears battled inside Sofia. In the end, her fear for Ludwig was stronger than her fear of singing in front of a room full of strangers. "Very well. I'll sing for your guests."

"Good. Then take the paper and get out of here," she said, shooing Sofia away. "Bring it back to me when you're finished."

Sofia began scanning the pages on her way down to the kitchen. Her breakfast plate was waiting for her on the table, and Mrs. Olafson, Elin, and Kirsten already had begun eating theirs.

"She gave you her newspaper?" Mrs. Olafson asked in surprise.

Sofia nodded. "Listen, the headline says, 'Ellis Island a Mass of Cinders and Blackened Ruins.'" She quickly skimmed the story until she read, *All escaped alive. No lives were lost.* She sank onto her chair in relief. "No one was killed," she murmured.

"Read it to us, Sofia," Elin said.

She cleared the knot of tears from her throat.

"The only indication of the existence of the immigration facility on Ellis Island is the smoke arising from the ruins. The immigrants who were rescued from the fire are all thankful to be alive. 'As far as I know, no one was seriously injured,' reported Dr. Senner, the immigration commissioner. 'All escaped alive. No lives were lost.' Since all records were destroyed in the fire, a board of special inquiry will try to determine what to do with the foreigners who were under detention at the time. Newly arriving immigrants will be examined aboard their ships, for now."

"Do you think your friend was still on the island?" Kirsten interrupted.

"I don't know. They were going to deport him when we left."

"Well, if they've lost everyone's records," Kirsten said, "maybe they'll have to let him stay in the country now."

"Do you think someone started the fire on purpose?" Elin asked.

"I don't know. I'll read the rest.

"The fire, which was ruled to be accidental and not arson, was believed to have originated from an electric light wire in the statistician's office in a corner of the main building. 'I have always been anxious about the construction of the buildings,' the commissioner said. 'They should have been fireproof.' A conservative estimate of the loss is one million dollars.

"Dr. Joseph H. White directed the rescue of the patients who were being treated at the island's hospital. The twenty men, twenty women, and seventeen children were taken to Bellevue Hospital on shore. The most severe case was a woman with typhoid fever who was carried out on the shoulders of attendants. Only one low wall of the hospital remains. All told, two hundred fifty persons were on Ellis Island at the time of the fire, including thirty-five employees. Two-thirds of those were male, and one-third were women and children. Most were awaiting deportation."

Sofia stopped reading. She closed her eyes.

"You're thinking about your friend, aren't you?" Kirsten asked.

Sofia nodded. "I wonder if he was still there. It must have been awful."

"Well, if he was still planning to swim ashore," Kirsten said, "maybe he was able to escape during all of the commotion. How would they know how many were detained, if all of the records were destroyed?"

The idea gave Sofia no consolation. She cleared her throat and continued reading.

"The fire was discovered when a night watchman making his rounds detected smoke. Upon further investigation he encountered thicker smoke and flames. He immediately notified the other watchmen and they hastened to get the inmates out of the building. The immigrants were all asleep, and when the men raised the cry of fire, a scene of indescribable confusion ensued."

"I can well imagine!" Kirsten said. "With so many languages and no one to translate, those poor people wouldn't have known what was going on."

"So great was the confusion and excitement that the rescuers met with great difficulty in getting the immigrants out. Some of them had to be forcibly ejected. One unnamed immigrant

assisted with the rescue of five children, two of them clinging to his neck, one under each arm and one holding onto his coat. Many of the women had to be carried out bodily. Several became hysterical. All were transported safely to boats anchored nearby. In the immigrants' haste to escape, all of their possessions were abandoned and lost to the flames."

Sofia stopped again. "If Ludwig lost all of his belongings, he might have lost my address, too. How will he ever find me? He would remember my name, but Uncle Lars' last name is different from ours."

"I don't know," Kirsten said, "but it's a good thing he gave you his violin or it would have burned up in the fire, too."

"*Ja* . . . good thing . . ." Sofia murmured. She tried to picture Ludwig sneaking away during the commotion and escaping to shore, but she couldn't do it. More likely, he was the unnamed immigrant who rescued the five children or who carried one of the hysterical women to safety. Ludwig would think of others before himself.

"Sofia? Are you all right?" Elin asked.

"I'm fine," she said, folding the newspaper into a neat rectangle. "I'd better take this upstairs to Mrs. Anderson."

"Sofia, wait," Elin said. "You never told us why Mrs. Anderson asked to see you yesterday."

"She . . . um . . . she asked me to sing for her dinner

guests." The thought of doing it made Sofia's heart race with fear.

"What did you tell her?"

"I . . . I told her that I would."

Chapter Twenty-Seven

AFTER LUNCH THAT day, Kirsten pushed the coin Elin had just given her back into Elin's hand. "No, keep it all. I don't want it."

"Are you sure?" Elin asked. Every payday she let her sisters keep twenty-five cents for themselves before sending the rest of their earnings to the men in Wisconsin. Today Kirsten's refusal worried her. Kirsten hadn't been her usual feisty self for several days. And she had been the one who had pleaded for spending money in the first place.

"I don't need anything this week. Send all of my money to Wisconsin."

"I guess I don't need anything, either," Sofia said. She dropped her coins back into Elin's hand.

"Then we'll all go without," Elin decided. "I'll send all of mine, too."

Uncle Lars had showed Elin how to wire the money to Wisconsin at the Western Union office, and she walked there each week to send it on her afternoon off. She and her sisters owed $120 for their tickets. After sending $11.25 the first week and twelve dollars this week, they now owed $96.75. At this rate, Elin calculated that they would need to work for at least eight more weeks. But with more than a dozen rooms left to clean in the mansion, not to mention the enormous ballroom on the third floor, she knew they would be busy for at least that long.

It was a long walk, but Elin took her time, enjoying the warm June day. She hardly knew what to do with the luxury of an afternoon off, all to herself, but she loved strolling in the fresh air after being cooped up in the mansion all week battling dust and cobwebs.

Elin wired the money, then walked to the boarding-house to see if any mail had arrived. "Make sure you ask Aunt Hilma about my German friend," Sofia had reminded her before she'd left. It seemed odd that Kirsten no longer begged to run over there every chance she got, looking for mail.

"There is just one letter," Aunt Hilma told Elin when she arrived. She gestured in the direction of the hall table with a tilt of her head, never pausing from her task of peeling potatoes. "And before you ask, no one has come from Germany."

Elin pushed through the swinging door into the hallway and was surprised to see that the envelope was addressed to her. The stamp in the corner was an American one. Who did she know in America? According to the return address on the back flap, the letter came from someone named Gunnar Pedersen in Wisconsin. He must be one of the men who had paid for their tickets. Elin carefully slit open the envelope and read the letter, written in Swedish.

Dear Miss Carlson,

Thank you for your letter. We were all very dis-appointed that you and your sisters will not be coming to our village here in Wisconsin. It means we will be lonely that much longer. To be honest, my four friends were angry and did not accept your apology so well. But I do accept it because I think I can understand why you and your sisters would hesitate to come so far to meet five strangers. So I will divide the money you sent last week among the angry ones first, so they can look for new brides right away.

But I also want you to know that you are still welcome to come up and see for yourself what our community is like. Maybe you will like it, and maybe you will like one of us. But if not, it would be nice if we could write to each other once in a while. Not because I will expect anything—but just because I am lonely, and it would be so nice to have your letters to read.

If you don't mind, I will tell you what I am like, and the next time you write you can tell me what you are like. I am twenty-one years old and I also have two sisters, but they are older than I am and are already married. I came to America with my family when I was ten years old and helped my father homestead our land. My father and I have sixty acres, but we may buy more land when we are able to. Our cows do very nicely in this cli-mate, which is much like home. On one section of

*our land there is a beautiful little valley sur-
rounded by hills that are covered with trees. This
is the piece of land that I picked to build my own
little house. Everyone in the community helps
each other build houses out of timber, but as our
farms prosper, we are able to make the houses
bigger and add more rooms and put on shingles
and paint them a nice color. That is my dream for
my house. I would like it to be big and warm and
filled with children.*

*For a pastime I enjoy making things out of
wood. People say I am pretty good at it—
although I know that might sound like I am brag-
ging, and I don't wish to do so. But I have made
furniture for my family, including a cradle for my
sister's first baby. Always, people are asking if I
can make a cradle like that for one for their
babies. So even though you won't be coming to
our village, I will have plenty of things to occupy
me this winter. I am saying this so you won't feel
bad for not coming.*

*I would like to continue to write to you, if you
are willing, because you sounded like a very
caring person in your letter. I would be interested
to hear what things you enjoy doing and how you
are living and if you like America as much as I
do. Also, what things you miss from back home
and what things you like about America so far.*

*I will close now, since I have filled up this piece
of paper, but I hope you won't mind that I am*

writing to you. And I hope we can become friends. Please know that I expect nothing else. It's just so nice to get a letter in the mail once in a while.

Sincerely,
Gunnar Pedersen

For some reason, the letter made Elin smile. She could picture Gunnar Pedersen's house nestled below the tree-covered hills and imagine how wonderful it would be to live on a farm near a forest again, in a place where it was quiet and peaceful, away from the noise and stench of the city.

It would be no trouble at all to write a short letter to him every week when she sent the money. But what would she tell him about herself? There was really nothing much to say. Maybe Kirsten or Sofia should write to him instead. Who knew? Maybe the correspondence would lead to romance for one of them. Gunnar Pedersen had asked Elin to write, saying that she seemed like a very caring person, but he didn't know the truth about her past.

Elin refolded the letter and put it back in the envelope. She arrived back at the mansion long before her afternoon was used up, but she had no place else to go. She found her sisters upstairs cleaning one of the many bedroom suites. Sofia was chasing dust balls from beneath the bed with a mop. Kirsten was washing the windows with a vinegar solution and crumpled newspapers. The tart smell made Elin's eyes water.

"*Hej*, I'm back," she told them. "Sorry, Sofia, but your German friend still hasn't arrived. And there was only one letter today. It was from one of the bachelors in Wisconsin. Shall I read it to you?"

"No thank you," Kirsten said. She continued to work without bothering to turn around. Kirsten's deepening depression worried Elin. She had noticed tears in her sister's eyes several times when she thought no one was looking, and Kirsten had all but stopped talking to them while they worked. She seemed as despondent as Sofia had been on the voyage to America.

"Is something wrong, Kirsten?" She shook her head. "I hope you would tell me if there is."

"I'm fine. Stop bothering me." She gathered up the pile of crumpled wet newspapers and left the room.

"Do you know what's wrong with her, Sofia?"

"No, not really . . ."

"Come on, Sofia. If you know something, please tell me. Kirsten was so eager to get a letter, ever since we arrived, and today she didn't even ask about one."

"Maybe one came for her the other day and she didn't tell us."

"But the only person from back home who might write to her is Nils, and he hasn't written to anyone. I'm certain she would have told us if he did."

"No . . . Nils isn't the only one."

"Please, Sofia. Tell me what's going on. How can I help Kirsten if I don't know what's wrong with her?"

Sofia stared at the floor with the dust mop in her

hand. When she finally replied, she spoke in a near whisper. "While we were waiting for you on Ellis Island, Kirsten told me that she was in love with Tor Magnusson."

"The shopkeeper's son? But he was Nils' friend, not hers."

Sofia shook her head. "Don't you remember how Kirsten always talked with Tor after church on Sunday? And he used to walk out to the farm to see her, even after Nils left home. Kirsten would always persuade me to do her chores so she could be with him."

"I guess I never really noticed," Elin said. She had been distracted by her own problems.

"Remember when Kirsten left you waiting at the train station on our last day in the village?" Sofia continued. "She went to Magnusson's store to tell Tor good-bye."

"Why didn't she tell me she was in love with him? I wouldn't have talked her into coming—"

"No, something happened. She didn't say what, but I think it might have had something to do with the way Papa died. Tor broke her heart, Elin. That's why she decided to come to America. When she told him good-bye that last day, she sounded very angry. She told him she was leaving and that he would never see her again. But Tor kept right on sweeping and didn't even seem to care."

"I'm going to talk to her."

Sofia grabbed her arm to stop her. "No, Elin. Don't.

I don't want Kirsten to know that I shared her secrets with you. Besides, it's not your job to take care of us."

"I promised Mama—"

"I know, I know," Sofia said, rolling her eyes. "You tell us that all the time. And you've done a good job, Elin, but we aren't children anymore. Even if Mama were still alive, she couldn't do anything for Kirsten. Mama couldn't have made Tor love Kirsten or agree to marry her, and neither can you. It isn't up to you to fix everything."

Sofia's words took Elin by surprise. Is that what she was doing? Trying to fix everything? If so, she wasn't doing a very good job. Elin sank down on the edge of the bed, feeling like a failure.

"But I want so badly to fix everything," she said. "I promised you and Kirsten a new home. I want one myself. I made you come all this way, and now everything has turned out all wrong."

She remembered writing in her diary about how naked she felt, like a newly shorn sheep, deprived of everything that had once warmed and comforted her. She had been so determined never to feel that way again and so hopeful that everything she had lost would be returned to her in a new way. But she and her sisters still didn't have a home to call their own. Elin knew she deserved punishment for what she'd done, but why was God punishing Sofia and Kirsten?

It wasn't up to her to fix everything. Yet Elin had been taking care of her sisters for so long that she didn't know how to stop. What other purpose did she have in life except that one? What would she do when her sisters didn't need her anymore? Elin realized that she was afraid to live her own life, afraid that she already had ruined it beyond redemption.

"You aren't God," Sofia said quietly. "It isn't up to you to control everything, Elin."

"I know. But God hasn't done a very good job of taking care of us."

"Maybe it only looks that way. Maybe—"

The bedroom door swung open and Mrs. Olafson stood there with a lunch tray in her hands. "There you are. Come here and look at this tray. Mrs. Anderson hasn't eaten one bite of her lunch, you see? This morning I brought up a breakfast tray and she sent it back the same way."

"Do you know what's wrong with her?" Elin asked.

"*Nej.* I'm afraid to open my mouth unless she asks me something. And look here," she added, pointing to her feet. Mrs. Anderson's cat walked in worried circles around the cook's legs. He looked up at Elin and meowed pitifully. "You see? He never acts this way. He never leaves her side. Something is wrong, I tell you."

"Maybe I'd better go find out," Elin said.

She dreaded facing her employer—the fairy queen, as Sofia called her—fearing that Mrs. Anderson might get angry and fire all three of them. But Elin crossed the hallway to her bedroom just the same, the cat waddling along beside her. The door was open a crack and Elin could hear Mrs. Anderson's cane thumping as she paced in front of the windows. Elin knocked on the door.

"Who is it?"

"Elin Carlson, ma'am."

"I didn't send for you."

"I know you didn't, ma'am, but we were wondering if you were all right."

"Why wouldn't I be?"

"Mrs. Olafson said you haven't been eating."

"My eating habits are none of her business—or yours. I'm paying you to clean my house, not to meddle. Go away."

The thumping resumed while Elin pondered what to do. In the end, her worry over the little woman's health outweighed her fear of being fired. She pushed open the door and stepped inside.

"Did I ask you to come in?" Mrs. Anderson was in her dressing gown. Her hair hung loose in two long white braids.

"No . . . but I wanted to see if you were all right."

"Well?"

"I think your cat is worried about you, too. He came to find us and was meowing for our attention."

"Traitor!" she said to the cat. Tomte had pushed into the room ahead of Elin and sat at his mistress' feet, tail twitching. "If you must know, I've been experiencing a little pain this morning—but don't you dare tell my son or his wife!"

"Shall I send for the doctor?"

"No, I don't need the nitwitted doctor." She paused, and when she spoke again, her tone had softened. "I have a tricky heart. I've known about it for years. That's why I was warned not to have any more children after Gustav was born. I had a bout of scarlet fever as a child."

"Is there some medicine you could take?"

"The doctor gave me pills, which I've taken. The pain will go away in a little while, but I'm feeling too nauseated to eat. That's all."

"My mother taught me how to brew tea with a little peppermint in it for nausea. Shall I fix some for you?"

"Hmmph. My ankles are swollen, too. You have a remedy for that?"

"Yes, ma'am. A bath of Epsom salts. I'll fix both of them for you, if you'd like." When Mrs. Anderson didn't object, Elin set about the task.

Mrs. Olafson had all of the ingredients for the tea, and Sofia hurried to the nearest pharmacy to buy Epsom salts. As soon as Mrs. Anderson immersed her feet in the deep, warm bath she found relief. And after sipping the tea she was able to eat a little toast and lingonberry jam.

"Do you know how to operate a Gramophone?" she asked Elin. "I would like to hear some music while I eat." She gestured to a machine on a little stand near the window. It had a crank on one side and a large funnel sticking out of the other.

Mrs. Anderson showed Elin how to insert a shellac

disc into the contraption and wind the crank, and a moment later "The Blue Danube Waltz" began to play. Elin couldn't wait to tell Kirsten and Sofia that she had found the source of the mysterious music they'd heard. But what a marvel that little machine was—an orchestra in a box!

"That's much better," Mrs. Anderson said when she finished her toast. "And now I would like to get dressed and go downstairs to the morning room."

Elin started to advise her to remain upstairs and rest, then thought better of it. The sun-filled morning room was much cozier and more cheerful than this enormous bedroom. She helped Mrs. Anderson get dressed and descend the stairs. The fairy queen sat down at the little desk where she did all of her correspondence and pulled out a list of names.

"I am going to give a dinner party for Midsummer's Eve," she told Elin. "I used to love celebrating it years ago, back home in Sweden. And when we moved to America, my husband insisted that we stay up all night on the longest day of the year. I've already had the invitations delivered."

"Do you think you should give a party if you're not feeling well?"

Mrs. Anderson glared at her. Her lips twitched with displeasure as if she were holding back an angry comment.

"I'm sorry," Elin said.

"Don't start telling me what to do, Elin. I have enough people trying to do that already."

"I just wanted to say that with your heart giving you trouble, perhaps you should take it easy for a few more days. Have the party another time."

"I don't expect you to understand, as young as you are. But you'll be my age someday . . . sooner than you think, in fact. The days fly by, faster and faster each year, like horses galloping toward the finish line. And one day you'll wake up and see an old woman's face looking back at you in the mirror."

Elin didn't reply. When Mrs. Anderson spoke again, her voice was uncharacteristically soft.

"I want to live my life for as long as I can, enjoying the things that give me pleasure—like giving this dinner party. If I'm about to drop dead from a bad heart, I'd prefer to do it while holding a glass of good wine in my hand and laughing with my friends rather than lying in a sickbed waiting to die."

Elin nodded silently in reply.

"Now," Mrs. Anderson said, her voice as loud and harsh as usual, "do you girls know how to serve guests at a formal dinner party?"

"No, ma'am."

"Do you know how to set a proper table? How to arrange all the silverware and glasses?"

"Sorry, no."

"Well then, I will have to teach you. I've invited eleven guests, plus myself. We will begin the evening in the salon with hors d'oeuvres and aperitifs."

Elin had no idea what those things were but didn't want to interrupt.

"The main meal will be served in the dining room, of course, and then we'll have coffee and dessert and some light entertainment in the salon. Altogether, I expect it will be an enjoyable evening. I've prepared a menu for Mrs. Olafson," she said, handing Elin a second piece of paper. "I want her to serve all the traditional Midsummer treats—pickled herring, new potatoes with dill and sour cream, strawberries and cream. One of you girls will have to help her in the kitchen, managing all of the food."

"Yes, ma'am. We will be happy to."

"She might need you to go to the market with her and help with the shopping, too. You and Kirsten will serve my guests, but Sofia is not to appear in a maid's uniform. I want her to be dressed up. Did she tell you that she is going to sing for us?"

"She told us. But I think she is frightened by the idea."

"Too bad. She made a promise. Does she have something nice to wear?"

"Her Sunday clothes are very . . . well, they're very Swedish, ma'am. They're the same clothes we wore on the day you hired us. You said we looked like peasants."

"No, no, no. That won't do at all. Take her down to Marshall Field's department store tomorrow morning and buy her something decent to wear. I'll give you my calling card and a letter of introduction. Tell them to add the bill to my account. . . . And by the way, why aren't you wearing a uniform today? Why are you dressed in street clothes?"

It took Elin a moment to remember why. "Because . . . well, because it's my afternoon off and—"

"You did all of this work for me on your day off?"

"Yes, ma'am."

"Humph. . . . I suppose I'll have to give you a half day off tomorrow, then."

"That isn't necessary, ma'am. I finished all of my errands today."

Mrs. Anderson struggled to rise, and Elin bent to help her, taking her arm. For once the fairy queen didn't wave Elin away. "We'll go into the dining room now, and I'll instruct you on the proper way to set the table and serve the meal."

She limped through the foyer, pausing to look into the library. She stood in the doorway for a long moment before turning away, then walked into the salon and looked all around. Finally, Mrs. Anderson crossed the hall to the dining room.

"You girls have done a lovely job," she said. Her voice was very soft and a little hoarse. "My home looks beautiful again. Thank you."

Chapter Twenty-Eight

THE DOORBELL CHIMES echoed through the foyer. Kirsten opened the huge front door for a young Swedish couple in their thirties, dressed in American clothing. "*God afton*," she said in greeting. "*Välkommen*. May I take your wraps?"

Mrs. Anderson had given Kirsten the task of

answering the door for her dinner guests and taking their coats and hats. Kirsten escorted the young couple into the salon, where Elin served appetizers and punch, then pulled Elin aside.

"I thought the fairy queen's guests would all be old, like her," Kirsten whispered.

"Shh. Mrs. Anderson has very good hearing, you know."

"And why do you suppose she invited her son and his wife? I thought they didn't get along."

"They don't. I think she wants to make a point with them, proving that she's in good health and capable of living alone."

"Is she, though? In good health, I mean?"

Elin shrugged. "Who knows?"

"It must be nerve-wracking for Sofia, hiding in the kitchen, waiting until it's time to sing. How's she doing?"

"She was busy helping Mrs. Olafson with dinner the last time I went out there. We'd better get back to work now."

Elin turned to serve the newest guests some punch, and Kirsten hurried back to the foyer. It was still light outside on the eve of the longest day, even though Chicago wasn't as far north as Sweden. Kirsten wondered if Tor was celebrating the festival back home, watching the young village girls dance around the maypole. Midsummer's Eve was a magical night for love. According to tradition, if you picked seven different kinds of wild flowers on your way home from the festivities and placed them under your pillow, you would dream of your future husband. Kirsten swore she had dreamed of Tor.

The door chimes jolted her out of her reverie. When she opened the door, the lone gentleman standing on the front step looked familiar. It took her a moment to realize that he was the man who had heard her crying at the boardinghouse last week and loaned her his handkerchief.

"Oh! It's you! . . . Um, Mr. Lindquist, isn't it?"

"Yes." He frowned, as if trying to place where he had seen her, his pale eyebrows furrowed in thought. They were several shades lighter than his sandy hair and mustache. Kirsten hadn't taken a very good look at him on the day they'd met, but now she noticed the fine lines around his eyes and realized that he was at least ten years older than she was.

"Ah, yes," he finally said. "You're the young lady from the . . . you're Mrs. Larson's niece, aren't you?"

"Yes." She looked down at the floor, embarrassed for losing her composure in front of him. "Please, come in. I'll take your hat and coat." He removed them, and she draped the coat over her arm. "Come this way, please. Mrs. Anderson and her guests are in the salon."

"Don't bother showing me. I'll find it." She watched him stride away and noticed how nicely dressed he was. His leanness made him seem even taller than she remembered. She thought it was curious that he had arrived alone, then realized that if he had a wife he wouldn't be living in Aunt Hilma's boardinghouse.

As Kirsten lifted his coat from her arm to hang it in the closet, something fell from his pocket and dropped to the floor. She picked up a palm-sized leather folder. Inside was a photograph of Mr. Lindquist posing with a woman and a small child. The woman was very pretty, with white-blond hair and delicate features. The little boy, who was about two years old, bore a strong resemblance to his mother, including his pale hair. Mr. Lindquist must be living in the boardinghouse while waiting for his family to arrive from Sweden.

The photo brought tears to Kirsten's eyes, reminding her once again of Tor and of the child he didn't know he had fathered. They should all be together, forming a family like the one in the picture. But it was impossible. Her dream of a life with Tor would never come true. She quickly dried her tears and returned the photo to Mr. Lindquist's coat pocket.

Meeting him a second time had rekindled Kirsten's grief, reminding her of the day she'd received the terrible letter from Tor's father. She closed her eyes and drew a deep breath to compose herself. She needed to get through this evening without breaking down. She could let her tears fall freely when she was alone in her bed later that night. That was when she always wrestled with the question that still had no answer: What was she going to do about her baby?

Eventually the party moved into the dining room, and Kirsten concentrated on serving dinner to Mrs. Anderson and her eleven guests. Her biggest fear was that she would spill something on one of the visitors and ruin their evening. The elaborate meal progressed slowly, taking several hours, and she eavesdropped on the dinner conversation while she worked. She learned that Mr. Lindquist worked for the Swedish language newspaper that Mrs. Anderson's husband had founded and that her son now managed. In fact, most of the dinner guests seemed to have some connection to the newspaper.

By the time Kirsten served dessert, her feet ached, but at least the work had kept her mind off her sorrow. "These are the last of the dessert plates," she announced as she pushed through the swinging door into the kitchen. "I think they're ready for—" She stopped short. Sofia had changed into the new skirt and shirtwaist that she and Elin had bought at the American department store. Elin had helped her pin up her hair. Today was Sofia's seventeenth birthday.

"You look beautiful," Kirsten told her. "This party should have been for you."

"We've been so busy with the dinner preparations," Elin said, "that we haven't had time to do anything to celebrate. We couldn't even shop for a gift."

"That's all right," Sofia said.

"I promised her that she could buy a treat for herself on her next day off," Elin said.

"But I don't need anything. These new clothes are the most wonderful birthday present I've ever had."

The long dark skirt was simple, yet elegant. The white silk blouse had rows and rows of tiny pleats and delicate ruffles that made Sofia look like a princess. But her face looked as white as her blouse.

"Are you all right?" Kirsten asked. "You look like you might faint. Maybe you'd better lie down for a minute."

"She can't," Elin said. "It's almost time for her to sing."

"I feel like I can't breathe. I don't know how I'll ever be able to sing."

"I didn't lace you up too tightly, did I?" Elin asked.

Sofia shook her head. She looked frightened to death.

"Don't worry," Elin said. "All the guests seem like very nice people."

"Except for her daughter-in-law, Bettina," Kirsten added.

"Well, yes. Except for her. But hear them laughing? Everyone is having such a good time. I don't think you need to worry. You have a beautiful voice, Sofia. They'll be thrilled to hear you."

"What are you going to sing?" Kirsten asked.

Sofia held up their mother's hymnbook. "Some of these songs. I dug Mama's book out of the trunk." Her hand shook like a branch in a windstorm. Kirsten could think of nothing to say to calm her sister's fears, so she simply pulled her into her arms and hugged her.

When it was time for Sofia to join the guests in the salon, Kirsten took her arm and walked with her to the door. "Close your eyes and pretend that you're singing to the man you love," she whispered.

Sofia nodded, then drew a deep breath and walked into the room.

Kirsten and Elin stood listening outside the doorway as Mrs. Anderson introduced Sofia. She made no mention of the fact that Sofia was her maid but simply stated that she was newly arrived from Sweden and was going to sing for them. One of the female guests agreed to play the piano for her. The room grew hushed the moment Sofia began to sing. She had a truly remarkable voice, and her singing sounded so effortless that no one would ever guess how nervous she was. The beauty of it sent shivers through Kirsten.

Sofia was so young and innocent and beautiful. She had her whole life ahead of her, filled with promise. But her future was going to be ruined when everyone found out about Kirsten's baby.

"Kirsten, you're crying," Elin said. "What's wrong?"

"Nothing's wrong," Kirsten lied as she wiped her eyes. "I'm just so proud of our little Sofia. She looks beautiful, doesn't she?"

Kirsten wondered how much longer she could hide her despair. Day after day, her thoughts were filled with the baby and with Tor and with her impossible situation. Her sisters had begun to notice her gloom and had heard her crying in the night. They were asking too many questions. Even though the truth was a heavy burden to carry alone, she couldn't bear to tell her sisters. After reading Elin's diary, Kirsten knew how much pain her sister had endured already. Now Elin and Sofia would suffer more scorn once the truth became obvious. If only she knew what to do.

Mrs. Anderson and her guests applauded when Sofia finished. They requested song after song, all the traditional Midsummer's Eve folk songs. Kirsten peeked into the room and saw that Sofia had begun to relax. Her shy smile told Kirsten she was enjoying herself.

"Is she available, Silvia?" one of the guests asked Mrs. Anderson. "I would love to have her sing for one of my parties."

"She's another Jenny Lind, the Swedish Nightingale," someone else said.

Shortly before the guests began to leave, Kirsten raced up to the third floor and retrieved Mr. Lindquist's handkerchief, which she had laundered, starched, and pressed. She handed it to him as she gave him his coat.

"Thank you so much for your kindness the other day, Mr. Lindquist."

"It was nothing."

He slipped his left hand into his pocket as he put on his coat and his pale brows arched in surprise. He quickly searched his other pocket and Kirsten saw his relief when he pulled out the leather folder. She had put it in the wrong pocket. He gave Kirsten an odd look as he transferred the photograph to the other side. She quickly turned away to retrieve another guest's coat from the closet as Mr. Lindquist bid his hostess good-night.

By the time Kirsten and her sisters finished cleaning up and washing all of the dishes, it was after midnight. Exhaustion numbed Kirsten, and she struggled to hold back her emotions. But Sofia beamed with happiness as she changed into her nightgown upstairs in their room.

"You were wonderful," Elin told her. "I wish Mama could have heard you sing tonight."

"Maybe she was listening up in heaven," Sofia said.

"She would have been so proud of you," Kirsten said. "I know I was proud of you."

"Tomorrow is my morning off," Elin said, "but I think Sofia should take it. It wasn't fair that you had to work on your birthday."

"You and Kirsten worked a lot harder than I did. Besides, I'd rather have the evening off that Mrs. Anderson assigned me this week so I won't miss my English class."

Kirsten knew Sofia was trying to learn English so she would be able to converse with the man she'd met on Ellis Island. Sofia still believed that he would be coming to find her, even though three weeks had passed. Kirsten had tried to warn her about the pain of heartbreak, but she hadn't listened. Now, as

Kirsten imagined Tor dancing around the maypole tonight with another girl, her thoughts spiraled into despair.

"Kirsten?" Elin had been speaking to her.

"I'm sorry. What did you say?"

"I said you should take tomorrow morning off and go to church. You've seemed so sad these past few days."

"I'm not *sad,*" she said irritably. "Why are you trying to make everyone go to church in your place? Why don't *you* want to go?"

"Because I think the party exhausted Mrs. Anderson, and I should stay home and take care of her."

Kirsten punched her pillow a few times to take out the lumps—and her frustrations—then climbed into bed. "Fine. If you are foolish enough to give away your time off, then I'll be glad to take it."

Kirsten didn't really want to go to church the next day, but she dressed in her Sunday clothes anyway and left the house. She could let her tears fall freely while she walked there, and afterward she could go to the little park a few blocks from the church and sit for awhile. She needed to figure out what to do.

Maybe she should take all of her money on their next payday and run away until after the baby was born. But where would she go? How would she live? She had no idea.

Kirsten reached the church and walked blindly up

the steps, deep in thought. Someone held the door open for her.

"Good morning, Miss Carlson." She looked up in surprise. Mr. Lindquist again. "I enjoyed your sister's singing last night. She has an exceptional voice."

"Yes . . . thank you for saying so," she mumbled. She hurried inside. Kirsten recalled the picture Mr. Lindquist carried in his pocket, and she hated him. Why couldn't Tor love her the way he loved his wife, carrying her picture everywhere he went? Why couldn't Tor be a loving father?

She couldn't sing any of the hymns. She barely paid attention to the liturgy. When she did bring her wandering attention back to the service, she saw that the pastor was preparing to baptize a baby. She gazed at the young, happy couple and could no longer hold back her tears. It had been a mistake to come here.

Kirsten stood and rushed out of the pew, not caring whose toes she stepped on as she fled from the church. She walked down the street blindly, letting her tears fall, not noticing or caring where she went. Without a surname or a father, her baby would never be baptized by the church. She would be excommunicated when they discovered the truth. She had ruined her life—and her sisters' lives.

Kirsten trudged onward as if plowing through deep snow in a blinding blizzard, with no hope of ever reaching her destination. She understood her father's despair, how he could feel so distraught that he no longer wanted to live. She didn't want to live, either.

She should end her life right now, while her sisters weren't there to stop her. All she had to do was step in front of a streetcar and her misery would end. She and her baby would die together. Tor and his family didn't want either of them.

She would act quickly, without thinking about it. Papa had tried to make his death look like an accident, and she would do the same. The streetcar rode on rails like a train, but it traveled right down the middle of the street alongside all of the horses and carriages. It couldn't swerve to avoid her. She saw one coming and stepped off the curb, closing her eyes as she walked straight into its path.

But instead of the vehicle's crushing impact, Kirsten felt hands gripping her waist, pulling her to one side. She lost her balance and fell facedown, landing hard on the cobbled street. The person who had saved her landed on top of her.

She felt stunned and bruised . . . and very disappointed to be alive. She spit dirt from her mouth and tasted blood where she had bitten her lip. Her hands and face were scratched and stinging from the brick cobblestones.

"Are you all right?" her rescuer asked in Swedish. "Did I hurt you?" She looked up as he struggled to his feet.

Mr. Lindquist.

"Oh no," she moaned.

He stretched out his hand to help her, but she covered her face instead. He bent down to lift her to her feet, then led her back to the sidewalk, reassuring the crowd that had started to gather. He spoke to them in English.

Kirsten began to weep. She longed to sink down in the middle of the sidewalk, but Mr. Lindquist wrapped his arm firmly around her and propelled her along, holding her upright. She couldn't see where they were going through her tears. Thankfully, he didn't say a word to her.

They finally stopped when they reached the little park near the boardinghouse. Mr. Lindquist led her to a bench and made her sit down. Kirsten knew she should thank him for saving her life, but she wasn't thankful. Her pain would have ended by now if she had died.

"Why did you follow me from church?" she asked when she was finally in control of her emotions.

"I could see that you were upset, and I had a feeling that you might . . . well, that you might try to harm yourself. It seems I was correct."

"How dare you!" she said angrily. "I didn't even know what I was going to do, so how could you possibly know?"

He paused, then said quietly, "Because I once tried to end my life, too." He pushed back his coat sleeve and lifted his shirt cuff to expose a jagged, glossy scar on his wrist. "When you've been as despairing as I have been, you can see despair in others."

"You should have let me die. My life is ruined. My

sisters—" She couldn't finish. She covered her face again.

He reached into his pocket, and she thought he was going to offer her his handkerchief. Instead, he pulled out the photograph that she had seen at the party last night and handed it to her.

"This is my wife, Flora, and our son, Torkel. He's four years old now." Mr. Lindquist paused, holding his fist against his mouth as if trying to contain his emotions. "Flora died two years ago in Sweden while giving birth to our second child. The baby died, as well. I didn't think I could go on without her. I didn't want to try."

"I'm sorry," she murmured.

"After I tried to kill myself, my friends and family advised me to move to America and start a new life, get away from the memories. I am supposed to meet someone new and then send for Torkel to come and live with me once I am settled. But my grief is unending. I have tried to forget Flora, but I can't. I still love her." He took the picture from Kirsten and returned it to his pocket without looking at it. He kept his hand in his pocket.

"I would like to send to Sweden for my son," he continued. "He's all I have left of Flora. But right now I'm not able to care for him as I should—and I don't mean just giving him food and clothing and a home. He needs love, Miss Carlson, and I have none to offer." He sighed and gazed down at his feet, waiting.

Kirsten knew it was her turn to confess, but she was afraid to. A man who loved his wife and child as much as Mr. Lindquist did would be appalled to learn that she had chosen to kill her child along with herself. His wife and baby would have given anything to live. But Kirsten owed him an explanation after he'd saved her life.

"I'm sorry for your loss, Mr. Lindquist. And when I tell you why I wanted to die, you will be sorry that you saved me." He waited, saying nothing.

"I was in love . . . no, I am still in love . . . with a man from back home in Sweden. Tor said that he loved me, but it was a lie . . . and so . . ." Kirsten couldn't bring herself to tell Mr. Lindquist about the baby. That secret was much too shameful. It was a moment before she could continue. She heard birds chirping in the trees and felt angry with them for being so cheerful.

"I left Sweden because Tor's father wouldn't allow us to get married. He's an important man in our village, and my father . . ." She stopped, unable to say the words out loud, especially when she had just tried to do the same thing he had done. "When Tor was forced to choose between my wishes and his father's, he cared more about inheriting his father's store than he did about marrying me."

"I see," he said softly. "I will spare you the lectures about how young you are and how you surely will find love again, one day. I've heard all those assurances myself, and I don't believe a word of them, either."

Kirsten drew a shuddering breath, then exhaled. "On the day we first met in the boardinghouse, I had just received a letter from Tor's father. I have been writing to Tor since leaving Sweden, but his father has been burning all of my letters without letting him read them. He told me to stop writing."

Mr. Lindquist was quiet for a moment before saying, "I suppose I'm in no position to criticize you for walking in front of a streetcar. Nor will I lie and say that the pain of lost love will go away any time soon. But it is true that I now regret trying to end my life. My son deserves at least one parent. And I believe that in your situation, Miss Carlson, you will one day be glad that your life didn't end today."

"You don't know if that's true," she said bitterly. "You don't know whether my life will ever get any better."

"It's true, I don't. But I watched you and your sisters last night and I saw that you share a lot of love for one another. I believe it would hurt them deeply to lose you."

Kirsten knew he was right. She and Elin and Sofia had wept at too many graves already. It would be hard for them to endure another loss. But if she lived, her disgrace would taint both of them.

"Suicide is a sin against the sovereignty of God," Mr. Lindquist continued. "I believe that now. By trying to end my life, I was saying that I knew more about the future than God did. I was taking my life into my own hands when sovereignty over my life and death belongs to Him."

"How can you still care what God thinks after He took your wife and child from you?" she said angrily. "He took my mother and father, too, and I still can't forgive Him!"

Kirsten had never acknowledged her anger before, but she saw the truth of her words the moment she spoke them. And her anger at God was the reason she was now in this predicament. She had felt so desolate, so unloved after her parents died and her brother left home, that she had turned to Tor for consolation. All she had wanted was for someone to hold her and love her, so she could feel something besides grief and loss. Everyone around her seemed to be dying, and she had wanted to feel alive again. God had deserted her, but Tor hadn't. And so she had turned her back on Him and turned to Tor.

"I won't say it has been easy to understand the Almighty," Mr. Lindquist said, "or to accept His will. But I do know that I must try. Life with God is often very difficult. But life without Him is unendurable."

Minutes passed as Mr. Lindquist sat staring into the distance. When Kirsten glanced up at him she saw that his deepset eyes were filled with pain. They were such a pale shade of blue that it was as if his tears had washed all of the color out of them. She noticed that he kept his hand in his coat pocket—the one with the picture inside it.

They would have to avoid each other from now on

after confessing their secrets. It would be too embarrassing to face each other again.

"I should go," she said. He laid his hand on her arm.

"Not yet," he said quietly. His hand felt warm and heavy.

How long had it been since she'd felt Tor's touch? A single tear fell as she realized that no man would ever hold her or kiss her again. She waited. Mr. Lindquist finally lifted his hand and pulled his other one out of his pocket at the same time, folding them together on his lap. He drew a deep breath.

"I would like to help you, Miss Carlson. I can see that you need someone to talk to and that you are unable to share your grief with your sisters. I can't offer any answers, but I am willing to listen."

"But why? You don't even know me. I work as a maidservant; I'm nobody. Why would you want to listen to me?"

"Because I would like to leave here today without worrying that you will attempt the same thing in the days ahead. God sent a friend into my life to listen to me after I did this," he said, pointing to his wrist, "and I've not felt the need to attempt it again."

"I-I don't know what to say, Mr. Lindquist."

"Perhaps you should begin to call me by my given name—Knute."

"You may call me Kirsten."

"I will meet you here whenever you have time off, Kirsten. You can rail at God and say whatever things you would like, and I assure you that I won't be shocked. I probably have said the same things—and worse. But it will help you to say them. It helped me. My anger is gone, if not my grief. When is your next day off?"

"Thursday afternoon."

"Good. I will take my lunch hour here on Thursday, weather permitting."

Kirsten didn't know what good it would do to talk to him, especially when she couldn't share what was really bothering her. But she agreed, knowing that she could always send him a note to cancel their meeting if she changed her mind.

"Whenever you're ready, I'll walk you home," he said.

"But if you walk all that way, you'll miss Sunday dinner at the boardinghouse."

He smiled faintly. "It's no great loss. And I'm still quite full from last night's meal."

They sat together on the bench a while longer, saying nothing. Kirsten waited until she was certain her tears were spent and her emotions were under control before letting Mr. Lindquist escort her home. As soon as the mansion came into view, she halted.

"I don't want my sisters to see us together. They'll ask too many questions."

"I understand. I'll see you on Thursday. And in the meantime, promise me you won't do anything foolish?"

"I promise."

He tipped his hat. "Good day, then."

. . .

That night in her bedroom Kirsten thought about Mr. Lindquist's offer. He had promised to listen to her troubles, but she didn't think she could ever bring herself to tell him the whole truth. Besides, he'd admitted that he might not have any answers.

Across the room, Sofia was reading her Bible while Elin wrote in her diary. Kirsten quickly looked away, ashamed that she had read that diary. She recalled Elin's courage and determination in saving all of them from Uncle Sven, and she knew Mr. Lindquist had been right about the love the three of them shared. Love wasn't shown with empty words like the ones Tor had spoken to her. Love was demonstrated by sacrifice, as Elin had done.

Kirsten was glad Mr. Lindquist had stopped her from killing herself. Her father's suicide hadn't fooled anyone, and hers wouldn't have, either. If she had died, Kirsten would have ruined her sisters' new life in America, just as their father's suicide had ruined their life back home. But she needed to figure out what to do about the baby soon, before that sin ruined their lives, as well.

Chapter Twenty-Nine

SOFIA HURRIED INTO the morning room on Thursday, wondering why Mrs. Anderson had called specifically for her rather than Elin or Kirsten. "You sent for me, ma'am?" she asked.

The fairy queen lowered the newspaper she'd been reading and took a sip of coffee. "There is an article in here that you may be interested in seeing." She pushed a different section of the paper across the table to her. Sofia wondered if it was more news about Ellis Island. But the paper was folded open to the social page.

"Go ahead and read it," Mrs. Anderson said, tapping one of the columns with her jeweled finger.

Sofia skimmed the article. It told all about the dinner party Mrs. Anderson had hosted and named all of the people who had attended. Then Sofia read: *The evening's entertainment was provided by a young Swedish nightingale named Sofia Carlson, whose astounding voice bore an uncanny resemblance to the legendary Jenny Lind's. We will be hearing much more about this phenomenal young talent in the months to come.*

Sofia looked up. She didn't know what to say.

"The author of that article is a friend of mine. She was here the other night. She also sent me this thank-you note." Mrs. Anderson held a small white envelope aloft. "She would like you to sing for her son's engagement party next Tuesday."

"I-I couldn't!"

"Oh, don't be such a nitwit," Mrs. Anderson said impatiently. "She's willing to pay you, of course. I understand that the usual rate for something of this sort is around five dollars."

"Five dollars?"

"Yes. That's more than a week's pay, simply for singing a few songs. Does that change your mind?"

"I . . . I . . ." Sofia couldn't imagine earning that much money just for singing.

"You're not going to give me a bunch of poppycock about having stage fright, are you? I could tell that you enjoyed yourself once you got started."

"No, ma'am. . . . I mean, yes, ma'am. I did enjoy singing for your guests." Sofia's nervousness had faded once she saw her audience responding favorably, and she had gradually gained confidence. The people had responded to her the same way they had at Ellis Island when Ludwig played his violin. The idea of going to a strange house frightened her, but how could she turn down the chance to earn more than a week's pay in one night?

"I will give you the evening off, of course," Mrs. Anderson said. "In fact, I will be attending the party myself. You may ride there with me."

"I-I don't know what to say."

"Thank you would be appropriate."

"Yes, of course. Thank you." Sofia hated to miss one of her Tuesday evening English classes, but the prospect of earning so much money was too good to pass up. Before she could say more, the front door chimes echoed in the huge foyer.

"That will be John Olson, my lawyer," Mrs. Anderson said. "Kindly send him in. And ask Mrs. Olafson to bring us some more coffee."

Sofia did as she was told, then hurried out to the

404

washhouse to tell her sisters the good news. They were heating tubs of steaming water to do the weekly laundry, including the linen tablecloth and dinner napkins from the party.

"You'll never guess what Mrs. Anderson wanted! A friend of hers heard me sing last Saturday and wants me to sing for her party, too."

Elin dumped an armload of kindling into the woodbin. Her face wore a worried expression. "I'm not sure that's a good idea, Sofia. We need to be careful about going into strangers' homes all alone."

Sofia tried to hide her hurt feelings. Why couldn't Elin be happy for her? "The woman is Mrs. Anderson's friend, not a stranger. And Mrs. Anderson will be taking me to the party. Besides, you didn't even let me tell you the best part."

Kirsten set down her laundry basket and draped her arm around Sofia's shoulder. "Tell us the best part."

"She is going to *pay* me to sing. Five whole dollars!"

"That's wonderful news," Kirsten said, hugging her. "We're so happy for you—aren't we, Elin?"

Her sister nodded, but Sofia could tell that she wasn't. Why couldn't Elin ever stop worrying? Sofia picked up the basket of wet linens and carried it outside to the clotheslines. Sofia loved working outdoors in the warm sunshine, hanging all of the linens on the line to dry. "Where are you going this afternoon for your time off?" she asked Kirsten as they worked side by side.

Kirsten hesitated for a moment, then shook her head. "Nowhere. I've decided to just stay home and rest." She helped Sofia and Elin finish the laundry, then went upstairs to her room as soon as they finished eating lunch.

"I know something's wrong with Kirsten," Elin said as she and Sofia cleaned one of the many spare bedrooms that afternoon. "If you have any idea what it is, I wish you would tell me."

"I don't know. And the more you nag her about it, the angrier she will get. She'll tell us what's wrong when she's ready to."

Sofia heard footsteps outside in the hallway and looked up. Mrs. Olafson stood in the doorway, breathless from climbing the stairs. "There is a young gentleman at the back door asking for Miss Carlson. He—"

"It's Ludwig!"

Sofia flew down the stairs, racing to the kitchen door before Mrs. Olafson could finish speaking. Ludwig had arrived at last! She threw open the door with tears of joy in her eyes—and could tell right away that the man facing the opposite direction, staring out at the huge lawn, wasn't Ludwig. He was much too thin. And his hair was fair, not dark and wavy like Ludwig's was. He turned to face her and he seemed just as surprised to see Sofia as she was to see him.

"I . . . I asked to speak with Kirsten. Is something wrong? Is she not at home?"

"No . . . I mean yes, she's home. . . ." Sofia's words

came out choked. She thought she recognized the man as one of Mrs. Anderson's dinner guests, but why would he come to the back door? And why would he ask for Kirsten?

"Is something wrong?" he asked again.

She saw the worried look on his face and quickly wiped her tears. "I'm sorry. I must have misunderstood. I'll go tell Kirsten you're here, Mr. . . . ?"

"Lindquist. Knute Lindquist."

But Sofia didn't have far to go. She passed Kirsten on her way inside. Elin and Mrs. Olafson stood waiting in the kitchen.

"What's going on?" Elin asked. "Who's here?"

"He said his name is Knute Lindquist. I saw him at Mrs. Anderson's party the other night."

"What does he want with Kirsten?"

"He didn't say."

Sofia sank down on a kitchen chair, paralyzed with disappointment. Kirsten had left the back door open, and Sofia could hear the two of them talking in low voices on the back steps, but she couldn't make out what they were saying. A few minutes later, Kirsten returned inside. She looked annoyed to find her sisters waiting in the kitchen.

"What were you doing? Listening to us?"

"We couldn't hear you," Elin said. "But who is he? Why is he here?"

"It's really none of your business. Yours, either," she told Sofia.

"I'm sorry," Sofia said. "But when Mrs. Olafson

told us there was a man here asking to see Miss Carlson, I thought it was Ludwig. I've been praying and praying for him to find me, and I can't understand what's taking him so long. He should have been here by now, and—"

"You need to accept the fact that you're never going to see him again," Kirsten said. "If you don't, you're going to get your heart broken." She fled up the back stairs to her room, her feet thundering on the wooden treads.

Elin let out a whoosh of air. "I wish I knew what was wrong with her."

Sofia barely heard her. "Even if Ludwig doesn't come for me," she murmured, "surely he'll come for his violin."

On the following Tuesday evening, as Sofia finished dressing to sing for the engagement party, Mrs. Anderson called her into her bedroom. "I wanted to see how you looked," she told Sofia. "Is that the only decent thing you have to wear?"

Sofia looked down at her new American clothing in dismay. "Yes, ma'am. I mean . . . I could change into my Sunday dress from home if—"

"No, no, no. Come here." She beckoned for Sofia to follow her into her dressing room. Mrs. Anderson opened a huge jewelry case on a stand beside her dresser and began pulling out glittering brooches and necklaces, one after the other, and holding them up to the front of Sofia's dress.

"Here. Pin this one on your collar." She handed Sofia a beautiful cameo brooch, framed with tiny seed pearls. "You'll have to fasten it yourself. My old fingers can't manage the clasp."

"Oh, but I-I can't wear this! I'd be afraid I would lose it."

"'I'm afraid, I'm afraid,'" Mrs. Anderson mimicked. "You're always afraid. When are you going to start living your life? Wear the stupid brooch!"

Sofia did as she was told, then accepted an exquisitely embroidered shawl that looked as though it had come from an exotic faraway land and had cost a lot of money. This time she knew better than to argue.

Somehow, Mrs. Anderson had ordered a horse and carriage for the evening, and the driver stood waiting for them outside the front door. Sofia was surprised to be treated as a guest at the party. Her hostess invited her to mingle with the others and to help herself to the buffet table. Many of the guests conversed in English or in a mixture of English and Swedish, and Sofia was able to understand some of what was said, even if she did find it exhausting to translate everything.

Couples danced to the music of a small orchestra, which included several violinists. As Sofia stood watching them play, wishing that one of them was Ludwig, a gentleman came to stand alongside her.

"They're very good, aren't they," he commented. She could only nod. "I don't believe we've met. I'm Eric Wallstrom."

"Sofia Carlson." Her voice was barely a whisper.

"Would you care to dance, Miss Carlson?"

"No thank you. I don't know how to dance." Kirsten should be there. She would enjoy this evening so much. She was the fun-loving sister—at least she used to be.

"Dancing is really very simple," Mr. Wallstrom told her. "They're playing a waltz. I could teach you how."

"No thank you. Will you excuse me, please?"

She hurried away, searching for a place to hide until it was time to sing, and nearly collided with Bettina Anderson. The woman grabbed Sofia's forearm to stop her, then looked her over from head to toe.

"What in the world are you doing here? Aren't you Mother Anderson's maid?" Before Sofia could reply, Bettina spotted the cameo pin. Her eyes went wide. "Where did you get that brooch? That doesn't belong to you!"

Sofia's hand flew to her throat, covering the pin. "I-It's . . . I mean . . . Mrs. Anderson told me to wear it."

"You're a liar! Take it off this instant, you little thief!"

Bettina tightened her grip on Sofia's arm and towed her out of the crowd and toward the hallway. Sofia fumbled to unpin the clasp with her free hand, afraid to cause a scene. But just as she started to hand over the pin, Sofia felt someone grip her other arm. It was the fairy queen.

"You put that brooch right back on," the elder Mrs. Anderson commanded. "What do you think you're doing, Bettina?"

"Your maidservant stole your cameo."

"She most certainly did not. I let her borrow it. You would do well to mind your own business from now on. Come, Sofia. I believe they are ready for you to sing."

Sofia didn't know how in the world she could sing after her confrontation with Bettina. She was still shaking from head to toe and could barely refasten the pin to her collar. But the hostess was already introducing her to the audience as Sofia made her way across the room to stand near the orchestra. She whispered a silent prayer for help as the musicians played the opening bars of her first song, then drew a breath and began to sing.

The first few notes sounded shaky, but Sofia quickly gained control. The bride-to-be had requested a traditional love song from back home, and the words made Sofia think of Ludwig. She closed her eyes and sang the words to him, pouring all of her love and longing into the music. When she finished, the applause went on and on.

After singing several more songs, she waded through a sea of people wanting to congratulate her as she made her way to the punch table to quench her thirst. A man in a three-piece suit followed her, jabbering in English, but she was too drained to comprehend what he was saying.

"Excuse me," she finally interrupted. "But I don't speak English very well yet."

"Oh. So sorry. My name is Carl Lund," he said, switching languages. "I wanted to have a word with you about your performance, Miss Carlson. I own the Viking Theater a few blocks from here. We do small productions, variety shows, a little vaudeville—all sorts of things. I would like to offer you a contract to sing in one of my variety shows."

Sofia stared at him, unable to speak. He had to be joking.

"Our shows are mostly for the Swedish-speaking community," he continued when she didn't respond, "and I think our audiences would enjoy hearing you. Has anyone told you that your voice is reminiscent of Jenny Lind's?"

"I-I only arrived in America a short time ago, Mr. Lund. I sang today as a favor for our hostess. I've really never thought of performing onstage."

"Well, perhaps you should think about it. You're a very lovely young woman, Miss Carlson, and you have a beautiful voice. People would pay a lot of money to hear you sing. If you would allow me to offer you a lift home, perhaps we could discuss it further. I could even show you the theater, if you'd like."

"No thank you. I came with Mrs. Anderson—Silvia Anderson. My sisters and I work as her maidservants."

"You can't be serious. A maidservant? You could

make a great deal more money singing in one of my shows, I assure you."

"I-I really don't think I'd care to, Mr. Lund. But thank you just the same."

"Well, here, take my card," he said, pushing it into her hand. "Give my offer some thought. I would love to hear from you if you change your mind."

Sofia stuck the card in her pocket, certain that she wouldn't change her mind. Nor would she tell Elin about Mr. Lund's offer. Elin worried too much as it was. Besides, Sofia had no interest in singing in a theater. Ludwig would be coming for her any day now.

"You made quite a favorable impression this evening," Mrs. Anderson said on the carriage ride home. "You should consider developing your talent. There is an excellent conservatory of music here in Chicago that just opened two years ago. It's run by William Hall Sherwood, a protégé of the great composer Franz Liszt. Have you heard Mr. Liszt's music?"

"No, ma'am. I'm sorry."

"Well, don't be sorry—*do* something about your ignorance. I'm a great believer in education, especially for young people such as you and your sisters. Women should always have a means of supporting themselves—and I don't mean as servants. If I had my life to live over again, I would attend college."

Sofia fingered the five-dollar bill in her pocket, still amazed by the staggering amount she'd been paid.

413

"My sisters and I can't afford to go to school, Mrs. Anderson. I'm taking English classes in the evening, but they're free."

"You need to think about your future. You won't be working for me forever, you know."

"I know. Once your house is clean—"

"That's not what I mean. I'm dying, Sofia. . . . No, don't get sentimental on me," she said when Sofia began to protest. "It's a fact. I'm eighty-six years old, and my time is almost up. Death is the one certainty that none of us can avoid. But I have two pieces of advice for you when my time comes and you no longer work for me. First, use your talent to support yourself. And second, whatever you do, don't go to work for Bettina. She'll poison all three of you."

"*Poison* us?"

"Not literally, you nitwit. With her greed and bitterness. She would destroy your charming innocence in no time at all. You saw how she reacted today when she recognized my brooch. Selfish woman! Why do you think she never bore children? She didn't want to share my son's money with them, that's why."

Once again, Sofia didn't know how to respond.

"The fact is, I'm dying," Mrs. Anderson continued, "and Bettina can't wait to get her hands on everything I own. Mind you, I've done things in the past that I'm not very proud of, just as she has. I'm not at all certain that St. Peter will let me through the pearly gates when my time comes."

"It's not what you've done that matters in the end,

Mrs. Anderson. It's what Jesus has done for you. The Bible says—"

"Hold it!" Mrs. Anderson held up her hand. "You're not going to preach another sermon, are you?"

"If you'll let me."

Mrs. Anderson laughed out loud. "Very well, then," she said with a sweep of her arm. "Give me your very best sermon. But I should warn you that an old curmudgeon like me has heard plenty of sermons over the years, and they haven't done one bit of good. I'm still a reprobate."

"I don't believe that's what you are, Mrs. Anderson. My aunt Karin's gander back home was always scaring me half to death, honking and flapping its wings. I didn't want to step one foot out of our cottage when he was on the loose. But it was all noise. He was just trying to protect what was his—his family, his nest, his home."

"Hmmph. So now I'm an old goose, am I?"

"Not at all. You have a good heart, Mrs. Anderson. You've been very kind to my sisters and me."

"So, you've seen through my flapping wings and honking noise—is that what you're saying?"

"Man looks at the outward appearance, but God looks at your heart."

"Well, my heart is black." She leaned back on the carriage seat, staring straight ahead. Sofia wasn't sure if she should continue the conversation or not, but Mrs. Anderson finally began speaking again after a long pause.

415

"Before we were married, my husband, Gustav, was engaged to another woman. He was madly in love with her and she with him. But I wanted his money, so I tricked Gustav into marrying me—never mind the sordid details. He had to leave Sweden in order to avoid a scandal that would have ruined him and his family. We began all over again here in America, and his newspaper did very well. He built a beautiful home for me and showered me with jewels. But I used him when I should have loved him. I was too filled with greed and self-loathing to love him or anyone else. That may not seem like a crime to you, but it is to me. Gustav loved that girl, and I stole something precious from both of them—for money, of all things. You can't put a price tag on love."

Sofia remained silent, thinking of her love for Ludwig.

"Perhaps that's why I hate Bettina so much," Mrs. Anderson said, as if talking to herself. "She married my son for his money, as well. I could hardly condemn her under the circumstances. But whenever I see her, I see myself. She'll realize—much too late, I'm afraid—that nobody in the whole world loves her, either."

They watched the houses and stores and side streets go by, listening to the clopping of horse hooves on the cobbled street. Sofia pulled the borrowed shawl a little more tightly around her shoulders. The chill she felt didn't come from the night air.

"Let's hear your sermon now."

416

The abrupt command to perform threw Sofia off balance for a second time that night. She struggled to refocus her thoughts.

"Um . . . I've been reading my mama's Bible and . . . and it says that we've all done bad things. But if we admit that we've done wrong and tell Jesus we're sorry for it and begin to follow His word, then His death will count in our place. He'll take all of our sins away so that when we get to heaven, the pearly gates will swing wide open to let us in."

"Even if we've done wrong all our life?"

"If we put our trust in Jesus—then yes."

Once again, Mrs. Anderson was silent for a while. "That's probably the shortest sermon I've ever heard," she finally said. "Why do the pastors take so long to say the same thing?"

"I suppose they want to earn their pay."

Mrs. Anderson barked out a laugh. "See? It always comes down to money, doesn't it? So tell me, what do you think it's like to die?"

"Well, my mama was sick for a long time, but she wasn't afraid. She believed that Jesus would call her home when He had a place prepared—"

"I asked what you thought, not your mother."

"Oh. Well, I think it will be a lot like coming to America."

"How so?"

"I didn't want to leave Sweden at first, because it seemed like I was leaving so many good things behind—and most of us don't want to leave this life behind, either. But America is so much better in so many ways, just like heaven is going to be. So now I'm glad I came. I've learned so much and grown so much, and I've fallen in love and . . . and now I never would want to go back."

"Even though you're working as a maid?"

"I had to work hard back home, too," Sofia said with a shrug. "But God seemed far away and distant there. Now I feel like He's right here beside me every day. I think He allows hardships in our lives so we will come to Him for help. And so we will learn to be better people."

"I envy you," Mrs. Anderson said softly.

There was so much more that Sofia longed to tell her, but they had reached home and the conversation came to a halt along with the carriage. She helped Mrs. Anderson climb down and didn't let go of her arm until they had climbed the stairs to her bedroom.

"Thank you for letting me wear your pin," she said, placing it in the old woman's hand. "And if you ever want to talk—"

"Good night, Sofia," Mrs. Anderson said, cutting her off. "And take tomorrow afternoon off. That's an order."

"Yes, ma'am. Thank you . . . *God natt.*"

Sofia had no idea what to do with an extra afternoon off and no English classes to attend. But the day turned out to be sunny and hot, so she decided to go for a walk. She explored the Swedish neighborhood and peeked inside a few shops, then stopped at the boardinghouse on her way back to the mansion.

"*Hej*, Aunt Hilma," she said after knocking on the back door. "I came to see if there was any mail."

"On the hall table." She didn't look up from the rutabagas she was mashing.

"By any chance, did the German gentleman come by for his Bible yet?"

Hilma shook her head. Sofia sighed and pushed through the swinging door. A letter addressed to Elin lay on the hall table. It was from one of the farmers in Wisconsin. She hoped Elin wasn't planning to make the three of them move up there, but why else would she continue writing to this man?

Sofia put the letter in her pocket and walked through the kitchen again. "Good-bye, Aunt Hilma. And thank you." She no sooner stepped outside when her aunt's maid appeared out of nowhere, blocking her path. "Oh, Inge! You startled me!" Sofia said. "I didn't see—"

"Shh! I don't want the missus to hear me." Inge glanced both ways before pulling Sofia inside the privy, speaking in an urgent whisper. "Please don't tell her I said so, but I think she's lying to you. I hear you and your sisters asking about the foreign man every time you come, and—"

"Was Ludwig here? Did he come?" Sofia's heart began to race.

"I don't know what the man's name was or if he's

the one you're waiting for, but there was a foreign man here last week. He didn't speak Swedish, so I couldn't understand him. And Mrs. Larson couldn't make heads or tails of what he was saying, either, so she closed the door on him."

"Was he asking for me?"

"How would I know? Like I said, neither one of us knew what he was going on and on about."

"Did he speak German?"

"It sounded like gibberish."

"What did he look like?"

"I didn't see him!" Inge seemed to be growing frustrated with all of Sofia's questions. "I was dusting the front parlor, and you know how the missus keeps the curtains drawn all the time? I knew she would be mad if I stuck my head out to have a look at him. She doesn't let me be seen, you know. But whoever he was, the missus ran him off and closed the door."

"Oh no! What if it was Ludwig? How will he ever find me? I'd better go talk to my aunt and make sure—"

"No, miss!" Inge barred the privy door, a look of panic on her face. "Please don't tell her I talked to you. If she catches me going behind her back like this she'll fire me—after she beats me black and blue first."

Sofia didn't know what to do. She longed to confront her aunt and find out more about the stranger, but she didn't want to get Inge into trouble. Besides, if it turned out to be another false alarm, as it had been when the man came to see Kirsten, she would have caused a lot of distress for nothing.

"Listen, Inge, if the man comes again, could you please, please tell him where I am? I'll write down the address—"

"I can't promise that, miss. I just happened to overhear them talking that day because I was cleaning the parlor. Usually she makes me stay in back. I don't ever get to see who comes to the door."

Hope and despair battled inside Sofia. If the man had been Ludwig, it meant he had made it safely to Chicago. But if Aunt Hilma had turned him away, how would he ever find her?

"I have to go," Inge whispered, "before I get in trouble."

"I understand. Thank you for telling me."

What if it had been Ludwig? Where would he go after leaving here? For all he knew, Sofia had stolen his violin and he would never see her or his instrument again. But surely he knew how Sofia felt about him. Hadn't he told her that he felt the same way?

If only Chicago weren't such a huge city. How in the world would they ever find each other?

Chapter Thirty

ELIN STOOD ON tiptoe on the ladder in one of the upstairs bedrooms, stretching to remove the heavy drapes from the curtain rod. Kirsten stood below her, supporting the dusty pile of cloth in her arms.

Suddenly Sofia burst into the bedroom, startling both of them.

"Aunt Hilma is lying to me!"

Elin dropped the curtain and gripped the ladder to keep from falling. It took her a moment to untangle herself and climb down so she could listen to Sofia's story. It didn't help that Sofia could barely speak through her tears.

"Inge said that a man came to the boardinghouse the other day and . . . and he was speaking another language and . . . and so I just know it was Ludwig— but Aunt Hilma sent him away!"

"Did Inge describe the man to you?"

"She didn't see him. But who else could it be?"

"Did you ask Aunt Hilma about him?"

"Inge didn't want me to. She didn't want to get into trouble for telling me behind Hilma's back. But the more I thought about it after I left, the angrier I got. Please come with me, Elin. We have to go over there and confront Aunt Hilma right now!"

"We can't do that," Elin told her. "We don't know for certain that it was your friend she turned away. We can't accuse Hilma if we don't know the truth."

"Besides, you said yourself that Inge would get into trouble," Kirsten added.

"For all we know," Elin said, "the man could have been looking for a room to rent and didn't speak Swedish."

They managed to calm Sofia down and dry her tears. But as Kirsten gathered up the drapes to carry down to the washhouse, she paused on her way out the door and said, "Don't believe everything your friend on Ellis Island promised you, Sofia. Don't let him break your heart. There are plenty of other men in America."

"I don't want anyone else!" She began crying all over again.

Elin rubbed her shoulder to soothe her. "Kirsten is only trying to protect you because she had her heart broken."

"Ludwig won't break my heart. He'll find me. I know he will!"

At last Sofia blew her nose and dried her eyes. "Are you all right now?" Elin asked. Sofia nodded and pulled a letter from her pocket.

"I forgot. This came for you. It's from that man in Wisconsin."

"Wait," Elin said. "Where are you going?"

"To the ballroom."

Elin decided to let Sofia go. It wasn't up to her to fix everything. She could hear the faint strains of music from Mrs. Anderson's Gramophone as she sat down to read the letter.

Dear Elin,

You asked me in your last letter to call you by your given name, so I will honor your wishes. I hope you will also call me Gunnar from now on. I wanted to let you know that the money you've been sending each week has been arriving safely.

My friends are not so angry anymore now that they know you intend to pay us back. They are planning to look for wives again and might take a trip to Chicago or Minneapolis when they have some free time. Our little community celebrated Midsummer's Eve, and it was obvious to everyone that we needed more girls to make the wreaths and to decorate the maypole, but we had a nice time just the same.

Summer is now well upon us, and this is a very busy time of year on our farm. You told me you grew up on a farm in Sweden, so I am sure you know how much work there is to do. Here in America my farm is much bigger and much more prosperous than the farms in Sweden were. My crops seem to grow all by themselves, and the soil is very rich and not as rocky as back home. I do miss eating fresh fish, though, because our home in Sweden was close to the sea. But there is a small lake near my farm, and I can catch my own fish to eat whenever I have time. What I need is someone to cook the fish afterward. I am not such a good cook and seem to burn every-thing.

The oats and potato crops are coming along very nicely, and our corn is more than a foot tall already. We are hoping that the weather stays nice so we can finish harvesting the hay. I think we will have a good crop of apples this year, too. One of our cows whose name is Maisie gives me the hardest time, though. She keeps getting out of the pasture somehow, and is always heading down the road to my neighbor's farm. Maybe she likes him better than me, I don't know, but I waste a lot of time chasing after her, let me tell you. None of us can figure out how she is getting loose.

I enjoy my work very much. I love being outside all day, feeling the warm sun on my face. Farming is hard work, but the rewards are so nice. I can drink fresh milk and eat cheese that came from my own cows and vegetables from my own garden. God provides plenty of rain and sunshine, and so life is good. Time passes quickly in the summer with so much work to do, so the evenings are not as lonely as in the wintertime. Did I tell you that we have built a small church for our village? We will have our own pastor here very soon.

I lived in Chicago for a few months when we first arrived in America, and I know what you mean about the busy streets and all the noise. I didn't like city life at all. I recall how terrible it smelled, too. But I enjoyed reading your letter very much and hearing all about the huge house you and your sisters are cleaning. I cannot imagine a house with that many rooms. Do you ever get lost in it?

I was sorry to hear that the elderly woman you work for isn't feeling well. I'm not saying that because I'm worried about not being paid if she dies, but because you seem to be growing fond of her. You also said that you wouldn't have a home to live in after she is gone. In your next letter, you will have to tell me about the big dinner party she gave for Midsummer's Eve. I especially want to hear about all the food everyone ate.

That's all for now. I am at the bottom of the page again. Maybe I will buy longer paper when I'm in town so I can write longer letters. I hope you have time to write to me soon.

Your friend,
Gunnar

As she read his letter, Elin was surprised to find she felt homesick for the farm she had left behind in Sweden. She missed being close to the land and watching things grow and could easily understand why Gunnar loved his work so much. Given the choice, she would much rather live on a farm than here in the city. But as with so many other things in her life, Elin didn't have a choice.

By the time she finished reading the letter, Kirsten had returned from the washhouse. "We got a letter from Wisconsin today," she told her. "Do you want to read it?"

"No thanks. He's your friend. He's writing to you." Kirsten had brought a pail of vinegar solution and a pile of newspapers back with her to wash the windows.

"The only reason I'm writing to him is because you and Sofia didn't want to," Elin said. "I feel sorry for him and the other men, don't you?"

"Not really. We're paying their money back."

"Even so, they were counting on us going up there, so I know they were disappointed. The least we could do is correspond with them." Elin picked up an empty ash bucket and knelt down to shovel the debris out of the ceramic tile stove. The soot made her sneeze.

"Was Sofia mad at me for what I said about having her heart broken?" Kirsten asked after a moment.

"You made her feel bad. Why do you have to say things like that? You never used to be so meanspirited, Kirsten. You were always so cheerful back home. What happened?"

"Things are different here in America. Why shouldn't I be different, too?"

Elin stood and went over to Kirsten's side. "Please tell me what's wrong. I can see that something is bothering you, and—"

"Something's bothering me, all right—you are! Why can't you leave me alone?"

"Because I'm worried about you. You used to be so full of life, and you would turn everything into an adventure. I used to envy you, running through the woods without a care in the world, seeing elves and fairies and gnomes behind every tree. You were always laughing, Kirsten. Even on the voyage to America you were the adventurous one, making friends with those cousins—giving me fits! Now you barely leave our room on your day off."

"That's because there's no place to go."

"Why don't you take English classes like Sofia is doing?"

"Why don't you?" The crumpled newspaper squeaked against the glass as Kirsten scrubbed the windowpane. Elin took it from her hand to force her to stop.

"Listen. We're sisters. All we have is each other. Why won't you talk to me? We used to be able to talk about everything."

"Oh really? I'm sure there are things you've never told me." The accusing look Kirsten gave Elin sent chills through her. Kirsten couldn't know about Uncle Sven, could she?

"Please, let's not fight."

"Then quit bothering me!"

"Shh . . . I don't want Mrs. Anderson to hear us."

"I'm done here." Kirsten gathered up the crumpled papers and left the room. In the silence she left behind, Elin heard the scrape and thump of Mrs. Anderson's cane as she paced in her bedroom across the hall. The Gramophone music had stopped. Elin took a few moments to calm down after arguing with Kirsten, then walked across the hall and tapped on Mrs. Anderson's door.

"Who is it?" she barked.

"It's Elin, ma'am. May I come in?"

"I suppose so, if you must."

Elin knew just by looking at her that Mrs. Anderson wasn't well. She did her best to hide it, but Elin could see by the way she pressed her lips together that she was in pain. Her breathing sounded labored, as if she had been running up and down the stairs instead of simply pacing.

"Shall I send for the doctor?"

"No. And stop pestering me about it. When I want a doctor I'll call for one." Mrs. Anderson's cat sat on a chair beneath the window, watching as she hobbled back and forth across the room.

"Is there anything I can do to help you?"

"Sit down and talk to me. Conversation helps distract me."

"Very well." Elin sat. She had no idea what to talk about. It was difficult to converse on command.

"You can start by telling me what's going on with you and your sisters. I hear the arguments, you know." She waved her hand in irritation. "No, don't start apologizing. That's not the point. But you came in here that first day like you were joined at the hip, and now I can see that you're at odds with each other."

"It's mostly Kirsten. She has been very depressed lately and won't talk about the reason why. She says there's nothing wrong—"

"But you don't believe her?"

"No. And the other day a man came to see her, and she wouldn't say why or tell us a thing about him. He's someone you know. He came to your dinner party. I think his name is Lindgren or Lindblad . . ."

"You mean Knute Lindquist?"

"Maybe that was it. He works for your newspaper."

"Not my newspaper, my son's. But you don't need to worry about Knute's character. He is an outstanding young man."

"I'm worried about my sister. Kirsten was in love with a man from our village back home. She won't talk about him, but Sofia said he broke her heart. Now she's meeting with this man who she barely knows, and . . . and I would hate to have her heart broken a second time."

"Knute Lindquist's wife died two years ago. He has been despondent ever since. Perhaps that's how they found each other, since your sister seems the same way, pining for that young man in Sweden."

"Is that a good idea? If they're both grieving and are both in love with someone else—is that any way to begin a relationship, do you think?"

"What does it matter what I think? What business is it of mine or yours what they do?"

Her words brought Elin up short, reminding her once again that she couldn't fix everything. "But she's my sister. I care about what happens to her. I'm just afraid that she will be hurt even more than she has been."

"You're very suspicious of people, aren't you? Why is that?"

Elin didn't reply.

"See? You have secrets," Mrs. Anderson said, pointing her cane at Elin. "So why can't your sister have them?" She pinned Elin with her eyes for a moment before resuming her pacing. "Knute is a good man, but I doubt very much if he intends anything more than friendship with your sister. He may never get over his wife's death. But the depth of his grief should tell you a lot about his good character and his capacity to love."

"But what does he want with Kirsten if he isn't looking for a wife?"

"What business is it of yours? Will arguing about it help Kirsten? Leave her alone. She is the one who has to live with her decisions, not you."

"I feel responsible for her. I—"

"Listen to me, Elin." She stopped pacing again. "Even parents aren't responsible for their children's decisions after a certain age, much less sisters. Believe me, I begged my nitwitted son not to marry that woman. Did he listen? No. Now he's living with his mistake. And what can I do about it? Nothing. That's part of being an adult—living with your mistakes."

"I would hate for either of my sisters to mess up their lives. I'm worried about Sofia, too. She's pining for a stranger she met on Ellis Island, a man she barely knows. We have a brand-new start here in America. We've left the past behind—"

"Have you, though?" Mrs. Anderson stood in front of the bedroom window gazing out, her back turned to Elin. "I believed that I was leaving the past behind, too, when I came to America. But only the scenery changed. I was the same person inside. I have secrets in my past, so I know how heavily they weigh you down, how they corrupt your judgment and erode your character."

She slowly turned to face Elin again. "Your sister Sofia talked to me about forgiveness the other night. I think you should talk to her, too, Elin. So should Kirsten. Don't be a fool like I was and hold your secrets inside all your life. I know firsthand how much power they have to destroy you. Don't wait until you're an old woman like me before you ask for forgiveness."

Elin stared silently at the floor. She didn't see how sharing the truth about Uncle Sven could possibly do her or her sisters any good. A moment later, Mrs. Anderson began walking again. Her cat jumped down from the chair to pace loyally beside her. She bent to stroke his head.

"Promise me you'll take care of Tomte when I'm gone," she said softly.

"If you're not well, I wish you would let me call for the doctor."

Mrs. Anderson gave her a venomous look. "You were here the day I fired my last nurse, weren't you?"

"Yes, ma'am. But—"

"Then let that be a lesson to you. Now kindly go downstairs and fetch today's mail for me. I believe the mailman has just arrived."

Elin returned with one letter, breathless from running up and down the steep stairs. "Shall I go back to my cleaning now?" she asked as she handed the letter to Mrs. Anderson.

"No. Sit down while I read this. It's from Bettina." Mrs. Anderson sat down, as well, frowning and pursing her lips as she read the brief note. "Well. It seems she is determined to evict me from my home. She wants me to know that she will be bringing another buyer here to look the place over." She stuffed the note back into the envelope.

"When?"

"Tomorrow. And there's nothing I can do about it. My son owns the house, Bettina was kind enough to remind me. He has every right to sell it."

"We haven't finished cleaning all of the rooms yet. And the ballroom is still—"

"It doesn't matter. I appreciate what you girls tried to do the last time, but I think it's finally time for me to go. I can't navigate those stairs much longer."

"We can move a bed down to the morning room for you, if you'd like."

"We'll see. You may return to your work now, Elin."

Bettina Anderson arrived the following afternoon an hour before the buyer was due to arrive. She made Elin walk through the house with her, inspecting it to make sure that everything was in order.

"I don't want any of your nonsense this time," she told all three sisters. "You stay in the bedroom with

Mother," she ordered Elin, "and you two stay in the kitchen. If you try to sabotage anything, I will see that you are severely punished. What's more, you'll never work as maids in this community again."

Elin played song after song on the Gramophone for Mrs. Anderson as the strangers toured her house. Afterward, Bettina knocked on the bedroom door. "The people liked it," she announced, her face stretched in a grin. "They've agreed to buy it."

"When?" Mrs. Anderson asked.

"It will take a few weeks for all of the papers to be drawn up and signed. But I will send the movers over right away for you and your things."

"Oh, no you won't. I'm staying right here until the deed is signed. I'm not leaving one day sooner than I have to. These girls will stay here, too."

"Good. They can finish all the work that needs to be done. There are still half a dozen rooms to clean, not to mention the entire third floor."

"I would have liked to waltz in my ballroom one last time," Mrs. Anderson said wistfully.

Bettina made a face. "Don't be absurd. Have you been up there? It's a mess."

"What will become of all my things? The furniture, the dishes . . . ?"

"You won't need any of them once you move in with us."

"What if I want my own things?"

"Be reasonable, Mother Anderson. There's no room in our home for all this stuff. Most of it is so old-fashioned. . . . I don't understand why you'd want any of it when you can have brand-new furnishings."

"But what will become of my things?"

"I really don't know. That's up to Gustav. He'll sell them at an auction, I suppose."

"And what about Tomte?"

"I've told you before, Mother Anderson, I won't have that animal in my house."

"And I've told you before, I won't go anyplace where Tomte isn't welcome."

"Well, then . . . I don't know what else to say. I have to go, now. *God dag.*"

Mrs. Anderson seemed dispirited after Bettina left, her usual spit and fire quenched. She wandered slowly from room to room with her cane, leaning on Elin's arm, surveying all of her possessions as if trying to figure out what to do with them.

"There was a time when I wanted this home and all these lavish things more than anything else in the world," she said. "They seemed so important to me. But now I know better. It's not the house that matters, it's the love that's inside it. A shack in the woods will be a home if you have someone to love." She turned to look up at Elin. "That's why you girls will never be homeless. You'll always have each other. I envy you for that."

Mrs. Anderson's son, Gustav, arrived later that evening. Elin was reading aloud to her when Kirsten escorted him up to the bedroom. She and Elin both started to leave, but Mrs. Anderson stopped them.

"No, you girls stay for just a minute. What brings you here, Gustav? You only come to see me when you want something."

He glanced at the girls, clearly irritated that they were overhearing the conversation. "I don't want anything, Mother. I came to ask why you're giving Bettina a hard time about selling everything and moving in with us. She only wants what's best for you."

"Nonsense. She wants my money."

"We both want you closer to us. I should think you'd enjoy having some companionship for a change instead of living here all alone."

"I'm not alone. I have my cat—who isn't welcome in your house, so I'm told." Tomte gave a high-pitched *meow,* as if outraged.

"You know he makes Bettina sneeze, Mother."

Elin felt uncomfortable as Gustav talked on and on, explaining all of the arrangements he had made for his mother. Mrs. Anderson listened in silence until he finally was finished.

"Before you leave, Gustav, I would like you to come up to the ballroom with me."

"What for?"

"And carry my Gramophone upstairs for me, will you? I want you girls to come, too. Kirsten, grab that box of music discs."

Mrs. Anderson needed Elin's help climbing the

stairs. She gasped for breath, pausing several times on the way up. Her son had gone on ahead with the machine and didn't notice how fragile she had become.

"These stairs are too much for you," Elin said, halfway up. "You should sit down and—"

"Leave me be!" She puffed and strained until reaching the top and walked into the ballroom, gazing all around.

Balls of dust skittered across the ballroom floor like ballerinas. Cobwebs hung in tattered streamers from the crown molding and chandelier. But beneath the skylight, a silvery puddle of moonlight illuminated the center of the dance floor. Sofia had come in from their bedroom to see what was going on and helped Kirsten finish lighting the wall sconces. Gustav stood with his hands on his hips, surveying the room, his nose wrinkled in distaste.

"What did you want to show me, Mother?"

"I don't want to show you anything, I want you to dance with me. One last waltz in my beautiful ball-room. Please?"

"Honestly, Mother! This place is filthy."

The fairy queen hobbled across the floor and took her son's hand, wrapping her other arm around his waist. "Your father was a marvelous dancer—did you know that? Put on the 'Blue Danube Waltz,' Kirsten, if you can find it."

Elin knew the song was one of Mrs. Anderson's favorites. The scratchy music that echoed around the ballroom sounded as if the musicians had recorded it in a furnace of crackling flames. But tiny Mrs. Anderson whirled around the floor as if listening to a live orchestra. She was as light on her feet as a young girl. She gazed up at the starry sky as they passed beneath the skylight, then closed her eyes as her son waltzed with her one last time.

"Thank you," she said when the recording ended. "You're a good boy, Gustav. If only you hadn't married a nitwit."

"If only you would try to get along with her, Mother."

"You can go home now," she said, standing on tip-toes to kiss his cheek. "Thank you for humoring me."

Mrs. Anderson wanted to stay upstairs in the ballroom for a while after Gustav left. She listened to song after song, seated on a chair beneath the little stage where the musicians once performed. Her wrinkled face wore a look of deep sadness. Afterward, it took Elin a long time to help her descend the stairs to her bedroom.

Elin wasn't surprised when Mrs. Anderson was too weak to get out of bed the next morning. She made Sofia deliver a message to her son to come right away. Bettina Anderson came instead.

"She does this every time we get ready to move her," Bettina complained as she strode through the front door. "She has pretended to be ill so many times that no one believes her anymore."

"I don't think she is pretending," Elin said.

Bettina glared at her. "Then you should have sent for the doctor, not Gustav."

"She doesn't want the doctor."

"I don't care what she says. I'm sending my driver for him."

When the doctor arrived, Mrs. Anderson had everyone leave the room while he examined her. Bettina waited downstairs in the morning room, drinking coffee and staring impatiently at the clock. Elin had just come in to replenish Bettina's cup when the doctor joined them.

"Her heart is failing," he said gravely.

"How much did she pay you to say that?"

"Be kind to her, Bettina. She doesn't have much longer to live."

Elin hoped the doctor was wrong. She slept on a chair in Mrs. Anderson's bedroom for the next few nights to be near her if she needed anything. Elin and Tomte, not Mrs. Anderson's family, were sitting at her bedside when she fell into a coma.

One week after her final waltz in the ballroom, Silvia Anderson died.

Chapter Thirty-One

IT RAINED ON the day of Mrs. Anderson's funeral. It seemed to Kirsten that it had rained on every funeral she had ever attended—and there had been too many of them. Most of the mourners carried umbrellas.

Kirsten and her sisters stood in the drizzle. She couldn't tell if their faces were wet from the rain or their tears. Probably both.

It seemed to Kirsten that the only permanent thing in her life was loss, as one after another the people she loved were torn away from her. She inched a little closer to Elin, linking arms with her.

Once again, they were without a home. But the sorrow Kirsten felt as she listened to the minister pronounce "ashes to ashes, dust to dust" wasn't only because of that. She had grown fond of the fairy queen.

Mourners filled the mansion afterward. Kirsten glimpsed Mr. Lindquist talking with Gustav Anderson, but she didn't speak with him. She helped her sisters serve the lavish buffet luncheon that Mrs. Olafson had prepared, and the work helped take her mind off her grief. It was easy to imagine a time when Silvia Anderson's husband had been alive and this huge, echoing house had been filled with people, just as it was now. Kirsten couldn't understand why Bettina Anderson didn't want to live here—unless it was from envy, unless she wanted an even finer home.

When the last mourner finally left, Bettina disappeared upstairs. Kirsten helped her sisters clear the dining room table and gather the scattered plates and glasses. She filled the kitchen sink with soapy water and began washing the dishes while her sisters dried them.

"Do you think we'll ever be allowed to be happy?" Kirsten asked them.

"Of course we will," Sofia said. "You make it sound as if we're being punished for something."

"It feels like we are," Elin said.

Sofia turned to her in surprise. "But we haven't done anything wrong."

Kirsten looked down at the dishwater, knowing that she had done something terribly wrong. It was only a matter of time before her sin would be discovered. When Elin also remained silent, Kirsten recalled reading the guilt-ridden pages of her diary. Maybe she and Elin deserved to be punished, but why was Sofia being punished along with them?

"We need to figure out what we're going to do now that Mrs. Anderson is gone," Elin said. "We're going to need new jobs, first of all. We're still working on paying off our debt for the tickets. And we need a place to live."

"Why don't we ask her son if we can stay here a while longer and help pack up Mrs. Anderson's things?" Kirsten said. "We haven't finished cleaning all of the rooms yet."

"That's a good idea," Sofia said, "but let's not ask Bettina. I don't think she likes us."

"Where is Gustav? Did he leave already?" Elin asked.

"No, he's in his father's study," Kirsten said. "I went in there looking for dirty plates and cups and saw him going through the desk drawers. I think you should talk to him, Sofia. Didn't he say he admired your singing?"

"I don't want to face him alone. Let's all go."

They agreed, and Kirsten grabbed a towel to dry her hands. But before they could leave the kitchen, Bettina Anderson stalked through the door. Her expression told Kirsten that she was furious.

"All three of you, sit down and don't move!"

They glanced at each other, then pulled chairs out from beneath the kitchen table and sat down. Kirsten's heart began thumping wildly when Gustav Anderson came through the door a moment later, a dark scowl on his face. The giant cat followed on his heels, as if aware that Gustav was his beloved owner's son. Tomte had been walking from room to room yowling morosely ever since the night his owner had died.

"Can't you shut that animal up?" Bettina asked no one in particular. Kirsten started to rise, reaching for the cat. "Sit down!" Bettina commanded.

"I can't do two things at once, ma'am."

"Then do as you're told and sit!"

Gustav cleared his throat. "We have discovered that several pieces of my mother's jewelry are missing."

Kirsten felt her stomach roll over. She had thought that her life couldn't get any worse, and now it had. Mrs. Olafson had warned them on their very first day that the previous maidservant had been falsely accused of theft, and now it was their turn. Kirsten was afraid to look at her sisters, knowing she might cry if she did.

Gustav pointed his finger at Elin. "Are you the one who became her nurse and spent all that time in her room?"

"Yes, sir. But I didn't take anything. I wouldn't steal from her. None of us would."

"I happen to know how badly the three of you need money," Bettina said. "You were stupid to think we wouldn't notice that her jewelry was missing."

"You'll make things a lot easier for yourselves," Gustav continued, "if you simply hand everything over before the police arrive."

"We've sent for them," Bettina said. "They'll be here any minute."

Kirsten's heart thumped faster at the mention of police. She finally risked a glance at Sofia and saw the terror in her eyes. "I don't care if you do send for the police," Kirsten said. "They'll find out we're innocent."

Elin laid her hand on her arm. "Hush, Kirsten. Don't waste your breath. They don't believe us anyway."

"You're right about that," Bettina said. "Don't forget, I have firsthand experience with your devious ways."

That's what this was all about, Kirsten suddenly realized. Bettina was still angry with them for scaring away the first buyers.

"My mother thought very highly of all three of

you," Gustav said sternly. "Once again, for her sake, I'm going to ask you to hand back what you've stolen."

"We didn't steal anything," Kirsten said.

"Fine. Don't say I didn't warn you." Gustav turned and strode from the room with the howling cat close behind him. Bettina remained in the kitchen as if guarding them, standing near the stove with her arms crossed.

A long time later, Kirsten heard the front door chimes ring, then voices out in the foyer. Two policemen followed Gustav into the kitchen. One of them spoke Swedish but the other didn't, and the discussion that followed was a confusing mess of languages. Bettina's fury grew by the minute.

"Mother Anderson always wore a large diamond and emerald ring with matching earrings," she said in Swedish. "Now they're missing. She wore diamond rings on several of her fingers, but they weren't on her hands when she died, nor are they in her jewelry case."

Kirsten recalled how the fairy queen had glittered with jewelry on the day they had first arrived, asking for jobs. It had seemed odd that someone would wear fancy earrings and rings while lying in bed. But now that she thought about it, Kirsten couldn't recall seeing any jewelry on Mrs. Anderson in the weeks before she died.

"What did you do with her emeralds?" Bettina demanded.

444

"We never touched her jewelry," Elin said calmly.
"That's a lie! I saw that girl wearing one of her
brooches a couple weeks ago," she said, pointing to
Sofia. "She was just as brazen as you please about it.
And I have witnesses, too. Everyone at the party saw
her wearing Mother's cameo pin that evening."
"She loaned it to me," Sofia said. "I gave it back—"
"Can you describe it, please?" the policeman
asked.

A blush of color rose to Bettina's cheeks. "Well . . .
the cameo isn't missing. But the other pieces I
described are. You can't let these little thieves get
away with this!"

"Let me talk to them alone, please," the Swedish
policeman said. Kirsten glanced at her sisters as
Bettina left the room. She wondered if she looked as
pale and frightened as they did. But in spite of her
fear, Kirsten's anger simmered just beneath the surface, waiting to boil over. Elin laid her hand over
Kirsten's again as if sensing her mood.

The policeman planted his hands on his hips. He
was growing angry, too. "You girls must have known
you would get caught. You'll save yourselves a lot of
trouble if you just hand over the items right now. If
you cooperate, the judge will take that into consideration when sentencing you."

"Elin wouldn't steal," Kirsten said. "Neither would
Sofia. And I know I didn't take anything."

But Kirsten knew that if it was their word against
Bettina's, they wouldn't stand a chance. Again, she

445

wondered if Bettina was getting even with them for playing that trick on her. If so, this mess was Kirsten's fault. She was the one who should be punished, not her sisters.

"Here are the facts," the policeman said. "There are no signs of a break-in. The jewelry is missing, and all three of you had access to Mrs. Anderson's room every day while she was ill, correct? That gives you opportunity."

"We didn't take her jewelry," Elin said in a trembling voice.

"I also know that you are in debt for quite a bit of money. That gives you motive."

"But we wouldn't steal," Sofia said. "Stealing is a sin."

"Stand up. All three of you."

Kirsten rose on trembling knees.

"Where's your room? We need to search it."

The two policemen made them stand aside and watch as they turned the bedroom upside down in their search. Sofia wept when they held up her friend's violin and shook it. Kirsten's anger grew hotter by the minute but she held back, knowing the police wouldn't find any jewelry. Bettina seemed disappointed when they came downstairs again, empty-handed.

"We told you we didn't steal her things," Kirsten said.

Bettina huffed in anger. "This house has two dozen rooms. There are thousands of places they could've hidden a handful of rings. I'm telling you these girls are devious."

"This is your last chance," the policeman said. "If you don't tell us what you did with the jewelry, you're going to jail."

"No, please," Elin begged. "You have to believe us. We didn't touch her jewelry."

"Maybe a night in jail will change your mind. Let's go." One of the men grabbed Kirsten's arm, harder than he needed to, and pushed her toward the door. The other policeman grabbed Sofia and Elin. Kirsten turned to Bettina.

"Please, let my sisters go free," she pleaded. "You know we didn't steal anything from you. If you're still mad at us for playing that trick on you, it was my fault, not theirs. Please don't take it out on my sisters. Please don't punish them."

"Was that a confession?" the policeman asked her. "Are you ready to hand back what you've stolen?"

"I didn't steal anything. Mrs. Anderson is mad at me for pretending that the roof leaked and—"

He shoved her through the door. "Tell it to the judge, miss."

The police wagon waiting by the curb had bars on the windows and rear door. The men loaded Kirsten, Elin, and Sofia into the back of it and drove away from the mansion.

"This is my fault," Kirsten wept as she looked out at the darkened streets. "I shouldn't have made Bettina angry."

"It isn't your fault," Elin said. She sat on the bench across from Kirsten, rocking Sofia in her arms. "No one is mean enough to do this just because of a prank—even Bettina Anderson. She must really believe that we stole from her."

"But who could have taken her rings?" Sofia asked.

Kirsten leaned back against the wall of the compartment, hanging on to the bench as the wagon bumped and jostled through the city. She closed her eyes. "I just want to wake up in my bed back home in Sweden and find out that this has all been a nightmare."

Too late, she recalled why Elin had worked so hard to get them away from their home in Sweden—and how life there had been a nightmare for Elin. She opened her eyes to face her sister. "I'm sorry. I-I didn't mean that."

No one spoke for the rest of the trip. When they reached the police headquarters, the Swedish-speaking policeman handed the captain his report and left. Kirsten stood in the bustling station with her sisters, listening to yells and laughter and catcalls, not understanding a word of what was going on. Sofia's meager knowledge of English was little use to them, and when all of their efforts to proclaim their innocence proved futile, Kirsten and her sisters were led down a dingy hallway to the rear of the station. The warden locked them in a cell.

"Why is this happening to us?" Sofia wept as she sank onto a cot. Elin sat down beside her and tried to comfort her, but Kirsten was too upset to sit. The cell reminded her of the detention room at Ellis Island—only with bars and a lock on the door. The beds, which hung from the wall by chains, had no mattresses or pillows, only a thin, grubby blanket for each of them. A bucket had been placed in the corner for their needs. At least they had the cell to themselves.

How in the world had they ended up here, with nothing but each other and the clothes on their backs? Kirsten tried to retrace their steps, remembering their once-happy family, their farm, their contented life in Sweden. But then the losses had started, and the funerals had begun, and with each upheaval, their lives had grown more and more difficult. Every time something good had happened in Kirsten's life—falling in love with Tor, finding a job at the mansion—a devastating blow had followed. Now she was pregnant, Mrs. Anderson was dead, and they were locked up in jail. She wanted to scream.

"I don't understand why this is happening to us," Sofia said again.

"I agree with what Kirsten said in the wagon," Elin said. "I'm sorry we ever left home. I thought America would be a land of golden dreams and new beginnings, but it isn't. This is all my fault. We never should have come to this country."

"Don't talk that way," Kirsten said. "It isn't your fault. I wanted to come to America too, remember?"

"Well, Sofia didn't choose to come. I'm sorry for bringing you here, Sofia. I'm so, so sorry."

"Stop it, Elin," Kirsten said. "We didn't do anything wrong. They'll find out that they've made a big mistake, and they'll let us out of here. You'll see."

She walked to the cell door and gripped the iron bars, peering out into the murky corridor. She wished she believed her own words.

Chapter Thirty-Two

"MAMA WOULD TELL us to pray," Sofia said. She had stopped feeling sorry for herself long enough to remember. "God promised He would never leave us or forsake us. He'll send help if we ask Him to."

"Praying won't do any good," Kirsten said. She stood with her back to Sofia and Elin, her hands clenching the bars of the cell door. "Prayer isn't like walking into a store and picking out what you want to buy. God isn't going to wave a magic wand and *poof,* we'll live happily ever after."

"God answered all of my other prayers," Sofia said. "I asked for you and Kirsten to get better and you did. I asked for help when I was all alone on Ellis Island, and He sent Ludwig."

"I must be doing something wrong, then," Elin said. "I don't think God ever answered any of my prayers."

"Oh, Elin. That can't be true."

"I prayed for Mama to get well, and she died. I

450

prayed for Papa to stop being sad and he killed himself. I prayed that Uncle Sven would stop—" She halted, stumbling over her words. "Th-that he would stop fighting with Nils, but that didn't happen, either."

"I know the Bible says ask and you'll receive," Kirsten said, "but I agree with Elin. I've asked, but I haven't received."

"Maybe what you're asking for isn't the best thing for you. Maybe—"

"Maybe we're being punished," Kirsten said.

Sofia shook her head. "For what?"

Kirsten didn't reply. Neither did Elin.

"Well, I think God *is* answering our prayers," Sofia insisted, "and we just can't see it yet."

"Sending innocent people to jail seems like a stupid way to answer their prayers," Kirsten muttered.

"I'm worried about both of you," Sofia said. "You're turning away from God and you won't tell me why. God is here with us, you know. He loves us and—"

"And this cell door is still locked," Kirsten said, shaking it until it rattled.

Sofia wondered how she could reassure them, especially when God didn't seem to be answering her prayers to find Ludwig. Sofia didn't want to lose her faith again, but this jail cell was the worst place she'd ever been in her life. She struggled to recall some of the other promises she had read in the Bible, wishing she could comfort her sisters. If only she had her mother's Bible.

"Jesus was falsely accused, too," she finally said. "He understands how we feel."

Kirsten gave a short laugh. "You're not helping me feel better, Sofia. Jesus' accusers killed Him, remember?"

"Yes, but He died for all of the wrong things *we've* done. He didn't have to die. You both keep saying that we're being punished for something, but even if that were true, God wouldn't want to punish us. He wants to forgive us."

Sofia waited for her sisters' response, but neither of them spoke. Kirsten still had her back turned. She saw Elin quickly wipe away a tear.

"What if we don't deserve forgiveness?" Elin asked.

"Nobody deserves it. God gives it to us for free, like a gift when it isn't even our birthday."

The door that led out to the police station opened, and the warden appeared. Sofia whispered a quick prayer. *Please, Jesus. Please let him be coming to unlock the door and set us free.* Instead, he yelled out something in English that she couldn't understand, and a minute later, the lights went out. Sofia crawled onto one of the cots and pulled the thin blanket around her shoulders. It took her a long time to fall asleep.

None of them felt like eating breakfast the next morning. The porridge was runny, the toast dry, and the stewed prunes tough and leathery.

452

"What are we going to do?" Kirsten asked again. None of them knew the answer. Sofia wanted to remind them again to pray, but her suggestion had met with disbelief last night.

"They'll have to let us go eventually," she said. "They can't prove we took Mrs. Anderson's things."

"Well, we can't prove that we didn't take them," Elin said. "Who else went into her bedroom besides us?"

"Mrs. Olafson brought her breakfast tray every morning," Kirsten said.

"You think Mrs. Olafson is the thief?" Sofia asked. "You must be joking."

"Accusing her is no more outrageous than accusing us."

The morning dragged endlessly. Sofia tried to pray instead of worry—an impossible task. She wondered if she would ever see Ludwig Schneider again.

Shortly before noon, the warden stopped in front of their door and stuck a key in the lock. He waved them forward as he swung open the cell door. Sofia slid off the cot. She wanted to tell her sisters that maybe this was an answer to her prayers, but she decided to wait and see.

Please, Jesus . . .

The warden led them out into the main area of the police station, where a gray-haired man in a three-piece suit stood waiting for them. Sofia thought she recognized him from somewhere—had he called on Mrs. Anderson? Had she seen him at church or at the

453

engagement party where she'd sung? Then she remembered.

"You're Mrs. Anderson's lawyer, aren't you? You came to see her at the mansion."

"That's correct. My name is John Olson."

"We didn't steal anything, Mr. Olson. Please, you have to believe us."

He held up his hand. "Give me one moment, please." He spoke to the police captain in English, too rapidly for Sofia to understand. She slipped her hand into Elin's while they waited, trying not to worry. Mr. Olson handed a piece of paper to the police captain, then bent to sign a paper that the captain handed to him. When he straightened up again, he smiled faintly at the three of them.

"Come with me, please."

Miraculously, they were allowed to leave the station. Sofia was surprised to find a bright, warm day outside after the dreary jail cell and the pouring rain during yesterday's funeral. She skirted around puddles as they walked down the block to Mr. Olson's carriage. He opened the door.

"After you, please, ladies." He gestured for them to climb in.

Amazingly, Elin didn't object. She was usually so suspicious of strangers. But she seemed too numb to argue, ducking through the door into the covered carriage as if sleepwalking.

"Are we really free to leave?" Kirsten asked. "We're not just out on bail or something, are we?"

"All of the charges have been dropped," Mr. Olson said. "I'm very sorry for the mix-up—and that you had to endure a night in jail."

"Did they find the missing jewelry?"

"In a roundabout way." He climbed in behind them and signaled to the driver. The carriage jolted forward and merged into the stream of traffic.

"Silvia Anderson entrusted me with several pieces of jewelry before she passed away," Mr. Olson told them. "She asked me to sell them for her. I have shown her son and the police a copy of the receipts. All of the missing items have been accounted for, and the money is on deposit in her bank account."

"Thank God," Sofia breathed.

"Mrs. Anderson also dictated the terms of her will to me, stating several bequests that she wished to make with the funds. I read the will to her family this morning—which is how I learned that you'd been accused of theft."

"They owe us an apology," Kirsten said. Elin shushed her.

"Mrs. Anderson's daughter-in-law intends to contest the will, however. She feels that the jewelry rightfully belonged to her and therefore the proceeds are hers, as well. It will be up to a judge to decide what happens to the money."

"So we're free to go?" Elin asked.

"Yes. Once again, I am very sorry for the misunderstanding."

"Where are you taking us now?" Kirsten asked.

"Back to the mansion. I have been asked to supervise while you gather your belongings."

"I hope Bettina Anderson is there," Kirsten said. "The very least she owes us is an apology after calling us thieves and making us spend the night in jail."

"That's not likely to happen." Again, Mr. Olson smiled faintly. "But Mr. Anderson did ask me to give you your final week's pay." He handed Elin an envelope with twelve dollars in it.

When they arrived at the mansion, Mr. Olson unlocked the front door and followed them upstairs to the third floor. Sofia had forgotten what a mess the police had made of their room after ransacking it. The entire contents of their trunk had been emptied and searched, then left in a heap. Sofia quickly examined Ludwig's violin, grateful that the police hadn't damaged it. She pitched in to help her sisters refold their bedding. When everything was packed, she gripped one of the trunk's handles to help Kirsten drag it downstairs.

"No, let's use the main stairs," Kirsten said when Sofia started toward the servants' stairwell. "It'll be easier. And we deserve a little consideration."

Sofia paused to change hands as they passed through the ballroom, remembering the night that Mrs. Anderson had danced with her son. She had truly seemed like a fairy queen that night, floating across the dance floor in the moonlight. Sofia remembered her kindness in loaning her the cameo pin and recalled the last conversation she'd had with Mrs. Anderson in the carriage. *"You've seen through my flapping wings and honking noise,"* she'd said. Sofia wiped a tear.

"I'm going to miss her," she said with a sigh.

"Why does life have to be so hard?" Kirsten asked.

The driver helped them lash the trunk to the back of the carriage. "Where would you like to go?" Mr. Olson asked.

"Our aunt's boardinghouse, I guess," Elin said.

"Wait!" Sofia suddenly cried as the carriage began to move. "What happened to Mrs. Anderson's cat? I didn't see him just now, did you? We promised we would take care of him."

"I have no idea," Mr. Olson replied. "Everything in the house belongs to her son now."

Sofia was devastated to think they had broken their promise. She struggled to hold back her tears. "She really loved that cat. . . ."

"Maybe Mrs. Olafson knows what happened to him," Elin said. "We'll walk over to her house tomorrow and ask her. I know where she lives."

"Why are you so worried about a cat?" Kirsten asked. "We don't have a place to live, either."

Aunt Hilma was even less pleased to see them this time than she'd been the first time they had arrived on her doorstep. "What are you doing here?" she asked. "The news is all over the community that you were sent to jail."

"They found out what really happened to the

jewels," Elin told her. "They know we didn't steal them, so they let us go."

"Disgraceful," Hilma muttered.

"We were cleared of any wrongdoing," Kirsten said angrily. "We didn't steal anything!"

"Well, I'm sorry, but you can't stay here."

"Where are we supposed to go?" Elin asked.

"You should have accepted those young men's offers in the first place and gone to Wisconsin. You would have had homes of your own by now. I suppose you can stay the night, but I want you to find someplace else to live as quickly as you can and be gone."

By the time Sofia helped Kirsten drag the trunk upstairs, she was exhausted. She and her sisters sat looking at each other.

"Now what?" Kirsten asked.

Elin shook her head. "I'm so sorry," she said softly. "We never should have left home."

PART III

Home

JULY 1897

"Jesus replied, 'If anyone loves me,
he will obey my teaching.
My Father will love him,
and we will come to him
and make our home with him.' "

JOHN 14:23

Chapter Thirty-Three

PASTOR JOHNSON AGREED to meet with Elin and her sisters the next morning in his study. She felt like a penitent on Judgment Day as she stood before him once again, pleading for work. The minister sat behind his desk with his hands folded, looking up at them, but since there were only two visitors' chairs, Elin and her sisters remained standing. She wished Uncle Lars had come with them again, but their uncle seemed to be avoiding them, as if he was as eager to be rid of them as Aunt Hilma was.

"You helped us find work before, Pastor Johnson, and we're very thankful," Elin began. "But now that Mrs. Anderson has passed away, we wondered if you knew of anyone else who needed maidservants."

"I'm not aware of anyone." He seemed surprised that they would ask him, as if he didn't recall helping them once before.

"The three of us don't have to work together in the same place," she said quickly, "although we would prefer it."

"And I can speak a little English, now," Sofia added. "It wouldn't have to be with a Swedish family."

"And it would help if the job included room and board," Kirsten said. "Aunt Hilma doesn't want us, even though we're her own flesh and blood."

Elin laid her hand on Kirsten's arm to shush her, afraid that the pastor would think less of them for

461

complaining about their aunt. He looked at the three of them with pity. His eyes were the same shade of gray as his tousled hair.

"I would like to help you . . . really I would. But I'm afraid that finding a job for any of you is going to be very difficult, if not impossible. Domestic servants are usually hired by word-of-mouth—the same way that gossip spreads. Unfortunately, everyone in our church community has heard the gossip about Silvia Anderson's jewelry. The stigma of theft will likely follow you."

"But we're innocent!" Kirsten said. "We didn't steal anything!"

"I know. But Bettina Anderson doesn't see it that way. Her mother-in-law named the three of you as beneficiaries in her will—"

"She did?" Elin said. "She named *us?* Her lawyer didn't tell us that."

"Well, it seems she did, and so Bettina still feels that you have stolen from her in a sense. She is going to make things very difficult for you, I'm afraid."

"That's not a very Christian way to act," Sofia said. "How can she attend church every Sunday and then turn around and treat people that way?"

"Very few of us act the way Jesus would like us to, Miss Carlson. I can preach the truth, but I can't enforce it. God gave everyone a free will."

"Tell her she can keep all of the money," Elin said. "We don't want it, if that's the way she feels. We just need jobs and a place to live."

"I don't know what else I can do for you," he said, lifting empty hands. "Chicago is filled with new immigrants looking for work. It's challenging enough for a man to find a good-paying job and a place to live, but it's especially difficult for young, unmarried women to find housing and the means to support themselves."

Something in the way he emphasized *unmarried* made Elin wonder if he knew about their refusal to marry the young men in Wisconsin. She could well imagine Aunt Hilma telling the pastor's wife and everyone else how she and Lars had done their best for their ungrateful nieces, but they'd scorned her help.

"You may have to go outside our Swedish community for work," Pastor Johnson continued. "Chicago is a big city, and if you can speak a little English it will certainly help."

"We don't know how to find a job," Kirsten said. "That's why we came to you."

"I'm sorry, but I'm not in the business of helping people find work. I have enough to do shepherding this flock." He rose to his feet and began sidling toward the door as he spoke, as if eager to show them the way out. "But I'll try to think of someone else who can advise you."

"I don't believe him," Kirsten said when they were outside in the bright sunshine again. "He isn't going to find someone to help us. His loyalties lie with Bettina Anderson. She probably donates money to his church."

"Our own family isn't helping us," Elin said, "so why should he?"

"Now what?" Sofia asked.

Elin had awakened long before dawn that morning, asking herself the same question as she'd stared into the darkness. She could think of only one other person who might be able to help them.

"Let's go talk to Mrs. Olafson. She needs to find a new job, too. Maybe she can help us."

"Ha! I wouldn't be surprised if she turned against us, too," Kirsten grumbled as they started walking away from the church. "I'm beginning to see that the community here is just like our village back home—taking sides, spreading gossip and lies . . ."

"Then let's not do the same thing," Sofia said. "Let's try to see people the way they really are from now on, not colored by what others say about them. Remember all the bad things everyone said about Mrs. Anderson? But once we got to know her, she wasn't so terrible after all."

They halted at the street corner, waiting for the traffic to clear before crossing. "Do you really think she left us some money in her will?" Kirsten asked. "I wonder why her lawyer didn't mention it to us."

"Probably because he didn't want us to get our hopes up," Elin said. "It turned out he was right not to mention it."

"How much money do you suppose she left us?" Kirsten asked. They were passing a storefront with dresses and hats on display, and Elin noticed that

Kirsten's steps had slowed as she gazed through the window.

Sofia tugged on her arm, pulling her forward again. "It doesn't matter," she said. "We'll never see a penny of it."

They walked another full block with the hot summer sun blazing down on them like a stove on a winter day. "Where does Mrs. Olafson live?" Kirsten asked as she mopped her brow with a handkerchief.

"She has an apartment above the Swedish bakery."

Elin found the bakery easily enough, but it took a few minutes to find the apartment's entrance in the rear of the building. The aroma of fresh bread filled the stairwell, bringing tears to Elin's eyes. The longing she felt wasn't for homemade bread, but for a home.

"I couldn't live here," Kirsten said, inhaling deeply. "This smell would make me hungry all the time."

"Maybe you'd get used to it," Sofia said.

Elin knocked on the apartment door, and when it opened, there was Mrs. Anderson's cat, circling Mrs. Olafson's feet, rubbing his flattened head against her legs.

"Tomte!" Sofia cried.

"We were so worried about you," Elin said as she crouched to pet him. The huge cat began to purr from all their attention, rumbling like a landslide. "We didn't know what happened to him."

"*Ja*, the poor thing mourned terribly after she died," Mrs. Olafson said. "The other Mrs. Anderson ordered the gardener to tie him up in a burlap sack and toss him into the river. Well, I couldn't let that happen, so here he is."

"I promised Mrs. Anderson that I would take care of him," Elin said. "I felt terrible for breaking my promise."

"Take him with you, if you want him. But come in, come in," she said, beckoning them inside.

"I will take him as soon as we're settled," Elin said. "But right now we don't have a job or a place to live. Were you able to find another job?"

"Oh, I got another offer right away. They can't pay me as much as Mrs. Anderson did, you see, and it's farther away from home, but it's the best I can expect at my age. I start working tomorrow, in fact."

Mrs. Olafson's tidy little apartment was as small as the main room of their cottage in Sweden had been and very hot inside, even with all of the windows open. The copper kettle on the cast-iron stove and the embroidered linens and pillow cushions on the white-painted furniture all reminded Elin of Sweden. She longed to find a home for her sisters, even if it was as simple as Mrs. Olafson's humble room.

The little woman gestured for them to sit at her table and brought out a pot of coffee and a plate of *lefse*, dusted with cinnamon and sugar. She talked while she worked. "I heard about your troubles with the missing jewelry, you see. I told my husband that I didn't believe you stole it from her. You girls would never do a thing like that."

"We didn't. But Bettina Anderson has a lot of influence in the community, and now no one else will hire us, even though the truth came out about the jewelry."

"Poor things. I'll keep my ears open for something—although it might be hard to place all three of you together, you see, working for the same family."

"It doesn't have to be together," Sofia said.

"And I'll take care of this poor cat in the meantime."

"Thank you, Mrs. Olafson. And God bless you."

They dragged their feet on the walk back to the boardinghouse. "I guess we'll have to look for work in a factory," Elin said. "We have to do something to finish paying for our tickets."

"Which factory? Where?" Kirsten asked, gesturing helplessly. "How do we go about it?"

"And where would we live?" Sofia added.

These were questions Elin couldn't answer. It was bad enough that she was in this predicament herself, but the fact that she was also responsible for her sisters—and for bringing them to America in the first place—made matters worse. She couldn't leave them destitute and homeless.

"I'll figure something out," she murmured.

All three of them worked in the boardinghouse that afternoon, trying to earn their room and board, at least. Once again, they slept on the floor in their cousins' cramped bedroom at night. The room was above the kitchen and as hot as a steam bath.

Another letter from Gunnar Pedersen arrived in the mail, but Elin waited to read it until her work was finished, wanting to savor his words and the pictures he always painted of life on his farm. He made it sound so nice—with plenty of hard work, to be sure—but at least he didn't live in this terrible city, where nobody wanted her and her sisters. Once again, Gunnar's letter made her homesick for their farm in Sweden.

Maybe moving to Wisconsin really was the best answer for them. There didn't seem to be any other solution. On the journey to America, Sofia had said she wanted to live on a farm again. Kirsten said she missed the trees and the stillness of the forest. Elin had wanted only to be safe from Uncle Sven. Maybe if she agreed to marry one of the bachelors, it would be the best way to give her sisters a home.

Elin took out a sheet of stationery and began to write:

Dear Gunnar,

So much has happened since I wrote my last letter to you. I'm sorry to say that our employer, Mrs. Anderson, has passed away. The days since her passing have been very sad ones for me, because I had grown very fond of her. But my sorrow is increased because once again, my sisters and I are without work and without a home. We spent much of today trying to find work in order to finish paying you and your friends the remainder of our debt. Unfortunately, we had no luck.

Tonight, I am very disillusioned with life in America. We can't seem to find the new start we were looking for when we decided to leave Sweden. And so, if it isn't too late, I would like to do what I should have done last May. I would like to accept your kind offer and come up to live in your settlement in Wisconsin. I will agree to marry whichever one of you will have me.

But please explain to your friends that I am the only one of us who is accepting your offer. It's my hope that you will consider my debt to be canceled if I do get married, and that you will apply the money we have already paid to my two sisters' fares. I'll find a way to finish paying for their tickets so that they won't be obligated to marry anyone. What my sisters need most of all right now is a home. I promised them when we left Sweden that they would have a home again someday, and you make life up in Wisconsin sound so nice. I hope that whoever agrees to marry me will make my sisters welcome in our home for as long as they need one. I can't promise that they will stay in your settlement and marry one of you, but I will stay. I promise to marry whichever one of you will have me. And I'll stay.

I'm very sorry for not accepting your offer right away, but my sisters were weary after the long journey to Chicago and didn't want to travel any further. I didn't want to force them to go. I hope you will write to me as soon as you can and let me know if I am still welcome, and if the offer of marriage still stands. If so, I will purchase our train tickets from our final week's pay at the mansion, and my sisters and I will come right away.

Yours truly,
Elin Carlson

Elin reread the letter, then folded the paper in half and slipped it into an envelope. When she looked up and saw Sofia reading her Bible, Elin recalled a verse in which Jesus said, *I go to prepare a place for you.* That's what she was doing: preparing a place for them, a home where she could take care of them. She doubted if they would believe this was the best answer for all three of them, but Elin knew from reading Gunnar's letters that it was. In time, Kirsten and Sofia would find husbands and settle down happily in homes of their own.

She licked the envelope shut and printed Gunnar Pedersen's address on the front.

She hoped sleep would come easier for her that night, having made this decision. It didn't.

"I'm going out to mail a letter," she said the next day after helping Aunt Hilma with the breakfast rush. But before dropping the letter in the corner mailbox, Elin first went to the Western Union office, where she had been wiring the money to Wisconsin. The clerk knew her by now, and he spoke Swedish.

"If I wanted to take a train to this place in

470

Wisconsin someday, could you advise me how I would do that? I don't know my way around Chicago very well, and I don't speak English."

"You would have to go to Union Station, downtown. They'll let you purchase a ticket in advance, and you can use it whenever you're ready to go."

Elin had no trouble following the clerk's directions to the train station, and since it was too far to walk, she rode on a streetcar for the very first time. She stood in line at the ticket window, then showed the agent Gunnar's address in Wisconsin when it was her turn.

"How much would it cost to travel to here?" she asked in Swedish, pointing to the address and holding out a handful of change.

The ticket agent jabbered in English. Elin shrugged and shook her head, wishing she had been as wise as Sofia and had studied English. He looked up something in a fat book, then jabbered again.

"I'm sorry. I don't understand. Could you write down the amount?" She mimicked holding a pen and writing. He finally seemed to understand and tore off a scrap of paper. He wrote $1.50 on it.

Elin quickly added it up in her head. Three fares would come to $4.50—her entire pay for the last week she had worked at the mansion, plus another fifty cents from her dwindling spending money. The ticket agent asked Elin something else—probably if she wanted to buy the ticket. She nodded and held up three fingers.

She would convince her sisters to go with her. She would make them understand that this was what they needed to do. Elin should have realized when they arrived in Chicago that this was the best choice and saved everyone a great deal of trouble. If she hadn't been so suspicious of everyone, as Mrs. Anderson said, perhaps she would have.

The thought of marrying a stranger made Elin shiver. But she would make this sacrifice for her sisters. At least they would have a place to live for now, until they were old enough to decide what to do next. They might choose to leave Wisconsin someday, but Elin would stay. She would keep her promise and marry whomever would have her.

Chapter Thirty-Four

KIRSTEN WORKED IN her aunt's boardinghouse all day, keeping one eye on the clock as the supper hour approached. When the time came for the boarders to return home, she removed her apron and hung it on a hook. "I'll be right back," she told Elin.

She slipped out of the back door as if visiting the privy but headed down to the street corner instead. Kirsten knew where the streetcar stopped near the boardinghouse, but she didn't know what time Knute Lindquist arrived home on it in the afternoon. The last time she had seen him was at the mansion after Mrs. Anderson's funeral, but she hadn't dared to speak with him. She hated her helplessness, hated taking advantage of his good nature by asking him for help, but he was the only friend she had in Chicago, other than her sisters. If God was punishing them by sending all this bad luck, Kirsten suspected that it was because of her, not Elin and Sofia. She loved her sisters. She needed to find a way to help them.

She waited for Mr. Lindquist for what seemed like a very long time, watching people get on and off the streetcars. They had places to go, work to do. They knew their way around Chicago and knew how to speak English. She envied their freedom.

Finally, just as Kirsten was ready to give up, Mr. Lindquist stepped off one of the cars. His face wore the dead expression she'd seen on the other passengers' faces, staring down at the ground, not really noticing his surroundings. He would have walked right past Kirsten if she hadn't called his name.

"Mr. Lindquist!"

"Miss Carlson? What are you doing here?"

"I've been waiting for you. I hope you don't mind, but I need to talk to you."

"Do you want to walk to the park?"

"I would hate for you to miss dinner at the boardinghouse. I know my aunt never saves food for anyone."

"It doesn't matter. Let's walk." His stride was longer than hers, and she had to hurry to keep up with him.

"Did you hear what happened? How we were accused of stealing?" she asked as they walked.

"Of course. The rumors were all over the news-paper office. I didn't want to believe they were true."

"They weren't true! Did you also hear that they found out we were innocent?"

"Yes, I heard."

"Well, we've been looking for another job, and we can't find one. No one wants to hire us, even though they know we aren't thieves. Pastor Johnson said Bettina Anderson hates us. I don't know what else to do, so I wanted to ask if . . . if you would hire me."

"Hire you? What for?"

"You said you wanted to send for your son, and I thought that if you did, I could take care of him for you. I could also keep house and cook for you, and—"

"I'm certain you could find a better job than that. I couldn't pay you very much. Surely there are better jobs."

"I don't need much money. Just enough to afford a room where my sisters and I can live."

"Would you like me to inquire about a job for you with another Swedish family?"

Kirsten didn't reply. She saw an empty park bench and walked over to it and sank down, determined not to cry. Even if Mr. Lindquist did find her another job, she would be fired when her pregnancy began to show. Her sisters would likely be fired, as well. She wished he hadn't saved her life.

Mr. Lindquist sat down beside her a moment later. "What's wrong, Kirsten?"

She had to tell him the truth. She had no other choice.

"I can't work for anyone else because . . . because when the truth comes out . . ."

"What truth?"

"I'm going to have a baby." She glanced over at him and wasn't surprised to see the shock on his face. She gave him a minute to absorb it.

"Now you know why I tried to kill myself. When people find out, my sisters will be disgraced, too. I don't know what else I can do except work for someone like you, someone who knows the truth. I've been trying day and night to figure out a solution, and I can't think of one."

"Where is the baby's father?"

"In Sweden. He doesn't even know about it. Remember how I told you that Tor's father is destroying all of my letters? I can't get in touch with Tor to tell him."

Mr. Lindquist didn't reply. He was silent for such a long time that Kirsten could no longer stand it.

"I do know right from wrong, Mr. Lindquist. I'm not an immoral person, just a very foolish and lonely one who made a terrible mistake. After my parents both died, I needed comfort so badly—and Tor said that he loved me. He promised to marry me."

Mr. Lindquist still said nothing. Kirsten had never met anyone who could sit so still, barely breathing, as if carved from stone.

"You must remember how desolate it felt when you

were grieving," she continued, "how you longed to talk to someone who understood you, someone who would hold you and let you weep."

When Knute still didn't reply, Kirsten said, "I've shocked you. I'll understand if you don't want anything more to do with me." She started to rise.

"Wait." He laid his hand on her arm to stop her, just as he had the last time. Once again, the weight of his touch was a painful reminder that Tor would never hold her again. Perhaps no man would.

"I do remember how it feels," he finally said, "and if anything shocks me, it's the fact that this young man would take advantage of your grief in such a despicable way. How old are you?"

"My birthday is in a few days. I'll be nineteen."

"Isn't there a family member or a pastor over in Sweden who could help you? I would be willing to help you compose a letter and explain your situation. This young man needs to come forward and take responsibility."

Kirsten swallowed, knowing that she would have to reveal even more of her shame. "There is no one in Sweden who can help me. Tor's father is an important man in the village, and he doesn't believe that my baby is his son's. No one in town will believe me, even the pastor, because my father's death was a suicide. My sisters and I left Sweden in disgrace."

"I see."

"I never would have bothered you, Mr. Lindquist,

except that I'm desperate. I thought maybe you would hire me to take care of your son and cook for you. All I need is enough money to rent a room where my sisters and I can stay. They're trying to find work, too, and we don't know where else to go or what to do."

"When will your child be born?"

"Around the New Year, I think."

"Do your sisters know?"

Kirsten stared down at her feet. "I'm too ashamed to tell them. But the baby is starting to grow, and . . ." Her voice trembled at the thought of how disgraced she would be, walking around in public in that condition. "If only I had a place to hide," she finished in a whisper.

"I understand."

Again, Kirsten noticed his unnerving stillness. Not a muscle twitched, his chest barely rose with each breath. Finally he spoke again. "I need to give the problem some serious thought," he said at last. "Perhaps I can ask discreetly if someone at work knows of a position for you and your sisters. Maybe there is even a family who is willing to adopt your child."

"Thank you," she said softly. But Kirsten knew that she had exposed her shame for nothing. Mr. Lindquist wouldn't be able to help her, either. She sighed. "We may as well go back."

He stood and helped her rise, then set off at his brisk pace. He chose the shortest route back to the boardinghouse. Once again, Kirsten had to hurry to keep up with him.

"You don't want someone like me taking care of your son, do you?" she asked.

"That's not true. I'm certain you would be very good with Torkel. But I am a widower. It wouldn't be proper for a young unmarried woman to work for me. I'm sorry."

"I understand." But she didn't. She was trying so hard not to cry. That's all she seemed to do around him. He would surely view her as a hysterical woman, playacting for his sympathy. Kirsten hated pity most of all.

"I am going to find a way to help you, Kirsten. Just let me think about it some more. I'll walk here to meet with you again after we've eaten dinner."

She didn't have much of an appetite that evening. Her sisters were solemn throughout the meal, too. Kirsten recognized their fear and desperation—they mirrored her own. Aunt Hilma would kick them out if they didn't find work soon.

"I'm going for a walk," Kirsten said after the dinner dishes were washed and dried.

"Do you want me to come with you?" Sofia asked.

"No thanks." Kirsten hurried away before anyone could stop her.

The summer evenings remained light until quite late at night, making the walk pleasant, even though Kirsten dreaded the outcome. Knute Lindquist wouldn't find a solution. There simply wasn't one.

She slowed her steps, closing her eyes to hold back her tears, walking blindly as she offered up a prayer.

Lord, I'm so sorry for what I did with Tor. Please forgive me. Please help me figure out what to do.

She saw Mr. Lindquist before he saw her, standing by the bench with his hands in his pockets and his back turned. The residual sunlight shone on his fair hair, turning it to gold. She was afraid to hope that he had thought of an answer for her dilemma, fearing instead that he would want nothing more to do with her. She crossed the grass to stand beside him, afraid to look at him, afraid to speak.

"We will be married," he said simply. "That is, if you are willing."

Kirsten stared up at him. This was not at all what she had expected to hear. "Married?" she breathed. It was inconceivable that he would even consider it.

"I could give your child a father and you could give mine a mother."

"But I-I never expected . . . Why would you do that?"

"Helping someone in need might be the only happiness I dare hope for after everything that has happened."

Kirsten was speechless. She didn't know this man. How could she marry him? It occurred to her that it would be no more unusual than marrying one of the strangers in Wisconsin, and at least she wouldn't be deceiving Mr. Lindquist into thinking the child was his. She would be able to help her sisters, and they would never need to know the truth about her baby.

"You're giving me more than you're getting in return," she finally said. "I would be willing to work for my room and board. . . . I wasn't expecting marriage. Why would you make such an extravagant offer?"

"I know it sounds strange, but I've felt alone in my grief for a very long time. The fact that you share such loss makes me feel as though we have something in common. If someone could have helped me through my difficult time, I would have been grateful. Now I have the opportunity to help you. I think it's time I thought about someone else besides myself."

She sank onto the bench as she tried to comprehend his offer. He sat down beside her a moment later.

"Marriage is for such a long time, Mr. Lindquist, and—"

"You're wrong. Nothing in life is as permanent as we would like to think."

"I'm sorry. I didn't mean—"

"I don't need an answer right away, Kirsten. You need to consider my offer carefully. I can't promise I'll be easy to live with, and you need to understand that I'm not expecting you to be my wife in every sense of the word. I could never love anyone the way I loved Flora. I would be too terrified to risk falling in love again. That's why I haven't married."

"I understand. And you need to know that I wouldn't be doing this just for my baby and myself.

I need to help my sisters. We still owe money for our passage to America. That's why we were working for Mrs. Anderson. I wouldn't expect you to pay our debt."

"We can work something out. If I were to send for my son, I would have to pay a nursemaid to care for him. Paying your fare would be no different."

"That's very generous of you."

"And your sisters can have a home with us for as long as they need one."

Kirsten drew a deep breath as if about to plunge into cold water. "In that case, I don't need to think about it. I want to accept your offer." Elin and Sofia would have a home. And a future.

"With any luck your sisters will think the child is mine," he said as he rose from the bench. "Everyone will. The child will bear my name."

Kirsten struggled to comprehend the enormity of Mr. Lindquist's proposal as they walked back to the boardinghouse. She wanted to ask him once again why he would do so much for her, especially since he knew the truth about her past. He was giving her a gift she had no right to expect, offering much more than he was receiving in return. She recalled what Sofia had said about God's forgiveness, comparing it to an unexpected gift when it wasn't even her birthday. Could God have answered her prayer for forgiveness so quickly? Kirsten didn't want to cry, but she was finding it hard to hold back her tears.

"I don't know how I can ever thank you," she said, her voice trembling.

"I know you will be a good mother for my son. The compassion and concern that you have for your sisters show me that you are a very loving person."

"I'm so grateful to you. More than you'll ever know."

When they came within sight of the boardinghouse, he stopped again. "I don't want to rush you, Kirsten, but people can count off the months, where babies are concerned. Once you are certain that you want to accept my offer, we probably shouldn't waste time."

"I am certain. I'll do whatever you say."

"Can you meet me here tomorrow during the lunch hour? If you still believe you've made the right decision after you've had a night to think it over, we can go to City Hall and apply for a marriage license. Then we'll talk to Pastor Johnson and arrange a quiet wedding in his study—unless you would like to do it properly and announce the banns in church? In that case, we will be married three weeks from now."

"I don't want to wait. Aunt Hilma won't let us stay in the boardinghouse that long. She would gladly kick us out tomorrow if we had a place to go. But are *you* sure you want to do this? I still don't understand why you would agree to marry someone like me. If anyone learns the truth about me it could ruin your reputation—your life."

He looked down at the ground. "I wouldn't call

482

what I'm living right now 'a life.' I don't want to exist this way forever, nor can I marry a woman who would have every right to expect me to love her in return. And I do want to see my son." He finally looked up at her. "I'm sure, Kirsten. Are you?"

"Yes."

"Then we'll go to City Hall tomorrow."

Chapter Thirty-Five

ONE OF THE few good things in Sofia's life was her English classes. And now that she wasn't working, she could attend class three nights a week instead of only one. She was hurrying to school after helping with the supper dishes that evening when she noticed a colorful playbill plastered on a fence near the school. It advertised a variety show at the Viking Theater. Where had she heard of that theater before?

Sofia was halfway through the door to her class when she suddenly remembered. The man she met at the engagement party owned the Viking Theater. He had heard her sing that evening—and had offered her a job! Of course! This was the answer she had been praying for.

Sofia could hardly sit through her lessons and barely heard a word the teacher said, wondering if the owner still wanted to hire her. What had she done with his business card? As soon as she returned home from school, Sofia searched the pockets of the skirt she had worn on the night of the party and found it.

His name—Mr. Carl Lund—and the address of the theater were printed on the card.

The relief Sofia felt lasted only a moment before fear replaced it. If her stomach had turned inside out when she'd sung for fifty people at the party, how would she ever be able to stand up on a stage beneath a spotlight and sing for hundreds of people? Fear had stalked Sofia all her life, and now the beast was howling so loudly that she could scarcely think straight. Then, out of nowhere, she remembered the verse God had given her on her first day on Ellis Island: *Sing the glory of his name. . . .*

Sofia pulled out her Bible and reread all of the verses Ludwig had shown her. When she came to the verse that promised, *And we know that in all things God works for the good of those who love him, who have been called according to his purpose,* she was certain that God had arranged for her to meet the theater owner. She needed to set aside her fear and go talk to him tomorrow.

She continued reading her Bible and, little by little, found the strength to trust God to help her sing onstage. He would keep her fear at bay, just as He had the last two times she had sung for people. With His help she could do this. She *would* do it. Elin had carried the load for all three of them long enough. It was time for Sofia to lean on God instead of on Elin; time for her to help her sisters instead of being helped by them. She turned out the light and prayed until finally falling asleep.

• • •

Sofia wondered the next morning how she would manage to sneak away to the theater. She didn't want to tell a lie, but she knew that if she explained where she was going, Elin would try to stop her. But Elin and Kirsten were both running errands of their own, and they left the boardinghouse before Sofia did. She prayed for God's help while she dressed in her new clothes.

Sofia walked to the address printed on the business card. It was too early in the morning for a show to be playing, but Sofia spoke with a man who was mopping the lobby floor, and he directed her to Mr. Lund's office backstage. The office door was open.

"Excuse me . . . Mr. Lund?"

"Miss Carlson!" he said when he saw her.

"You remember me?"

"Yes, of course I do." He rose from his seat behind the desk and hurried over to welcome her inside. "I'm delighted to see you—but I must say I'm surprised. Please, come in . . . sit down. Can I get you anything?"

Sofia shook her head, feeling tongue-tied and weak-kneed as she took the seat he offered her. He raked his fingers through his hair as he returned to his place behind the desk, as if he were the one who needed to make a good impression.

"What brings you here, Miss Carlson? Have you reconsidered my offer?"

"I have. I'm sure you've heard that my employer, Silvia Anderson, has passed away."

"Yes. I was so sorry to hear the news. She and her husband were very active in the Swedish community. I do a lot of business with the newspaper he founded."

"Well, now that she's gone I need another job, so I decided to talk to you about singing in your theater—if you still want me, that is."

"Yes! Absolutely! I would be delighted. Where shall we begin?"

"I'll be honest with you; I don't know anything at all about the theater. I've never even been inside one, even in Sweden. And so I need to know what it is exactly that you would like me to do—before I agree to anything."

"I understand. Listen, would you like to see the theater?" He stood, walking around his desk once again. Sofia stood, too, her knees a little less shaky than when she first sat down. "Come this way, please."

He led her out of his office and through a warren of dusty, cluttered hallways behind the stage, talking as they walked. "My audiences seem to enjoy my variety shows the most. They're a combination of several acts, including musical numbers, a comedian, maybe a juggler or a magician. What I would like you to do is sing a solo as one of my acts, probably as a warm-up for a more well-known performer."

He stopped backstage beside a rack full of clothing. "You would wear a costume—like one of these.

Probably something very Swedish. And you would stand in front of a backdrop with a Swedish scene painted on it." He pointed to a stack of enormous paintings leaning against the brick wall. The one on top depicted a farm scene.

"W-what would I sing?"

He looked her over for a moment. "I think I would like you to start with the Swedish love song you sang first at the party. You brought tears to everyone's eyes. Eventually, you will need to expand your repertoire once the audience grows tired of it. But I'll bill you as our own Swedish Songbird—alluding to Jenny Lind, of course, the Swedish Nightingale."

"I could never sing like she did."

"I think you have the potential to," he said quietly.

He parted a maroon velvet curtain and motioned her forward. She was suddenly onstage. It was dark in the theater, but the rear lobby doors were open and daylight streamed through them. Sofia looked out at row after row of red plush seats. More seats lined the gilded balcony above them. A wave of panic nearly knocked her to the floor. She felt as if a giant were sitting on her chest, making it hard to breathe and impossible to speak. She swayed, nearly losing her balance. Mr. Lund didn't seem to notice.

"I have plans to expand my productions in the near future," he continued, "adding musical reviews and plays. If you can learn the parts and work with other singers and actors, you would be able to earn even more money. It's up to you how much and how often you'd like to sing. But for now, I can pay you seven dollars a week for five evening shows and two Saturday matinees—a dollar per show."

"Oh my!" That was three dollars more per week than she'd earned as a maid—just for singing. Sofia wondered if there was a catch, if there was something Mr. Lund wasn't telling her. He seemed so kind and sincere . . . and so eager to hire her.

"I believe you could reach star status once you gain experience and expand your repertoire," Mr. Lund said. "I'm certain you would draw a big crowd. Your name would move up to top billing on all of our posters."

Sofia remembered the playbill she had seen outside the school. "You mean . . . there would be signs everywhere? With my name on them?"

"That's right. Initially, your name will appear near the bottom, I'm afraid, in smaller print. But I don't see why you can't earn top billing someday, Miss Carlson."

Sofia knew this job was the answer to her prayers. Not only would she be earning seven dollars a week and helping her sisters, but her name would be on posters all over town. Ludwig might see one of them and finally find her.

"Do you ever hire violinists to play for your shows?" she asked.

"We certainly do. That's the orchestra pit down there." He pointed to a jumble of chairs and music stands in a dark hole below the stage. Ludwig could work there, too, she thought as they walked back to Mr. Lund's office.

"I don't want to rush you," he said when they were seated again, "but as soon as you sign a contract, you can begin working—and I can begin paying you."

"I-I also need to find a place to live before I agree to work for you. My two sisters and I arrived in America only two months ago, and now that Mrs. Anderson is gone, we have to no place to live."

"Do they sing, as well?"

"They've never shown any interest in singing, so I can't speak for them. But if I agree to work for you, I would need to know if seven dollars is enough money to afford a place to live. Otherwise, I would have to find a job where room and board are included."

"Well . . . if you don't mind a rooming house, I do know a place that you could afford. Whenever I hire traveling troupes, they usually stay at an establishment I recommend nearby. It's a cross between a hotel and a boardinghouse. It's not luxurious, but the rent is reasonable and quite affordable on the salary I'm offering you. I'm sure you'll find it will meet your needs. I can direct you to it, if you'd like."

"Thank you. I would appreciate it." All of the pieces were falling into place. This job was the answer to Sofia's prayers. She drew a deep breath. "I would be very happy to sign a contract with you, Mr. Lund."

"Wonderful!" He took a printed form from his desk

489

and filled in the blank spaces with the date and Sofia's name and the salary he had agreed to pay her. She read every word before signing her name on the bottom.

"Thank you," she said as she handed it back to him.

"No, thank you, Miss Carlson," he said. "I'll see you tomorrow at ten o'clock to start rehearsing."

As he was seeing her out, Mr. Lund called to one of the stagehands working in the back of the theater. "Tura, could you escort Miss Carlson over to the hotel for me? You know the one our theater people use, don't you? She wants to ask about a room."

"Sure thing, Mr. Lund."

Tura was a disreputable-looking man with shaggy, unkempt hair and a filthy beard. He wore his shirt unbuttoned, revealing his bare chest. Elin would be horrified if she saw Sofia with him. But she followed Tura out the rear door and through a warren of back lanes and alleys, praying that Jesus would keep her safe. Sofia couldn't believe she was being this brave, for once. God must be answering her prayers.

"I'm taking you on a shortcut I know," Tura said. "But see? That's the main thoroughfare just a block down that way. Now do you know where you are?"

"Yes. Yes, I do." It wasn't very far from Aunt Hilma's boardinghouse and still well within the safety of their Swedish neighborhood. But the ramshackle hotel turned out to be very shabby and rundown. It resembled a hotel inside with a large registration desk, a tiny lounge area, and long, mysterious hallways and stairways that led into the darkness. It smelled like mildew and dirty feet. A large sign in Swedish told Sofia that the hotel rented rooms by the day or the week.

"How much to rent a room for one week?" she asked the man slouched behind the desk.

"With board or without?"

"Um . . . with board."

"Three dollars for the room, twenty-five cents a day for three meals. That comes to $4.75 a week with full board."

"Oh. That's a lot." She paused to add up the additional cost of meals for her sisters and it came to $8.25 altogether—more money than she would earn. But at least they could live here together for now, even if they did have to buy their own food.

"May I see one of the available rooms, please? I need one with a full-sized bed. I'll be sharing the room with my two sisters, if that's allowed."

He lumbered to his feet. "You can share it with an entire circus for all I care."

Sofia followed him up a creaking staircase and down the hall to room 23. The man unlocked the door for her and stood aside, waiting in the hallway while she looked around. It was not what anyone would call a home. The room had one large bed with an iron headboard, a plain wooden chair, and a mirrored dresser with three drawers. There were no rugs on the plank floors, and the single window had a view of a horse stable across the dirt alleyway. But the room would be less cramped than the one she now shared with her sisters and two cousins.

"The washrooms are down the hall," the man said when she finished looking around. "You'll have to share."

"There aren't any linens on the beds," Sofia said.

"Twenty-five cents extra if you want laundered linens."

"Oh. Well, we have our own bedding."

She could work hard and earn extra money, Sofia told herself as she followed the man downstairs again. She and her sisters could move out of this place eventually and find something better. But for now, Sofia could help relieve Elin's worries. And maybe Kirsten would stop being so sad all the time.

She gave the man three dollars for a week's rent using the money Gustav Anderson had paid her for her final week of work at the mansion. Then she hurried back to the boardinghouse to tell her sisters the good news.

Chapter Thirty-Six

WAITING FOR A reply from Gunnar Pedersen and the other men in Wisconsin was agonizing. Elin longed to tell her sisters that she had found a way to rescue them, to show them the train tickets she had purchased and restore their hope in finding a home. And she longed to tell grouchy Aunt Hilma that they would soon be out of her way for good and no longer a burden to her. But Elin decided to wait until she heard back from Gunnar and all of her plans were in place, just as she had waited to hear from Uncle Lars when she was back home in Sweden. Meanwhile, she tried to help Aunt Hilma with her work as much as she could and accompanied her to the farmers' market that morning.

"Look at all of this beautiful fresh fruit for sale," Elin said. "Would you like Kirsten and me to help you make a batch of jam from it?"

"Are you sure you know how to make jam?" Hilma asked. Elin nodded, holding back an annoyed reply. "Well, I suppose my boarders would appreciate it," Hilma said.

But instead of picking the best peaches and berries, Hilma filled her basket with fruit that was bruised or overripe, then bargained for a cheaper price. "You'll need to make the jam this afternoon," she told Elin.

By the time they finished shopping and returned to the boardinghouse, both Kirsten and Sofia had disappeared. Elin's first impulse was to worry. Then she reminded herself that her sisters knew their way around the neighborhood. They would be safe without her.

Elin was busy with her jam-making, sweating over a roaring stove and a kettle of boiling fruit, when Sofia returned. "Where have you been? And why are you all dressed up? Where's Kirsten? I need help."

"Kirsten didn't go with me. Let me change my

clothes, and I'll help you with that." Sofia pitched in as soon as she'd changed into work clothes, feeding more wood into the fire and melting the paraffin to pour on top on the jars.

"Where did you run off to?" Elin asked her when they had a chance to pause.

Sofia glanced at Aunt Hilma, then whispered, "I'll tell you later."

At last the jam was finished, and Elin and Sofia went outside to sit on the back steps and cool off. "Do you remember helping Mama make jam?" Elin asked as she fanned her face with her kerchief.

"I remember picking berries with her. And I remember watching you and Mama make jam. But most of my memories of Mama are of how sick she was. And of how long she suffered."

"I miss her so much," Elin sighed.

Sofia turned sideways on the steps to face her. "Listen, Elin, I have some really good news to share. This morning I—" Before she could finish, Kirsten sauntered into the yard.

"What are you two up to?" she asked. Her face looked flushed and happy, and she was smiling. She seemed just like the old Kirsten that Elin remembered from back in Sweden, ambling home from a walk in the woods with a pail full of berries.

"We just cooked a batch of jam for Aunt Hilma," Sofia said. "That's why we're sweating. We came out here to cool off."

"And Sofia was about to tell me her good news."

Kirsten's smile widened. "I have some good news to share, too. But I'll let Sofia go first."

Sofia resembled one of Aunt Hilma's overripe peaches that was about to burst. "Well, my news is that we can move out of here," she said with hushed excitement. "I found a job! I found a place for us to stay, too. And I'll be making enough money for us to live on, if we're careful."

Elin stared in disbelief. "How? Where? Do I know this family?"

"I'm not working for a family. I'm going to earn seven dollars a week singing in a variety show at the Viking Theater."

Elin felt as though Sofia had punched her in the stomach. "The *theater?* Sofia, why would you even consider such an outrageous idea? Singing in a theater? You'll ruin your reputation!"

"What reputation? Papa disgraced us in Sweden, people here think we're thieves, our own aunt and uncle don't even want us. Besides, come and see the theater, Elin. It is respectable. Remember when I sang at the engagement party for Mrs. Anderson's friend? Well, the man who owns the theater heard me sing that night. His name is Carl Lund, and his variety shows are for families here in the Swedish community. He also told me about a rooming house where we can all stay for only three dollars a week, and it isn't much different from this one, only—"

"Sofia, stop! You're talking a mile a minute and . . . and I can't even comprehend what you're saying!

You can't be seriously considering this. We're simple farm girls from Sweden. You can't sing in a theater!"

"Elin's right," Kirsten said. "And besides, you don't need to work there, Sofia. That's what my good news is—I found a home for all of us, too. Everything will be taken care of in just a few more days." She paused, and a huge smile spread across her face. It was such a relief to Elin to see Kirsten happy again. Elin was certain her news must be wonderful.

"My friend Mr. Lindquist has asked me to marry him—and I've accepted. He says you both can live with us, and—"

"What!" Elin felt as though she'd had the wind knocked out of her a second time. "You barely know this man. You can't marry some stranger you just met!"

"I'm really sorry that you haven't met him yet, but he isn't a stranger to me."

"Kirsten, no. Please don't do this. A few months ago you were ready to run off with one of those cousins we met on the voyage. Don't be foolish. At least get to know this man a little better before you talk about marriage. We're not that desperate for a place to live."

"It's already done. Knute and I applied for a marriage license today."

"And I signed a contract to sing for Mr. Lund."

Elin doubled over, moaning as pain knifed through her stomach again.

"What's going on out here?" Aunt Hilma asked, coming to stand in the doorway. "You want the whole neighborhood to hear you scrapping?"

"We're sorry," Sofia said. "We'll talk someplace else." She stood and offered Elin a hand to help her up. "Let's take a walk around the block and discuss this calmly."

Elin felt weak as she walked between her sisters, her arms linked with theirs. She searched for the right words, desperate to hold them close and prevent them from making such disastrous choices. "Both of you, please stop and think this through. I know you mean well and that you're just trying to help, but I can't let you go through with these outrageous plans! You'll ruin your lives—for nothing."

"I'm not ruining—"

"Let me finish, Kirsten. I already came up with a plan to take care of you, and it's already in motion. If it works out, you'll have a home with me that will be just like the one we had in Sweden. Neither one of you will have to get married until you're ready, and you won't have to work for a living, either."

"That's impossible," Kirsten said. "What's your wonderful plan?"

Elin waited until they rounded the corner and started down the next length of the city block. "I wrote to Gunnar Pedersen in Wisconsin. I told him that I would agree to move up there and marry who-ever would have me if they would allow the two of you to live with me, too."

"No!" Kirsten said, halting her steps.

Elin pulled her along again. "Listen, I told Gunnar I would finish paying for your two tickets, and you would both be free from any obligation to get married or to stay there."

"That's even more foolish than what we've done," Sofia said. "You don't want to move to Wisconsin and marry a stranger any more than we do."

"Gunnar isn't exactly a stranger. We've been writing to each other, and he seems very nice. And from the way he describes his farm, it's going to be just like our farm back home."

"That makes absolutely no sense," Kirsten said. "You're telling me it's a mistake to marry Knute so that we can all have a home, yet you want to do the same thing! And move to a strange place, no less. It would make much more sense if we all stayed here."

"I already made the commitment to Gunnar. I mailed the letter to him and bought train tickets for all three of us."

"And I already signed a contract at the theater and paid for a week's rent."

"Knute and I took out a marriage license. He's going to find a house for us. You don't have to go, Elin. You can stay with Knute and me."

"Or you could live in the rooming house with me," Sofia said.

Elin stopped, too weary to walk another step. She slowly shook her head. "I gave Gunnar my word. I can't disappoint him a second time. It wouldn't be right."

They stood looking at each other. "This is awful," Sofia murmured. "Now what are we going to do?"

"Why did you make plans without talking to me first?" Elin asked.

"You did the same thing," Kirsten said. "You didn't ask us about moving to Wisconsin."

"This is awful!" Sofia repeated.

"Don't worry, either of you," Elin said. But her heart was racing so fast she was afraid it would give out. "It's my fault that we're in this mess, and I'll figure a way out of it. I'll talk to the man at the theater, Sofia, and explain that you're only seventeen, that you didn't know what you were doing when you signed that contract. And I'll explain to Kirsten's friend that she needs more time to get to know him. I'm sure Aunt Hilma won't throw us out on the street with no place to go. Please, this mess is my fault, but I can fix it."

"How is any of this your fault?" Sofia asked.

"It's my fault that we left Sweden, my fault for making you come. I should have planned better. I should have—"

Kirsten gripped her shoulders. "Stop punishing yourself, Elin. You don't need to feel guilty for rescuing us. Saving us from Uncle Sven was the most courageous thing you've ever done!"

Horror rocked through Elin. She couldn't breathe. "How do you know about that?" she whispered.

Kirsten looked away. "I-I read your diary . . . when you were in the hospital."

Elin turned her back on her sisters and ran blindly down the street. The pain in her stomach was so fierce she thought she might vomit. She felt violated, humiliated. She wanted to die.

"Elin, stop!" Kirsten called after her. "Listen to me!" Kirsten caught up with her and pulled her to a halt. "What Uncle Sven did to you wasn't your fault." Elin twisted out of her grasp.

"What's going on?" Sofia asked. "Elin, what's wrong?" She tried to embrace her, but Elin pushed her away, too.

Shame and guilt piled on top of Elin. She thought she'd left the past behind in Sweden, but as Mrs. Anderson had warned her, only the scenery had changed. Elin wanted to run and run and never stop, but her sisters hemmed her in, blocking her escape.

"Listen to me," Kirsten said. "I know that reading your diary was wrong, and I'm sorry, Elin. Believe me, I am. But at the time, I had an impossible decision to make, and I didn't know where to turn for help. You were in the hospital and I couldn't pray about it, so I thought that if I read your journal, maybe it would help me figure out why you decided to come to America and whether or not I should let them deport me."

"Why would they deport you?" Sofia asked.

Kirsten closed her eyes. Her face twisted in pain as her tears began to fall. "Because I'm pregnant," she whispered.

"No. . . . Oh no," Elin moaned. It couldn't be true. Terror prickled through her at the thought that the baby was Uncle Sven's—that he had taken things much further with Kirsten than he had with her. If it was his child, then it was Elin's fault that he had turned to Kirsten. Elin had been avoiding Sven for the final months they'd lived in Sweden.

She should have killed him.

"I'm sorry," Kirsten wept. "And I'm so ashamed of what I've done. I found out about the baby when I was in the hospital on Ellis Island, and I didn't know what to do. They were going to deport me—and maybe I would have let them if I hadn't read your diary and found out about Uncle Sven. So I lied and told them that Tor and I were secretly married. And that he was coming to America, too."

"Tor? You mean Tor Magnusson is the father?"

"I'm so ashamed," Kirsten wept. "I know that what we did was wrong, but Tor said he loved me. And after losing our family, I just wanted someone to hold me and make my grief go away. I'm not trying to give excuses, but—it just happened. And I didn't know I was pregnant until after we arrived in America."

"Tor is the one who should be ashamed," Elin said. Her relief that the father wasn't Uncle Sven transformed into anger toward Tor Magnusson. "If only I had known before we left. I would have made him marry you."

"Tor's father wouldn't let us get married because of Papa. I wrote to Tor and told him about the baby, but

501

Mr. Magnusson is burning all of my letters. Tor doesn't even know."

"This is such a mess," Elin murmured.

"It was a mess, Elin, but Knute Lindquist is an answer to my prayers. He saw me crying, and I was so desperate that I ended up telling him everything. He's a widower with a young son, and he offered to marry me and save my baby and me from disgrace. He's saving both of you from my disgrace, too. He didn't have to do that. But he is a good man, and I'm going to marry him."

No one spoke. It seemed to Elin that the air around them was too thick to breathe. Her heart ached for Kirsten.

Sofia laid her hand on Elin's arm. "Would somebody please tell me what you're talking about? What did Uncle Sven do?"

Once again, a wave of relief washed over Elin. If Sofia didn't know, then it meant that he hadn't touched her. But her relief was quickly followed by a tidal wave of shame.

"He was an evil man," Kirsten said.

"But it was my fault," Elin said. "I-I turned to him for comfort after Papa died. . . ."

"It wasn't your fault," Kirsten said. "You trusted him, and he took advantage of you."

"Just like Tor took advantage of you," Elin finished. "And for the same reasons. I was so distraught after Mama and Papa died, and I trusted him. I'm so sorry."

They clung to each other and wept, huddled together on the sidewalk, oblivious to their surroundings. When they finally pulled apart and dried their eyes, Elin was surprised that life around them continued as before.

"So," Sofia said with a sigh. "We'll start all over again, beginning today. Our past is forgiven when we give it to God, and from now on there is no more shame for any of us. Do you believe that, Kirsten?"

"Yes."

"Do you believe it, Elin?"

"Yes . . . but I still don't know what we're going to do—"

"We're going to trust God, just like Mama did. Even when she was dying, she trusted Him and never doubted His love, remember? Things might still be a mess right now, but He can make everything right. He already is making it right. We thought everyone in our family was gone and that it was just the three of us, but now our family is starting to grow again. Kirsten's baby is part of our new family. Mr. Lindquist will be, too. We're going to be fine. You'll see."

Elin couldn't help smiling when she looked at Sofia and heard the optimism in her voice. She truly had changed since leaving home. "But you don't have to work in that theater, Sofia. You'll come up to Wisconsin with me, won't you? You can have a home up there just like the one we left behind. When we were on the boat you said that was what you wanted."

"I've changed my mind since then. I met Ludwig and—"

"Oh, Sofia. Please don't keep waiting for him," Kirsten said. "Don't you think he would have been here by now if he was coming?"

"I'm not giving up. He'll find me, I know he will. And in the meantime, the job at the theater is the answer to my prayers. I signed a contract, and I'm going to keep my word. I love both of you, but I think it's time for me to grow up."

Elin still wasn't sure that Sofia and Kirsten were making the right choices, but both of them seemed determined to carry through with their plans, with or without her approval. They all started walking again, taking their time. Elin didn't want to return to the boardinghouse yet and deal with Aunt Hilma after the emotional upheaval she'd experienced today. Her sisters seemed fragile, as well. They kept walking.

Kirsten was pregnant. Elin still couldn't comprehend it, nor could she shed the feeling that it was somehow her fault. She had promised Mama that she would take care of her sisters . . . but Sofia had said it wasn't up to Elin to fix everything. And Mrs. Anderson had said that even parents weren't responsible for their children's decisions, much less sisters. Being an adult meant living with your mistakes.

Kirsten and Sofia had their own lives to live—and Elin had hers. The thought frightened her. What purpose would she have without her sisters to care for?

They rounded the corner and the little park came into sight.

"Don't go to Wisconsin, Elin," Kirsten said. "You can live with me."

"Or with me," Sofia said. "The rent is all paid. We can move in right now, in fact."

"No, let's squeeze one more free meal out of Aunt Hilma first," Kirsten said with a smile.

"We did make all that jam for her today," Sofia added. "Do you think she'll give us a jar to take with us?"

"Ha!" Kirsten scoffed.

It was good to see her sisters laughing again after all the tears they had shed. But Elin realized that she hadn't answered their question about moving to Wisconsin. "I don't know if I can stay here with you or not," she finally said. "I told Gunnar Pedersen to write and let me know if the offer of marriage is still good—and if I would still be welcome up there. If he and the others want me to come, I can't renege a second time."

They moved out of the boardinghouse that evening after supper, dragging their trunk through the streets once again, this time to the room that Sofia had rented. Kirsten would live there until Knute found a house and arranged their wedding with Pastor Johnson. Elin would stay until she heard from Gunnar.

"Maybe those farmers are fed up with us by now," Kirsten said. "Maybe they just want their money, not you."

"Maybe," Elin said. But she knew from Gunnar's friendly letters that he would likely accept her offer, even if the other farmers didn't. She couldn't turn him down and dash his hopes again, even if it meant leaving her sisters behind.

Kirsten paused to rest, setting down her end of the trunk. "I'll be glad when we finally have a real home so we don't have to drag this trunk around anymore. It would have been easier to haul a dead troll all the way from Sweden than this thing. At least a troll would have been soft enough to sit on."

They had stopped to rest in front of a dress shop, and Sofia gazed at the gowns in the window. "You know what?" she said. "I think Kirsten should buy an American dress for her wedding. Her birthday is tomorrow. I still have one dollar left after paying our rent. Do you have any money, Elin?"

"I spent all of it on train tickets to Wisconsin. They might let me cash them in, but I don't know."

"Do you still have your money, Kirsten?"

"I do, but what about food? Don't we need to eat?"

"No, I think a new dress is much more important," Sofia said. "Don't you, Elin?"

Elin looked at her sisters' hopeful faces. She didn't want to be as stingy as Aunt Hilma, and she was tired of worrying. "Yes, I do," she said. "As soon as the stores open tomorrow morning, I think we should all go shopping."

Chapter Thirty-Seven

"HAPPY BIRTHDAY, KIRSTEN," Elin said the moment Kirsten opened her eyes.

She sat up and looked around sleepily before recognizing the hotel room that Sofia had rented. It had bare walls and an odd musty smell that had intensified overnight. The bed they shared was too cramped for all three of them, so they had slept crosswise with their feet hanging off the side. It wouldn't be comfortable to sleep that way for very long, but Kirsten knew she would be leaving soon. She and Knute were getting married in three days. She wanted to savor these last few days with her sisters.

"Yes, happy birthday," Sofia said. "This is going to be a wonderful year for you, I just know it."

Kirsten turned nineteen today. When she and Knute had applied for their marriage license she'd learned that he was twenty-nine. The sorrow he carried with him made him seem much older.

"I'm hungry," she said as she buttoned up her skirt. The smell of toast was drifting up from the hotel dining room, below them. "I can't believe Aunt Hilma didn't at least give us some bread crusts when we moved out last night."

"I was hoping for some of the jam Sofia and I made," Elin said.

"We'll buy food while we're out," Sofia said.

"We're going shopping this morning to buy Kirsten some new clothes, remember?"

They finished getting dressed and were trying to decide which store to visit first when someone knocked on their door. Kirsten, who was standing closest to it, unlocked it and opened it a crack.

"Knute! What are you doing here?"

"I'm on my way to work, but I wanted to tell you that I found a small house for rent yesterday. The landlord will be there at eleven o'clock this morning if you want to go over and see it. If you think it is suitable, you may pay him this rent money, and he will give you the keys." He pushed an envelope into her hands.

"Of course it will be suitable," she said, laughing. "Anything is better than this creepy place—or the jail cell we stayed in for a night." He didn't smile at her attempts to be lighthearted. Kirsten tried to recall if she had ever seen him smile. "Listen, Knute, I'm in no position to be choosy, so—"

"I am not a very good judge of kitchen facilities. I was concerned that they may not be adequate."

He was so serious and intense that Kirsten's mood sobered, as well. "I see. In that case, I'll be happy to walk over and have a look at the house."

"I wrote the address on the envelope. The house is close to the streetcar line that I take to work. And it's only a few blocks from the market. Here, take some money for the streetcar. It's a long walk from here."

She let him dump some loose change into her hand,

thinking she would walk to the house instead and buy breakfast for her sisters with the money. Besides, she didn't want him to know that she had no idea how to travel by streetcar. Kirsten closed the door after Knute left and turned around to tell her sisters the good news.

"Look!" she said, waving the envelope. "Knute found—"

"We heard everything," Elin said. "Sorry. It was impossible not to hear."

"That's all right. Do you want to walk over there with me at eleven o'clock and see it?"

"I can't," Sofia said. "I have to rehearse at the theater this morning at ten."

"I'll go with you," Elin said. "Where is it?"

Kirsten looked down at the address. "Knute said it's a long walk. He said to take the streetcar, but the exercise will be good for me. I don't want to get too fat. Remember how huge Mrs. Jansson from back home used to get every time she had a baby?"

"You won't get that big," Elin said, laughing. "Mrs. Jansson was huge even when she wasn't expecting."

"How could you tell?" Sofia asked. "She was always expecting! Didn't she have about two dozen children?"

"It sure seemed like it," Elin said. "But none of them ever stood still long enough for anyone to count."

Kirsten felt tears stinging her eyes as she listened to her sisters' laughter. "I'm going to miss you both so much," she said softly.

"Don't start talking that way yet," Elin scolded. "We have three more days until your wedding, and I don't want to run out of tears before then."

"Let's go shopping." Sofia stood and herded Kirsten and Elin toward the door. "Wait until you see how nice it is to have something new. You'll feel like a real American once you look like one. I felt like I had finally left Sweden behind when I put on my new clothes."

They couldn't afford to shop at Marshall Field's, where Sofia had shopped. Instead, they went to a store in their Swedish neighborhood that sold everything from ladies' dresses and men's hats to dishes and household goods. Kirsten purchased a simple black skirt made of patterned brilliantine for $1.35 and a white taffeta waist for $1.65, spending all but one dollar of her pay.

"We can get by on one dollar until Sofia gets paid," Elin said. "We can buy day-old bread at the bakery and bargain for damaged fruit and vegetables at the farmers' market the way Aunt Hilma does."

The clerk folded Kirsten's new clothes and wrapped them in a brown paper bundle tied with string. "I'm going to save these clothes until the wedding," Kirsten said.

It took her and Elin half an hour to walk to the house Knute had rented. Sofia showed them the Viking Theater on the way but had to remain behind to rehearse.

"I still can't imagine our shy little Sofia singing on a stage in front of hundreds of people," Kirsten said as she and Elin walked on. "Who would have ever thought?"

"I'm still not too sure I like the idea." Elin said. "I hope she's safe and that nothing happens—"

"She'll be fine. She has grown up so much since we left home, hasn't she? Sofia used to be so quiet and shy and prissy; now she's reading the Bible all the time and telling us to pray about everything."

"She reminds me of Mama."

"Yes . . . Mama would be very proud of her."

Kirsten found the white-shingled house on a quiet side street a few blocks from the main thoroughfare. It was small and square with a peaked roof and a tiny front porch, and it sat perched on a patch of grass like a rock in the middle of a stream. The landlord sat waiting for them on the porch steps with the key. Kirsten recognized the first word he said to them—the American greeting *hello,* but that was all as he babbled on and on in a friendly way.

"I don't speak English," she said, shaking her head. "Sorry. May I see inside?" She smiled and pointed to the door. "Inside . . . ?" He finally seemed to understand. He unlocked the door for her, then stood aside as she and Elin went in to look around.

The three downstairs rooms—living room, dining room, and kitchen—were lined up in a straight row from the front door to the back door. The house had wooden floors and plenty of windows to let in sunlight and fresh air. A staircase led to two small bedrooms beneath the eaves.

"This is a very nice kitchen," Elin said as she looked around. It had a sink with indoor plumbing, a small cast-iron cookstove, and a cupboard for dishes hanging on one wall. "It's just right for the two of you."

"There will soon be three of us," Kirsten said. "Knute is going to send to Sweden for his son. And the baby will make four of us, of course." It was still hard for Kirsten to imagine that a real live baby was growing inside her. When she did remember, the idea of giving birth and caring for a newborn terrified her.

"It's a nice little house," Elin said. "You're going to take it, I hope."

Kirsten came out of her reverie. The landlord stood with the key in his hand, waiting for her answer. "Yes," she told him, using one of the few English words she knew. "Yes . . . yes."

She handed him the money Knute had given her and kept the envelope with the address printed on it. The landlord gave her the key, then pulled a second key from his pocket and handed it to her, chattering on and on in English. She hoped he wasn't giving important instructions about how to take care of the house, because she didn't understand a word he said.

"Thank you," she told him in Swedish. "Thank you very much." When he was gone she turned to Elin. "We need to be smart like Sofia and start learning English."

"You should learn," Elin said. "I probably won't need it up in Wisconsin."

Kirsten exhaled. "I wish you would change your mind about going there. I need you, Elin. Especially with a baby on the way and—"

"I know, I know. But let's not worry about it until I hear from Gunnar Pedersen. Shall we take a look at the backyard now?"

The little plot of grass had a scrawny oak tree in one corner and a square patch of weeds that might have once been a vegetable garden in the other. A clothesline stretched from the back porch to a pole on the side of the yard. Kirsten pictured a row of flapping diapers on it and suddenly felt alone. And scared.

"This will be a nice place for Knute's little boy to play," Elin said.

Kirsten nodded, but the truth was, the yard looked desolate and bleak to her. She remembered how she and her sisters had roamed the woods near their farm at home, searching for fairy glens and pretending that a pile of boulders was a giant's castle. She turned and went back into the house.

"Where will you get furniture?" Elin asked as they walked through the empty rooms again.

"Knute is going to look through the advertisements in his newspaper. He says people are always buying new furniture and selling their old things."

"Really? Don't Americans hand things down to their children and grandchildren like we did back home? It means so much more when the tables and chairs were in your family for years, don't you think?"

"Yes, but a lot of Americans immigrated here from someplace else, remember? They had to leave all the furniture behind, just like we did."

"I guess you're right. Things change . . . and life goes on."

Kirsten didn't want to think about change—there had been too many changes in her life as it was—but she knew that she had to. Elin was right. Life went on.

"It's a nice little house," Elin said again. "You'll make it into a home."

On the night before the wedding, Elin unpacked the trunk and divided up the things they had brought with them from Sweden, letting Kirsten have first choice of what she wanted for a wedding present. Kirsten decided on the silver candlesticks that had belonged to their grandmother. Elin chose the copper coffee kettle. Sofia took Mama's hymnbook and the wooden bowl painted with rosemaling. Then they divided up the linen towels and aprons and table runners that Mama had embroidered and the wooden utensils that Papa had carved.

"Just think Mama's fingers made every stitch," Elin said as she caressed the colored thread.

Sofia wiped a tear. "I'll bet she never dreamed these things would travel so many miles from home."

"What's wrong, Sofia?" Elin asked her.

"Dividing all these things . . . I think I'm finally realizing that we won't always be together."

Kirsten struggled against her own tears. "Both of you should move in with Knute and me. This rooming house isn't a very nice place."

Sofia shook her head. "It would be too far for me to travel back and forth to the theater every day. I'll look for a nicer place when I have a little money saved."

"Besides," Elin said, "your house isn't very big, Kirsten. And you need time alone with your husband."

Kirsten finally lost the battle with her tears. "I hate being apart! We've never been separated before. All my life, for as far back as I can remember, the two of you have been there."

"I know," Elin said, pulling Kirsten into her arms. "I know. And for as long as I can remember, I've been watching over the two of you. But even if we'd stayed in Sweden, we would have all married husbands one day and moved to homes of our own. I'm just sorry that the time has come so soon."

Kirsten didn't sleep well that night. And judging by the way her sisters tossed and turned, they didn't, either. She couldn't stop thinking about Tor, wishing she were marrying him in their church back home. It must feel very different to be marrying someone you loved and to be looking forward to a lifetime together. It scared her to think of all the years that stretched ahead of her as Knute Lindquist's second wife. She wished she could run away.

But she quickly turned her thoughts to the baby that was growing inside her and knew she had to go through with the wedding. She closed her eyes and thanked God for Knute Lindquist.

"I shouldn't have wasted money on these clothes," she said as she dressed for her wedding the next day. "They won't fit me too much longer anyway." She hopped up and down in front of the dresser, trying to see herself in the mirror.

"What are you doing?" Elin asked her.

"I can't see how I look."

"You look beautiful," Sofia told her. "Doesn't she, Elin?"

"Yes, now sit down and let me pin up your hair. And no more hopping around, or it will all come falling down."

"Don't make it look too neat," Sofia said with a smile. "She won't look like Kirsten unless her hair is flying all over the place."

When it was time to leave, Elin and Sofia loaded all of Kirsten's things into their three satchels and carried them for her. Kirsten's knees felt wobbly as she walked to the church. Knute was already there, waiting for her. She wondered if he was as nervous as she was and if he was thinking of Flora, remembering their wedding day. She wouldn't ask him. She didn't want to stir the ashes of his grief.

It seemed to Kirsten that Pastor Johnson was reluctant to perform the simple ceremony, even though Knute had spoken to him about it several days ago. "I would still advise against this marriage," he said as he ushered everyone into his study. He addressed his words to Knute, not her. "Why not take your time and do this properly? At least have the banns read in church."

"My son is coming from Sweden soon. We want everything to be ready when he arrives."

"Are you certain you want to do this, Knute?" he asked again. "You barely know Miss Carlson. And there is quite an age difference."

"Miss Carlson and I are both very certain." He turned to Kirsten as if to make sure. She nodded and smiled in spite of her fear.

The pastor's wife handed Kirsten a small bouquet of flowers that she had picked from her garden. Elin, Sofia, and a friend of Knute's from work gathered around them to serve as witnesses. Kirsten's heart pounded so wildly as the pastor read the vows that she barely comprehended a word of them. She answered "I do" in all the proper places, closed her eyes as Pastor Johnson prayed for them, and before she knew it, they were pronounced man and wife. It seemed ridiculous that a few words and a simple piece of paper could bind her to this man she barely knew for the rest of her life. But it was true. Kirsten was now Mrs. Knute Lindquist.

The pastor's wife applauded as Knute gave her a

brief kiss. There would be no wedding reception. Neither of them had many friends or family members in Chicago.

Knute shook hands with the minister and with his friend, and then everyone followed him outside to the carriage he had hired to drive to their new house. Kirsten and her sisters cried as they hugged each other good-bye. Knute loaded Kirsten's satchels into the carriage.

"I just remembered," he said, turning to her. "When I asked Mr. Anderson for the afternoon off, he said that he wanted to speak with you and your sisters in his office tomorrow."

"Why? What does he want?" Kirsten asked.

"He didn't say. But he would like all three of you to be there tomorrow at two o'clock."

"I wish he'd told you what this is about," Elin said.

"It's useless to worry," Sofia said with a sigh. "We can face him with a clear conscience."

Kirsten smiled, trying to put on a brave face as she climbed into the carriage with Knute. "Good-bye! I'll meet you at the newspaper office tomorrow." She waved until her sisters were out of sight.

Knute had purchased a few things for the house since Kirsten had visited—a table and two chairs for the dining room, a desk and small horsehair sofa for the living room, some pots and utensils for the kitchen. The house still looked empty. Kirsten gazed around, trying to shake the feeling that she had made a huge mistake. She reminded herself that her mistake had been in trusting Tor. Knute was a good man.

"Thank you for marrying me," she told him. "You didn't have to—"

"Listen, Kirsten. It's done now, so please don't mention it anymore."

She followed him as he carried her bags upstairs and set them down on one of the beds he'd purchased. It looked much too narrow for two people to sleep on.

"I thought I would let you and Torkel have this larger bedroom," he said. "I plan to put another bed in here for him—and you'll want a cradle for the baby. I'll sleep in the smaller bedroom."

She stared at him in surprise. He had warned her before they'd married that he didn't expect her to be his wife in every sense of the word, but the reality of it still stunned her. "But . . . I mean . . . I didn't realize that we would sleep apart."

"I don't think it would be right if . . ." he said, his voice trailing off. "I'll let you get unpacked."

She sank down on the bed, listening to his footsteps fade as he hurried downstairs. She couldn't deny that she felt hurt and rejected. But what did she expect? After all, it was a marriage of convenience for both of them. She had entered into it knowing that Knute didn't love her, knowing that his wife would always occupy first place in his heart. And if she was honest with herself, Kirsten knew she wasn't in love with him, either. Even so, she couldn't help feeling disappointed that Knute didn't want to be with her and that they would never truly be husband and wife.

Think of the baby, she told herself. She had done this for her baby and for her sisters. She wiped her tears and stood to make her bed, using the linens she'd brought with her from Sweden. When she'd finished unpacking, placing her clothes in the dresser drawers and her toiletries on top of it, she went downstairs. Knute was working at the desk in the living room. He had already filled it with his papers and books. She noticed a packing crate with more books on the floor beside it.

"I have made arrangements for Torkel to come as soon as possible." He didn't look up at her when he spoke.

Kirsten sat down on the stiff sofa, perched on the very edge. "How will he get here? He can't travel this far all by himself."

"Flora's family will travel with him as far as Gothenburg. He has been living with them. And as it happens, the friend you met at the wedding today wants to bring his mother to America. She will travel with Torkel the rest of the way."

"Won't it be hard for them when they get to Ellis Island? My sisters and I were stuck there for almost two weeks, and it was so crowded and confusing and—" She stopped, suddenly recalling that the immigration facility had burned to the ground.

"They will be traveling with first-class tickets, not

in steerage," Knute said. "They won't have any problems."

Kirsten ran her fingers along a worn place on the arm of the sofa, thinking she should crochet a doily to cover it. She could tell that both she and Knute were nervous as they tried to make conversation. She hoped it would get easier once they grew to know each other better.

"You must be excited to see your son again," she said. "How soon will he arrive?"

"In about three weeks, if all goes as planned."

She could think of nothing more to say. Neither, apparently, could Knute. "Well," she said, rising to her feet. "I suppose I should get busy if we're going to have our dinner on time. Are there any groceries in the cupboard?" She felt like a child playing house, preparing to fix mud pies. She had never been in charge of her own kitchen before.

"I didn't know what to buy, but I can give you some money." He stood to pull out his wallet. "Do you know where the shops are?"

"Yes. I think we passed some on the way here. What would you like to eat?"

"Anything is fine. I'm not particular."

"Well, then . . . I guess I'll be back in a little while."

She took an empty satchel in which to carry her groceries and walked two blocks to the store, fighting the urge to cry. The sun was shining. She had everything she needed for a happy life: a roof over her head, food to eat, and a good man to take care of her.

God had answered her prayers. Her baby would have a father and a name. Most important of all, she had a home again. Yes, for the first time since leaving Sweden, Kirsten finally had a real home.

So why did she feel so empty inside? Why did she still long for something more?

Chapter Thirty-Eight

THE THUNDERING PRINTING presses made the floor tremble. Sofia felt the vibrations tremble through her as she waited with her sisters to speak with Gustav Anderson. Dozens of reporters sat behind paper-strewn desks in the busy newspaper office, pounding on typewriters. The presses occupied the large room below the office area, churning out newspapers with relentless noise.

"How long do you think it would take to get used to this racket?" Sofia asked. Elin shrugged.

"I couldn't stand to work here," Kirsten replied.

"Doesn't your . . . doesn't Knute work here?" Sofia asked. She craned her neck, looking around the room for him. "I don't see him."

"I don't know where he is or what he does here." Kirsten and Elin seemed very nervous as they waited to learn why Mr. Anderson had asked to see them. Sofia leaned toward her sisters so she wouldn't have to shout.

"We don't have to be afraid of him, you know. We didn't do anything wrong."

"That was true the last time we talked to him, too," Kirsten said, "and we ended up in jail. Remember?"

"Maybe he wants to apologize to us."

"Ha!" Kirsten said. "Maybe fairies are real, too."

Sofia gave up trying to ease the tension and sat back to wait, watching the chaos in the newsroom. At last Mr. Anderson's door opened, and she heard him clear his throat.

"Thank you for coming, ladies. Please, step inside."

"Into the lion's den," Kirsten murmured as she rose to her feet. Elin shushed her.

But there was nothing lionlike about Gustav Anderson. In fact, he was so small and prim and sharp-featured that he reminded Sofia of a mole. His office had no windows, which probably explained why he was so pale-skinned. The dim interior made him seem even more molelike.

"Please sit down," he said.

They obeyed, sitting in the three chairs he had placed in front of his desk. Mr. Anderson took his seat behind it. Elin and Kirsten looked as stiff as kindling wood as they waited to hear what he had to say. He gazed into the air above their heads, as if unwilling to look them in the eye.

"I owe you an apology for accusing you of thievery," he said quietly.

Sofia's mouth fell open in amazement. She fought the urge to give Kirsten a nudge.

"Under the circumstances, I hope you will understand how easy it was to reach the conclusion that you had taken Mother's jewelry. No one else had access to her bedroom, and the jewelry was clearly missing. Nevertheless, I do apologize for the error."

None of them spoke, apparently too shocked to respond. Finally Sofia answered for all three of them. "We forgive you, Mr. Anderson."

"Thank you." He cleared his throat again. "Along with her will, my mother entrusted her lawyer with a letter addressed to me. Most of it is very personal, but she also talked about the three of you. I know that Mother had a gruff exterior and that she probably would never admit it, but she grew very fond of the three of you in the short time you worked for her."

"We were fond of her, too," Elin said softly. "We miss her."

Gustav took a moment to shuffle papers around on his desk. He scowled as if trying not to show his emotion, his focus resting everywhere but on the three of them. Sofia thought his behavior was surprising for a wealthy businessman in the comfort of his own office. He cleared his throat again.

"My mother told me in her letter that she envied you girls. She said you had two things that all of her wealth could never purchase: love for each other and faith in God's forgiveness. She said she learned a great deal from you, and so she wanted to do something for you in return. That's why she sold her jewelry and left the proceeds to the three of you in her will."

Sofia's pulse quickened. She moved to the edge of her seat, wondering what her sisters were thinking.

"As you've probably heard, my wife wants to contest Mother's will." He looked up at them, eye to eye, for the first time. "I have ordered her to stop the lawsuit. You will receive the bequest that my mother wanted you to have."

Sofia leaned back in her chair. She didn't know which surprised her more, the fact that she would receive the money or that Gustav had stood up to Bettina. Neither she nor her sisters seemed to know what to say, so they remained silent, waiting. Gustav picked up a piece of paper, consulting it.

"Which one of you is Elin?"

"I-I am."

"Mother said that of all the nurses who have cared for her over the years, you were the finest. She said you have an intuitive gift for healing. Before she died, she spoke to someone at Augustana Hospital. The institution is more than ten years old, but about three years ago they started a school to train nurses. Mother has arranged for you to be enrolled in their two-year nursing course this fall. She has provided for all of your expenses in her will."

Tears filled Sofia's eyes as she reached for Elin's hand.

"If only I had known . . ." Elin murmured.

"You're not moving to Wisconsin," Sofia heard Kirsten whisper. "You're going to stay here and be a nurse." Elin slowly shook her head.

"You must be Kirsten," Gustav continued, nodding in her direction.

"Yes, sir."

"Mother described you as intelligent and quick-witted. She was always a firm believer in higher education for women, even though she wasn't educated herself. And so she has arranged for you to attend North Park College up on Foster Avenue. The school is only a half-dozen years old, but they provide a variety of programs for young people from the Swedish community, including English classes."

Sofia watched a tear roll down Kirsten's cheek. Mr. Anderson must know that it was too late, that she had already married Knute Lindquist.

"I wish I could thank her," Kirsten said.

"The scholarship is available whenever you decide to use it." He turned abruptly to Sofia. "You are Sofia, the one who sang at her dinner party."

"Yes." Her voice was barely a whisper.

"Mother thought very highly of your musical talent. She cleared the way to have you enrolled at the Sherwood Music Conservatory on Michigan Avenue. She provided money for all of your costs, including living expenses."

"Oh!" There was so much that Sofia wanted to say, but she couldn't seem to utter another word.

"Finally, Mother stipulated that any outstanding debt for your tickets to America be paid in full, as well."

Sofia didn't know whether to laugh or cry. With their debt paid, Elin was free to stay in Chicago.

Kirsten was the first one who was able to speak.

"I-I believe I speak for my sisters when I say that . . . that we don't know what to say!"

"It isn't necessary to say anything at all. This was Mother's doing, not mine." He stood as if he wanted them to leave now that he'd appeased his conscience. Sofia and her sisters rose, also. "My mother's lawyer, whom I believe you've met, will handle all of the details of her bequest from now on. You should consult with him to make any further arrangements, not with me."

"Thank you, Mr. Anderson," Elin said. "We're very grateful to you and your mother." As soon as they were through the door, he closed it behind them. They walked out to the street without saying a word and stood in front of the building, too stunned to start walking, too amazed to decide where to go.

"If only we had known about the will sooner," Kirsten finally said. "It would have changed everything."

"At least you can quit working in that theater now," Elin told Sofia.

She shook her head. "But I don't want to quit. In the first place, I already signed a contract. And in the second place—" She stopped, deciding not to tell her sisters that she wanted her name to appear on posters so that Ludwig could find her. Kirsten would say that Sofia was foolish to wait for him, that he would have been there by now if he were coming. But Sofia knew Ludwig would find her. *"I will search for the one my heart loves,"* he had promised.

527

"And in the second place," she continued, "if I talk to Mr. Lund, maybe he'll let me study at the music conservatory and sing in his show at the same time."

Elin sighed. "But promise me that you'll look for someplace else to live. There must be a respectable boardinghouse for women like the one Aunt Hilma runs for men. Mr. Anderson said that all of your expenses would be paid for."

"That means Sofia can eat, too," Kirsten said, smiling. "And it won't have to be moldy fruit."

"I promise I'll find a better place," Sofia said. "You and I will live there together, Elin, while you study to be a nurse. Mrs. Anderson is right—you're going to make a wonderful nurse. I'm so relieved that you can stay here with us now that our tickets are paid for."

But Elin's expression was sorrowful as she turned away from Sofia. She started walking down the street, away from them. "What's wrong?" Sofia asked when she caught up with her.

"It's too late. I promised Gunnar and the others I would come to Wisconsin if they still wanted me to. I gave my word, just like you signed a contract and Kirsten spoke her marriage vows. You have to keep your commitments, and if I hear back from Gunnar, I'll have to keep mine."

"But you were only moving up there in order to repay our debt," Kirsten said. "All they want is their money, right?"

"No, that's not all. Gunnar and the others are

lonely. They want to get married and start families. They want real homes, too, just like we do."

"But we need you here with us," Sofia said.

Elin stopped walking and put her hands on Sofia's shoulders. "No. The truth is that you and Kirsten are all grown up now. You don't need me hovering over you anymore, worrying about you and telling you to be careful. Look at all the things you and Kirsten were able to do on your own."

"But that doesn't mean we want you to leave!"

"I know. But let's live one day at a time, Sofia. We'll wait to hear from the men up in Wisconsin, and we won't think about saying good-bye until then, all right?"

"I think we should stop by the boardinghouse on our way back to the hotel and see if a letter came," Kirsten said.

"It's much too soon to hear back," Elin said. "It will take a while for my letter to get all the way up there and for Gunnar to reply."

"Let's stop anyway," Kirsten said. "I want to tell Aunt Hilma that we're rich now, and gloat in her face."

"Be nice, Kirsten."

"Why?" she laughed. "We don't need her any-more."

They found Aunt Hilma in the boardinghouse kitchen as usual, making a pot of fish chowder for the boarders' dinner. "Oh good," she said when she saw the three of them. "Here you are. I was afraid I would have to send Carl and Waldemar over to that hotel where you're staying after supper. Now you've saved me the trouble."

"What did you want us for?" Elin asked.

"I don't want you. A telegram came for you today and I figured it must be important. It's on the hall table."

Sofia and Kirsten waited in the kitchen while Elin went to retrieve it. She didn't open the envelope until they were well away from Aunt Hilma and her gossiping tongue.

"Who is it from?" Kirsten asked. "What does it say?"

Elin's face looked pale as she tore open the envelope. "It's from Gunnar Pedersen. It says, 'The offer is still good. We can't wait to meet you. Please come right away.'"

"Oh no," Kirsten moaned.

Sofia wanted to sink down in the middle of the sidewalk and weep. She knew Elin would keep her word. They were going to lose their sister. "It's our own fault," Sofia wept. "We took matters into our own hands instead of waiting for God to answer our prayers."

"Well, God shouldn't have taken so long," Kirsten said.

"Can't you write to Gunnar and explain about the nursing school?" Sofia asked.

"No, that wouldn't be fair." Elin lifted her chin in the air, and Sofia knew she was trying to be brave.

"I'm going to go up and meet them—and with any luck, none of them will want to marry a scrawny, plain-looking girl like me."

Chapter Thirty-Nine

ELIN TRIED TO hold back her tears as she stood on the station platform with her sisters—to no avail. The locomotive chuffed steam and spat out soot, eager to be on its way. Elin wasn't eager at all.

"It's so hard to let you go!" Sofia sobbed.

"I know," Elin told her. "I know. And it would be impossible to leave you and Kirsten if you both weren't so grown up now and able to make choices for yourselves."

"We're trusting God," Sofia said.

Elin nodded, biting her lip. "That's the wisest choice of all."

Kirsten gave their battered trunk a kick. Her husband had hired a carriage so they could transport it to the station. "Well, it's not as heavy as it used to be, but you're still stuck with it, Elin. Promise me you'll chop it up for firewood this winter—and make soap out of the ashes."

"I'm not going to chop it up," Elin said, smiling through her tears. "I'll keep it to remind me of you."

"Promise you'll write to us every day?" Sofia asked.

"Maybe not every day. How will I get any work done?"

"Here. I want you to have this." Sofia pulled their mother's Bible from the pocket of her skirt and handed it to Elin.

"But you need this. You read it all the time."

"I'm going to buy a new one in English. It will help me learn faster."

Elin held the little Bible out to Kirsten. "Do you want it? I feel selfish taking it. It was Mama's."

Kirsten pushed it away. "No, you keep it. Knute has a Bible I can read. I saw it there with all his other books."

Sofia handed Elin a small piece of paper, folded in half. "And I want to give you this. It's the last Bible verse that Ludwig gave me before we parted."

Elin opened the paper and her eyes filled with tears as she read the words: *May the Lord keep watch between you and me when we are far away from each other. Genesis 31:49.*

The train whistle blew.

Of all the good-byes Elin had said, this one was the hardest. She could never remember a time when Kirsten and Sofia hadn't been in her life. She boarded the train with an aching heart and watched from the window until her sisters were out of sight. She felt like she was traveling to the ends of the earth.

Tears blurred Elin's journey through the city, past smoking factories and tenement houses and stock-yards. But soon the train reached the city limits, and the view through her window expanded, revealing scattered houses and barns, and acres and acres of flat farmland and prairie. It was the first time she had been out of Chicago since arriving last spring, and she had nearly forgotten what trees and blue sky looked like.

She rode for hours. The train stopped every once in a while in a small nameless town with a small wooden station. Elin remembered how she had gazed out at the scenery back in Sweden and had tried to memorize her homeland, fearing she would forget what it looked like. And she had forgotten, for a while, when living in Chicago. But now, as she neared the little village where Gunnar Pedersen lived, Elin looked out at the gently rolling hills carpeted in green, at the neat squares of cultivated land, at the tidy barns and grazing cows, and she remembered what home was like.

It looked just like this.

At last the conductor came up the aisle and removed her ticket from its clip in front of her seat. She didn't understand what he was telling her in English, but she knew from observing the other passengers along the way that when the conductor took passengers' tickets, they always got off at the next stop. She tried to tidy her hair and smooth some of the wrinkles from her skirt, feeling nervous about meeting Gunnar Pedersen and the other men for the first time. She wondered what they would look like—and what they would think of her.

When the train halted, only one person stood waiting on the platform. Elin knew it was Gunnar.

He looked younger than she had expected yet much bigger, a giant of a man with burly shoulders and forearms like logs. His smooth, round face broke into a smile when Elin stepped off the train, and he swept off his hat to greet her, revealing comb trails through his damp sandy hair. His eyes were as blue as the sky.

"*Hej*, I'm Elin Carlson. You must be Gunnar." She offered him her hand, and it was swallowed up in his own.

"You didn't tell me you were so pretty. And as tiny as a little sparrow."

Elin had the feeling that Gunnar would have stood there all day with her hand in his, staring at her. But she glanced to one side and noticed a baggage clerk wheeling her trunk down the platform from the baggage car.

"That's my trunk," she said. "I hope it will fit in your carriage."

Gunnar never took his gaze from her face. His grin widened. "It'll fit. I brought the farm wagon. I hope you don't mind."

She recalled that her trip to America had begun in a farm wagon, and she shook her head. "I don't mind. It will be just like home." She gently pulled her hand out of his, breaking the spell.

Gunnar lifted the trunk as if it were filled with feathers. Elin smiled, imagining what Kirsten would say about that. He loaded it into the back of his wagon, then helped Elin climb up on the seat. He took his place beside her. The bench was small and he was very big, forcing them to brush against each other as they drove down the road. But even though Gunnar was a stranger, Elin was surprised to discover that she didn't feel at all afraid or suspicious of him. He smelled good, like sunshine and fresh air and newly turned earth.

"We decided you should stay with my parents for now, on their farm," Gunnar said. "I live with three other bachelors, so it wouldn't be right for you to stay with us. My mother is looking forward to meeting you and having someone to talk to in the kitchen. I think I told you that my sisters are both grown and married with families of their own. Mama has gone all out cooking for you. Wait until you see! Although you don't look like you eat very much, so I hope you're hungry. When we have time, I'll drive you over to my land and show you where I plan to build my own house. I want to build a big white farmhouse someday, like that one over there. It belongs to Per Wallstrom and his family. They were among the very first settlers here, and—I'm sorry, I'm talking too much, aren't I?"

Elin smiled up at him. "That's all right. My sisters tell me I'm too quiet. Kirsten does most of the talking, and—" She choked up thinking about her sisters. "I'm sorry."

"No, that's all right. You miss your sisters. That's understandable."

"I've been taking care of them all my life."

"Maybe when you tell them how nice it is up here they'll decide to come, too."

"It is beautiful here. And so much like home. But I don't think Kirsten and Sofia will be coming. They have lives of their own in Chicago. But please keep talking. I would love for you to tell me about everything we'll see along the way."

"Are you sure? You'll let me know if I'm boring you, won't you?"

Elin laughed. "Your letters were always very interesting. I'm quite sure you won't bore me."

The wagon passed several farms and stretches of woodland until finally coming to a halt outside a tidy cluster of log buildings nestled in a little valley. The tree-covered hills surrounding the farm were so lush and green and beautiful they made Elin's chest ache. Mrs. Pedersen came to the door to greet them with her apron on, and for a moment she reminded Elin of her own mother.

"*Välkommen!* We are so happy to have you, Elin Carlson. Gunnar has been walking around on eggs for days, waiting for you. I'll bet he never imagined that you would be so pretty—eh, Gunnar?" She gave her son a wink.

As hard as the decision had been, Elin knew that coming here had been the right one. The Pedersens were a happy, boisterous family, the food so wholesome and good that she could easily see how Gunnar had grown so tall and strong. Elin enjoyed working in the kitchen beside his mother all day. The workspace was spacious and well stocked, with a dry sink and an iron cookstove and a well-worn farm table that was just the right height for kneading bread. An embroidered sampler next to the corner cupboard read *God Bless Our Home.*

Elin spent the evenings sitting on the porch with Gunnar, listening to him tell stories, or writing letters to her sisters. Within days, she felt like she was back home in Sweden—except for missing Kirsten and Sofia, that is. She wished all three of them had come to Wisconsin in the first place, when they'd first arrived in America. This was the new beginning they had been searching for, the home she had promised them.

And as unlikely as it seemed, Gunnar Pedersen gradually inched his way into Elin's heart. She began to notice how her pulse quickened whenever he arrived home for the evening meal. She found herself glancing in the mirror to fix her hair as she heard his boots tromping up the porch steps. And when she saw her reflection, she was surprised to see that she was smiling.

Three weeks after Elin arrived, Gunnar and his father came home from a trip into town with an envelope from Western Union, addressed to Elin. She opened it to find a letter from Mrs. Anderson's lawyer.

"Is everything all right, Elin?" Gunnar asked. "I hope I'm not being too nosy for asking, but I was worried all the way home that it might be bad news."

"No, it's good news," she said, handing the envelope to him. "It's the remainder of the money that my sisters and I owe for our passage to America. You and your friends can divide it among yourselves. We're all paid up."

He looked down at the envelope, not at her. He wasn't smiling. "Yes . . . I'll do that."

Gunnar was very quiet as they ate their dinner. When Elin finished helping with the dishes, she went outside to look for him. She found him in the springhouse, sitting on the edge of the well.

"It's nice and cool in here," she said.

"*Ja.* It always is."

She sat down on the wall beside him. "I thought you would be happy to get your money back."

"Not if it means you're going away."

"I don't want to go away, Gunnar. This feels like home to me." Elin was as surprised as he was to discover that it was true.

He looked up at her for the first time. "But . . . but if everything is paid up . . . and where did the money come from?"

Elin told him about Mrs. Anderson's will, and how it provided money for Kirsten to attend college and for Sofia to go to the music conservatory, as well as for their tickets.

"What did she leave you?" Gunnar asked. Elin looked away. She didn't want to tell him. "Come on, she must have given you something. You were the one who took care of her, weren't you?"

538

"Yes."

Elin smoothed the hem of her apron. She had learned during the past few weeks what a patient man Gunnar was. He would sit here in the springhouse with her until dawn if he had to, waiting for her to tell him. She may as well get it over with.

"She gave me a scholarship to a nursing school. It's a two-year program."

"Is that something you want to do?"

"I don't know. . . . My mother was a midwife back home. Before she died she used to take me with her sometimes, to help with the newborn babies. I loved working with her, and she said she would train me to deliver babies, too. But then she died." Elin paused, listening to the crickets chirp in the grass outside.

"When I was in the hospital on Ellis Island," she continued, "the nurses fascinated me. It seemed like they could ease people's pain and soothe their fears, just by sitting at their bedside. And then I took care of Mrs. Anderson—" Her voice choked again as she remembered the fairy queen. She couldn't finish.

"Then why didn't you stay and become a nurse?" Gunnar asked. "If your tickets were all paid for, why did you come up here?"

"Because I gave you my word before I found out about the will. I didn't want to renege on my promise a second time. I didn't think it would be fair to you."

"Elin," he said, shaking his head. "It seems you are always thinking about other people—your sisters, my friends and me. What about your own feelings, your own dreams?" She answered with a shrug. "You're entitled to have them, you know."

"No . . ." she said aloud, then stopped. Elin didn't believe she was entitled. Ever since Uncle Sven had moved in with her, she'd believed she had forfeited her right to be happy by the bad choices she'd made.

But what if Sofia was right and God really would forgive her? What if her life wasn't over—but just beginning?

"I'm a farmer, deep in my soul," Gunnar said. "It's what God made my heart to love and my hands to do. If He made you to be a nurse, then that's what you should do."

"But I promised you. You sounded so nice in your letters, and you were kind enough to forgive me and to wait for your money. . . . And I'm happy here, really I am. It feels like home."

Gunnar reached for her hand. Elin didn't pull away. Her hand felt comfortable sandwiched between his huge rough ones.

"I think we have feelings for each other, Elin. I felt it already when we were still writing letters, didn't you?"

"Yes. When you met me at the train station I felt like I already knew you."

"Then this is what we will do," he said, giving her hand a gentle squeeze. "You will go back to Chicago and learn to be a nurse, and I will wait for you. It's only two years. We could use a good nurse up here, you know. I think there might be lots of babies coming, one day."

"But that's not fair to you."

"You are worth waiting for, Elin."

She couldn't reply. For the first time in years, Elin dared to believe that she was worthwhile. She looked down at the scrapes and scars on Gunnar's hands and wanted to kiss his rugged knuckles. She lifted the corner of her apron to wipe her tears. "Thank you," she whispered.

"When does your school start?" he asked.

"In September."

"And it lasts for only two years?" She nodded. "That's not such a long time. Two growing seasons. You are welcome to stay here with my family and me until September, but then I think you should go back to Chicago. You'll have a home here with me when you're finished with school—if you want one, that is."

"You are so kind, Gunnar Pedersen. Will you write letters to me while I'm gone?"

"*Ja*, of course I will. In fact, if I have a good crop this year, maybe I'll come down and visit you in Chicago after the harvest."

Elin smiled. "You can meet my sisters. They are very special to me. . . . And so are you."

Chapter Forty

KIRSTEN MISSED HER sisters. The days seemed long and endless, the house too quiet. She had nothing to do but shop and cook and do laundry and no one to talk to while she did it. Whenever she glimpsed her grandmother's silver candlesticks, they reminded her of Sofia and Elin. And home.

Each day she waited eagerly for Knute to come home, watching the front door as she cooked their dinner. Then when he did arrive, she found it difficult to carry on a conversation with him. They sat at their tiny table like mannequins, unsure what to say to each other. As soon as the meal ended, Knute would sit down at his desk or bury his nose in one of his books.

Kirsten was sitting in the living room with him one evening, trying to crochet and making a tangled mess of it—and wishing Elin were there to untangle it for her—when she suddenly asked, "Would you mind if we got a cat?"

He looked up from his book. "What did you say? . . . A cat?"

"Well, not just any cat. He belonged to Mrs. Anderson, and my sisters and I promised her we would take care of him after she died, but none of us could because we didn't have a place to live, and now that I do . . ."

"I don't mind, Kirsten. You may get a cat." He returned to his book.

542

She walked over to Mrs. Olafson's house the next evening after supper to fetch Tomte. "Yes, take him," Mrs. Olafson said. "The poor animal is here alone all day, you see, while my husband and I are at work. The neighbors say he cries all the time."

"How did you carry him over here from the mansion?"

"I stuffed him in a picnic basket and tied the lid shut. And I do mean 'stuffed.' He's such a fat old thing he barely fit inside—and he didn't like it one bit, I'll tell you that!"

Kirsten covered her mouth to hide a smile as she pictured the wiry little woman hobbling down the street with the enormous cat crammed into the basket. Tomte probably howled in protest all the way.

"But the cat lost weight, you see, since his missus died," Mrs. Olafson continued. "He'll fit inside the basket now—but he still won't like it and he'll still be a load to carry."

He was as heavy as a basketful of watermelons. Kirsten had to stop and rest several times, but she managed to lug him all the way home. She and Tomte quickly became a comfort to each other. He followed her around the house all day as she worked and slept beside her in the narrow, lonely bed at night.

Three weeks after Kirsten's wedding, Knute's little boy, Torkel, arrived from Sweden. Knute went alone to the train station to fetch him. Torkel was small for a four-year-old and as thin as his father was. He didn't seem to remember Knute at all, and was crying for his grandmother when Knute carried him into the house and set him down.

"*Hej*, Torkel," Kirsten said, crouching in front of him. "It's so nice to finally meet you." He shrank back from her in fear. She stood again. "What shall I tell him to call me?" she whispered to Knute.

"I don't know. Let him decide."

Suddenly the cat jumped down from the sofa where he'd been sleeping and yowled in greeting. Torkel let out a piercing scream. He clung to his father's pant leg in fear and wouldn't stop screaming—which made the cat yowl all the louder. Knute lifted the boy in his arms again. Kirsten picked up the cat.

"Torkel, stop that," she said. "What's wrong?"

"He has teeth! He'll bite me!"

"Tomte would never bite you."

"You'll have to get rid of the cat," Knute said.

"Don't be silly. Tomte won't hurt him. Look, Torkel, he's afraid of you, too. See how flat his ears are? He can't understand what all that racket is about."

"Torkel shouldn't have to be afraid in his own home," Knute said.

"Well, this is Tomte's home, too. Torkel needs to get over his fear. The cat would never hurt him. Please give them time, Knute."

"I'll give them two days. Now please put the cat outside until the boy calms down."

But Torkel was such a nervous child, Kirsten didn't

think he ever would calm down, even without the cat. And since the cat wanted to be with Kirsten, he meowed inconsolably when she locked him up. Knute asked for cotton to stuff in his ears.

"This cannot continue," he said.

"It won't," she promised. "You'll see."

As soon as Knute left for work the next day, Kirsten closed all of the windows so the neighbors wouldn't hear Torkel screaming and let Tomte come inside the house. Torkel was sitting at the table eating his breakfast, but the moment he saw the cat he ran to the comfort of Kirsten's arms for the first time.

"Shh . . . shh . . ." she soothed. "It's all right, Torkel. He isn't going to hurt you."

It felt wonderful to hold his warm little body and kiss away his tears. And with no one else to turn to for comfort, Torkel quickly grew accustomed to her. By lunchtime, she loved him like her own child.

And by the time Knute arrived home from work that evening, cat and boy had reached an uneasy truce. Torkel no longer screamed whenever Tomte was in the room as long as Kirsten held him in her arms. She had to lock Tomte away again in order to fix supper, but afterward, when the dishes were done, she lifted Torkel in her arms and let the cat come inside.

"See how much progress we've made?" she asked Knute. He scowled and returned to his book. Kirsten carried Torkel to the sofa and sat down with him on her lap. "Stay down," she told Tomte, holding out her hand. The cat sat at her feet, looking up at her, meowing pitifully.

"Do you know why he cries like that?" she asked Torkel. "It's because he also lost someone he loved very, very much, just like you did."

Knute lowered his book and looked up at her in alarm. "Kirsten, wait. Do you think it's wise to—"

"Tomte was very, very sad," she continued, "just like you must have been. That's why he cries. He knows just how you feel."

"Did his mama die, too?" Torkel asked.

"*Ja*," she said, hugging him close. "Mrs. Anderson was his mama. And you know how good it feels when I hold you like this? Well, Tomte wants me to hold him, too. Do you think we could let him come up here and sit with us?"

"Will he bite?"

"No, he won't bite. I promise."

Kirsten let Tomte jump up on the sofa and gradually coaxed the two of them to make friends. Knute watched them warily. Torkel was still afraid to pet the cat, but Tomte began purring when Kirsten scratched his chin.

"Why is he making that noise?" Torkel asked.

"That's the sound he makes when he's happy."

"Why is he happy?"

"Because you made friends with him. And you know what? From now on, whenever you and Tomte need someone to hold and I'm busy making dinner, you can hold each other."

Even though he'd made friends with the cat, Torkel was still a weepy, fearful child, clinging to Kirsten wherever she went. When she set up the laundry tubs in the backyard to do the washing, he never ventured from her side as she scrubbed clothes and hung them on the line to dry. He was afraid to sit down on the grass and get his clothes dirty and didn't seem to know how to play.

"Your grandmother obviously coddled you," she said, sighing in exasperation. "She must have treated you like you were made of glass."

Late that afternoon, when all of her work was finished, Kirsten grabbed the largest kitchen spoon she could find and dug a hole in the weedy garden patch, then dumped out the tub of laundry water. "Come on, let's make mud pies." She stuck her hands into the gooey clay, oozing it between her fingers. "Try it, Torkel. The mud feels nice and squishy."

"No," he said, backing away. "I'll get dirty."

"You're a little boy. You're supposed to get dirty." She reached for him, but he squirmed out of her reach. "Come here!" She stood and chased him, catching him in her muddy hands and carrying him, kicking and crying, back to the mudhole.

"Hey, I'm the one who should be crying, not you. I'm the one who has to wash your muddy clothes." She plunged his hands into the muck against his will, holding him tightly until he calmed down.

Eventually, he stopped crying and began carefully trailing his fingers through the mud.

"There. Isn't that fun? And look what I found." Kirsten pulled out a fat, wiggling earthworm and held it up. Torkel took one look and let out a piercing scream.

"A snake!"

He scrambled to his feet and ran all the way to the house and through the back door before she could stand up. She ran after him with the worm in her palm, laughing and calling to him. "Torkel come back. It's not a snake; it's only a worm."

Kirsten came through the back door at the same moment that Knute came through the front door. Torkel barreled into Knute and clung to his father's leg with his muddy hands, screaming.

"W-what in the world . . . ?" Knute sputtered.

Kirsten looked at the mud-smeared father and son and couldn't help laughing.

"Kirsten, he's getting me filthy! You're both filthy, and . . . Why are you laughing?"

"It's only mud. It will all wash away." When she finally could control her laughter, she pried Torkel off of Knute's leg and held him tightly. "Listen, Torkel. Do you think I would do anything to harm you? Do you?"

He sniffed and finally shook his head.

"All right, then. I'm going to open my hand and show you something. It isn't a snake. It's a harmless little earthworm. Worms live in the dirt and they help the plants grow."

"Do they bite?"

"No, they don't bite. They don't even have teeth." He clung to her in fear while she slowly opened her palm.

"How do they eat their dinner if they don't got teeth?"

"Well . . . I don't know. Maybe your papa knows." She looked up at Knute. He still didn't seem to know what to make of her. Torkel looked up at him, too.

"I suppose they must eat things that don't require teeth," Knute finally said. "Unlike humans, who do need teeth to eat their dinner. Speaking of which, might I expect to see mine anytime soon? Or will we be eating mud pies tonight?"

Kirsten thought she saw a glint of humor in his colorless eyes. He was almost smiling. "No mud pies," she said, laughing. "Torkel and I are going to put the worm back where it belongs and wash our hands, and I'll have your dinner ready in no time."

She hummed a tune as she and Torkel carried the worm back to the mudhole. It had been a very good day.

"Now that Torkel is less fearful," she told Knute a few days later, "I would like to take him to the zoological garden in Lincoln Park. Maybe my sister Sofia will come with us."

"Do you think he's ready?"

"Of course he's ready. It will be fun. For both of us."

"Then you don't need my permission to go."

"The thing is, Knute . . . I feel so stupid for asking, but . . . I don't know how to get to the zoo. I mean, I know where it is and that we'll need to take a streetcar, but I don't know how to ride on one. We didn't have streetcars in our village back home. And I haven't learned enough English yet to know how to ask questions."

"It's simple, really."

He explained everything she needed to know and even drew a map for her with the street names on it. He gave her enough money for Sofia's fare, too.

Torkel was wary at first, clinging to Kirsten as if they were glued together. "Does it have teeth?" he asked as they approached each animal's cage.

"Yes, some of these animals have teeth. But all of them are locked in cages so they can't get out. And look—that bear is sound asleep."

"Why is he sleeping?"

"Because it's very hot outside and he has nothing else to do."

When Torkel finally ventured a few feet away from Kirsten, Sofia whispered in her ear. "Do you think he'll ever stop being so fearful?"

"Of course he will. He's already much better than he was at first. But do you know what, Sofia? You used to act just like him."

"I did not!"

"Yes you did," she said, laughing. "Our cottage could have caught on fire and you still wouldn't have gone outside if Aunt Karin's gander was on the loose.

And now look at you—singing on a stage in front of hundreds of people."

"I was scared stiff when I first started singing, but it gets a tiny bit easier every time. I'm going to get tickets to one of the shows when Elin comes back in September. I want both of you to come and hear me sing."

"I would love to." A pigeon swooped down to land in front of Torkel and he ran back to the safety of Kirsten's arms. "You'd better get a ticket for Torkel, too," she said, laughing.

Sofia smiled. "You could join the circus as a two-headed person."

Torkel met Knute at the door that evening and told him how much fun they had at the zoo. "Next time you should come with us, Papa. The animals have teeth, but they didn't bite us."

"I can't come, son. I have to go to work."

"The zoological garden is open on the weekends, too," Kirsten said.

Knute didn't reply. He pried Torkel's hands off his leg and went upstairs to change his clothes. Kirsten wondered how long he would continue to hold his son at arm's length.

That night, she sat on the sofa with Torkel and Tomte, telling the story she had made up that had quickly become Torkel's favorite. It was about a fairy queen who lived in a huge castle with a little gnome to do her cooking, two sprites to take care of her, and one to sing for her. She had an enchanted cat named Tomte who could talk.

"Tell me more about the fairy queen," Torkel begged when she finished. "Please?"

"Well, let's see . . . did I tell you that the fairy queen loved to dance?"

"She did?"

"Yes. She had a magical box with a tiny little orchestra inside it, and she would take it up to her enchanted ballroom and dance to the music every night. The ceiling of the ballroom was made of glass, and the fairy queen loved to look up at the moon and stars while she danced."

"Who did she dance with?"

"She used her fairy magic to turn a little brown mouse into a handsome prince, and she danced with him until the sun came up and he turned into a mouse again. There. Are you happy now?"

"*Ja*. But why can't I make that noise like Tomte makes when he's happy?"

"Because you're a little boy, not a cat. You make a different noise when you're happy."

"What noise do little boys make?"

"This noise!" Kirsten lifted his pajama top and tickled him until he giggled helplessly. The sound brought tears to her eyes.

When she came downstairs again after Torkel was in bed, Knute looked up from his book. "Thank you, Kirsten. You're good for him. You give him the love that I'm not able to."

"He needs your love, too, Knute."

And so do I, she wanted to tell him. But he returned to his book without replying.

Kirsten watched her husband from across the room and longed for him to hold her and talk to her. She didn't think she could bear to be unloved for the rest of her life. He had told her before they married that it would be this way. But if little Torkel was finally beginning to heal, surely God could heal Knute's heart, too—couldn't He?

Now that Torkel was growing accustomed to playing in the mud, Kirsten wished they had a forest nearby that they could explore, too, like the one back home. She stood on her back porch one afternoon, surveying her dwarf-sized yard in frustration. She didn't have a forest, but there was one oak tree.

"Come on, Torkel," she said. "Let's climb that tree."

"I might fall down!"

"You might, but that's part of the fun." She carried him, kicking and protesting, to the scrawny tree. "Now watch. I can climb it, and I'm a girl. Little boys like you should be able to scamper up in no time."

She pushed back her sleeves and began to climb, skirt and all, showing him how it was done. Fat old Tomte clawed his way up behind her, howling as if begging her to get down. When she got as high as she dared to go without breaking the spindly branches, Kirsten called to Torkel again.

"See? Look at me! This is fun! Tomte isn't afraid. Come on up, Torkel!" He turned and ran toward the house. Kirsten shinnied down and ran after him.

Little by little, she convinced him to climb. "Pretend you're an explorer," she coaxed. "This is the mast of your sailing ship and you can look out for miles and miles and watch for pirates." Every day he became a little braver and climbed a little higher. Eventually he conquered his fear and was able to scramble up almost as quickly as Kirsten could.

"Let's surprise your father when he gets home and show him how high you can climb," she told him when he was ready. She left him in the top of the tree and went to the front door to wait for Knute.

"Come out back with me," she told him when he arrived. "Torkel has something he wants to show you."

Knute took one look at his son, swaying in the top branches of the tree, and his face turned pale. He ran to the tree, horrified. "Torkel! Come down from there this minute!" Knute grabbed him in his arms as soon as he was within reach. "Kirsten, how could you? He could have fallen!"

"But he didn't," Kirsten replied. "Maybe you want to live your entire life in fear, but it's wrong to make Torkel live that way, too!" She turned and stalked into the house.

Later, when Torkel was asleep and Kirsten's temper had cooled, she went into the living room to talk to

Knute. "Could you please put your book down for a minute?" she asked. He closed it and laid it on his desk. "I'm sorry if Torkel and I frightened you today, but I'm not sorry that I taught him how to climb a tree."

"He could have fallen. He could have been hurt."

"But he didn't fall, and he wasn't hurt. He had fun."

Knute rose from his chair and Kirsten thought he was going to walk away from her. Instead, he began to pace in front of the window.

"Whenever we love someone," Kirsten said, "we always take a risk. There's always the chance that we'll be hurt or that we'll lose them. But would you have refused to fall in love with Flora if you'd known the loss you would suffer?"

"Of course not," he said, never taking his focus from the window. "Those were precious years."

"So how do you know that you aren't missing out on a great deal of joy with Torkel? Or with me?" When he didn't reply, she moved a few steps closer to him. "Knute . . . are you ever going to hold me in your arms?"

"I can't," he murmured.

"You aren't being disloyal to Flora if you do. Don't you think she would want you to be happy again, the way Torkel is happy? The vow you made to her was only until death parted you."

He finally turned around to face her. "That's what scares me, Kirsten. You're expecting a baby. What if you die in childbirth the way Flora did? I can't risk loving you if the same thing is going to happen and I end up losing you."

"Life has losses. I've lost people I've loved, too. But God will give love back to us if we open our hearts to Him. I love Torkel as if he were my own child. And I want to love you, too. I can't live without love, Knute."

"I'm not sure I even know what love is anymore. Do you?" He turned his back again.

"Well, I know it isn't a bunch of beautiful words people say to each other. And it's not always a feeling, either. I listened to Tor's words and had very strong feelings for him, but it turned out not to be love. I think love is an action. It's what we do for other people. You reached out to me when you saw my distress, and you saved me from the streetcar. You did the loving thing again when you married me. I think that kind of love is a much stronger foundation to build upon than empty words and misleading feelings. You did the loving thing. And I can't help loving you for that."

He sighed and stared down at the floor.

"I'm not expecting you to feel the same love for me that you had for Flora. But you already have shown me love, and I want to return that gift by being a wife to you, in every sense. I want to comfort you with my arms and with my heart the way I comforted Torkel. It's all right to let yourself heal, Knute. It doesn't mean you loved Flora any less."

Kirsten went to him and made him face her, then

gently took him in her arms. At first he just stood there with his arms by his sides as if he were made of stone. But when she laid her face against his chest, he finally responded. His arms encircled her. He held her loosely, but he was holding her. It was a beginning.

She stood on tiptoes and kissed his cheek.

"Thank you, Knute."

Chapter Forty-One

THE FIRST TIME Sofia had walked onstage to perform before an audience, her legs had trembled so badly she thought they would collapse. The accompanist had to play the introduction to her song three times before she managed to open her mouth and draw in enough air to sing. When she finally did, her wobbly voice sounded like she was singing in the back of a wagon on a bumpy road.

"I know I was terrible," she told Mr. Lund afterward. "I'm so sorry, but I was terrified."

"That's all right, Sofia. It was your first time. You'll get used to it."

"How will I get used to it? When I looked out and saw all those people—"

"Next time close your eyes and forget about them. Pretend you're singing to someone you love."

Walking onstage the second time had been just as frightening as the first. Sofia's costume was drenched with sweat from standing beneath the hot lights, and she still felt like her knees were going to collapse, but she closed her eyes and thought of Ludwig. She remembered how his violin music had soothed and calmed her, and she pretended that he was the only person in the audience. She sang just for him.

"I still feel like I'm going to be sick each time," Sofia told Kirsten as they sat in her living room. Torkel played near their feet with the cat. "But singing is a lot less work than cleaning Mrs. Anderson's mansion all day—and the pay is better."

She and Kirsten got together at least once a week to share their letters from Elin. "It sounds like she really likes it up there in Wisconsin," Sofia said.

Kirsten looked skeptical. "Maybe she's just saying nice things about the place so we won't worry about her."

"I don't think so. . . . And did you notice that she talks about Gunnar Pedersen in nearly every paragraph?"

"You don't think she's falling in love, do you?"

Sofia laughed. "Well, why not?"

When they learned that Elin would be coming back to Chicago to attend nursing school, they hugged each other in joy.

"I'll help you look for a new place where you and Elin can live," Kirsten told her. "Now that you can speak English and I know how to travel by streetcar, we should be able to find a nice boardinghouse by the time she comes home."

Kirsten brought Knute's little boy with her wherever she and Sofia went. Torkel didn't cling to

Kirsten quite as much as he did at first, but Sofia still liked to tease them about becoming a two-headed circus act. Together the three of them found a rooming house reserved for women near Augustana Hospital. Sofia could take a streetcar to the theater or to the music conservatory, where she had begun taking lessons. She began counting the days until Elin came back.

At last that day arrived. Kirsten and Torkel went with Sofia to meet Elin at the train station. Sofia wept with joy as she finally hugged her sister. Kirsten laughed out loud when she saw their battered trunk once again.

"I thought we were finally rid of that thing—and here it is!"

"Elin and I will carry it," Sofia said with a smile. "You shouldn't be lifting heavy things anymore."

"Yes, look at you," Elin said. "You're starting to get a little thick around the middle."

"I guess I won't be climbing trees much longer."

"Climbing trees?" Elin asked. "Why in the world would you want to climb trees?"

"Somebody had to teach Torkel how to do it."

"Oh, Kirsten. I'm so glad you haven't changed!"

Sofia lifted one end of the trunk and waited for Elin to lift the other. "I wish you could see Gunnar Pedersen lift this for me," Elin said as they began hauling it out of the station. "You would think it weighed nothing at all."

Sofia looked at Kirsten and smiled. "We can't wait to hear all about your friend," Sofia said.

"He's a good man," Elin said. "He loves the land and he works very hard, but he's kind and gentle, too. I can't wait for you to meet him. He wants to come down here for a visit after the harvest." Elin spoke in her usual serious way, but Sofia couldn't help smiling at the tenderness she heard in Elin's voice.

"It sounds like you have feelings for Gunnar Pedersen."

Elin didn't reply until they reached the street and set down the trunk again. "I do," she said quietly. "We're going to keep writing to each other. And I think I want to move back to Wisconsin when I finish school. Gunnar says they'll need nurses up there."

Sofia's smile faded at the thought of Elin leaving again. "But in the meantime," Sofia said quickly, "Kirsten and I found a place where you and I can live. We've hired a cab to take us there now."

"And I'm going to give the driver a big tip," Kirsten said, "so he'll carry the trunk all the way up to your room."

They all climbed into the back of the carriage and Torkel nestled onto Kirsten's lap. Within a few minutes, he had fallen sound asleep from the rocking motion. "You should see what a wonderful mother our Kirsten has become," Sofia said.

"I can see already," Elin replied.

"He called me Mama for the first time the other day," Kirsten said in a whisper. "I was worried that

Knute would be upset, but he wasn't. He said he was glad. He said Torkel needs a mother."

"And Kirsten has turned her little house into a real home," Sofia added.

Kirsten looked down at Torkel and brushed his silky hair off his forehead. "It feels like a real home to me, especially now that we're becoming a family."

Elin took Sofia's hand in hers. "I hope you aren't upset, but I think I've found a home, too—up in Wisconsin."

"I'm not upset," she said softly.

"That's what we wanted all along, wasn't it?" Kirsten asked. "To have a home again?"

"Yes, that's why we left Sweden," Elin said. "But what about you, Sofia? What about a home for you?"

She took a moment to put her feelings into words. "I haven't found a home in the same way that both of you have—but I don't feel sad about it. To me, this whole adventure wasn't about reaching a destination and finding a home—it was about the journey. Think about how much we've learned, how much we've all changed and grown since leaving Sweden. And everything we've endured has brought us closer to God."

"And to each other," Elin said, squeezing her hand.

"Yes, that, too—even if we do have to be apart. Remember how Kirsten said we would all marry rich husbands when we got to America and sit in the warm sunshine all day eating strawberries and cream?"

"I remember," Kirsten said, smiling.

"Well, if God had given us a home like that right away," Sofia continued, "we never would have turned to Him. We wouldn't have needed Him, and so we wouldn't have known that the new homes and new families we've found were gifts from Him."

Sofia paused, swallowing her tears as she thought of Ludwig. "God will give me a home, too, when the time comes. But until then, I'm happy to continue the journey, because I know that God is with me. When I was alone on Ellis Island, He showed me Psalm 66. It says to sing the glory of God's name, and that's what I've been trying to do. It also talks about how God sometimes tests us. It says, 'You brought us into prison—' "

"Don't remind me!" Elin said.

" 'And laid burdens on our backs. . . .' "

"You mean like this trunk we've been lugging around?" Kirsten teased.

"Yes," Sofia said, laughing, "like our faithful trunk. And it says, 'We went through fire and water, but you brought us to a place of abundance.' I think we're finally finding that place."

"Amen," Elin murmured. "Amen."

The carriage plodded slowly through the congested city streets. Finally the traffic began to thin and Sofia sat forward in her seat, growing excited as they neared the Swedish neighborhood.

"I've asked the driver to take a little detour," she said. "There's something I want to show both of you." When she spotted the billboard she was looking for, plastered on the side of a building, she asked the driver to stop. Kirsten and Elin were astonished to see her name on it: *Sofia Carlson, the Swedish Songbird.*

"And I have another surprise for you. Mr. Lund gave me free tickets for both of you. You're going to come and hear me sing tomorrow at the matinee."

"I haven't seen her show yet," Kirsten said. "I can't wait."

Elin hugged her tightly. "Me either."

Sofia was surprisingly nervous the next day as she prepared to perform for her sisters. She always wanted to do her best, but especially at this performance, with people she loved in the audience. She drew a deep breath as the curtain opened and walked to the center of the stage. With the spotlight shining on her, she couldn't see Elin and Kirsten in the darkened theater, but she knew they were there, cheering for her. The pianist played the prelude to the Swedish love ballad that had become Sofia's theme song. She closed her eyes, thinking of Ludwig, and sang the words just for him.

As she neared the end of the song, Sofia thought she saw a shadowy figure moving toward the stage down one of the aisles. She tried not to let it distract her as she poured her heart into the final heart-stirring chorus. Then, in the brief silence before the applause began, the shadow in the aisle called out to her.

"Sofia! . . . Sofia Carlson!"

Her heart began to race. She shaded her eyes and hurried to the edge of the stage to peer down. An usher was trying to pull the man away from the stage, away from her.

"Sofia!" he called again.

Ludwig.

It was him! It was Ludwig! *Oh, thank God he's here at last!* But a second usher was hurrying down the aisle to help wrestle Ludwig out of the theater.

"Let him go," she cried. "That's Ludwig!"

Sofia raced to the side of the stage and down the steps to the auditorium, praising God for bringing Ludwig back to her. The applause went on and on, and she realized that the audience must think this was part of the show—two lovers were being reunited, just like in the song.

She could barely see through her tears of joy, and without hesitating, she ran straight into his arms. She had forgotten how tall he was, how handsome. He lifted her off her feet as they hugged each other.

"Ludwig!" she wept. "Ludwig, it's really you!"

"I find you! At last I find you." It took her a moment to realize that he had spoken in English. And that she had understood him.

The audience was on their feet, cheering and applauding, believing this was the climax of her act. Sofia took Ludwig's hand and bowed again, then led him up the stairs the way she had come and through the curtain to the backstage area.

"Great ending to your number!" Mr. Lund said as he came forward to shake her hand. "The audience loved it! How did you think of it?"

Sofia shook her head, still too emotional to reply.

Mr. Lund's eyes went wide. "You mean that was *real?*"

"Yes," she managed to say. "This is Ludwig. I haven't seen him for . . . for . . . I thought I'd lost him."

Mr. Lund smiled and patted her arm. "Why don't you go in the back and talk."

Sofia and Ludwig held each other again in the privacy of the dressing room. At last she wiped her tears. "I know English, a little," she said.

"I, too. But I learn how to say one thing in Swedish." He held her face in his hands and looked into her eyes. "*Jag älskar dig.* I love you, Sofia."

"And I love you, Ludwig."

She went into his arms again and he held her tightly. "I thank God I find you," he said in English. "I am looking for a long, long time to find you. In the fire, I lose everything. I know your name but not your house in Chicago. I am walking all around, looking and looking. I will knock on all of the doors in Chicago if I have to. I pray to God for help and then I see a big sign: 'Sofia Carlson.' And I am wondering if it is you—and it is!"

"The newspaper is telling about the fire on Ellis Island," she said, looking up at him. "I am fearing you are there."

"The ship is going to take me back to my country and I am thinking to swim, but before I do, there is the fire. I help some little childs to escape and the American officials see this, and they say that because I am strong enough to save those childs I am strong enough to live in America. They let me stay, but I have no money. My money burns in the fire, too. Some people from my country who are in New York, they find for me a violin to play and a job making music so I have money to come to Chicago. I tell them I have to find my Sofia. I cannot forget her."

"I knew you would find me."

"I love you, Sofia. All this time, I am hoping you love me, too."

"I do!" she wept. "I do!"

They talked until the show ended. Then Sofia led Ludwig to the lobby, where she had promised to meet her sisters. "This is my sister Elin, and you already met Kirsten," she told him in English. "This is my friend Ludwig Schneider," she said in Swedish. "He came for his violin and his Bible."

"We thought so," Elin said, smiling.

Ludwig reached for her hand and held it up to show them. "I come to find my Sofia," he said, "and I will not let her go again." And even though he spoke in English, Sofia knew that her sisters understood.

"See? I knew he would find me," she told them. "I knew he would."

Center Point Publishing
600 Brooks Road ● PO Box 1
Thorndike ME 04986-0001 USA

(207) 568-3717

**US & Canada:
1 800 929-9108**
www.centerpointlargeprint.com